Red
Reins

S.G. COURTRIGHT

Published by 27th Avenue Publishing, Salem, Oregon

www.sgcourtright.com

Printed by CreateSpace

Library of Congress

Cover design by: James T. Egan, Bookfly Design
Copyeditor: Kira Rubenthaler, Bookfly Design

DEDICATION

For Dad

I miss you every single day.

ACKNOWLEDGMENTS

I owe a world of thanks for the support and encouragement of my friends, family, and the loyal fans of Red's Horse Ranch.

My sincere accolades go out to Bookfly Design—Kira Rubenthaler for the impeccable copyediting, and James T. Egan for the beautiful cover design.

Warmest thanks to Ian Doremus, for a great website.

And to Bob Passaro for the expert guidance in publicity.

Special thanks to Rich Cason, Norma Jean Elmer, John Goldwyn, Merel Hawkins, Nora Hawkins, Debbie & Ken Lind, Joe Spence, and Janie Tippett.

I am delighted to end my story with a pencil drawing by the most talented Mike C. Dominguez.

CHAPTER 1

Any ordinary person would be asleep at 4:35 a.m., but Red Higgins was anything but ordinary.

It was well before dawn when he left the warmth of his cabin to journey out into the crisp morning air. The path was dark, but he had no need for a light. Even if he were blind, he could easily find his way around the eighty-acre ranch bordering the Eagle Cap Wilderness in northeast Oregon.

Red looked older than his sixty-five years—a result of too much sun, whiskey, and hard living. His graying beard and short-clipped hair held just a trace of their original red color. However, age hadn't robbed him of any of his six feet three inches, and although he carried a slight paunch, his narrow hips and long legs gave him a slender appearance. As a whole, if it weren't for chronic back pain and his fondness for drink, he would be in fine shape for his years.

He wore his everyday uniform of a long-sleeve western shirt, worn Wranglers, dusty boots, and a cowboy hat, tan when new, now misshapen and sweat stained from years of use. For a jacket, he had chosen the tattered cotton canvas over the new one hanging next to it. A long, curved pipe hung from the corner of his mouth. Whether lit or not, it was with him always, even when he was soaking in his bathtub, and he only put down the pipe to eat or sleep.

Tan Dog, named for her color, ran down the path ahead of him. She was his favorite dog, and the only one he allowed to sleep in his cabin or be welcomed into the lodge. Her three rambunctious brothers, also named for their different colors, were banned from the buildings and slept under the shed awning behind the lodge. Sometimes her brothers woke early and went with them on the morning ride, but today they were still asleep, leaving Tan Dog his only companion.

They passed the lodge, the old bunkhouse, the caretaker's cabin, and finally the corral outside the gray barn. Red flipped the barn lights on, grabbed a saddle, pad, and bridle from the tack room, and carried them to a stall, where he set all but the bridle on a wooden saddle rack. Then he turned the latch and slid the door open.

The sudden light made Sugar, his sorrel quarter horse, blink. She pinned her ears back and turned her rump to him.

"Well, good morning to you too, Miss Grumpy," he said, walking around her.

Sugar turned away, keeping her rear to him.

"I realize you've never been one for mornin's, but do we have to go through this blessed dance every flippin' day? Now turn around, or you'll be getting the business end of these reins."

Red had owned the mare since she was five months old, and the sweet treat she was named after had always been his bargaining chip with her. He reached into his jacket pocket for a couple cubes and held them out on his palm. "Would your favorite treat sweeten your sour disposition?"

Sugar kept her head tucked in the corner.

"You really are in a piss-foul mood this mornin'." He looked down at Tan Dog sitting at his feet, staring up at him, panting. "At least you've got a smile for me." She barked once and he tossed the cubes to her. After catching them in midair, she turned and ran across the aisle where she sat down to crunch her snack.

Red patted Sugar's rump. "Okay, sourpuss, it seems you're in need of an attitude adjustment, and I think I know just the thing." He pulled a metal flask from his pocket, twisted the cap off, and took a long drink. She finally turned to face him when he waved the flask toward her nose.

"I thought that would get your attention." He poured a splash of whiskey into his cupped hand. "Now get your sorry mug over here."

Sugar stepped forward and licked the whiskey from his palm.

He placed the flask in his pocket and stroked her white blaze. "Sometimes it takes a little starting fluid to get the old engine running, isn't that right, girl?"

CHILLED AIR BRUSHED RED'S cheeks as he rode Sugar around the barn, across the grass landing strip, and onto the trail that would lead him up the canyon wall. He knew once he got to the ridge high above the ranch, he would be out of the cold air that settled across the canyon during the early morning hours in June.

Small clouds blew from Sugar's nose as he rode her up the trail to where Tan Dog waited, smiling and panting. Tan Dog paced and then sat down near Sugar's front legs when Red stopped on the ridge overlooking the canyon. He watched as a sliver of sunlight crept up over the Wallowa Mountains, illuminating the snow-covered peaks in the distance.

This was Red's favorite spot. From here he could watch as the heavens woke the day, bringing life to his ranch below. He dropped the reins across Sugar's neck, fished a match from his shirt pocket, and leaned down, striking it against the heel of his boot. The scent of sulfur rose from the spark and lingered in the crisp air. Holding the flame to his pipe, he puffed the tobacco to life and shook out the match. His puffs slowed to an easy rhythm as he rested his hands on the saddle horn, waiting for the rising sun to pull back the curtain of darkness from the canyon below.

Red felt at peace. He knew that later in the week, when the teenage boys arrived, these moments would become even more sacred. And in spite of the rabble-rousing the troubled kids could muster on any given day, during the early morning hours he would still find nothing but grace and majesty across his ranch.

Tan Dog jumped up growling and ran toward a patch of dry brush.

"Tanny! Come back here! Let the squirrel get some grub for her babies."

She turned around and ran back to him.

"Damn you, Tan Dog. You sure can wreck a guy's reverie."

Tan Dog gave a happy bark and wagged her tail.

These were Red's most cherished moments—before his ranch hands emerged from the staff bunkhouse in search of coffee, before planes started arriving, before hikers ventured from their tents in the forest outside his property—a time for him to be alone and to survey all that was his.

Red sat on his horse watching the sunrays sweep across the long, narrow canyon, slowly illuminating a panoramic view of the ranch into focus. Along the opposite foot of the canyon wall, the Minam River flowed fast and deep from snow melt. Beyond the river, the thick forest surrounding the canyon appeared foreboding in the shadows, but as the rising sun cast light across the trees, it revealed a lush blanket of green. He looked at the lodge where the rays touched the roof, turning the frost into a bed of sparkle. From there, his gaze traveled out across the sprawling meadow where a low-lying fog turned his grazing horses ghostly.

He'd first laid eyes on the property from this spot. No roads were permitted to cross the surrounding wilderness, so the ranch could only be reached on foot, on horseback, or by small plane landing on the narrow airstrip running down the center of his property. He had always felt that the effort it took visitors to get to his hidden haven was a small price to pay for such beauty and tranquility.

The sun rose higher, bringing into view Red's private two-story log cabin and a row of duplex and single guest cabins sitting along the riverbank. His eyes landed on the newest cabin with its rich red color and bright white chinking between the logs. He puffed on his pipe as he thought about the young campers who had been at the ranch four summers ago when it was built.

He and his men could have built the cabin quicker, but Red saw the project as a means to work one-on-one with a boy named Jake, who suffered from serious anger and trust issues. It certainly wasn't an overnight transformation, but with the same authority and patience he used in training a horse, Red had been able to win the boy's respect. As summer came to an end, Jake left the ranch with a sense of accomplishment in building with his bare hands a cabin that would stand for years. Since then, Jake had returned by choice each summer to work as a wrangler.

Behind the row of guest cabins and across a small meadow, a lone cabin stood apart from the others. Sitting near a pond, this ancient old cabin housed the boys who came for summer camp. In the grass between the camper's cabin and guest cabins was a large stone fire pit circled by seats made of log sections sitting on end. Each night Red would gather his guests around a roaring fire and entertain them with wonderful stories, some true, some not.

Nestled between the barn and Red's personal riverfront cabin, the lodge served as a dining hall and a central gathering spot for visitors and ranch staff. The long shed behind the lodge housed a restroom, three storage rooms, and a cold house. A separate washhouse sat off on its own.

Two of the oldest buildings on the ranch, stood a few yards off the corner of the front lodge porch. The first was once a bunkhouse, now turned into a storage shed after a larger cabin was built for the ranch staff. Beside the storage shed was a one-room prospector's cabin. For years, this small building had served as the fulltime home of Leroy and Edith Meyer, the ranch caretakers. Both in their mid-seventies, the couple lived there year-round, taking care of the ranch when the other staff members left for the winter. An outhouse behind their cabin had a sign on its side: "Occupancy 40—one at a time".

Red knew by the smoke rising from a thicket of pines that his staff would soon be leaving their bunkhouse-style cabin to start the morning chores. Almost hidden in the trees was another, smaller cabin, used by Jim Lee, the ranch cook everyone called Lee. He was the only staff member to have his own cabin, more for the safety of the other ranch hands than for Lee's comfort. Red's men enjoyed pulling pranks on each other, which the hot-tempered Chinese cook tended to respond to with knife-wielding anger.

Red spotted Lee coming out from the trees, following the path to the lodge. Soon smoke would be billowing from the twin fireplaces, warming the lodge and signaling to the ranch hands that breakfast would soon be served.

Jake Mercer and Billy Kirkpatrick emerged from the staff cabin, heading toward the barn to saddle their horses. Since it was their job to ride out at dawn to bring in the herd of thirty horses and mules, and one donkey, off the meadow before planes started landing, their horses were kept in the barn for easy access. In their early-twenties, they were his youngest and lankiest ranch hands. Jake had a more muscular build than Billy, but the most striking contrast between the two was in their coloring and hairstyle. Blue-eyed Billy had fair skin and unruly blond hair that poked out in curls under his hat. Jake's skin was a golden tan, and his brown hair was cut short, almost military.

As Jake and Billy got closer to the barn, Red noticed how Billy had to hustle to keep up with Jake's long, controlled strides. Red could tell by the animated movement of Billy's arms that he was telling another of his long-winded stories. Jake shook his head and laughed as the two disappeared into the barn.

Had anyone told Red four years ago that those two, once sworn enemies, would one day be the best of friends, he would have said they were out of their minds. This was one time he was glad to be wrong.

Red glanced up and saw an eagle soaring high above the canyon. The chiseled lines on his face deepened as his blue, bloodshot eyes squinted against the brightening sun.

He gave Sugar a pat, sat up tall in the saddle, and gathered the reins. "Well, girl, let's get you back to your oats." As he began down the trail, he glanced back to Tan Dog sniffing around a mouse hole. Taking the pipe from his mouth, he whistled. "Come along, Tanny. There's a biscuit waiting for you back at the cabin." They hadn't made it far down the trail before he heard the sound of an approaching engine. He pulled to a halt and spotted a distant plane glimmering in the sky. *What the hell?* He looked at his watch. *Who the devil would be comin' in this early?*

The ranch landing strip started at the end of his property and ran down the center of the meadow, stopping before it reached the trees on the other end. To ensure no planes were taking off, it was necessary for incoming pilots to fly over and circle before making a landing on the one-way-in, one-way-out airstrip.

Red gnawed on his pipe. *Surely the pilot will see the horses and realize he shouldn't land.* Down on the short-mowed landing strip, he spotted no fewer than a dozen of his herd grazing in a light haze of ground fog. The hum of the plane grew louder. *Holy Smokes!* He spurred Sugar into a gallop down the steep trail, slowing only when the mare struggled to keep her footing on the tight turns around a series of switchbacks. Tan Dog raced to keep up with the mare as they hurtled down the ridge.

I can't believe this is happening again. It had been ten years since a rookie pilot had disregarded the rules for landing at the ranch, coming in early without notice and without circling over first. He and his passenger were lucky they were able to walk away from the crash, but the horse they hit hadn't been so lucky. The gelding had been one of Red's favorites, and he didn't like to think of how it suffered before he had the chance to put the horse out of its misery. He could only hope this pilot was more responsible, but he wasn't going to take the chance. *I can't lose another horse to a plane, even worse if someone got killed.*

Once they reached the canyon floor, he raced Sugar down the landing strip toward the grazing herd. He was galloping past the barn when the four-passenger Cessna 182 flew directly over and banked sharply at the end of the canyon. His concern grew when he realized he didn't recognize the plane flying back over him. *At least the fool knows enough to do a flyover before landing.*

"Get the lead out, boys," he shouted to Jake and Billy as they rushed from the barn, pulling their horses behind them. Red heard the plane fly up out of the narrow canyon. He had no way of knowing if the pilot had seen the herd through the thinning haze, but if he hadn't it would only be minutes before the plane turned to make its final approach.

"Get these horses off the field!" Red looked behind him and saw the plane circle high above the canyon walls. *Damn, he's comin' back!* He leaned down low over the mare's neck. "Come on, girl, you'll have to do better than that." Dirt flew from Sugar's hooves as she stretched her neck out and pushed for more speed. Even as they neared the meadow, he still didn't know if they would make it in time.

Not having time to saddle up, Jake and Billy jumped on bareback and galloped after Red. Once they reached the horses, the young wranglers split—one going off to the right, the other the left. "Haw! Haw!" they shouted and waved their arms, spooking the horses into joining the rest of the herd that Red was running toward the corral.

Jake rode up to Red, helping him push the horses, while Billy herded six more from the other side of the meadow.

They were almost off the runway when Red noticed a horse standing in the deep ditch along the landing strip. "Get that one, Jake," he shouted, pointing at the gelding.

Jake yanked on the reins, turned his mare sharply, and

jumped her off the embankment, but the mare stumbled on the loose rocks. "Shit!" Jake shouted as his horse fell.

Red looked over his shoulder and saw Jake's horse get up and run off to the gelding. Jake had disappeared in the tall grass. "You take the herd in, Billy," Red yelled. "I'll see to Jake and bring in the stragglers." He slid Sugar to a halt, spun her around, and ran the mare to where Jake's horse had fallen. As he neared the location, he was relieved to see Jake get to his feet. "You up for hitchin' a ride?"

Jake nodded and grabbed hold of the saddle horn, allowing Sugar's momentum to swing him up in the saddle behind Red without stopping. He held tight to the back of the saddle as they rode up onto the airstrip and galloped toward his mare. Once he was close, Red slowed enough for Jake to safely slide off.

"Take the gelding in," Red shouted as Jake caught the mare's reins. "And take a head count."

"Where are you going?"

"I only saw four mules." Red whirled his horse around and scanned the meadow.

"It's Ned and Nellie." Jake pointed to the missing mules coming out of the woods.

"I've got 'em!" Red ran Sugar down the runway with Tan Dog following on her heels. He didn't need to look behind him. He'd heard enough planes to know when one was coming in for a landing. *Can't the fool see me?* He tore the coil of rope from the side of his saddle, widened the loop of the lariat, whirled it, and threw it over Nellie's head.

He wrapped the rope around the saddle horn and spurred Sugar off the landing strip, pulling Nellie behind with Ned right on her tail. He heard the whine of the engine and screech of wheels touching ground. *Damn, that was close. Too close.* Once he reached a safe distance, he stopped and watched the plane turn around and come to a stop at the end of the runway.

Now they decide to wait? Red shook his head. "Come on, Nell," he said, towing the mule at a walk behind Sugar. "Come along, Ned. Let's get you two long-eared nuisances up to the corral. I may need this rope to string up that pilot." Ned lagged behind before suddenly shooting past Sugar. Red looked down at Tan Dog, wagging her tail as she trotted beside him. "You look plenty pleased with yourself. You didn't happen to nip at Ned, did you?" He turned in his saddle and looked back at the waiting plane. "I know a pilot you could bite."

"That was close," Jake said as Red led the mules through the corral gate.

"That it was." Red tossed Nell's rope to Jake before riding Sugar back through the gate. The mare was foaming with sweat as she stood heaving for breath under him. He gave her a pat. "Double helpin' of oats for you this mornin', old girl." He dismounted and loosened her cinch.

"Jake, walk Sugar until she cools. Then give her a good rubdown. Billy, you take care of your horse and Jake's. And give Sugar's stall a cleaning for me."

The young men nodded.

Red turned his attention to the plane, which had taxied up and parked in the grass between the barn and the lodge. Tan Dog stood at his side, barking. "Never you mind, Tanny. If anyone's takin' a chunk out of this guy's hide, it's gonna be me."

Once the propeller came to a stop, he strode toward the plane, watching as the passenger door opened. The second he saw the shiny boots, designer jeans, and perfectly styled dark hair, he knew exactly who was stepping out. "I should have known it was you, Hollywood. You never were any good with tellin' time." Red watched the pilot get out to inspect his tires. "Here I was about to grab your pilot by the ears and pull him out through his wing window." He shook hands with a smiling Gil Harper.

"He wanted to go around again, but I told him you'd get the animals off in time."

"I see time hasn't lessened your enjoyment for causing me grief." Red used his sleeve to wipe sweat from his brow. "Damn near took ten years off my life with that stunt."

Gil grinned. "As rough as you're looking, I'd say you don't have it to spare."

"Watch your sass, boy. I may be long in the tooth, but I can still knock the likes of you on your ass."

"I have no doubt about that." Gil laughed. "Exactly how old are you now anyway?"

"I lost count sometime around Moses and his burnin' bush, but as far as I reckon, I'm as old as my tongue and slightly older than my teeth."

The dimples on Gil's tanned face deepened. "I hadn't realized how much I've missed your poetic prose."

Red took a match from his shirt pocket, struck it on his belt buckle, and scanned Gil's attire as he tried to puff the tobacco to life. The sight of Gil's sharply creased jeans and bright silk shirt brought a smirk to his face. "You didn't need to get all gussied up just for us." Failing to light the used tobacco, he flicked his wrist, extinguishing the match.

"I asked my wife to pick me up some suitable clothing for going to the mountains." Gil's broadening smile added charm to his handsome face. "This would be Shelly's idea of ranch attire."

"The last time I saw such fine glad rags was on a senator who came to the ranch."

"Did he come to hunt?"

"No, he was more hunted than hunter. From what I understand, his mistress decided to introduce their baby to his wife. I guess the wife didn't take to the news, because the senator hightailed it out of DC and hid here for a week. He might have been able to shut out the world for a spell, but trouble was still waitin' for him when he went home to divorce papers and a paternity lawsuit. Some things even the ranch can't fix."

Gil's smile faded as he glanced at the angry face glaring from the window of the plane. "I sure have hopes it can do something for Nathan. Otherwise, I'm at the end of my rope."

"Funny, that's the same thing your dad said to me when he dropped you off for a summer."

"Yeah, well, take the trouble I caused, times it by ten, and you got my boy. But the fault's not all his. He's the result of too much money and not enough of my time."

"You have to know you aren't alone in this problem." Red could see pain in Gil's expression.

"I can't say that makes me feel any better. I'm at a loss as to what to do. I knew rotting in a juvie center wasn't going to do Nathan any good. So, I sold my soul to the devil to get him sent here instead. And the honorable Judge William B. Bradley made it clear that come next election, he fully intends to pick my pockets clean."

"Ouch, that could end up bein' a costly proposition."

"Yeah, tell me about it."

"Were you thinkin' your boy couldn't survive detention?"

Gil huffed. "Hell with survive, he'd probably thrive. My son has the uncanny ability to charm his way into controlling any situation. If he weren't causing riots, he'd probably end up running the place."

Red took the pipe from his mouth, dumped the ashes on the ground, and scraped dirt across them with his foot. Pulling a packet of tobacco from his pocket, he packed his pipe and returned the packet. "Has the silver tongue of a true politician, does he?"

"Most of the time, but once in a while someone takes offense to the silver foot he puts in his mouth. And when that happens, it really means trouble. There's not a lot of gray with Nathan. People either love him or hate him."

Red held the pipe between his lips as he took a handkerchief from his jeans pocket and wiped the sweat from the inside band of his hat. "We'll see if we can't put his tongue to rest and his feet to better use while he's here." He placed the hat back on his head and shoved the handkerchief in his pocket. Then he struck another match and lit the pipe. "What exactly did he do to earn a one-way ticket to the ranch for wayward boys?"

"What didn't he do?" Gil looked annoyed. "He was only fifteen the first time he got expelled from school. Ever since then, he seems to go out of his way to piss off the authorities—any authority. The last two years, Nathan's been in the back of more police cars than I can count. His latest run of trouble started with an evening of barhopping, earning him his third MIP, a DUI, and a suspended license. That didn't slow him down. He immediately got caught driving again. Then he and his partner in crime, Trey Campbell, decided to pick a bar fight with a Marine over some girl they didn't even know."

"What were two seventeen-year-olds doin' in a bar? Seems to me they would have gotten tossed out on their underage asses."

"Having the celebrity factor in their establishment is more important to bar management than following the law. They may get fined for underage drinkers, but the cost doesn't come close to the amount of money the bar makes when the story hits the tabloids. They couldn't buy the publicity that one picture of Trey brings them. And Nathan is right there beside him, smiling like the jackass he is."

Red used his toe to smash the burned out match in the dirt. "Sounds like your son's friend isn't the best of influences."

"I'm sure Trey's parents think the same of Nathan." Gil scowled down at his feet. "In the beginning, Trey's fame was the driving force behind their foolishness, and Nathan was just along for the ride. As time went on, Nathan expanded on his role as Trey's sidekick, becoming the mastermind of poor choices. The more outrageous their behavior, the more my son and his friend generated media interest. It only got worse when the constant coverage of their bad behavior attracted the attention of television executives. For the last year and a half,

Trey and Nathan have been costars in a reality show called *On the Prowl.*

"I can't say I like the sounds of that," Red said.

"Yeah, well, allowing Nathan to do the show wasn't one of my smarter decisions. Then things only went from bad to worse when the show producers began ignoring the contract clause stating the boys were to be kept from doing anything illegal or of possible endangerment to themselves or others." Gil paused to drag a hand through his hair. "That was my fault. I've been in the business long enough to know ratings trump contractual agreements every time." He stared down at his feet. "I can't believe I was actually dumb enough to think a couple cameras could act as a babysitter. It didn't slow the bullshit down, it fueled the fire. Trey's parents and I finally wised up and pulled the boys from the show, but that didn't stop them from engaging in this last asinine stunt." Anger growing, Gil shook his head. "Being in a bar was dumb enough. Then the bright idea to take on the war vet got them sent to the hospital, where drugs were discovered in their systems. There seems to be no limit to their stupidity."

"I've read that the male brain doesn't become fully developed until sometime after thirty," Red said. "Sounds like these boys are determined to prove that theory."

Gil groaned. "Great, another thirteen years of this shit and I'll be the one locked away in a rehab center."

Red caught sight of Nathan glaring at him from the plane window. He returned his stare with an impassive expression. "Have you gone that route with your son?" His gaze held on the boy until he saw him turn his back to the window.

"Yes. In fact, I thought the judge was most lenient when he sent them to separate rehab centers, but it only took two days for Nathan to charm a nursing aid into helping him escape. He busted his best friend out, and they drank the case of beer they paid a man to buy for them. Then they jumped into the aid's car and went on a joy ride through Beverly Hills with Trey recording the entire thing on his damn phone. Somewhere along the way they made a right turn in front of a bicyclist, running him off the road and crashing the car through a fence, tearing up the owner's yard. That time the judge wasn't so tolerant, but it would have been far worse if they hadn't stayed at the scene."

"You got that right."

Gil rubbed his forehead. "As much as I'd like to think my son waited for the cops out of responsibility, it was probably only because he was too drunk to run. Unfortunately, he wasn't too drunk to keep his flapping jaw shut. When the cop asked him if he had any idea how fast he was going, Nathan's answer was, 'If I guess right, do I win a prize?' Needless to say, the cop didn't see the humor, and neither did the judge when he read the police report."

"I see he takes after you in the smart-mouthed department."

Gil frowned at Red. "I was never that bad."

Red raised an eyebrow. "I believe that's called selective memory. I remember every kid and every stupid thing they did while here. In your case, it might take me some time, but I'd be happy to make you a list."

"No, thank you. I'd rather live with my delusions. But at least you can't say I dragged my best friend down with me. It gives me no pleasure to admit Nathan is the instigator in most of Trey's troubles. The two have been inseparable since preschool. Their first day on the playground, Nathan took the role of leader, and like the actor he's become, Trey has followed Nathan's direction ever since."

Red rubbed his chin. "Trey Campbell—isn't he the latest teenage heartthrob?" He noticed Gil's questioning look. "What? You think just 'cause we don't have any fancy gadget phones up here, we can't keep up with the outside world? I can read, you know."

Gil grinned. "Do you still read while taking bubble baths in your pretty pink bathtub?"

"Well, sure, and what you got against pink, anyway?"

"It's just funny that a person who wouldn't be caught dead wearing the color soaks in a pink tub."

Red points to his face. "I'm an autumn. Pink doesn't go with my hair and skin colorin', so I don't wear it—don't mean I can't soak in it."

Gil laughed. "Some things never change. You're still a contradiction of hard and soft."

"I'd rather see myself as a blend of wisdom and generosity."

Gil rubbed the back of his head. "I don't know about the wisdom part, but I do remember how generous you were with the head slaps."

"I couldn't very well slap your face—that would be humiliating. Now a good slap to the back of your thick head— that's just a wake-up call."

"I remember getting more than my fair share of wake-up calls."

Red shrugged. "Some heads are thicker than others."

"Speaking of thickheaded kids, I suppose I should work on getting mine out of the plane."

"We can always yard him out with rope, if he gives you any trouble."

Gil turned toward the plane. "It might take that. He's not at all happy about coming here."

Red stood at the end of the wing with his thumbs hooked in his pockets, smoke puffing from his pipe as he watched the exchange between father and son grow heated. When he saw Nathan kick at Gil, he'd had enough. He called to Jake and Billy as they came out of the barn. "You two each get a rope out of the tack room. I've got a job for you." He watched them disappear back into the barn and then walked to the plane. "Let me have a word with the boy," he said, motioning Gil away from the door.

Looking defeated and embarrassed, Gil walked toward his old mentor.

"Don't look so concerned." Red gave Gil's shoulder a pat. "You know I won't hurt him."

"It's not him I'm worried about."

"Would you feel better if I carried a club?"

"No, but you might want to wear a cup," Gil said, rubbing the ribs Nathan had kicked. "And don't be surprised if he throws some colorful words at you. He's not in the best of moods."

"I'm sure it couldn't be anything I haven't heard before." Red climbed up into the front seat and turned to look at Nathan. It surprised him to see how much the boy looked like his father when he was seventeen. He had Gil's raven hair, angular features, dark-blue eyes, and dimples so deep they were still noticeable even though he was glaring.

"Hello son, my name is Red Higgins. I understand you'll be spendin' the summer with us."

Nathan folded his arms tightly over his chest and pinned his dark, angry eyes to Red's. "Look, if I were into the country scene I'm sure this would be a great place, but there's no way I'm wasting a summer in Hillbillyville." He sneered. "My plans are set for South Beach, and that's where I'm going."

Red watched the snide boy slump back in his chair with his feet up on the seat in front of him. *Boy, aren't you full of attitude.* He took his pipe from his mouth and studied it. "From what I gather, the judge gave you two choices: juvie or here."

"The judge can kiss my ass."

"I doubt you're his type."

"Hey, I've seen *Deliverance*. I know what you mountain men do to guys like me, and you can just forget about making me your boy toy."

Red chuckled. "Don't flatter yourself. You aren't my type either." His expression turned serious when he asked, "Do you really think your father would send you someplace where you'd be abused?"

"He'd do anything to get rid of me."

"From where I stand, it appears your father has gone to extreme lengths to keep you from incarceration, and that doesn't exactly support your theory."

"Yeah, well, he's not as noble as you think. I'm an embarrassment to him, and he just wants to stick me somewhere I can't get his star in trouble where there aren't any tabloids."

"I wouldn't say that's all of it. I realize you don't see your behavior as the problem. But once we get your noggin' pulled out of your ass, you might actually be able to see your way to becoming a productive human being. You'll be surprised how differently you see things when your head's where it belongs."

"If you think I'll fit in here, then you're the one who needs to get his eyes checked. I mean, look around this shit hole." Nathan pointed to the barn and the corral. "This place has to be the inspiration for every stupid country song ever written. I'm not a goddamn cowboy, and I have no intention of ever becoming one. Everyone just needs to get out of my fucking face and let me live my life."

Red's brow rose, but his voice stayed controlled. "If the way you live your life had no effect on others, then I'd be inclined to step aside. Unfortunately, from what I've heard told, you leave a heap of destruction in your wake, and that just isn't right."

"Whatever, dude." Nathan rolled his eyes. "You don't know anything about me."

"I know that if you ever call me dude or roll your eyes at me again, you'll be wearin' your ass as a hat, young man." His dark stare made Nathan squirm in his seat.

"Whatever, du—whatever." Nathan turned away from him and looked out the window. "I'm sure whatever Dad's told you, is a huge exaggeration of what really happened." He shrugged. "It's not like I killed anyone."

"Dumb luck may have kept that from happening, but you can't argue how close you came to doin' just that."

"So I got a little jacked up, and a guy fell off his bike. Dad's making way too much of it. He doesn't know what it's like to be young. I'm sure he never did anything his father wouldn't approve of."

Boy, if you only knew. Red clamped down on his pipe, fighting a smirk. "Is that right?"

Nathan turned to look at him. "Yeah, that's right. And it's what makes me and him so different—I don't give a shit what my dad thinks or wants." His smug expression returned. "Believe me, mister. You won't want me to be here when I don't want to be."

"Is that a threat or a challenge?"

Nathan didn't answer. The haunting gaze of Red's scowling face had all but squelched his cocky attitude. He squirmed in his chair again.

There was a growl in Red's voice as he said, "What you want is neither here nor there at this point. You gave up your right to choose when you earned an audience with the judge." His demeanor lightened slightly. "Now, as much as I've enjoyed our conversation, why don't we get you out of this plane and settled into one of my cabins?"

Nathan stared straight ahead. "I'm *not* getting off this plane."

"Well, son, sounds like you're beggin' to be taught your first lesson." Red tossed his head in the direction of Jake and Billy waiting outside the barn door. "See the young men with the lariats in their hands?"

Nathan stared out the window. "So?"

"Those two are just itchin' to throw those ropes over you and drag you out by your heels. Now, if you were to walk out of here on your own two feet, you'd be keepin' them from their fun, and you'd still have your dignity. But it's up to you."

Red stepped down from the plane and glanced back at Nathan. "I'll let you have a moment to decide."

Jake and Billy looked eager as they walked from the barn. "You want us to get him, boss?" Jake asked.

Red held up a hand. "Let's give him time to mull over how

he's gonna play this." He walked to the end of the wing, where Gil waited with his hands tucked in his pockets.

"I see you're still in one piece."

Red shrugged. "Like most, he's more bark than bite." He stood with Gil, watching the plane door. "So how's the movie-makin' business?"

"It would be better if I didn't have to replace Trey Campbell as the lead in my next production. That kid is box-office gold right now, but since he'll be spending the next sixty days in a rehab center, I have no choice. And it's going to cost a fortune to reshoot everything we already had in the can."

"Sounds to me like havin' the boys apart might be a good thing for both of them."

"I know I'll be happy not to see anything of them in the tabloids for a while."

"I remember another young actor whose questionable behavior became fodder for more than his fair share of gossip rags."

"Yeah, and the kicks from your pointed boots did a great job of helping me outgrow that nonsense."

Red stared at Gil's sulking son. "As obstinate as your boy is, I might need to buy me some boots with steel toes." He smirked. "Come on Hollywood, I'll buy you some breakfast." Red took a couple steps with Gil and then hesitated, looking back. "But before I do, maybe I should ask Nathan if he's coming out on his own." He walked to the plane. A moment later, he came away, nodding to Jake and Billy as he strolled back to Gil.

"Did he give you an answer?" Gil asked as they started down the path to the lodge.

"Yup." Red grinned. "Two words."

CHAPTER 2

Red sat in a worn wooden rocker under the covering of the lodge porch. Dinner had passed, evening chores were completed, and there were no guests to entertain around the campfire. He welcomed the peace, knowing in a matter of days the opening of the summer season would bring an end to his quiet evenings.

He stretched his legs out with his ankles resting on the railing and tipped back his hat for a better view of the hawk taking its last flight across the backdrop of the setting sun. He felt a kindred spirit for the solitary bird soaring above the trees.

A personal search for solitude had brought him to the Wallowa ranch in the first place. However, unlike the hawk, his freedom could not be sustained without allowing the public to invade his secluded space. So he went on a building campaign, adding guest cabins to the few that were already there as well as a bunkhouse cabin for the staff, and he doubled the size of the lodge by adding a dining hall with a second rock fireplace and a larger, more modern kitchen in the back.

Many years had passed since he hung the Red's Horse Ranch sign on the gatepost. Since then, the ranch had served the dual purpose of mountain resort and boys camp during the summer and outfitters post and hunting lodge throughout the fall.

It wasn't long before the popularity of Red's ranch attracted the attention of dignitaries, athletes, and movie stars. John Wayne, Burt Lancaster, Lee Marvin, movie producer, Samuel Goldwyn Jr. and his sons, John, Tony, and Frances, Supreme

Court Justice William O. Douglas, as well as the entire LA Rams football team, were just a few of the celebrities he had played host to over the years.

The hawk made one last cry as it disappeared into the trees where it would take refuge until dawn lit the skies again. Red knew many of these regal birds had come and gone over the years, but there had always been at least one at the ranch. So, too, had the ranch owners changed over the years, and he had to wonder who would take his place once he took his final flight out of the canyon.

"There you are," said Bud Emery as he walked out the front door of the lodge. He was a short man with dark hair showing under the band of his hat. Unless he took it off, which he seldom did, no one would ever suspect how sparse his hair was on top.

Bud had spent the last twenty summers of his nearly sixty years working at the ranch. The first time he'd come was to bring his dying father for one last trip to the place he called God's country. Bud had never understood his father's attachment to the ranch until he spent the week there with him. Since his father's passing, he had come every summer to escape the pressure of the California-based chemical business he inherited from his family.

"I should have known you'd be out here sucking on your pipe." Bud stepped onto the porch, leaving the door to slam shut behind him. "I swear that thing's gonna grow attached to your lips."

Red shrugged. "I can think of worse vices."

"Yes, so can I, and the other ranch hands and I would like to partake in two of them right now."

"And what would those be?"

"Drinkin' and poker," Bud replied. "I sent Billy to the barn to find Jake. And Woody should be here as soon as he finds his lucky socks that went missing somewhere in the cabin."

"I see no harm in the boys blowin' off a little steam before the season starts."

"So are you going to join us, or did you want to be alone to contemplate your navel?"

"When have I ever turned down a chance to fleece my men of their earnings?" As Red stood, Tan Dog jumped up from where she had been sleeping at his feet and beat him through the door.

Bud looked down at the dried, cracked leather and permanently curled up toes on Red's boots. "Maybe you could use some of the winnings to buy new boots. They look like something a wicked witch would wear."

"They may look like crap, but as long as the soles keep my feet off the rocks, I'm good to go. Hell, I damn near got them broken in at this point."

"I don't think it'd kill you to let the moth out of your billfold from time to time," Bud said, following Red into the big room that served as a gathering space. As they took a seat on the pair of overstuffed chairs sitting in front of the smoke-stained rock fireplace, a questioning expression came over his face. "And what are these earnings you were referring to? I've been working here for twenty summers, and I don't recall ever getting a paycheck. Same goes for Woody," he added as he watched Tan Dog circle twice before lying down on the bear pelt in front of the fire.

Smile lines pulled at Red's eyes. "As I recall, you were the one who came to me looking for a place to hide from your business during the summer. If there's somewhere you'd rather spend your vacation, have at it. Or if you want to change our arrangement, I'd be more than happy to pay you. Of course, then I'd have to charge you for room, board, and booze." He paused to stroke his beard. "Now that I think about it, I'm pretty sure I'd come out ahead on that deal."

Bud groaned. "Never mind, we'll leave it as it stands."

"I don't see how you could possibly need more money anyway," Red said, using the bear's head as a footrest. "Hell, if I had your money, I'd burn mine."

"I'm not as flush as you might think. My business does well, but after my ex-wives, the piranhas, get done feeding on me, I'm lucky to crawl away with my limbs intact."

The screen door slammed shut and Red nodded to Woody Taylor as he walked in. "Evening, Woody."

"Evening, Red." Woody looked down at Red's feet. "You do know you're rubbing a bald spot on that poor bear's head?"

Red shrugged. "He's never complained about it." He rose from his chair and followed his men through the wide entry into the dining hall in the next room. "Bud was just regaling me with his women woes."

Standing just shy of six feet, Woody was between Red and Bud in height, but his barrel-shaped chest and belly was twice the size of either of theirs. His features were round with plump cheeks and a bulbous nose. His hair had turned more salt than pepper since he retired from his position as a NASA aeronautical engineer two years earlier at the age of sixty-two. He had started coming to the Wallowa's twenty-one years ago after attending an outdoor show where Red was promoting his resort to hunters and fishing enthusiasts. Since then, the ranch had become Woody's annual vacation destination. As his seniority grew at NASA, so did his time in the Wallowa's, only missing a few summers when launch schedules prevented him from leaving work.

"I've lost count. How many exes do you have, Bud?" Woody asked as he took a seat in one of the six chairs at the only round table in a room filled with eight-foot dining tables. Red chose a chair across from Woody, facing the large window.

"Three." Bud pulled a chair out and sat next to Woody. "My lawyer and accountant make a hefty living just dealing with them."

"You know what they say about marriage." Red paused to empty his pipe tobacco into an ashtray. "It's the leadin' cause of divorce."

Woody grinned. "I keep telling Bud that if he'd bed 'em, not wed 'em, his harem of ex-wives wouldn't keep growing."

Bud snorted. "Hell, at my age, I can't bed 'em unless I do wed 'em."

"Temptation is an evil mistress at any age," Red said, holding a flaming match to the freshly packed tobacco.

"I don't have to worry about avoiding temptation," said Woody. "As I grow older it avoids me."

Bud grinned. "That's because you're older than dirt."

"You may be trailing behind me a few years, but you'll be steppin' on sixty soon enough. The difference between you and me is that I keep gettin' better looking with age, where you just get uglier. Hell, if my wife weren't so opposed to me dating, I'd have women throwing themselves at me."

"Ha, that's a good one." Bud chuckled. "What do you think would attract women the most: your thinning gray hair, bad back, bulging waistline, or false teeth?"

"I don't have false teeth, you jackass. And your hair may have stayed darker than mine, but take off your hat and let's compare who has the most. The good news is what you've lost on your head has taken root on other areas. I give it a year before the hair comin' from your ears is long enough to use as a comb-over."

Red slid the cards from the box and looked at the two men sitting across from him. "Now girls, there's no need to fight. You're both pretty." He shuffled the deck. "Speaking of pretty, where are the young bucks?"

"I'd say that's them now," Bud said as the lodge door opened to the sounds of boots on boards.

The rattle of spurs quickened, becoming a loud jingle as the young wranglers pushed each other and raced for the same chair.

"Do you two numbskulls have to compete for everything?" Woody rolled his eyes when Billy tripped over Jake's foot and fell to the floor.

Laughing, Jake pulled the chair out, but before he could take his seat, Woody stretched his leg under the table, kicking the chair out from under him. "How funny is it now?" Woody asked as he looked down at Jake on the floor.

The young men jumped up and continued to scuffle until Jake threw Billy to the floor again and jumped in the chair next to Red.

"If you two are done with the slap and tickle, you think we could get on with it?" Red frowned at Jake.

Jake gave Billy a hand up.

"You boys get lost on the way here?" Bud asked. "My elderly mother could move faster than you, and she uses a walker."

"Hey, we have to do twice the chores since Edith and Leroy took off for their vacation," Billy said, taking a seat on Red's other side. "Where'd they go, anyway? I have a hard time imagining Leroy sitting somewhere in a swimsuit, drinking one of those frilly umbrella drinks."

"As skinny as he is, he'd look like a piece of jerky in a Speedo," Woody said.

"Wow, that's something I don't need to see." Jake turned his grin to Billy. "You do realize that's exactly what you'll look like when you're old."

"So? You'll probably be as fat as Edith."

Red's frown deepened as he looked at his wranglers. "That's enough pickin' on the Meyers. They work hard takin' care of the ranch through the winter. I don't think it's askin' too much to let them have a few days to visit her sister in La Grande. Of course, if it's more than what you boys can handle, you're welcome to pack up your skivvies, and I'll find someone who isn't afraid of a little work."

"Ah, don't do that," said Bud as he rolled up his checkered shirtsleeves. "Billy looks so sweet cleaning cabins in Edith's apron."

"Real funny." Billy glared at Bud and then at Jake. "Glad you think this is so hilarious. Have you forgotten who's on laundry duty tomorrow?"

Red cut the deck. "By the smell of Jake, it's not too soon."

Billy laughed. "Yeah, Jake, you smell like a farting dog made love to a skunk wearing sweaty gym socks."

Jake looked down at his soiled jeans. "I ran out of clean clothes."

"Did you roll with the hogs?" Bud scooted his chair away from Jake.

"Nah," Woody began. "That's the unmistakable smell of calf scours. Once you've smelt it, the odor never leaves your memory bank."

"I take it Gertie's calf still has the runs?" Red asked as he dealt the cards around the table.

"You mean Buttercup?" Jake smiled.

Confused, Red paused. "Buttercup?"

"That's what Lee named her." Billy shook his head, grinning. "I've never seen him get attached to any animal, but he's always in her stall speaking in what I assume is a form of Chinese baby talk. It's funnier than hell to hear."

"In answer to your question, yes, Buttercup is definitely still a fountain of crap," Jake grumbled. "But I think the medicine is starting to slow it down. I just haven't found a way to shove a pill down her stinking throat without getting covered in shit."

"With luck, maybe you'll win Billy's apron from him." Woody grinned at Billy. "The boy looks fresh as a daisy."

"That's a real fine red shirt you have there, Billy," Bud said. "Nice of you to get all prettied up for us."

"It's the only clean shirt I have. I'm running out of clothes too."

Woody glanced up from his cards. "That's definitely not a work shirt. Bet it set you back some."

"It's a Marc Jacobs I bought at a Nordstrom in Portland." Billy ran his hand down his sleeve. "You can't find this quality at any of the stores around here."

"I wanted to buy the same one in blue." Jake picked up his pile of cards. "But I don't have hundreds of dollars to blow on one shirt."

Red puffed on his pipe and shook his head. "Any shirt that cost more than a day's pay is like a horseshoe costing more than the damn horse."

"Cowboy philosophy." Billy looked over at Jake. "We never get enough of that."

"Here's one for you." Red looked stern. "Never miss an opportunity to shut up."

"Speaking of fancy boys," Bud said. "When are you going to put the Hollywood kid to work?"

"I'd rather wallow with the pigs than do any more spring cleaning of the cabins." Billy's expression turned hopeful. "I vote the ranch newbie take it over."

Jake's face lit up. "You can add feeding the animals and milking the cow to his chore list. And he can doctor that damn calf as well."

Annoyed, Red said, "He isn't Cinderella, although you two are doing a great impression of the ugly stepsisters. The boy only arrived this mornin'. I think we can give him another day to get acclimated."

Woody swooped on the card that landed in front of him and positioned it between two others in his hand. "I don't know. He's already proven that idle hands are the devil's playthings. You should have seen the shape of the storage room after he went scrounging for food this afternoon."

"The little thief actually picked the lock," Billy said. "From the amount of wrappers he left thrown about, he must have eaten an entire box of candy bars. And that was after Bud caught him sneaking food out of the kitchen."

"Lee nearly spit nails when he saw the mess." Bud chuckled. "You know how possessive he is about his kitchen and supplies. If that boy trespasses into his territory again, we just might find his hide making company with the deer heads on the wall."

"He's stubborn enough to cut his nose off to spite his face." Red's gaze landed on Jake and then Billy. "You two knot-heads came around eventually. With time, he will too."

Billy smirked. "Where is our resident delinquent, anyway?"

"Confined to his cabin for the rest of the night." Red set the deck in the center of the table and picked up his cards.

Bud looked up from arranging his cards. "Fat chance of him staying put."

Red puffed on his pipe with his eyes glued to his cards. "Most likely not."

The door to the kitchen swung open, and Lee walked into the dining hall still wearing his cooking attire. The crisp white Nehru jacket and pajama-like checkered pants rivaled the uniform worn by chefs in the finest restaurants in Portland's Pearl District. If it weren't for stains on Lee's apron, no one would guess he spent the day in front of a stove. Although his clothing seemed much too formal for the mountains, it showed how seriously he respected his position on the ranch, going so far as to cover his head in a white cook's cap. A gold medallion hung around his neck, and unlike the rest of the boot-wearing staff, his feet fit snuggly in brown soft-skinned loafers.

Lee had first come to the ranch in search of the legendary gold a group of bandits were rumored to have hidden somewhere in the Wallowa's after killing and robbing thirty-four Chinese miners along the Snake River in 1887. After a month of living in a cave, Lee ran out of supplies and came to the ranch looking for work. He didn't know much English and Red wasn't able to understand him, so Lee left without a job.

At dawn the next morning, Red walked into the kitchen and found Lee turning hotcakes on the grill. Before Red could say anything, Lee reached into the oven and brought out a plate with a huge ham-and-cheese omelet. To that he added a huckleberry muffin, two hotcakes, and a pile of bacon, then handed the plate to Red. Confused, Red watched as Lee used his apron to grab the hot handle on the coffeepot brewing on the stove and filled a mug. He handed it to Red and walked across the kitchen to hold the door for him.

"What's got you so perplexed?" Leroy had asked Red as he came into the dining hall.

Red stood staring down at his plate. "I'm not sure what just happened, but I think I hired myself a cook."

Twenty-six years had passed since that first breakfast. Now in his mid fifties, Lee came to the ranch each June and returned to his home in Baker City after the end of hunting season in November. He was known for having a passion for three things: hunting for gold, cooking, and gambling. He only did one of these things well.

"I still don't get why Lee wears that dumb hat. It makes him look like an ice cream vendor," Billy whispered as Lee walked across the dining hall carrying a platter of cookies.

"You could always ask him," Woody said.

Billy glared. "Do I look stupid to you?"

"Well, actually…" Woody was interrupted when Billy and Jake nearly tipped the table over as they reached for the cookies Lee set in the center.

"Thanks, Lee," Jake mumbled with his mouth full.

Billy bit into his cookie and reached for another, only to have Lee slap his hand. Shaking the sting from fingers, he waited until Lee went back to the kitchen before grabbing another.

"If you're that hungry, you can have mine," Woody said, watching the young men gulp down the plate-sized cookies.

"You're not having one of Lee's famous cow-pie cookies?" Bud asked. "I hope it wasn't because I mentioned your girlish figure."

Woody stuck out his stomach and slapped his paunch. "My doctor seems to agree with you. He's put me on a diet. If it tastes good, I'm supposed to spit it out."

Billy glanced at the kitchen door before grabbing another

cookie.

"Wish I could still eat like Billy." Woody watched Billy shove the second cookie in his mouth. "His idea of a balanced diet is a cookie in each hand."

Lee came back into the room, no longer wearing his cap or apron and carrying a fifth of Johnnie Walker Red and a stack of glasses. He sat between Billy and Bud in the last open chair, poured himself a generous amount of whiskey, and then passed the bottle to Bud.

"Wait, there aren't enough glasses," Jake said.

"You want me to get you boys a Coke?" Bud asked.

"I've been shooting whiskey since I was fifteen," Billy said. "But never at the ranch. Even though there wasn't anyone around to bust us, Red still wouldn't let us drink until we turned twenty-one."

"My place, my rules," Red said, puffing on his pipe.

"Hey, Billy and I turned twenty-one last year," Jake protested. "In a few months, we'll be twenty-two."

Red glanced up from arranging his cards and saw the hopeful expressions of his young hands. "All right, but if you prove you can't hold your liquor, it will be the last whiskey you drink on my property." He barely got the words out before Billy and Jake sprang from their chairs and raced for the kitchen to get glasses.

Red eyed the label on the bottle. "Well, Lee, I see you raided my special stash."

"I make cookies, you bring drink," Lee said in a heavy accent.

Red plucked a card from his hand and took another from the top of the deck. "I take it we're out of beer again?"

Lee took a long sip of his whiskey, ignoring the question as he studied his cards.

Red frowned at him. "Your legs may be short, but I'm pretty sure they're hollow."

SEVERAL HOURS INTO THEIR card game they heard a loud crash.

"What the hell was that?" Red said.

"Sounds like it came from the kitchen," Billy said, setting his cards on the table as he jumped from his chair to race Jake.

The men followed them through the swinging kitchen door.

"In here." Jake pointed to the pantry door.

Red looked in at the pile of canned goods, torn bags of sugar and flour, and the broken shelves that once held them. He watched a flour-covered Nathan push cans and shelves off as he struggled to get to his feet.

"Son of a bitch!" Nathan shouted, rubbing his leg.

"I teach him!" Lee snarled as he slid past Red.

"Hey!" Nathan jumped back from the short man waving a meat cleaver and shouting in Chinese.

"No need for that." Red grabbed the cleaver from Lee's hand. "Come on out of there, Lee. I need to have a chat with the boy."

Woody chuckled as Lee passed him. "Nice job chaining up the refrigerators. Tomorrow I'll put a lock on the pantry for you."

Red pulled a collapsible stepladder from where it was tucked beside the door. "If you had used this, you might have had a better outcome."

Nathan shook the flour from his head, exposing his dark hair along with his temper. He glared at the laughing wranglers from behind long lashes coated in white.

"You do know that you don't have to sneak food if you just eat with the rest of us?" Jake asked.

"I'm not going to eat with cowboys," Nathan snapped. "I'm losing brain cells just being in the same room with you."

"Oh, that's not good," Woody said. "From what I see, you don't have many to spare."

Nathan sneered at him, but with the cover of white powder over his face, the expression only looked comical. He ignored the laughing men as he brushed the flour from his shirt and lifted it to wipe his face.

Bud nudged Woody with his elbow. "I'm afraid that may have gone over his head, him being so smart and all."

"Yeah, funny how the guy covered in flour is calling the rest of us dumb," said Billy.

"What kind of a hellhole did my dad send me to?" Nathan snarled as he tipped his head to the side and knocked flour from his ear.

"The kind where you mind your manners and do what you're told," Red said. "You can count that as lesson number two. Now go out and shake off. Then you can sweep this mess up."

Nathan walked out, slamming the door behind him.

Jake turned to Red. "You don't actually believe he'll come back?"

"Nope, he's as hardheaded as you were at seventeen."

"Are you going to let him get away with that?" Billy asked, frowning at the closed door.

"I'll treat him the same as I did you when you were a camper."

Billy grinned. "In that case, he's toast."

"Don't worry about the mess, Lee." Red patted his shoulder as he walked past him. "The boys and I will see to it that Nathan has it cleaned up before the mornin'."

Lee nodded and followed the men back to the dining hall, where they played poker well into the night.

"I'm out," Red said just after 1:00 a.m. He threw his cards on the table and pushed his chair back.

"Hey, where are you going?" Billy asked as Red rose from his chair. "Come on, just one more hand. I'm about to double my money."

"Boy, the best way to double your money is to fold it over and shove it back in your pocket." Red nodded to his men and walked from the table.

"Great, more cowboy philosophy," Billy grumbled.

"You callin' it a night, Red?" Bud asked.

"Nope, I figure I best go wake young Hollywood and put a broom in his hand."

"He's gonna love that," Woody said, throwing chips onto the pile in the center of the table. "He'll be dead asleep by now."

"That will be one rude awakening." Bud chuckled.

Red grinned. "Why do you think I waited so long?"

RED FINALLY MADE IT to his cabin shortly after 2:00 a.m. Nathan hadn't been cooperative when he tried to rouse him. He'd had to yell like an army drill sergeant to get the boy out of bed to clean the kitchen. That hadn't been nearly as annoying as watching a seventeen-year-old fumble with a broom as though the concept was completely foreign to him.

"I now see why you wear shoes with no laces," Red had said when Nathan dropped the broom for the second time. "If hanging onto a broom is tough, I can only imagine how hard tying your shoes would be for you."

An hour later, the room was clean enough for Nathan to go back to his bed and Red to the bottle of whiskey waiting for him in his cabin.

Tan Dog walked through the door he held for her, trotting to the fireplace, where she lay on the rug of Nez Perce design. Red's two-story cabin was large in comparison with the other cabins on the ranch. It had a big, open living space with a river-rock fireplace and a seating alcove surrounded by picture windows overlooking the Minam River. The living area sat between two bedrooms and a bathroom on one side and Red's private quarters on the other. Along the wall near the front door rose a staircase made of rough-cut split logs and a wood-patterned railing. On the second floor, open to the living space below, a catwalk connected two large bedrooms on either side of the cabin. Many celebrities had stayed in these bedrooms as

Red's personal ranch guests.

What Red enjoyed the most about his cabin was the unique design of the walls. Instead of lying horizontal, logs were placed vertically along the middle half of his walls, moving back to the traditional horizontal placement on top. This architectural feature drew raves from his guests.

Red closed the front door and walked past the matching cow-print couch and the chairs with wide wooden armrests sitting in front of the fireplace. Along the wall behind the couch was his built-in bar. There he opened a cabinet, slid a large container of popcorn kernels to the side, and reached into the corner, feeling for the case of whiskey. "There you are." He pulled the bottles from where he had hidden them. Three were missing. *Dagnabbit! Now I'll need to find a new place to hide the rest of you from Lee.* Red took a bottle, leaving the others on the bar. As he turned, he discovered Tan Dog looking up at him. "You wouldn't be beggin' for a biscuit, would you?"

Tan Dog barked.

"All right, I guess you did help with herdin' young Hollywood from his cabin." He picked out a dog biscuit from the container he kept on the bar counter and tossed it to her. She caught it between her teeth and wagged her tail as she carried the treat back to the rug. He followed her, carrying the bottle and a glass. "The way you were nippin' at his heels, I think there might be a little blue heeler in you."

He set the bottle and glass down on the end table and walked around Tan Dog to the firebox, where he gathered wood and kindling and stacked it in the hearth. He struck a match and held it to the kindling, watching as the flame caught and spread. Once he had the fire blazing, he gave Tan Dog's head a rub before stepping over her. As he made his way to the couch and his waiting bottle, he heard the thump, thump, thump of her tail against the wood floor. "Good night, girl." He sat down and opened the bottle. "Just you and me, old friend."

By the time the last embers sent shadows flickering across

the log walls, the better part of the bottle was gone. Burned out pipe in one hand, nearly empty glass in the other, he sat slumped with his head resting on his chest as he drifted into whiskey induced sleep.

CHAPTER 3

Red slumbered on his sofa, dreaming of years earlier, when he was a young firefighter in Portland.

"My boys!" the young mother holding her infant screamed as the twenty-five-year-old Red Higgins led her from the burning house. "You have to get them out," she pleaded, clutching his arm.

Red looked at the flames shooting from the kitchen windows in the two-story Northeast Portland home. He knew the houses in the low-income neighborhood had been built in the nineteen twenties with highly combustible materials and no fire blocks between the floors. Like so many others of its time, this house had insulation made of ground newspaper, a perfect fuel for the fire. He was well aware of how quickly the home would become engulfed in flames.

"Where are your boys?" Red asked the distraught mother.

"I don't know. They must have run when the fire started." She wiped a stream of tears from her cheek. "It's all my fault. I shouldn't have left the candle burning where the boys could get to it. You can't let them die. They're all I have!"

"Don't worry, I'll get them." He patted her arm.

The captain was giving orders to his engine crew when Red slung an air pack over his back and ran for the house. "Don't you think to go back in there," the captain shouted. "We'll find a way in from the back."

"No time," Red said, running up the porch steps.

"That was a direct order, damn it."

"Might as well save your breath, Cap," the engineer said as he rushed to couple another hose. "You'd have a better chance of stopping a freight train with a pile of wet noodles."

Just as Red reached the door, a window over the porch blew out, sending shards of glass raining down over the lawn as he disappeared into the smoke-filled house.

"I hope he makes it out alive," the captain grumbled under his breath. "So I can kill him myself."

Inside, the kitchen was in full blaze. The roaring crackle of the fire and the steady rhythm of breathing from his air pack made it impossible for Red to hear the children. Upstairs, downstairs, he wasn't sure where to look first, so he stood in the center of the living room, closed his eyes, held his breath, and listened. When he finally heard their faint cries, he raced up the stairs to the second floor, where he was met with smoke so thick he couldn't see the hallway in front of him.

"Mommy," a child cried.

He took in a breath of air before tipping back his air mask. "I'm comin'," he shouted, coughing. "Where are you?" Red breathed from his air pack and called out again. "I'm a fireman. Your mommy sent me to get you."

Still hearing no response, he worked his way down the hall to the first open doorway. "You don't need to hide," he said as he moved on to the next door. "Your mommy isn't angry with you. She knows the fire was an accident. Say, I have a couple toy fire engines for you boys. They're yours if you come out to my truck with me. Your mama's waiting for you there."

The next door was directly over the kitchen, where the fire had started. He didn't bother to feel for heat, the red glow coming from under the door was evidence as to what was behind it. He groaned. "Shit!" *I've got to find those boys!*

Red turned away from that door and quickened his pace as he felt his way down the hall to a closed door on the opposite side. "Are you in there?" The door was cool. He opened it and found this room hadn't filled with smoke yet, but still he didn't see the children. With a glance back at the growing halo of light coming from the previous door, he quickly moved to the room at the end of the hall. He entered what appeared to be one of the boy's bedrooms, closing the door behind him.

"Come on, boys, we need to get out of here," he said, sliding the closet door open. He knew from experience that children often became frightened and confused in a fire and would hide somewhere they felt safe rather than seek an escape. "I'll tell you what, if you boys can make the sound of a fire truck, I'll let you play with the siren in the real one." Sweat ran down his face as he dropped to his knees and looked under the bed.

"Wheeeeee..." the small voice rang from under the cloth-covered nightstand.

Red pulled the cover up and motioned to the children. "Come on, boys, your mama's waitin' for you." When the boys didn't move from where they huddled, Red took off his helmet and held it out to them. "Which of you wants to wear my helmet?"

Red watched as the bigger boy, who looked about seven, helped his younger brother to his feet. The younger boy placed one hand in his brother's and the thumb of the other hand in his mouth.

"Mama doesn't like it when you suck your thumb, Timmy," the older brother said, pulling his brother's thumb from his mouth.

"I don't think your mama cares about that right now." Red handed his helmet to Timmy. Then he grabbed the blanket off the bed to plug the gap under the door.

"How would you boys like to be real firemen?" Red asked as he pushed the window open and waved an arm out, signaling for his fellow crewmen to set a ladder against the house. "We'll have to do a grab and go," he called to the firefighter climbing the ladder.

The man nodded, dropped his equipment, and raced up the ladder.

Red turned to the boys. "Who wants to go first?" When he moved forward, Timmy ducked behind his brother. Red looked at the older boy. "What's your name?"

"Tony."

"How about showing your brother how to do it, Tony?" Red watched the boy nod and step closer, but before he could grab him, a loud crash of a beam falling across the hall, made the boy jump back to his brother.

Red motioned to the boys. "The nice fireman will help you down the ladder." At the sight of smoke seeping in around the door, Red turned to the man leaning through the window. "Isn't that right, Mel?" Then he whispered, "We're about out of time."

Mel smiled at the boys. "That's right. You just climb aboard, and I'll give you a piggyback ride down."

The boys looked at each other and rushed to the window.

"Do I get to wear a hat too?" Tony asked.

"Sure." Red took the helmet from Mel's head and placed it on Tony's. Then he swept the boy into his arms and positioned him on Mel's back. "Now hold Mel's neck real tight, and wrap your legs around him like a monkey. That's it. Good."

"I'm scared," Tony cried as he tightened his hold and buried his head in Mel's back.

"Just hang on, son," Mel said, taking the first careful step down the ladder.

"Me too," Timmy cried as he tossed Red's helmet on the floor and rushed to the window. His tiny arms reached out as he sobbed. "I go with Bubba."

The tears running down his red cheeks made Red feel terrible for the frightened boy. He knelt down and spoke softly. "Listen, sport, I'm going to climb out this window onto the ladder, so I can take you down to Tony and your mama. Can you stand right here at the window for me?" Timmy nodded, rubbing the tears from his eyes. "Atta boy." Red gave Timmy's head a rub and stood up. He climbed out the window and was reaching for Timmy when the boy ran to pick up the helmet. "Come on, Timmy, we've got to go. Now!"

As Timmy walked back with the helmet on his head, Red heard the whooshing noise coming from the bedroom door and realized the fire on the other side had grown to a critical state. He called down to the firefighters below, "We might have to jump for it." When he turned back to grab for Timmy, he was gone. Red's eyes darted to the blanket that now lay in the center of the room, and then to the door where Timmy was reaching for the handle.

"No!" Red screamed, lunging forward. Time slowed to an excruciating pace as the fire sucked air through the window. He knew what would happen next, and grabbed the windowsill, struggling to pull himself back inside. It was too late. Before he could put a foot on the floor the doorway exploded in a flash of smoke and flame. The last thing he saw was Timmy's tiny body flying through the air. Then the searing heat hit him, and he tucked his head under his arm and hugged the ladder as broken glass and splintered wood flew at him.

"Let go, Red," his captain shouted from below. And then he was falling, falling...

RED SAT UP WITH a start, dropping both pipe and whiskey glass. He wiped his sweat-soaked face with the back of his hand. He could still feel the scar from the shard of glass that had sliced across his temple, leaving a permanent reminder of that horrific day. *Forty years and I'm still tortured with that damn nightmare.* Rubbing his eyes, he reached for the whiskey sitting on the end table, and drank straight from the bottle. He was in the process of setting it down when a sight made him drop the bottle to the floor. Startled awake, Tan Dog jumped up and walked to the spilled whiskey, sniffing it as Red stared at the shadowy figure standing near the fireplace. His heart began to pound as he fought to focus on the dark outline of a young boy. "Timmy?"

He heard a loud knock and took his eyes off the boy to look at the front door. When he looked back, Timmy was gone.

"You in there, boss?" Billy asked, knocking again.

"Yeah, what is it?"

"Sorry to bother you, but the Hollywood kid has made a run for it."

Red groaned as he stood and stretched his sore back. "Of course he did. I couldn't possibly go a summer without chasin' some ass wipe through the mountains." *That boy is definitely his father's son.*

CHAPTER 4

The chill in the air made the old cowboy's bones ache. Red didn't need to look at his watch to know the time. It always got coldest just before dawn.

Summer was known to come late to the high Wallowa Mountains. Deep in the canyons, below the rugged snow-covered peaks called the Eagle Caps, the month of June brought a battle between the changing seasons. Here the days warmed away the patches of snow left behind by winter, while the nights still clung to the cold.

Sugar shook her head as Red pulled her to a halt.

"I know how you feel, old girl. If it weren't for that knot-headed teenager, you'd be back in the barn, snug as a bug in a rug. Instead, we're out here in the blessed cold, givin' chase after another runaway fool."

Tan Dog ran ahead, sniffing the trail.

Sugar snorted and pawed the ground, blowing clouds of breath into the night air.

"Whoa, girl. It shouldn't be long now."

He stepped down from his saddle, took the reins from around the horse's neck, and gave her white blaze a vigorous rub. "Patience has never been one of your virtues."

Sugar nuzzled his coat pockets in search of the sweet treats he always carried.

He held out the last two sugar cubes on his palm. "I swear you've got a bigger sweet tooth than Billy." As she chomped, he scratched her chest. "Hit the spot, did I? I'm not sure what you like more, sugar or scratching."

Sugar nuzzled his pockets again.

"Here now, stop that. There's no more. You'll have a big helpin' of oats when we get back to the ranch. Until then, I'll thank you to keep your nose off of me." He shoved her head away from him, but she came right back and continued her search, sliding her nose from one pocket to another. Annoyed, he jerked on the reins. She threw her head up, knocking his hat off. "Well, that just tears it, you gluttonous animal." He leaned down to pick up his hat. "You can nibble twigs and tree bark to your heart's content, but you'll be leavin' me alone. I should have known better than to turn you on to sugar when you were a foal." He led her to a tree and tied her to a low-hanging branch. Then he walked to a large boulder where he settled down to wait the arrival of his runaway.

Tan Dog came back from exploring, jumped up on the boulder, and sat, panting beside him. Then she lay down and rested her head across his leg.

As Red stroked her head, his thoughts drifted to Nathan. Gil hadn't exaggerated his son's foul temperament. Ever since being dragged from the airplane, Nathan had showed nothing but contempt for him and his staff, and Red had pegged the boy as a runner from the first sight of his angry eyes and brooding face. The thought of how similar Nathan's reaction had been to his father's when he had been dropped off so many years earlier made Red smile. It was a common reaction for troubled teens to view the ranch as a prison and him as the warden.

Tapping his pipe on the rock, he emptied the ashes on the wet ground. He packed new tobacco and was about to light a match when he heard a yelp, followed by a stream of foul words coming from the top of the steep trail. The curses grew louder as Nathan tumbled and slid down the path.

Red jumped from his boulder, worried that the boy might slip down the muddy slope toward a cliff. Relief washed over him when a tree stopped Nathan from going over the embankment behind it. A dip in the icy river was the last thing Red's sore bones needed.

The hair bristled along Tan Dog's back as she stood by Red, silently watching as a moonlit Nathan struggled to get to his feet and turned to kick the tree that had saved him.

Red couldn't help but grin when Nathan caught a toe on the tree's root and fell on his face. Somehow it seemed a fitting bit of justice for the kid's disrespect.

Nathan got to his feet again and carefully picked his way down the trail. Once the path leveled off along the river, he began to quicken his pace, but he didn't get far before the strike of a match stopped him. Out of the darkness, behind the eerie glow of the flame, a face appeared. Nathan sucked in a breath of surprise and stared at the figure holding the match to the long curved pipe. He gulped as he scanned the area, looking for the growling dog hiding behind the cloak of night.

"Sure as hell took you long enough, boy," Red grumbled between puffs. He turned and walked the short distance to his horse and drew the reins from the tree. After a quick check of the cinch, he stepped up into the stirrup and swung his leg over the saddle. With both hands resting on the horn, he showed no expression as he looked down at Nathan. As he puffed, clouds of smoke floated downward in the heavy early morning air.

"Yuck," Nathan said, waving the smoke from his face. He stepped back where the moon broke through the trees, shining a spotlight on him.

When Red saw that Nathan was covered in mud, he untied a coat from the back of his saddle and tossed it down to him. "Damn fool kid," he said, moving Sugar forward with a gentle nudge of his heels.

Nathan jumped away from the horse. "I'm not riding that thing."

"I didn't offer you a ride. You came in on foot, you'll go out on foot," Red said with his pipe clenched in his teeth.

"And I'm not going back up that stupid hill." Nathan pointed to the trail he had tumbled down.

"Only a fool would take a steep trail like that during the spring thaw," Red called over his shoulder as he rode onto the path heading in the opposite direction. "As you just proved, going down wouldn't be any too smart either." He turned in the saddle to look at Nathan. "If you want a guide out of here, you'd better shake a leg."

Red followed Tan Dog around a clump of trees and out of Nathan's view.

Nathan hesitated a moment alone in the dark before rushing down the trail after them. "Could you slow down?" he asked, panting.

"Nope. I'm holding her back as much as I'm going to. Sugar don't much care for leaving her warm barn in the wee hours of the mornin', so I'd say you're plenty lucky she's moving as slow as she is. Thanks to you, it'll be too late for her to go back to her stall. And this is one old horse that knows how to hold a grudge."

"Like that stupid animal understands anything."

"You don't think Sugar knows who caused her to be out here at this hour? Come a little closer to her hind end, and I bet she'll be happy to set you straight on that."

"How stupid do I look?" Nathan snapped.

Red looked back at the muddy boy. "I hope that was a rhetorical question."

When they finally broke out of the trees into the open meadow, Tan Dog raced on to the lodge.

Red glanced over his shoulder and saw that the exhausted teen was barely shuffling along behind him. When the distant outline of Nathan's cabin came into view, Red felt the boy closing on him, and he noticed the smile that came to Nathan's face when he saw the log building. No doubt the longing for a bed had something to do with the boy's change of attitude.

Red hid a grin when Nathan glanced nervously at Sugar,

keeping a safe range from the horse's huge rump as he ran past. He bet if Nathan never saw the backside of a horse again, it would be too soon.

The sun was just starting to rise over the peaks when Nathan reached the fork where the path branched off toward his cabin. There he stopped and turned to Red. "I came to a place where the trail split. How did you know what direction I'd go?"

Red pulled Sugar to a stop and with a single finger tipped his hat up off his forehead and gazed down at Nathan. "Since down is easier than up, what other choice would a spoiled, lazy kid make?"

"So if I'd gone up, I would have made it out of this toilet?"

"Only if you knew where you're goin', and seein' that you don't, I wouldn't try it anytime soon." Red tapped his hat back in place and turned Sugar toward the lodge. "After you get cleaned up, you can head for the dining hall and get some breakfast."

"I'll pass on both breakfast and cleaning up," Nathan called out. "I'm going to hit the sack and not get up until sometime tomorrow."

Red turned in his saddle. "Sorry to throw ants on your picnic, but you forfeited your sleep when you decided to take a jaunt through the woods."

Nathan spun around so quickly he stumbled. "Listen, and listen good, no one tells me when to sleep. I'm not a child. I'll be the one to determine when I go to bed and when I get up."

"Is that right?" Red asked, unconcerned as he nudged Sugar forward.

"That's a fact," Nathan shouted.

Red watched Nathan take the thin path across the grassy meadow and disappear into his cabin, slamming the door behind him. He reached back and gave Sugar's rump a pat. "Well, girl, looks like I'll be giving young Hollywood another lesson." He dismounted, tied Sugar to the hitching rail in front of the lodge, and walked to the porch, where he waited for Jake and Billy to walk from the barn.

"So where did you catch up to him?" Jake asked.

"Same old place, just took his sweet time gettin' there," Red said, chewing his pipe as he stared darkly at Nathan's cabin. "After you boys get the horses off the meadow, you can give young Hollywood a wake-up call for me. Since he kept me from my sleep, I'll be keeping him from his."

"Sure, boss," Jake said.

"It'll be our pleasure." Billy rubbed his chin. "I still owe him for kicking me in the face when we were dragging him from the plane."

"I'll leave the choice of how to do it up to you." Red pointed a finger at the two smiling wranglers, warning, "But don't do any physical damage, hear me?"

"Shoot," Billy said, turning to Jake. "Why is it that he always has to throw water on our fun?"

"Water." Jake grinned. "Now that's a good idea. And there's a whole lot of it in the pond behind his cabin. That should wake him up."

Red shook his head, watching the young men walk from the porch. *It's like tellin' two otters not to play with their food.*

RED WAS POURING WHISKEY in his second cup of coffee when he heard a plane fly low over the lodge. *What the hell?* He rushed outside. Mug in hand, he stood on the porch, watching as the plane made a tight turn at the end of the canyon, again flying low over the buildings on its way back out. At first, he was confused as to why the plane had buzzed over the lodge instead of the meadow. That was something pilots only did when they were trying to get the attention of someone on the ground.

It wasn't until he saw the panic on the faces of his young wranglers galloping madly toward the meadow that Red noticed the herd.

"Get those damn horses off the runway," Red shouted as

Jake and Billy raced past on horseback.

"Whoa there, Sugar," Red said when the excitement of horses running past made Sugar prance and pull at her reins. "Settle down, girl." But his attention was no longer on his mare. It was on the figure moving well beyond the dust the horses had kicked up. He watched as Nathan carefully picked his way up the bank and out of the tall swamp grass lining the pond. His frown deepened when he saw Nathan was wearing nothing but underwear. He could tell the boy was cold by the way he walked hunched with his arms tightly clutched across his chest. *Idiots*, Red thought. It wasn't the manner in which the young wranglers had chosen to wake Nathan that annoyed him. It was their failure to follow his orders to first round up the herd that had his blood boiling.

He watched as Nathan began walking in the opposite direction of his cabin. *Where the devil is that boy going?*

Turning toward the lodge, Nathan walked gingerly through the grass, dodging sticks and rocks that could poke at his bare feet. His steps became more assured once he reached the freshly tilled soil in the garden where there were fewer sharp obstacles in his path. Red lost sight of him as he disappeared behind the caretaker's cabin. When Nathan came out on the other side, he turned again and followed the corral fence, dodging horse manure as he slowly made his way toward the barn.

Bud and Woody came out of the barn and ran to untie their horses from the hitching rail outside the corral. They jumped into the saddles and galloped across the meadow to help gather the horses. Red followed them with his eyes and then turned to look at the plane circling miles away over the end of the canyon. He could see that his herd would be well out of the way by the time the plane came back. Convinced that all was safe for the plane to land, he started back into the lodge, but a strange feeling made him stop and look at the open corral gates Nathan was approaching.

"Hey, watch out, boy!" When he got no reaction, he shouted again, but still he failed to get Nathan's attention.

Red glanced to the end of the canyon, where the plane was coming back, and then to the running herd. "Oh hell!" He tossed his mug on the porch and ran to his horse. He pulled the cinch up tight, sprang into the saddle, and whirled Sugar on her haunches, spurring her into a gallop.

Seeing that the herd might be too close for him to save Nathan, Red used his reins to slap the mare into moving even faster. Dropping the reins across her neck, Red bent down and grabbed Nathan under an arm, hauling him up and holding him tightly to Sugar.

"Hey!" Nathan squirmed.

"Stay still." Red held Nathan with one arm and picked up his reins.

After a glance at the approaching herd, Red dug his spurs into Sugar. She snorted as her muscular hindquarters propelled her forward, leaping out of the way of the speeding herd crossing at her heels.

A few safe strides away, Red drew hard on the reins, bringing his horse to a jolting stop.

Sugar shook her head in protest of the sharp pull to her mouth and stood breathing heavily through flared nostrils.

Red let go of Nathan, and he collapsed on the ground, gasping for breath.

"Boy, you surely are a mess of trouble." Red gave his winded horse a pat on the neck, turned her toward the lodge, and then stopped to look back at Nathan. "Answer me one thing. Why the devil were you goin' to the barn?"

Nathan coughed and held his side. "That's where your two thugs took all my clothes." He groaned as he struggled to his feet. "God, I think you broke my rib."

"The horses would have done far worse than that."

As Red rode away from Nathan, he fought the urge to rub a growing pain of his own. Moving his arm only made it hurt worse. *Great, I threw my back out again.* He leaned forward in the saddle. "I don't know about you, Sugar, but I think I'm too old for this shit." As he sat up tall again, he felt a painful pinch in his back. *That boy might be the death of me.*

He rode to the lodge hitching rail, threw his leg over the saddle, and stepped down. Cringing from the shooting pain when his feet hit the ground, he took a moment to let his bones settle before loosening the girth strap on Sugar's saddle. The instant relief had the mare exhaling. He patted her rump. "Maybe we're both gettin' too old for this."

He wrapped the reins around the rail and moved to the back of his horse, where he paused at the sight of Nathan rubbing his sore ribs as he limped into the barn.

"Good, at least I'm not the only one in pain."

CHAPTER 5

Red leaned against the porch post, watching as the plane taxied off the landing strip and parked in the field about one hundred feet from where he stood. Recognizing the Cessna 182 as a frequent visitor to the ranch, he walked out to greet the pilot with Tan Dog trotting at his side.

Once the propeller came to a stop, Russell Elmer opened his door and stepped out with a big smile on his face. "Your boys sleep in a little this morning?" Russell asked as he came around the wing to shake Red's hand.

"Sorry about that. Good news is you scared them into never letting that happen again, and if it does, the ranch will be in need of two new wranglers."

Russell slapped a hand to Red's shoulder. "Aw, no harm, no foul."

"Who do you have with you?" Red asked when he saw the passenger struggling to pull something out of the plane.

"That's my friend, Burr."

"Burr," Red repeated, watching as the man heaved a huge bag of dog food off the front seat. "That's a name you don't hear every day."

"Burr was at my place designing a new irrigation system. So I asked if he wanted to ride along. He owns a plane he uses for his irrigation business, and I thought since many of his trips take him right over the ranch, he could act as my backup in case I can't make a run for you. He's a darn good pilot and flies a great little machine with short takeoff and landing wings. He won't have any trouble getting in and out of here. His Cessna 172 can land on a postage stamp." Russell turned to Burr as he came around the plane. "Burr, I'd like you to meet Red, the owner of the ranch."

Burr balanced the bag on his shoulder and extended his hand. "Nice to meet you," he said, giving Red's hand a firm shake. "Russell's told me a lot about your place here." He repositioned the bag when it started to slide.

Red took the pipe from his mouth and used it to point at the ground near Burr's feet. "You can drop that. My boys are on their way out to take care of it."

"We had the plane so packed with supplies Burr had to sit on top of the dog food." Russell chuckled as he tossed a bag of chicken feed on top of the bags Burr set down. "At least the ride home should be a little more comfortable without his ear pressed to the ceiling."

Red rested an arm on the plane's wing strut and puffed on his pipe as he watched the two men pull supplies from the backseat. When Burr suddenly stopped a few feet from the pile, Red looked for the cause of his apprehension and saw Tan Dog sniffing the supplies. "She won't do you any harm."

"It's not her I'm worried about," Burr said, staring at the pack of muddy dogs romping their way. "I have a meeting in La Grande later this morning. Any chance I'll make it without paw prints?"

"Here now, you dogs get." Red blocked Burr from the pack. "Get," he repeated, waving them away. Tan Dog stayed by Red's side as her siblings ran off to chase after the mule-pulled wagon coming from the barn. He reached down to pat her head. "Those mutts have a very short attention span. Out of a batch of four puppies, Tan Dog here got all the brains, leavin' her brother's empty-headed."

"You call her by her color instead of a name?" asked Burr.

"That is her name," Russell said. "Her brothers, Gray Dog, Brown Dog, and Black Dog, are named for their colors as well."

Red shrugged. "Keeps it simple."

"Now I see why you need so much dog food," said Burr, throwing a bag of oats on top of the growing pile. "If you expect me to haul in this much at a time, I'm going to need to buy a bigger plane. No way would mine get off the ground with the size of this load." He paused to look at one of the bags of feed. "Do you have turkeys up here?"

"No, no turkeys. Oh, you're referring to the turkey chow. That's for my peacocks."

"Peacocks?" Burr looked confused.

"Yeah, Red's more zookeeper than rancher," Russell said. "If a critter's known to be mean or obnoxious, Red's going to have at least two of them. And boy, are those birds obnoxious. Scared the livin' daylights out of me the first time one of them screamed. I actually thought a woman was being attacked. The nasty things enjoy perching above doorways, where they lay in wait for some unsuspecting person to walk out. I don't think the sound is something you ever get used to."

"They're not that bad," said Red.

Russell laughed as he pulled another bag from the plane. "Who are you kidding? I've been witness to several occasions when one of their bloodcurdling screams nearly made you jump out of your skin."

Red shrugged. "Don't need to spend money on a stress test when you got those birds around. They do a fine job of testin' the old ticker."

Russell flung a bag of chicken feed on top of the stack. "Burr may be right about needing a bigger plane. I'm kind of surprised all this fit in mine."

Red watched Burr set two cases of Beer down next to the pile. "We appreciate anything you can help bring in, but we certainly don't want you to do more than is safe."

"Safe is the only way I fly." Burr smiled. "My wife would kill me if I died in an airplane crash."

"We can't have that then." Red chuckled.

"You must have a constant run of supplies coming in to keep this place going," said Burr.

"If it weren't for Russell and a few other local pilots, we'd have to pack everything by horse and mule from the Moss Springs Trailhead above Cove, and then only if we could get someone to deliver all the supplies there."

"Big items, like tanks of propane, are still packed in on animal," Russell added. "He used to cut most of his own lumber in the old sawmill at the end of the ranch. Unfortunately, that heavy snowstorm we had a couple years back collapsed most of the roof. Now when he needs lumber, it has to be brought in by strapping small stacks to both sides of two animals walking in tandem. Switchbacks can make that real interesting."

"I can imagine," Burr said. "I guess you have to be creative when you don't have any roads coming to your place."

"As far as I know," Red began, "the last people who attempted to drive to the ranch were a couple of young men in the nineteen twenties who were skunked enough to mistake the frozen Minam River as a road. I hear they made it quite a ways before downed trees stopped them."

"I remember one item that was even too large for pack animals to haul," said Russell.

Red grinned. "He's talking about my tub. It was quite a spectacle for my guests to see it flyin' through the air under a helicopter. We dropped it into my new cabin before the roof was put on. It's the first and last tub the ranch will ever have."

Russell laughed. "Red's partial to bubble baths."

"A man's got to soak his trail-weary bones," Red said, looking at Burr. "Don't you agree?"

"You're talking to the wrong guy. I've been on enough horses to last me a lifetime. Now my daughter would spend all her time on the back of a horse if she could, and she nearly does in the summer time. Not me. I've got a great view of trails from my plane, and that's about as close as I ever need to come."

"You must not be a hunter," said Red.

"Nope. Last time I went hunting was when my brother and I made the mistake of going out with two of our brothers-in-law. When we happened upon a herd of elk, I witnessed exactly what buck fever means. One look at the animals and those two went berserk. Once the shooting frenzy started, my brother and I dove on the ground, and that's where we stayed until the smoke cleared. It turned out to be a real sour experience. I gave my guns to my brother and never touched one again after that."

Red nodded. "I can see why."

Burr pointed to the wire running through the trees to the lodge. "Russell tells me you have generators for power. But it looks like you've got a telephone line."

"We have two phones—one in the lodge and one in my cabin. Sometimes they work, more times not. It's kind of hard to take reservations without a phone line, so I strung one all the way to Cove. But it only takes rain or a windstorm to take the damn thing out. I swear my crew spends half their time ridin' the line to make repairs."

"You don't have the convenience of cell phone or internet service at Red's ranch, but at least he saw to having showers and flush toilets in each of the guest cabins," Russell said as he carried a load from the plane. "The lodge also has restrooms, and there are two full baths in Red's personal cabin."

"Just because you're in the mountains, doesn't mean you can't be comfortable." Red watched Russell set a box of whiskey next to the cases of beer and tobacco Burr had carried from the plane.

"That's the last of it," Russell said.

Red eyed the alcohol. "I think we'd better haul those things ourselves. I wouldn't want the boys gettin' into it." He reached for the bag of tobacco and walked toward the lodge, clearly leaving the heavy boxes for Russell and Burr.

In the process of stacking the beer cases, Burr knocked a paper bag over. It fell open and several Indian arrowheads slid out. He gathered them up and placed them back in the bag, which was filled with them. "I take it he's a collector of arrowheads?" Burr set the bag next to the pile and picked up the beer cases.

"More like a planter," Russell said laughing. "Red spreads them around the ranch so his guests can find them. He's famous for telling stories around the evening campfire and especially enjoys making his visitors believe his ranch was once an Indian village."

"Was it?"

"Some artifacts have been dug up, so I guess his stories could be true. But if they weren't true, it wouldn't stop him from telling 'em that way. Red never lets the facts get in the way of a good story."

As they sped to catch up with Red, Burr glanced at the case of whiskey Russell carried. "I sure wish I had a camera to record this moment. I bet a picture of you carrying whiskey would bring a few raised eyebrows from your fellow Mormons."

"I don't think I'll be condemned for just carrying it, but I'll pray twice as hard next Sunday, just in case." Russell smiled at Burr as they caught up to Red. "I've thought of having my entire congregation pray for Red's soul, but I don't think we have enough members to cover all his sins. You think the Methodists could help with that?"

Burr nodded. "I'll see what I can do."

"You're not the first to voice concern for my soul," said Red. "And I certainly don't mind having all the bases covered. So far I have someone of the Methodist, Mormon, Catholic, and Jewish faiths, all puttin' in a good word for me. I also know a Baptist, but he's angry over hunting territories, so I'm pretty sure he's lookin' to send me in the other direction. Just for good measure, maybe I should find a Buddhist monk. Either of you know one?"

The men laughed.

"Well, I know Russell's out, but I'd be happy to offer you a nip of whiskey with your mornin' coffee, Burr."

"Thanks, but I don't touch the stuff either. Coffee sounds good though."

"That we have plenty of, but I have to warn you, we serve cowboy coffee here."

"What's that?"

"Strong enough to float a horseshoe," Red replied. "I've always found a little whiskey does well to thin it just right. But if it suits you better, we have milk and sugar."

They were passing the flagpole in front of the lodge when Burr set the cases on the ground and slapped a hand to the top of his head.

"Is a pest tryin' to make a meal of you?" asked Red.

Burr wiped away the dead bug. "I swear if there's a single mosquito within fifty miles, it's going to make a meal of my bald head. I must taste like candy to them."

"It probably hitched a ride with us from my place," Russell said.

"From the size of it, that could be true," said Burr. "If there's one thing Russell's farm grows better than wheat—it's bugs. His mosquitoes are big enough to stand flat-footed and look a turkey in the eye."

Red took his pipe from his mouth. "Better take up smokin', even turkey-sized mosquitoes stay away from me."

They stepped on the porch, but before they reached the door, Lee came bustling out of the lodge. Without saying a word, he grabbed the cases of beer from Burr, ignoring Red's look of consternation as he slipped back inside, letting the door slam shut behind him.

"Now Lee there is the one I have to worry about," Red said. "I can assure you he wasn't being helpful just then. By the time he reaches the storage room, two cans will be gone and the better part of a case ferreted away for later." Red held the door for his visitors, looking at Russell as he passed. "I don't suppose you could convert him?"

"I'd have a better chance of converting the devil," Russell said. "You forget how long I've known Lee."

Red shrugged. "Well, it was worth a try."

They didn't make it to the dining hall before the sound of a twin-engine plane drew the three men back out to the porch. They watched as the plane buzzed over the airstrip, signaling that it would be landing on the next approach.

"Looks like you'll be having more company for breakfast," Russell said, watching the plane land and taxi up next to his.

As the propellers went still, Red wondered why the pilots made such a hasty exit from the plane.

"Are any of you Red Higgins?" the pilot shouted as he and his copilot walked briskly toward the lodge.

Red noticed how they both kept glancing back at the plane. "I'm Higgins." But before he could take the hand the pilot offered, the plane started rocking.

Clearly concerned, the pilot dropped his hand and turned his eyes to the bouncing aircraft. "I've got a delivery for you, but you might want to get a tranquilizer gun before you pull one of them out."

The men shuddered at the scream coming from within the plane.

"You got a mountain lion in there?" Russell asked.

The copilot shook his head. "More like a Tyrannosaurus."

"The big kid must have sweated a full bucket worth since we lifted off from Los Angeles," said the pilot.

"Poor kid was scared spit-less," the copilot added. "He didn't move a muscle the whole way. That is, until our wheels touched solid ground. Then he was on his feet and taking his aggression out on the two boys who thought it was a smart idea to tease someone four times their size."

The men watched as the plane continued to rock from side

to side.

"Well, I guess we better put a stop to this before they tear the wings off that bird," Red said, waving Bud and Woody from the barn. "One of your passengers is the grandson of an old friend of mine. Boy's name is Carlton Maxwell. I'd hate to have to report that his little grandson got hurt in transit."

"Carlton? Little?" the copilot said, furrowing his brow. "How long has it been since you've seen the boy?"

"I guess it has been a few years. Last time I saw him he was knee-high to a gnat. Why do you ask?"

"Believe me, the fuse to his temper is the only thing short about him now," the pilot said. "The kid wreaking havoc on my plane is Carlton."

The plane rocked harder, followed by another scream.

Red's brow went up. "Exactly how big is he?"

"Big enough that I won't be getting in his way," the pilot replied.

Just then the door to the plane dropped open, revealing steps that the kid who was thrown from the plane didn't have a chance to use. A moment later another boy hurled through the door, landing on the ground next to the first. Then Carlton came into view.

"Good Lord, that boy is big enough to have his own moon," Bud said as he and Woody came to Red's side.

"Who's the baby-faced giant?" Woody asked.

"His name is Carlton," Red answered. "And since I'm pretty sure he could bench-press the two of you at the same time, you might want to watch what you say to him. Apparently he doesn't handle teasing all that well."

The men watched as Carlton squeezed through the narrow doorway and walked down the steps with his angry eyes set on the two boys scrambling to get to their feet.

"Who are the two kids he's fixin' to kill?" Woody asked.

"From the descriptions I was given, the skinny redhead with the freckles is Sean Bennett," Red said. "And that would make the bigger, dark-haired one Carlos Mendez." Red kept his eyes glued to Carlton. "I was going to have you deal with this, but now that I've had a look at him, I think it's a job better handled by our young lads."

"Amen," Woody said, looking relieved. "I don't think I'm up to wrestling a bear. Especially one that looks that angry."

"I second that," Bud said, watching Carlton chase the smaller boys around the plane. "I doubt we could knock him down with a hammer."

"They're lucky he isn't any faster, because if he gets his hands on them, I'm certain he's going to tear their heads off and spit down their throats," said Woody.

"So tell me, is his father a sumo wrestler, or did his mother lace his bottle with steroids?" Bud asked.

"Seein' that you think this is so funny, maybe you'd like to handle it after all." Red glared at Bud.

Bud shook his head. "I'm very sure I wouldn't. Come on Woody, let's go get the boys and find a place to watch the show from a safe distance."

As his men walked away, Red turned to his visitors. "I see no reason to chance injury to my seasoned hands when we have young bucks in need of a little punishment."

Russell laughed. "What did they do to piss you off?"

"They're the numb-headed boys that didn't get the horses off the field this mornin'. I think a few bumps and bruises fit their crime." Red's eyes shone with mischief as he paused to puff clouds of smoke into the air. "Hell, this kind of nonsense is best left to the young anyway. They mend so much faster than we old duffers."

Moments later, Jake and Billy ran up, eagerly seeking orders.

"Stop the big kid from tearin' the other two apart, and then collect all of their shoes," Red instructed. "You might want a rope. Take mine."

Jake ran to the hitching rail, took the rope from Sugar's saddle, and came back to get Billy.

Billy glanced at Carlton and then at Jake. "Glad there's two of us."

"I think four would give us better odds," Jake said. "Do you see the size of him? He has to be six four and close to three hundred pounds. We barely make that together."

"You gonna stand around and gab about it, or go get it done?" Red asked.

"Maybe he'll listen to reason," Billy said, looking concerned as he and Jake walked out to the plane.

They soon discovered Carlton wasn't open to discussion.

"Geez, that went well," Russell said, watching Jake help Billy up off the ground. "What was that about him listening to reason?"

"They might as well have been hanging on to the tusks of an elephant," said the pilot.

The men watched Billy and Jake limp back to the porch.

"You two on coffee break?" Red asked with arms crossed over his chest.

"I don't think we can take on the Hulk alone," Billy said. "His forearms are bigger than my thighs."

"Yeah, boss, he's like wrestling with Sasquatch," Jake said.

"Like I told you," Red scolded, "If you had used the rope, you wouldn't have to be close to him. Now go out there and get this done."

Billy looked at Jake. "I'll rope his legs, and then you topple him like the giant in 'Jack and the Beanstalk.'"

"How about I rope him, and you do the toppling?"

"Hey, you're bigger than me," Billy protested.

"Are you two tryin' to piss me off?" Red asked. "Maybe you'd rather spend the day diggin' a new hole for the outhouse?"

"That wouldn't be so bad," Billy said. "Safer than this."

"It's not the diggin' you should worry about," said Red. "It's what you uncover when you move the outhouse off the old hole."

Billy made a face. "Yikes, I forgot about that."

Jake handed the rope to Billy. "Come on, you throw the rope and I'll tackle him."

"Breakfast and a show, I'm glad we didn't miss this," Russell said as he, Red, Burr, and the two pilots, watched Billy throw the rope and Jake ran at Carlton.

"Good God, they're wrecking my plane," the pilot said as Jake rammed Carlton back into the aircraft.

Red emptied his pipe by tapping it against the flagpole. Then he filled it with tobacco and lit it, puffing smoke into the air. "You can always go help them if you want."

One of the young wranglers screamed in pain.

"No, I think I'm good." The pilot cringed. "I'll charge any damages to the two rich kids' daddies. After all, they're the ones that started this with their teasing."

Burr watched as the younger boys shook from their shock and ran for the trees. "What's the deal with these boys?" Burr's expression was both, puzzled and concerned.

His face void of any emotion, Red took a moment before answering, "Seems I've become a babysitter for society's delinquents."

"Red's taken on cleaning up and straightening out the likes of Hollywood brats and the embarrassments of wealthy parents," Russell said.

"Like a therapy center in the mountains?" Burr asked.

"We call it camp," Red said dryly. He shook his head when he saw Jake and Billy scuffling on the ground with Carlton. "Not a plum nickel of sense between the two of them. But sometimes ignorance can sure come in handy around here."

The men watched the young wranglers walk back to the lodge, leaving Carlton tied up on the ground, while the younger boys stayed in the trees.

"Damn, Red," Jake said, limping on one leg. "Any more dealings with King Kong and we'll be expecting hazard pay."

"Got that right," Billy said, dropping the pile of shoes at

Red's feet.

"I'm sure breakfast will cure you," Red said.

The young wranglers hobbled through the lodge door, letting it slam behind them.

"Well, how 'bout it?" Red turned to his guests. "You fellas up for some breakfast?"

The men followed Red into the dining hall. No sooner had they sat down at one of the long tables than Lee appeared with two cast-iron frying pans. One had sizzling bacon, sausage, ham, and eggs; the other held fresh-baked biscuits. Lee set them on planks of pinewood, pulled his oven mittens off, and left them on the table. "Hot," he said and turned to leave.

Russell chuckled. "Lee's always been a man of few words."

"Unless he's cursin' at you," Red said. "I don't always understand his words, but I'm pretty sure he calls my mother names and he wishes me a one-way trip to the underworld. I'd advise you not to get on his bad side. Then again, I'm not so sure he has a good one."

The men laughed.

Burr poured a cup of coffee and passed the pot on. He looked down the length of the table to where Red sat like a king at the end. "Why did you take the shoes from those boys?"

"So I won't have to spend another night out chasin' through the hills after a darn fool runaway." Red spooned scrambled eggs onto his plate and slid the pan to Russell. "City kids see these mountains as Siberia, and their first thought is to look for an escape. Since none of them have a lick of sense, they never think it through before headin' into the forest. If I don't catch them quick enough, and depending on which way the numbskulls decide to go, I can end up chasing them all night."

"Seems like they'd be afraid to wander a strange place after dark," Burr said, helping himself to more bacon.

Red poured the pilot a cup of coffee before filling his own. "You'd think. The boy I tracked down last night didn't even have a coat. When I found him, he was wearin' a thin jacket and covered from head to toe in mud."

"How many kids do you have over the summer?" Burr asked as he scooped up a forkful of eggs.

"We had four last year. Got five coming this year."

"Don't the boys usually arrive a little later in June?" asked Russell.

Red pulled the flask from his pocket and poured whiskey into his coffee. "Usually that's true." He took a sip from his mug without bothering to stir it. "The parents of this crop of hoodlums seemed more anxious to get them out of their hair."

The men spent the next twenty minutes in talk about airplanes. The conversation suddenly died when they saw Bud and Woody leading the three boys across the grass in front of the lodge.

"There go your delinquents," said Russell, looking out the big dining-hall windows.

"Speaking of delinquents." The pilot turned to Red. "Since we've delivered ours, we best get our plane back in the air.."

Burr nodded to Russell. "We had better go too. I need to get me back to work."

Burr and Russell followed Red and pilots out to the flagpole, where the copilot paused to shake Red's hand, thanking him for breakfast. When Red turned to the pilot, he found him studying the grassy airstrip.

"Don't worry, if John Wayne could get his DC-3 out of here." Red used his pipe to point at their aircraft. "I think that bitty plane of yours can make it."

"A DC-3?" the pilot said. "Wait, did you say John Wayne?"

Red nodded. "Burt Lancaster was probably the most frequent celebrity, but Wayne was here quite often, huntin' mostly. Of course that was years ago. Russell helped me add another five hundred feet to the runway to fit their planes. As long as you leave before the heat of the day and keep to a slight right turn on your way up, you'll be fine." Using his pipe again, he pointed to a rock face on the hillside at the end of the runway. "Of course, that rock there seems to do a pretty good job of stoppin' planes when their pilots screw up. You'll want not to do that."

CHAPTER 6

Red waved to Russell Elmer's plane as it sped down the runway. Blocking the sun with his hand, he watched the plane rise from the ground, making a slight turn as it climbed through the narrow opening between the canyon walls. He puffed on his pipe, grinning when he saw the wings waggle, a pilot's way of waving goodbye from the air. As the plane disappeared from sight, he walked past the lodge, and followed a path through a grove of trees leading to the lone bridge in the canyon.

Until the snowmelt eased, the wooden bridge was the only safe crossing over the Minam River. In a few weeks, what was now a raging river would turn to a slow flow of shallow water easily crossed on foot in some areas, and deep enough to swim in others.

He stepped onto the plank decking, ignoring the layer of dried horse manure as he made his way to the center. Resting his arms on the flat tops of the railing, he took in the view of the turbulent current flowing a few yards from the back of his cabin. His gaze moved across the river to the doe and fawn licking the block of salt he had placed there to attract deer. He often enjoyed watching them while taking his morning coffee in his cabin.

The scream from the hawk flying in circles directly above him drew his attention upward. Preoccupied, he didn't notice the man coming across the bridge.

"If I were a rodent, I'd take that as fair warning that this would be a good time to tuck my ass underground," the man said as he walked to Red. "I stopped by your lodge. Bud said he saw you heading this direction."

"Good mornin', Harold. How are things at the Minam Lodge?"

"Oh, fair to middlin'," replied Harold Turner, owner of the neighboring resort. "But I do have somethin' I wanted to pass by you."

Red noticed how serious Harold's expression had turned. "Sure, come on, I'll buy you a cup of coffee." They walked to the lodge and into the dining hall, where they each filled a mug from the large coffee pot. "Let's sit in the gathering room." Red motioned Harold to the stuffed chairs in front of the blazing fire. As they sat, Red pulled a flask from his pocket and held it out. "You look like you could use some of this."

Harold poured a shot of whiskey into his mug, handed the flask back to Red, and watched as he emptied the rest into his cup. "I see you're havin' a little coffee with your whiskey this mornin'."

Red looked down at his mug. "Too much coffee if you ask me." He examined the metal container and set it on the table next to his chair. "I think I'm gonna have to get me a bigger flask." He took a drink and made a face. "Yup. Definitely too much coffee."

Harold chuckled as he raised the coffee cup to his lips. "I guess I better get to what I came for, so you can go refill that thing." His expression turned serious again as he asked, "Have you had any animals come up missing?"

"No, what's missin' at your place?"

"Percy, my golden Lab. When he and my Rottweiler, Lola, went out the other night, Lola came back alone with a deep gash on her shoulder. By the looks of it, I'm thinkin' they might have tangled with a cougar. I had my men search the area the better part of yesterday, but we didn't find any signs of Percy."

"Did you come across any tracks?"

"No, not so far, but a fourteen-year-old daughter of one of

my guests swears that when she looked out her cabin window last night she saw eyes lookin' back from a tree."

"Did she mention the eyes having the glow of a cat?"

Harold took another sip of coffee and shook his head. "We couldn't get past the tears and hysterics. She was completely inconsolable, but I'm not so sure it wasn't all an act."

"What would be the purpose of that?"

"When she arrived with her family yesterday, she was going on about a boyfriend she wasn't happy to leave behind. If she heard talk of a cougar, she might have concocted a story to get her parents to take her home. If so, it worked. They're flyin' out today. But with my dog missing, I can't ignore the possibility her story may be true, and if it is, that's one brazen cat." His brow furrowed as he looked at Red. "This isn't the first time I've had animals go missing. Over the past few years I've lost several calves, a number of cats, and a toy poodle belonging to one of the guests. The thing I can't figure, if this is a cougar, why isn't it pickin' off your animals as well?"

"Not with the pack of crazy dogs I have," Red said. "They're part Rhodesian Ridgeback, which were bred to hunt lions. I suspect even a mountain lion would have a difficult time getting past them."

"Good. Any chance you could bring them over and scout around my place? I'd really like to get this stopped."

"Unfortunately, Ridgeback is only half of their breeding. They're also a quarter Weimaraner, which explains their tendency to chase anything that moves and their confounded lust for mud. The last quarter is pure mutt, which explains how they came to be of different colors." He looked down to where Tan Dog lay at his feet. "We could give it a try, but unlike Tanny here, her brothers aren't exactly long on attention or brains. The sight of a chipmunk or even their own tails could be enough to take them off task." As he ran a hand down her side, Tan Dog thumped her tail against the floor. "But I'll take the dogs and a couple of my men out to canvass your ranch and surrounding area for tracks." He gave Tan Dog another pet. "So sorry about Percy, maybe he'll show up yet."

"I doubt it. Lola and he were inseparable."

"I hope Lola recovers okay."

"Yeah, me too. My wife flew her to the vet in La Grande. The wound was pretty deep, so I expect Lola will have to stay there for a few days." Harold stood up. "Thanks for the coffee. I'd better get back. Let me know if you see any signs of a cat." He looked down at Tan Dog. "That's a good dog you got. You might want to keep her close."

"No worries there. She's seldom farther than a breath away from me."

"I'd keep it that way." Harold paused at the door, looking back at Red. "Heard we're in for some lousy thunderstorms over the next two evenings. You might want to batten down the hatches."

Red nodded. "I'll get the men on it."

Harold walked through the door, holding it for Woody as he came up on the porch. The two men spoke for a moment, and then Harold walked off and Woody went into the lodge.

"Hey, Red," Woody said, sitting in the chair Harold had vacated. "What was Harold doing here?"

At the sound of Woody's voice, Tan Dog wagged her tail.

Red stared at the fire. "Thinks a cougar killed one of his dogs and took a slice out of the other."

Woody looked concerned. "Damn, that's not good. We don't need a big cat prowling around this close to opening."

"Harold had his first guests come in yesterday, but they're already hightailin' it out of here after their girl claimed she saw the cougar. He asked us to take the dogs out and see if we can't hunt the damn thing down."

"Good thing we keep the calf inside the barn," said Woody.

"And that's where she'll stay 'til we know a cat's not gonna make lunch out of her. I meant to find you and see how the new campers settled in with young Hollywood. Did Nathan try to throw any of that alpha dog nonsense at them?"

"No." Woody laughed. "You should have seen the look on his face when Carlton walked in. At least he's not so numb in the head that he doesn't realize Carlton could easily wipe his ass with him. So far, Nathan's cutting a wide berth around him—didn't even squawk when Carlton took his bed."

Red shook his head. "Nathan is lazy, cunning, connivin', and well experienced in manipulation. He may be taking his time to size them up, but I'm sure it won't take him long to lead the rest into some kind of mutiny. We better keep a close watch for a few days."

"You want me to have Jake and Billy stay with them at night?"

"I think they could use a little breathing space. We'll watch from a distance and only step in if we find it necessary. The busier we keep them, the less likely they'll have energy to fight with each other, or allow Nathan to talk them into doing somethin' stupid." He paused for a moment. "So what's your impression of Sean and Carlos?"

"If it weren't for Sean's freckled face and red hair, I'd think he was a clone of Billy. He hasn't shown any of Billy's temper yet, but he's wired for sound and runs at the mouth just like him. Carlos seems more reserved, even laid-back. I can't get a read on him yet. He and Sean seem to be growing tight. I'm not sure if that's a good thing or bad. And at this point, it's a toss of the coin whether they become Nathan's minions or adversaries."

"Time will tell. Either way it's likely to be a pain in our butts." Red stood to empty ash from his pipe into the fireplace. He replaced the tobacco, lit it, and leaned against the hearth, puffing on his pipe. "It might be dangerous to let grass grow under their feet. We better not let them have time to plot. Rain is headed our way tonight, so after lunch let's put them to work patchin' the roof and replacing the rotten logs on their cabin. You and Billy supervise them, and I'll take Bud and Jake out on a cat hunt."

THE SOUNDS OF the distant evening thunder lured Red outside, where he settled in a porch chair, raised his feet against a post, and waited for the darkening skies to bring the storm.

"I thought you'd be out here," Bud said as he stepped out the door. "You're attracted to electrical storms like a bug to light."

"I like the price of the show." Red watched the bolts of lightning race across the sky. "I thought you were playin' cards with the men."

"I was, but when Billy and Lee's argument over cheating escalated into Billy tossing the table, I was done."

"Who was doing the cheating?"

"Both. And neither is any good at it."

Red grinned as he watched another web of lightning flash across the clouds, basking the canyon in momentary light. Then he saw his nervous herd. "The horses are as jumpy as a cat in a room full of rockers." He watched the frightened horses run from one end of the corral to the other. "Good thing you boys brought them in off the meadow."

"I don't exactly enjoy spending the day tracking spooked horses through the mountains." Bud sat in a rocking chair. "One good bolt of lightning and they'll stick their tails in the air and jump the fence."

"If we're lucky, the storm will have the opposite effect on the campers," said Red. "I doubt there's much chance they'll dare venture away from cover with the lightning we have headed this way."

"At least it should keep the cougar from coming anywhere near the ranch. Too bad we didn't see any signs of it."

Red pushed his hat up off his forehead. "I'm beginning to wonder if it exists at all." A thought had him looking at Bud. "Did you get the new boy settled?"

"I did, and I can't say I enjoyed it. Felt like I was leading young Noah to slaughter when I shoved him in with all those older and much bigger boys. He may only differ in age by a few years, but it can be a big difference when a fourteen-year-old gets tossed in with boys of sixteen and seventeen. When I left, he had the look of a mouse surrounded by hungry cats. I have to wonder if he isn't headed for a grueling summer."

Red took the pipe from his mouth and studied it. "You know, I haven't had a litter of pups that didn't have a runt. The funny thing is the runt always seems to grow to be the fastest and smartest of the pack. Isn't that right, girl?"

Tan Dog raised her head slightly and thumped her tail against the porch.

Red reached down and stroked her ears. "I think it's because they have greater pressure to survive than the others. Hopefully the same will hold true for the boy."

"I don't know. If I were him, I'd make fast friends with Carlton and stick to him like stink on shit."

"Sounds like you speak from experience."

Bud nodded. "I spent a fair amount of time inside a school locker. Like Noah, I was small for my age, probably no more than ninety-five pounds soaking wet. I became a favorite target of a group of bullies who took great sport in tormenting me on a daily basis. Then came the day I got my skivvies pulled up over my head in front of sweet Lucy Daniels. There I stood with my tighty whities over my ears, staring at the pity in the eyes of my crush. Something just snapped, and I jumped the biggest bully, climbing him like a crazed spider monkey. I still got the worst of it, mind you. Bled like a stuck hog, but I never had a moment of trouble after that. Guess the hoodlums thought I was nuts and not worth messing with. Or maybe they were afraid I'd bleed all over them, like I did on their leader. Surface veins can be a real problem for a boxer, but they sure come in handy for scaring off a bully. Maybe I should take Noah aside and give him a few pointers."

Red watched another bolt of lightning race across the dark

sky. "Just keep an eye on him and see if he can't find his own way first. If that doesn't work, then I'll let you teach him that monkey thing."

Drops of rain began to hit the porch roof. With a boom of thunder, the skies opened up, pouring rain down on the ranch.

"Good thing you had the campers start on the repairs for their own cabin first," Bud said over the pounding rain. "Those walls had more holes than a slice of Swiss cheese."

Red looked out through the waterfall coming off the roof. "I don't think they would have enjoyed sharing their cabin with critters, and in rain the likes of this, the dry of their cabin would draw wood rats like whores to a navy ship."

Bud chuckled. "I'm kinda sorry to hear we put a stop to that. It might have been entertaining to hear them scream like little girls."

RED WOKE TO clear skies, fresh air, and the scent of vegetation washed-clean from the downpour the night before. He gazed out over the glistening dew covered meadow.

"Would you like me to fetch you a cup of coffee," Woody asked as he joined Red on the porch. "Billy made a fresh pot."

"That swill isn't coffee," Red grumbled. "I'd make a stronger cup by tying a bag of grounds to my ass and dunking myself in the river."

Woody laughed. "The only person I know with the same fondness for that tar you call coffee is my mother. Still drinks a pot a day."

"How old is she now?"

"Just turned ninety and as cantankerous as ever." Woody shook his head. "The woman never has gotten the irony in calling me a son of a bitch." He paused at the sight of the activity in the corral. "I see Bud's giving our resident hoodlums a little payback instead of breakfast."

"It took some effort to talk him out of stringin' them up by their thumbs," said Red.

"Whose bright idea was it to empty all the hay out of the barn last night?"

"The others were quick to point the finger at young Hollywood," Red replied. "I wouldn't say any of them are fans of his at the moment."

They watched as the forks of the Jackson lift lowered down to chomp another bite of loose hay. The line of boys then pulled a rope, raising the load up under the hay hood where Noah grabbed the forks and pulled the lift along a track into the hayloft.

"Bud was happier when I told him he could make the boys take the place of horses in pulling the hay forks."

Woody chuckled. "Every year I think we've seen it all, and then the new batch has to go and prove me wrong. But even I have to admit using a pile of hay as a landing pad for riding the lift out of the barn was an ingenious idea. It certainly was another first."

"I believe that was the last time they'll think playin' in hay is fun. They're lucky the barn wasn't full, or they'd be working 'til way after dinner."

"They'll love being told they get to do it all over again when this year's hay is ready to be put up." Woody thought for a moment. "I realize Nathan's a little slow between the ears, but I wonder if the others have finally figured out this nonsense always comes around to bite 'em in the ass."

"From the angry looks Carlton keeps giving Nathan, we may not have to worry about him coming up with anymore harebrained ideas."

Hours passed.

"Well, that's the last of it," Woody said as the final load was lifted. "I bet those boys are famished after missing breakfast."

"I wouldn't fret over that," said Red. "If I had my way, they'd be eating dry tuna on toast. They certainly don't deserve any special treatment."

"Doubt Lee's very happy about keeping lunch for them."

"No, and I'm sure he'll let them know about it."

The men watched as the boys trudged by the lodge, worn-out and sweaty. Nathan walked ahead of the others, around the Meyers' cabin and the old bunkhouse, taking the path back to their cabin to get cleaned up for their midafternoon lunch.

"Looks like we've got some conspiring going on." Woody nodded toward the four boys whispering behind Nathan. They watched as the boys suddenly bolted forward, tackling Nathan to the ground. Each grabbed a leg or arm and together they swung him into the pond. "How many times do you think that boy's gonna end up in the water this summer?"

"I don't know, but I doubt that's the last," said Red.

The laughing boys walked on, leaving Nathan cussing as he fumbled to get out of the pond.

"You think the others have finally learned their lesson on following Nathan's stupid ideas?" Woody asked.

"Not a chance."

RED AND BUD WERE walking out of the barn when they heard a plane fly over and circle back.

"That's Russell Elmer." Red watched as the plane came back again and landed. "He said he'd be givin' Edith and Leroy a ride back today."

"No offense to Edith, but it sure has been quiet with her gone. I can't say I haven't enjoyed it," Bud said, standing with Red, waiting for the plane.

Red nodded. "I admit it has been nice not having her and Lee go at it, but it seems like something's missing without her."

"I guess the garden does look a little bland without Edith's floral dresses and that big fake-bouquet hat of hers. I especially like the way she completes the ensemble with army boots and knee-high socks."

"She is a snappy dresser," Red said as they walked out to greet the plane parking in the field near the lodge.

It took a bit of effort for Edith to squeeze her plump body

through the small door of the plane, but she finally succeeded in stepping down to the ground. Although Leroy was rail-thin, his extraction wasn't any easier since he was crammed in the backseat with their stack of bags.

"Here, hand me that bag in your lap," Edith ordered Leroy. "Don't drop that one," she told Russell as he unloaded a bag from the other side of the plane. "That has breakables in it."

"You got an anvil in here?" Russell asked, setting the heavy bag down.

"I'm guessing there's a month's supply of hooch in that bag," Bud whispered to Red.

"Half a month at best," Red said softly. "We are talking Edith and Leroy. Why do you think Edith has to make a trip to the dentist every two weeks?"

"Since her teeth never look any better, I'm guessing it isn't for oral health. She could eat an apple through a picket fence with those things. But even with a few missing, she seems to have plenty enough to chew Leroy's hide."

Red and Bud watched as Leroy struggled to carry several heavy bags, while Edith followed with nothing more than a purple purse in hand.

"Edith seems to be in a mood," Red said. "I wonder what's got her feathers ruffled."

Edith stopped to scold Leroy for dropping a bag.

"I suppose we could help," Bud suggested.

Red grabbed Bud by the arm, stopping him. "And get in the middle of one of Edith's browbeating tirades? Not on your life."

"I never get to see my sister enough," Edith complained as she walked behind her husband. "And every time I do, you have to go and act like a jackass. Would it have killed you to give her a compliment once in a while? I don't know why you have to be such a Grumpy Gus whenever you're around her. You know how lonely she's been since losing Marvin."

Leroy rolled his eyes at Red and Bud as he walked by,

mumbling under his breath, "Lucky bastard."

"What was that?" snapped Edith.

"I said, yes, dear."

"I'm just sayin', since Marvin's passing left you as the head of the family, it seems you could at least try to be nicer." Edith stepped around Leroy when he paused to rearrange his load.

Leroy frowned at his wife's back and then looked over at the men. "Ha! Head of the family—my ass! If I'm the head, Edith must be the neck 'cause that confounded woman turns me anyway she wants."

RED SIPPED WHISKEY as the soft rumble of thunder moved across the sky for the second night.

"Well, look at you sittin' out here like you ain't got a speck of sense," Edith said as the porch door slammed behind her. "I swear, someday a lightning bolt is gonna go clean through you and melt your boots right to this here porch."

Red puffed another stream of smoke into the air. "As long as I go with my boots on, I reckon I won't kick up a fuss as to how I'm sent off to heaven."

Edith raised a brow at him. "Heaven? When your time comes, I'm thinkin' you'll be goin' the other direction."

"Oh well, it's all good. If I had the choice, I'd take heaven for the climate and hell for the company. But it sure is nice to know you have concern for my welfare, Edith."

"Concern, my sweet petunias," she huffed. "Your dyin' would just leave me with one more mess to clean up. Be just like you."

"I'll try not to put you out." Red looked at the plate Edith held. "Are those your famous biscuits?"

"They are. And if Leroy doesn't get out here with the cocoa, the youngsters will be eatin' 'em cold." She pulled the door open and shouted, "Leroy, get your bony butt out here."

"You screechin' like a crazy woman don't get the cocoa poured into the thermos no faster," Leroy grumbled as he came out the door. "I burnt my hand, thanks to you."

Looking stern, Edith placed a hand on her hip. "I hope you didn't waste much of it. I had just enough for them five boys. And where are the cups?"

Leroy frowned at her. "Cups? You didn't say nothin' 'bout no cups."

"I suppose you expect them to drink out of their shoes?"

"Damn, woman," he growled as he disappeared back into the lodge.

"Here, I'll let you have a biscuit while we're waitin'." Edith lowered the plate to Red. "I was gonna make them earlier, but Lee ran me out of the kitchen. I had to wait until Mr. High-and-Mighty was gone for the night."

Red hesitated before taking the top biscuit from the stack.

Edith shook her head. "I tell you, if he don't stop spittin' Chinese insults at me, I'm gonna stick him with a handle and use him as a mop."

"Now, Edith, you know how territorial Lee is about the kitchen. It is his work space, after all."

"Well, it's mine when he's not here, and I don't appreciate him gettin' in my face every time he decides I've left some little thing out of place."

Leroy came through the door. "Okay, I've got the damn cups. Can we get this done so I can go to bed?"

"I'm warnin' you, Leroy. You had better put a smile on your face and be nice to them boys." Edith's expression softened as she turned to Red. "I'm excited to meet Gil Harper's boy. I feel like he's the grandson I never had," Edith gushed. Then she whirled on Leroy, poking a finger in his chest. "And you're gonna act like a grandfather, not a cranky old fart. You hear me?"

Leroy rubbed the spot where she'd poked him. "I'll grin like a donkey eatin' cactus if gets me to my bed."

Red looked up at the sky. "If you don't want those biscuits getting soggy, you two better make a run for it before the rain hits." He watched Edith and Leroy walk off the porch and onto the path leading to the boys' cabin. Then he looked down at the biscuit in his hand. He held it out to Tan Dog, but she sniffed it and turned away. *You know her cooking is bad when a dog won't eat it.* He tapped the biscuit on the arm of his chair. *I sure hope none of the boys break a tooth.*

He was alone for only a few minutes before Jake and Billy came up on the porch. "What the devil happened to you two?" he asked when he saw the feathers in their hair.

"When we got back to the staff cabin, we found all of Edith's chickens inside." Jake brushed feathers from his head.

Red grinned. "And so it begins. These boys were quick to get to the pranks."

"Damn campers think they're real funny," Billy said, wiping feathers from his shoulder. "They're about to find out how funny we can be."

Jake bent to brush feathers from his pants. "We just saw all five of them sneaking behind the lodge with Nathan leading the way."

Red nodded to Bud and Woody as they came from the barn. "It seems Nathan has recruited the others to help him steal food." He looked down at Tan Dog. "They must have had the same opinion of Edith's biscuits as you did, girl."

"I wondered how long it'd be before they raided the kitchen," Bud said, reaching out to pick a feather off Jake. "You two lookin' to tar and feather them?"

Billy frowned. "No, but that's not a bad idea. The little assholes turned chickens loose in our cabin. And you're not going to be happy with what's all over your bed."

Woody turned to Red. "Whatever your plan is—I'm in."

Red gnawed on his pipe, thinking. Then he looked at Jake and Billy. "You two go in and watch the kitchen. If they get in, scare the piss out of them with pots and pans. The men and I will cover outside, in case they go for the supply rooms." As Jake and Billy disappeared into the lodge, Red turned to his men. "Well, the way I see it, they had their fun. Now I say we have some of our own."

"What'd you have in mind?" Bud asked.

"Why don't you boys take the skins from the tack room and sneak around to the back of the kitchen. An encounter with a couple bears should make them think twice about leavin' their cabin after dark."

"It'll be our pleasure," Woody said, laughing.

"I'll fire off a shot or two to help drive the message home," said Red.

The men nodded and walked to the barn to prepare their prank.

While Bud and Woody plotted, Red took a rifle from the rack on the wall of the lodge and picked up a screwdriver from a cabinet drawer. He walked across the gathering room to the wall of logs, stuck the screwdriver in the crack, and pried open a short section of the log. He reached into the hidden compartment for a box of ammunition, loaded two rounds into his rifle, and secured the rest back in the hiding place.

Inside the tack room, Bud and Woody laughed as they gathered the bearskins and rushed out into the aisle of stalls. There they tossed their well-worn hats on a pile of hay and threw the hides over their backs. With the bear heads hanging down over their faces, they started for the door, stopping when Woody threw an arm out across Bud. "Should we growl?" he asked, tipping his head up so he could see Bud from under the hide.

Bud shrugged. "I suppose so."

The grown men looked completely out of character as they practiced and argued over who had the better growl. After finally agreeing on the proper technique, they walked out into the cover of darkness, and crept to the back of the lodge. Bud peeked around the corner and whispered to Woody, "Nathan's trying to jimmy the kitchen lock with the others watching."

"Good, that gives us an element of surprise." Woody

adjusted the head over his face. "Let's take cover."

Distracted by shoving at each other for a better view, the boys were oblivious to what hid in the trees behind them.

Bud and Woody crouched in a thick cover of brush. With only the bear heads visible, Woody growled loudly while Bud shook the brush.

The boys whirled around.

"What was that?" Sean whispered.

They froze in a huddle, and another growl made them clutch each other. Then Carlos pointed. "Is that a bear?"

"Run!" Sean shouted.

In a tangle of arms and legs, the boys scrambled to make their escape, sprinting even faster when a gunshot rang out.

"What was that?" Billy said as he and Jake ran out the backdoor.

Red walked out of the shadows with the rifle cradled across his arm, and Bud and Woody came out of the brush, laughing.

"That'll teach them to go sneaking around at night," Bud said, chuckling as he and the others followed Red to the corner of the supply shed, where they had a clear view of the boys racing down the path to their cabin.

"I wonder how many soiled themselves?" said Woody.

"Good thing there really isn't a bear after them. They would have been eaten by now," Bud said, watching as the boys appeared under the light on the porch, fumbling to open the cabin door.

Woody laughed. "Now, how do they think they're all going to fit through that door at the same time?"

"I'll be," Bud said. "Did you see Noah dive between their legs?"

Red grinned. "I told you the runt always has the best survival instincts."

CHAPTER 7

"Daylight's burnin' in the swamps," Red shouted as he flipped the campers' light on at dawn.

Tan Dog followed him in and immediately circled the room, sniffing the piles of clothing and possessions scattered about the cabin.

As he walked between the two rows of beds, Red scanned the groaning boys, covering their eyes.

"What the hell is that supposed to mean? Nathan asked from beneath the pillow he held over his head.

"It means you should be half finished with your chores by now," said Red. "And there won't be any breakfast until they're done. Get your clothes on and meet me outside for your assignments. You have to earn your keep at this camp."

"Camp, my ass," Nathan grumbled as he slowly sat up. "It's nothing more than a fuckin' work prison. Ouch! Hey, cut it out!" he cried after Red slapped the back of his head.

"That will be the last time you use that particular word. We have guests coming to the ranch soon, and you will not insult them with such language." Red bent down, his face so close to Nathan's his pipe nearly brushed the teenager's nose. "You got that, boy? Or do I need to rattle the cobwebs from your head?"

Nathan flinched and leaned away from Red. "Okay, okay. I got it." He bent to pick his jeans up off the floor and began to pull them on. He had one leg in when Tan Dog grabbed the other and pulled back, growling. "I said I got it. Call your dog off."

Red whistled, and Tan Dog released the jeans, ran to his side, and sat, panting up at him. "I guess she doesn't like back talk any more than I do. Come on, girl." She followed him outside, where they waited. A few moments passed before the boys began to trickle out one at a time. It didn't matter to Red that none had bothered with a comb, but when Carlos came out wearing jeans hanging below his rump, exposing his crimson boxers—that mattered a lot. "Pull your pants up, boy."

"They're supposed to be like this. It's the style," Carlos said.

"Not around here it isn't," Red said, annoyed. "You either pull those things up over your drawers, or I'll do it for you." He took his belt off and handed it to Carlos. "Now get those things hitched up, and don't let me see you like that again."

Carlos fed the belt through the loops, pulled it tight, and fastened the buckle. "This looks stupid," he said, looking down at the bulky gathers around his waist.

Red harrumphed. "And yet you looked like such a genius with your bloomers hangin' out."

Sean, the last to appear, came out of the cabin, groaning. "Man, it's barely light out." He grabbed his growling stomach, whining, "Man, I'm so hungry. Can't we eat first?"

Red shook his head. "No, as I told you, chores are to be done first. It will be light in a few minutes, which means you're already late."

"You mean we have to get up this early every morning?" Sean looked shocked.

"Of course. This isn't early for the animals." Red pointed at Noah and Carlton. "A basket is waiting for you at the chicken coop. You two collect eggs and take them to the kitchen. Then report to Bud at the barn, and he'll show you how to muck stalls." He moved on to Carlos. "Woody is gonna teach you to milk the cow and separate the cream. Go find him in the barn. He ignored the grimace Carlos made as he turned to the last two boys.

"I have something special for Mr. Foul Mouth and the

Whiner. Come with me. I'd like to introduce you to some feeder hogs." Red picked up the garbage bags he had left along the path and handed one each to Nathan and Sean. Then he picked up a bag of hog chow and slung it over his shoulder. "Follow me."

"Shit that smells. What's in here?" Nathan looked inside the bag. "Gross!"

"Table scraps," Red said, turning to walk down the path. "What's garbage to you is a smorgasbord to a hog."

"Wait," Nathan shouted, running after Red. "Look, these are five thousand dollar shoes. They're not on the market yet and definitely not the kind you wear to slop hogs."

Red glanced down at Nathan's scarlet sneakers. "They'll wash."

"Are you crazy? You can't throw them in a washer. A person would have to be completely stupid to do that."

Red continued walking. "What's stupid is paying five thousand dollars for somethin' you wear on your feet."

"What are you doing?" Sean asked when Nathan stopped and stared down at his feet.

"Mourning the loss of what were perfectly sweet shoes."

They followed Red across the grassy area between the campers' cabin and the guest cabins, walking toward the end of his property. As they trudged single file along the thin path, Sean glanced back to Nathan. "Do you have any idea where he's taking us?"

"Not a clue. But wherever it is, I know I'm not going to like it."

When they finally caught up to him, Red was standing near a four-person rowboat on the bank of the largest of three ponds on his property. This one was farthest from the lodge and guest cabins.

"Welcome to Pig Island," Red said as he tossed in the bag of chow and shoved the boat into the water. Hanging on to the rope attached to the bow, he motioned to the boys. "Come aboard." He steadied the boat as the two got in and sat on the second bench seat. Using his foot, he pushed the boat from the bank, jumped in, and took a seat on the front bench facing the boys. "This isn't a motor boat," he said, pointing to the paddles. "Get rowin'."

"Damn," Sean said as they approached the bank of the island, where ten hogs fought for position around the low metal feeder sitting a few yards from the water. "When you said feeder hogs, I was thinking, well, you know, like the little pig in the Babe movie. These are a lot bigger than I thought they'd be."

Red turned to look at the hogs. "Leroy has been feedin' them through the spring. They only weigh a little over one hundred pounds right now. By the time we butcher them, they'll weigh anywhere from 240 to 270."

"What's the difference between a pig and a hog?" asked Sean.

"From the smell of it, I'd say the size of their stink." Nathan held his nose.

"A pig is anything under sixty pounds," Red replied. "Anything over that is a hog."

"Can't they swim?" Nathan asked.

"Sure, if they needed to, but since they're fed here and have plenty of mud to wallow in, they don't have a reason to leave. Once the weather turns warmer, the island becomes the safest place for them. Predators won't cross the water, and it keeps them from damaging the ranch with all the rooting they do. And I very much doubt our guests would appreciate hogs running loose."

"Why do they keep biting each other?" Sean looked concerned.

"They don't need a reason, but it only gets worse when competing for food. Best to spread the scraps out so they don't all end up in one place."

Sean gulped when a hog tore a gash in the shoulder of

another. "They won't bite us, will they?"

Red saw how the boys nervously stared at the island. "Make sure you don't give them the chance. The trick is to throw some of the food as far as you can. That keeps them away from you and busy long enough to spread the rest."

"Wait." Nathan turned big eyes on Red. "Can't we just throw it out from the boat?"

"No, you need to take it closer to the center, drawing them away from the feeder." Red pointed to the bags. "You'll be fine. Pick up the scraps and get ready."

"Is it too late to sign up for something else?" asked Sean. "Like maybe gardening or cleaning toilets?"

"You don't need both of us," Nathan said, sliding his bag to Sean.

Sean shoved both bags over to Nathan. "No you don't. You do it."

"You'll both do it," Red said, his tone serious. "And don't mess around. These hogs see you as nothin' more than walking dinner."

A few yards from the bank, Red reached into Sean's bag, pulled two large handfuls of table scraps out, and threw them about twenty feet toward the center of the island. The squealing hogs raced after the food, biting at each other as they went. "Okay, it's safe to run the boat ashore." The boys rowed the bow up onto the bank. "The scraps will keep them busy long enough for me to get the feeder filled with hog chow. That means one of you throws the scraps, while the other fills the feeder with chow. If you do it right, it shouldn't take more than a couple minutes. You're to feed them twice a day—before you have your breakfast and again before dinner. My men are capable of doing this alone, so there won't be any excuses for the two of you."

"God it stinks," said Sean as he stepped onto the muddy bank, dragging the plastic bag with him.

"A hog farmer would tell you that's the smell of money."

Red picked up the hog chow and waited for Nathan to step out of the boat. "Boy, you're slower than molasses on a winter mornin'. Could we get this done already? And you might want to remember those animals are carnivores. You fall down, they will eat you. So watch each other's backs and no screwing around."

"Great, this just keeps getting better," groaned Nathan as he searched for safe footing along the bank. What looked to be solid ground mushed beneath his weight, oozing mud over the top of his shoes. "Shit!"

"Quit worrying about your precious shoes and get in here," Sean said, dodging brush as he made his way up the slope. He stopped a few yards from where the hogs were milling around, searching the ground for the scraps Red had thrown. He began emptying his bag, throwing some and pouring the rest in front of him. The last morsel fell from the bag just as the hogs took notice of him. "I'm out of here!" He turned and ran for the boat.

Preoccupied with picking his way around the muddiest areas, Nathan didn't see Sean run through the brush toward him. "Watch it, you jerk," he shouted when Sean collided with him, knocking him to the ground. "God, you're such an asshole!" He jumped up from the mud.

"Gross, you're covered in pig shit." Sean held his nose. "Maybe you should swim back."

Nathan raised his fist and took a step toward Sean, but he slipped and fell down again.

Sean looked down, laughing. "Looks like your fancy kicks could use some shoe chains."

"Shut up," Nathan shouted, slipping again when he tried to get up.

"I'd help you up, but I don't see why both of us need to have shit on our hands." Sean walked past him.

"Yeah, well, maybe you'd like to be covered in this." Nathan reached into his bag, pulled out a handful of sloppy scraps, and threw them at Sean's back.

"You idiot!" Sean exclaimed, picking food from his clothing.

Red had already filled the long metal feeder with hog chow and was back in the boat, watching the boys. "Stop your nonsense and get this done already." Then he noticed two of the hogs racing for them. *Ah, hell.* "Get out of there!"

Sean looked over his shoulder and turned to run, but it was too late. The two hogs slammed into his legs, knocking him off his feet. He struggled to get up, but the squealing hogs kept stepping on him as they battled over the food. "Get them off me."

Nathan dropped his bag and ran for the boat.

"Help him," Red shouted as Nathan came down the slope.

"I'm not going to be hog chow," Nathan said, lifting his leg to get into the boat.

Red raised a paddle up, keeping him from getting in. "You never leave a man behind. Here, take this paddle. I'll bring the other."

Nathan looked back at the hogs and gulped.

"Come on, boy, don't make me drag you."

Finally taking the paddle, Nathan followed Red. When two additional hogs joined in the battle with the others, he stopped and looked back at the boat.

"Don't even think about it," Red said, grabbing Nathan by the arm and pulling him up the slope to Sean. "You take those two. I'll get the others."

"Say what?" Nathan stared at the fighting hogs.

"Use the paddle to push the hogs away from Sean!"

Red smacked the hogs' snouts with the paddle until he broke them apart, but they only separated for a moment before coming back at each other. He blocked one with the paddle and kicked the other in the shoulder. It ran squealing from Sean. Red ran the other off by slamming the flat of the paddle against its side.

On the other side of Sean, Nathan struggled to break up

another battle. He stuck the end of the paddle against the hog's side and pushed, but it did nothing to stop the two hogs from tearing into each other. He pushed harder and finally succeeded in pushing one of the hogs off Sean, and the other followed it, biting. As the two continued to bloody each other, a third came to quietly gobble the food scraps.

As the hog went after a partial slice of bread lying across Sean's leg, its teeth tore through his jeans, scraping his flesh. "Ouch! It bit me!" He rolled over and came face-to-face with another hog.

"Watch out, you've got lunch meat in your hair," Nathan shouted as he swung his paddle against the side of the hog that bit Sean. It squealed and jumped back.

Sean sucked in a breath and scrambled back away from the hog at his face. As the hog came toward him, a paddle suddenly slammed down in front of Sean, blocking the hog.

"Get," Red said, hitting the hog's snout with the paddle. As the hog retreated, he reached down and helped Sean to his feet. "Nathan, get Sean to the boat."

Nathan hesitated for a moment, then draped Sean's arm over his shoulder and supported him as he hobbled to the boat.

Red used the paddle to hold the hogs back until the boys got to safety. Then he picked up Nathan's bag, flung the scraps from it, and strode to the boat. He sat next to Nathan with Sean sitting on the bench facing them. Using the paddle to push back from the bank, he looked at Sean. "How's the leg."

Sean pulled his pant leg up, exposing the bleeding wound.

"It's not too deep. We'll get you up to the lodge where it can be washed up and bandaged." Red puffed on his pipe, stroking the paddle through the water on his side of the boat, while Nathan stroked on his side. "I bet that's a lesson you won't soon forget."

Sean looked down at his leg. "I think I'll have a scar to remind me."

"Good, maybe it will also remind you not to be such a

douche bag," said Nathan.

Red paused his rowing to slap the back of Nathan's head.

"Ouch," Nathan shouted, rubbing his head.

"I'm sure you don't need to ask what that was for."

CHAPTER 8

"Hey, Woody," Red said as he came out of the lodge. "Did you have any trouble getting Carlos to milk the cow?"

"No trouble getting him to do it, but a lot of trouble getting him to get it done. I couldn't stand to watch any longer. At the speed he's going, I doubt he'll have her milked out by dinner tonight. I was about to go check on him again."

"I'll take care of it in a minute." Red sat down in a porch rocking chair. "He couldn't be any worse than the two I had feeding hogs."

"I take it that was an epic fail?"

"You can say that. They may have to burn their clothes. Once they finish their showers and get changed, I'm gonna put them to work on somethin' where they might actually have the ability to stay on their feet."

"Looks like you don't have to wait long," Woody said at the sight of Nathan and Sean strolling toward the lodge.

Nathan had changed into another pair of fresh jeans, while Sean had chosen to wear shorts.

"What do we have here?" Woody asked as he stared at Sean's bloody leg.

"A hog bit me." Sean dabbed the wound with a tissue. "Will I need stitches?"

Woody rose from his chair and bent to examine Sean's wound. "Nah, it's nothing more than a scratch. But it does need disinfecting. Come on inside and I'll help you get that cleaned up."

"Thanks, Woody." Red held the door for them. "Not you," he said, stopping Nathan. "You're comin' with me."

"Now what?" Nathan groaned as he followed Red on the path leading to the barn. "Let me guess. You have a bear that needs its teeth brushed. No, I know. You want me to give a skunk a bath." They walked past the donkey grazing near the front of the barn. "Or maybe you want me to give an enema to a constipated donkey."

Red glanced back at the donkey and then at Nathan. "Believe me, you'd be safer with the skunk or bear. But if you aren't attached to your teeth, go ahead and have a go at Satan's backside. Just let me get a chair first. I'll want a front-row seat to that show."

"You named that little thing Satan?"

"Yes, and for good reason. What he lacks in size, he makes up for in mean."

"If he's so mean, why do you keep him?"

Red shrugged. "Entertainment."

Continuing on to the barn, he held the door and waved Nathan inside. "Grab a pitchfork and give Noah and Carlton a hand with cleaning stalls."

"Great, like I haven't been in enough animal shit for one day."

"That's the spirit."

"I didn't...never mind." Nathan grabbed the pitchfork Red handed him and walked into the open stall. As he disappeared into one, Billy stormed out of another.

"What's got your undies in a wad?" Red asked when he saw the angry look on Billy's face.

"Lee. That little troll won't pay me the money he owes me from the poker game."

"Watch the name-calling," Red warned.

"He's a cheat and a squelcher."

Red frowned at him.

"You can't blast me for that. Those were descriptions of his character, not names." Billy kicked the dirt with the toe of his boot. "I'm so sick of him always reneging on a bet. Even after getting caught cheating, he refused to pay up. Just ask the guys. They'll tell you what he did. Sometimes I could just kill him."

"The way I hear it, you were right there with him in the cheating department."

"I was just giving Lee a taste of his own medicine." Billy turned and glared down the aisle toward the stall where he had left Lee feeding the calf a bottle. "God, I hate that asshole. It wouldn't hurt my feelings if he went back to China."

"What have you got against the people of China?" Red grinned.

The tension in Billy's shoulders softened slightly. "Yeah, I guess they don't deserve him either." He walked past Red, pausing at the door. "I think I'll talk to Woody and see if he could build a rocket ship to take Lee on a one-way trip to outer space."

As the door closed behind Billy, Red heard Lee cooing to the calf in Chinese. He strode to the open door and peered into the spotted calf's stall. "I hear she has a name."

"Buttercup." Lee held the bottle in one hand and stroked the head of the suckling Jersey calf with the other.

"We could assign one of the boys to feed her."

Lee frowned. "No, they not do it right."

"Could I try?" asked a voice behind them. "I've never been around a baby cow before."

Red turned and found Carlton standing in the aisle. "You want to feed the calf?"

"Yeah." Carlton's chubby face beamed with eagerness.

Lee hesitated, studying the boy a moment before handing the bottle over to him. After making a few corrections to Carlton's feeding technique, Lee walked from the stall, telling Red as he passed. "Send boy to kitchen. He works with me."

"You may not know it," Red said, watching Carlton run a finger down the calf's face. "But an invitation to work in the kitchen isn't something Lee takes lightly. That was quite an endorsement."

Carlton shrugged. "I'm okay with that. I like to cook." He smiled down at the calf. "And I like to feed the baby cow. Could I do it every day?"

"Her name is Buttercup." Red watched the calf drain the last of the bottle. "You'll have to take that up with Lee. He seems to have adopted her." He took the empty bottle from Carlton and slid the stall door closed behind them. "You go get cleaned up and report to the kitchen."

"Where are you going, Carlton?" Noah asked as he and Nathan came out from a stall picking straw from their hair.

"I'm going to help Lee cook breakfast."

"Can I come?" Noah asked, turning a hopeful look to Red.

"Sure, I don't see why not."

Carlos walked out of the milking stall, carrying a pail. "I think I finally got the hang of it." He beamed.

Red looked inside the pail, frowning at the bits of straw and manure floating in the milk. "So, how many times did you knock the bucket over?"

Carlos looked sheepish. "Three. Okay, maybe four."

"I'd say you need a little more practice. Pour that into the cat dish by the kitchen door." The wet stain on Carlos' jeans caught Red's eye. "And then you might want to take a shower."

"I fell off the stool." Carlos looked down at his soiled jeans. "A few times."

Red followed the boys to the cutoff to their cabin, walking on alone to the back of the lodge. As he came around the corner, he saw Leroy poking a finger in Lee's chest. Lee's face was flushed with anger. Red groaned. *Now what?*

"I'm sure you men could find something better to do with your time," Red said as he walked past them.

Woody came out the kitchen door just as Lee stormed inside, slamming the door behind him.

"What was that about?" Woody asked Red as his gaze turned

from Lee to Leroy.

"Don't want to know, not going to ask," Red replied, watching an angry Leroy disappear around the corner of the lodge.

"I guess it's safest to stay out of the line of fire." Woody chuckled. "You'd think they would have learned to get along after all these years."

"Oil and water." Red shook his head. "They just don't mix."

"Speaking of oil and water," Woody said, watching the four boys walk toward their cabin. "Is Nathan getting along any better with the others? Or is he still stirring the pot every chance he gets?"

Before Red could answer, he saw Nathan throw a leg in front of Noah, tripping him. Nathan laughed when Noah fell.

As Carlton walked past Nathan, he threw an arm out and, without stopping, gave him a hard shove off the path.

Nathan let out a yelp as he fell backward, landing with a splash in the pond.

Red looked at Woody. "Does that answer your question?"

CHAPTER 9

For Lee Chang, it had been a very long day. But then, it always took a little time to find his rhythm after being off all winter.

It was long past dinner when he walked to his cabin, leaving Carlton and Noah to clean the kitchen and remove the three pies baking in the oven. He knew that without his supervision, the boys wouldn't clean his work space to his liking, but his mood was too dark to be anywhere near people. It had been one hell of a day, beginning with the young, long-haired hikers he had run off after finding them stealing food from the supply shed, ending in a massive fight with Edith over her meddling in his affairs.

He didn't bother to change his clothes when he got to his cabin. The call for alcohol was too great, and the case of beer he had stored in his antique ice cabinet wasn't going to do the job. Instead, he went straight for the whiskey bottle hidden in the firebox. Ignoring the glass on the mantel, he picked up the bottle, opened it, and took a long drink. Then he carried it to the only seat in his tiny cabin and collapsed into the leather armchair. He took another drink and looked down at his red berry stained cooking jacket. Then he noticed the juice on his medallion and wiped it on his sleeve.

Edith had taken him by surprise when she threw the pie at him. Just the thought of her made him tip the bottle back and take several more gulps. Oh, how he loathed that woman. Every year he had to battle Edith Meyer to win back his kitchen after months of it being solely her domain. She was twenty years his senior, yet she could still go toe-to-toe with him in an argument. He hadn't expected her to be that fast or have good aim. At least he'd been ready when she threw the next two pies. And now all three lay splattered across the walls and floor of *his* kitchen.

He took another drink and looked at the label—one of the bottles Red had hidden in his cabin behind the boxes under his bar. This wasn't a night for the cheap swill Red poured at the lodge. Only the good stuff would ease Lee's temper. It irked him to no end that Edith would elbow her way in on the pie-baking lesson he was giving to his newfound prodigy. For the first time, he had finally found the perfect kitchen helper. Carlton took to cooking as easily as he did eating, and more importantly, he kept his mouth shut while working.

Then Edith had to come in and throw her weight around, sticking her nose in his business and correcting everything he had told the boy. Who did she think she was, telling him how to bake pie? She still used lard in the crust, for God sake. It had to be her jealousy of his superior baking talents that led to the destruction of half of his master pieces. He also knew how quickly the staff and campers would devour the three remaining pies, leaving none for the visiting hikers who would stop by to sample the delectable pastries that he was known for making. Now he'd have to get up early to make more. Edith wouldn't care that she'd thrown his schedule off. The woman had no respect for order.

Three-quarters of a bottle and several hours later, Lee decided to check on Buttercup. The ground swayed under his feet as he forced his legs to stand. He clutched the bottle in one hand and grabbed the back of the chair with the other, steadying himself before staggering to the door. He stepped out into the dark. In his drunken condition, he hadn't thought to bring a light. With his blurred vision, it probably wouldn't have made much of a difference anyway.

As he walked through the barn door, he wondered why the

lights were still on. He supposed the damn fool campers were to blame. He blinked, struggling to focus his eyes as he lurched down the row of stalls. Sugar was snorting and pacing nervously in her stall. Moving on to the next stall, he noticed the door was halfway open. "Buttercup?" he called, standing in the doorway.

Lee stared at the red spattered walls and followed the trail down to the blood-soaked stall floor and the mutilated carcass of Buttercup.

Lee gasped, dropping the whiskey bottle as he stepped into the stall. Then he heard movement behind him and turned. But before he realized what was happening, a knife thrust into his gut. The blade entered above his pelvis and pulled upward, slicing him open to the chest before jerking away. Swaying on unsteady legs, Lee looked down at his gaping wound and wrapped his arms across his abdomen to keep his insides from pouring out. The knife hovered in the air, Lee's blood dripping from the tip, and then the blade plunged into his chest.

CHAPTER 10

"Lee's not in his cabin, boss," Jake said as he walked into the lodge after dawn.

Red struck a long match across the rock face of the gathering room fireplace and held it under the stack of wood. "Yeah, I figured as much. Every time he and Edith go at it, Lee gets a snoot full and wanders off into the woods to lick his wounds. As heated as last night's brawl got, it's likely we won't see him for a couple of days." The match failed to catch the kindling and burned out. He tossed it into the firebox as he had the previous four.

"Why is it that a single match can burn an entire forest, and it'll take an entire box of them to start a damn fire in a fireplace?" Red grumbled as he struck another match. This one finally caught the kindling.

"A few days from opening weekend is a fine time for Lee to do one of his disappearing acts," said Jake. "We're gonna need a cook. You want me to tell Edith she's on kitchen duty?"

Red lifted the half-burnt match to his pipe and held it to the tobacco until it caught. "No, I'm fairly sure she's in no condition to work. Edith and Leroy were hittin' the hooch pretty hard last night."

"How is that different from any other night with those two?" Jake asked, smiling.

"Anger and drinkin' never make for good bedfellows. I don't think I've ever seen Edith that angry. She was mad enough to kick a cat." Red tossed the match in the fireplace. "For years now, she's been threatening to kill Lee, and with the state she was in last night, I wasn't so sure she wouldn't actually do it. I even had to stop her from takin' one of the rifles from the display case."

Jake scratched his head. "I thought the display guns were never loaded."

"They aren't, but that wouldn't stop her from using one for batting practice on Lee's head. She was going after the gun John Wayne gave me. That rifle is special to me and I'd just as soon keep in one piece. After getting the keys to the gun case away from her, I hid them somewhere she won't find them."

"Sounds like you're more concerned for your gun than Lee's head."

A slight smirk came to Red's face. "I can always get another cook, but I can't replace that rifle." He walked past the gathering room chairs, motioning for Jake to follow him into the dining hall. There he paused at the side table, checking the progress of the percolating coffee pot. "Where's Billy?"

"He and Bud are bringing the horses in off the meadow."

"Well then, how about helping me break a few eggs?"

"I'm not much of a chef, but I know enough to scramble eggs and burn bacon." Jake followed Red into the kitchen. "I could use a little quiet time away from Billy anyway."

Red opened the refrigerator and handed Jake a bowl of eggs. "He does have the gift of gab."

"Gift?" Jake put the eggs on the counter. "I'd say it's more like an affliction. You know that he even talks in his sleep? Between his jabbering and Woody's snoring, it's damn hard to get any sleep in the staff cabin."

"I can imagine. I got my fill of communal sleeping as a firefighter."

The kitchen had two large stoves sitting side by side, one with a large flat grill top where Red laid strips of bacon. As the bacon began to sizzle, he reached over and took an iron pan down from a hook over the other stove. From the refrigerator, he took out the bowl of fresh-churned butter Woody had taught Carlos to make and spooned a small amount into the frying pan. He turned the gas on under the pan and returned to his grill.

As Jake whisked the eggs and poured the mixture into the pan, Red thought he noticed a more fluid maturity in the way Jake moved. It was something he had witnessed in other young men as they began to fill out. *Not yet the case for Billy.*

His thoughts went to his early morning ride, when he had watched his young wranglers as they walked to the barn.

Looking down from the ridge, Red had shaken his head when he saw Billy trip over a rock. *That boy never knows where his feet are.*

Billy, a recent business graduate from Oregon State University, still hadn't fully grown into his long, skinny legs. He was as awkward as a newborn colt, but at least he'd grown up from the high-strung ball of fury he was at seventeen when his wealthy father first sent him to the ranch. It hadn't been easy to teach him to control his hot temper, but by end of summer, and with the help of a number of tosses in the pond, Billy had finally cooled.

Sadly, a very different reason would bring Billy back the following year. His carefree world would never be the same after a fateful rainy day in October when his younger sister went missing from a local shopping mall. As the months passed without finding her, desperation turned to devastation for Billy and his parents. Finding the tragic loss too much to bare, Billy sought solace at the ranch the next summer.

Four seasons later, and Billy was still working at the ranch, and come fall, he would start a new career in sales for his father's Portland shipping business. *Maybe he'll finally put his motor mouth to good use. I pity the poor fool that tries to best him in negotiation. If there's anything that kid has plenty—it's wind. But with all his energy, I sure can't see him tied to an office chair.*

From his spot on the ridge, Red had smiled as he looked

down at Jake, his true success story. *This kid didn't come from money...far from it.* He remembered when he'd gotten the call from Jake's grandfather, a fellow retired Portland firefighter. Jake had been seventeen when his grandfather rescued him from his estranged daughter and son-in-law. Red could still hear the pain in the grandfather's voice when he told him of the abuse Jake had endured from his drug-addicted parents, suffering years of neglect from his mother and serving as a punching bag for his father.

Then one day, Jake finally snapped, unleashing his rage on his father, nearly beating him to death with his own fists. The authorities had determined it to be self-defense and placed Jake in his grandfather's care. Unfortunately, Jake was damaged goods at that point, and his grandfather was at a loss as to what to do with the troubled boy. Thinking the structured environment of a Catholic high school would be helpful, he enrolled his grandson in Jesuit High School in Beaverton. It took Jake no time to get expelled after he got into a fight on his first day. Then there was the pack of beer he stole from the corner grocery store, and the rock he threw through a neighbor's window after she asked him to turn his music down. The final straw came when the grandfather discovered Jake had begun hanging out with known gang members. That was it. His only hope was Red.

Jake's story was Red's most triumphant. He had known from experience that handling a wild boy wasn't that much different from breaking a colt. It was all about winning his trust, and that came from a firm hand and gentle encouragement. Jake had been more withdrawn than any boy he'd ever had at the ranch. Red was well experienced with extinguishing explosive tempers like Billy's, but the daily abuse Jake had suffered left him hard, distant, and resistant to authority. So Red made him his personal project, working side by side building a duplex-style guest cabin from the ground up.

He hadn't been overly concerned with the teenager's refusal

to work on the cabin the first two days. He knew that his rule of no food until work was done would eventually make the boy come around. So when Jake showed up at the worksite on the third morning, Red wasn't surprised and didn't comment on his arrival. He simply went about stripping the bark from a log while Jake watched, and then, without a word, he handed the drawknife over to him.

The change he saw was gradual, but by the end of the summer, the mean, angry, anti-social boy had turned into an even-tempered, responsible, hardworking young man with a newfound ambition.

That first summer at the ranch had given Jake something he'd never had before: stability, purpose, and pride. Red only needed to look at Jake's expression every time he saw his name written in the porch concrete, to know what the cabin they built together meant to him.

Red's thoughts were brought back to the present when Billy and Carlos burst through the kitchen door. Startled, he turned from his grill. "What the devil?"

"Bud needs you in the barn, boss," Billy said, breathing heavily from his run.

"It's horrible! There's blood and guts everywhere!" Carlos shouted. He slapped a hand over his mouth and ran for the garbage can.

"What the hell are you talkin' about, boy?"

"It's the calf," said Billy. "She's been slaughtered in her stall."

"Carlton wasn't done with collecting eggs, so Bud told me to feed her the bottle," Carlos said, wiping his mouth on his sleeve. "When I finally figured out what the bloody pile in the center of the stall was, I got the hell out of there."

"Yeah, he nearly ran Bud and me over when he came screaming out of the barn," said Billy. "He only stopped long enough to toss his cookies."

"Is it okay if I go lie down for a while?" Carlos asked,

holding his stomach.

Red nodded. "I think that would do us all a favor. And take that garbage bag with you." He watched Carlos leave through the back door and handed the metal spatula to Billy. "Here, take over for me." Red walked into the dining hall and out the front door. His long strides quickly took him off the porch and past the Meyers' cabin.

"Good mornin', Red," Leroy said as he came out of his cabin.

"If what I've been told rings true, this will prove to be anything but a good mornin'," grumbled Red as he motioned to Leroy. "Come with me, we've got trouble."

They walked into the barn and down the aisle to the stall where Bud stood looking down at the mutilated calf.

"Damn strangest thing I've ever seen." Bud shook his head as he stared down at the mangled remains. "Whoever did this took their sweet time with it."

"From the amount of blood in here, I'm thinkin' there can't be a drop left in her," Leroy said, looking around the red-spattered stall.

Red dodged the spots of blood-soaked straw as he moved closer to the calf carcass. "Is her head missing?"

"The whole thing's such a mess I can't tell." Bud pointed to a corner. "That looks to be a leg over there."

"Leroy, get me a pitchfork," Red said.

Leroy pulled a pitchfork from the pile of loose hay at the end of the aisle and carried it into the stall. "Here you go."

Red used the tines to roll the body over.

"She's been gutted." Bud pointed to the cut running down the calf's belly.

Red slid the fork under the body and moved it off to the side. "This is more than just a slaughter. It was a dissection, and a pretty precise one at that. See how each organ sits alone." He pointed the tines to where the lungs, heart, stomach, and intestines had been hiding under the body. "He took his time with those—there's not a single nick in them." Red picked up the calf leg lying near his feet and inspected the end. "It's cut clean at the joint." He held the leg out for Leroy and Bud to have a look. "No saw marks or tearing."

Leroy nodded. "Someone knows their way 'round a knife."

"And has a good and sharp one at that," Bud added.

"What's that by your foot?" Red asked, pointing to something in the straw near Bud.

Bud rolled it over with the toe of his boot, exposing a bumpy surface. "That would be a tongue."

"What a waste of a good animal." Leroy's mouth turned down even more than usual. "It don't make no sense. Maybe it was a vagrant lookin' to get him some veal, and he was interrupted before gettin' the job done."

Red rested the pitchfork against the stall wall. "I don't think food was the motivation behind this mess."

"So you're thinking this was done for sport?" Bud asked.

"I'd say spite," Leroy said, turning his head to spit chewing tobacco.

Red considered for a moment. "It has passed my mind that this could be retaliation for Lee runnin' off the three long hair hikers he found rummaging in the supply room yesterday. If it was them, they might not be too far away. Keep an eye out for three teenaged boys. They can't be hard to spot. One has a blue checkered bandana tied around a mass of dreadlocks and the other two have long stringy hair in bad need of soap and water." He turned and took a step, pausing when his foot came in contact with something under the bedding. He bent and brushed the straw away. "Well, that tears it." He stared down at Buttercup's head. "I think the sick bastards might have taken an ear as a trophy."

"That being the case, it was a good thing you didn't come upon them this morning," Bud said. "Or you might have ended up missing one of your own."

"This must have been done before I came to take my ride,"

Red said. "It would explain why Sugar was kicking up such a fuss this mornin'. At first I thought she was just in one of her pissy moods. Even then, it was odd for her not to stand still for saddling, and even stranger when she nearly dragged me out of the barn. When she tried to gallop out from under me when I only had a foot in the stirrup, I began to wonder if she'd gotten into some locoweed." He looked down at the calf carcass. "The smell of blood must have been making her nervous. She wouldn't go into the barn when we got back, so I left her out in the round pen. I was so fed up with wrestling with her I didn't even think to look in on the calf."

"Best you didn't." Leroy paused to spit tobacco juice near his feet. "The killer could have been hidin' somewhere, and you might have gotten the sharp end of a cutter."

"I'd think you would have noticed Tan Dog sniffing at the stall. Didn't she show any interest?" Bud asked.

"No, she caught the scent of somethin' long before we got to the barn and raced off toward the ponds." Red frowned. "Come to think of it, I haven't seen her since."

Leroy spat again. "I bet you'd find the knife that done this in the gear of one of those hooligans you babysit."

Red bristled. "I very much doubt any of them would have done this."

"What about the big kid?" Leroy asked. "He could tear the legs off the calf with his bare hands."

Bud's brow furrowed. "You know, Lee was training Carlton to cut up chicken."

"Just because he's big doesn't make him a killer," Red said. "I was witness to the way Carlton loved on this calf when Lee had him help feed her. The boy is nothin' more than a giant teddy bear with added stuffing."

"And a hot temper," Leroy added.

"Only to people that peck at him," Red corrected. Then he turned a stern look on his men. "You two know a thing or two about butchering. Should I suspect either of you?"

Bud frowned. "You've got a point. Speculating about who did this isn't going to accomplish anything."

"I still think one of the camp kids did it," Leroy mumbled.

"I'll tell you what." Red tossed his head in the direction of the calf. "You clean this up, and I'll ease your mind with a search of the campers' cabin later. But if it was done by kids, my money would be on the hikers. All I know, is my gut says it was someone completely unrelated to the ranch. If not the hikers, it could be any one of the many people camping in the woods outside the property. And if it were done by someone passin' through, I doubt we'll ever discover who." He frowned when a muddy Tan Dog appeared in the stall doorway. "There you are. I guess I don't need to ask where you've been."

Leroy grabbed Tan Dog by the collar, stopping her from going into the stall. "And what would you be wantin' me to do with this here mess?"

Red followed his gaze to the mutilated calf. "Toss the carcass to the hogs. Then burn the straw out past Pig Island where no one will see." He walked out of the stall with the men following him.

Leroy closed the stall door, released Tan Dog, and walked off to get the wheelbarrow on the far end of the aisle.

"Come on, girl," Red called. "You can't be goin' in the lodge like that. Let's get you hosed down. Then I have a call to make to the sheriff." He paused at the door, looking back at Leroy. "Let's keep the young campers out of here until you get this cleaned."

"YOU'RE GONNA HAVE TO stay out here until you dry, girl," Red said, stopping Tan Dog from going through the lodge door. "Go on with you now." He watched her sulk across the porch, where she flopped down next to a rocking chair. She laid her head on her front paws and looked sadly up at him. "You can stop feelin' sorry for yourself. The last time you came in after a romp in the mud, it took a week for the place to stop smellin' like wet dog. And that's an odor only a dog appreciates."

Leaving Tan Dog sulking, Red entered the lodge and headed for the coffee pot in the dining hall. As he turned the corner, he saw Nathan hanging several feet off the floor near the kitchen door. If the sight surprised Red, he didn't let it show as he poured a cup of coffee.

"Red, get me down from here," Nathan pleaded, kicking his legs in the air.

Red carried his coffee to the doorway, where he studied the teenager who hung by his belt on a hook made of horseshoes.

"Dude, I'm getting a serious wedgie here," Nathan whined. "It's cutting off the circulation to my balls. Come on! Get me down before I lose them."

Red rubbed his chin, considering. "I rather doubt you were put up there without reason. So, who'd you piss off?"

Nathan stopped kicking. He glared at Carlton. "Sasquatch. But I didn't do anything to deserve it."

"Somehow I don't think that's likely." Red turned to look at the large boy quietly eating his breakfast at a table with the other campers. "Anyone who picks on Carlton has to be a few feathers short of a whole duck." He turned back to Nathan. "I'd call you stupid, but that would be an insult to stupid people, Dude." Leaving him hanging, Red ignored Nathan's protests as he walked across the room to the staff table. He sat down, pulled the flask from his pocket, and took a generous gulp of coffee, making room for the whiskey he poured in the cup.

Bud came through the doorway and sat next to Woody. "I see a village is missing their idiot this morning."

"Carlton took offense to Nathan picking on Noah again." Billy grinned. "You should have seen it. Carlton jerked him out of his chair and carried him by the back of his pants. I tell you, it was the funniest thing I've ever seen."

Woody laughed. "After the morning we've had, we could use

some comic relief."

Red looked across the room to the boy who sat in silence as the others chattered noisily. "Carlton may be a man of few words, but he certainly has his own way of drivin' the message home."

"Unfortunately, Nathan isn't what you'd call a fast learner," said Bud. "So we're probably in for some more entertainment before the summers over."

"No doubt," Red said. "The kid has a Titanic intellect in a world full of icebergs."

"Billy told me about the calf," Woody said. "Sorry bit of news that was. I got the phone line back up, so I'm available to see to the cleanup in the barn."

"Leroy's taking care of it right now." Red took a sip of coffee. "But there is something I wouldn't mind you doin' for me."

"Sure, whatever you need."

"You can tell Lee about his calf when he comes back from wherever he took off to."

Woody groaned as he stood and walked toward the kitchen.

"Where you going, Woody?" Jake called.

"Knowing how Lee felt about the calf, I suspect the news will spark his temper. Just to be safe, I'm gonna hide all the knives."

Red smirked. "Not a bad idea."

CHAPTER 11

"Still say it's one of them damn kids," Leroy said aloud as he worked alone in the stall. "Them brats wouldn't think twice 'bout killin' no baby cow," he grumbled, throwing a pitchfork full of bloody straw into the wheelbarrow.

As he stabbed the fork into another heap of straw, the tines made the clinking sound of hitting something metal. He shook the pitchfork and out fell a hunting knife. "What the hell?" He stared down at the special field-dressing knife he had made by hand. There was no mistaking the titanium blade he had spent hours grinding to a razor-sharp edge, or the upward curving trailing point at the tip.

He picked up the knife and closely inspected the rough ridges on the elk-antler handle. Like fingerprints, no two antlers were alike, and after the hours of sanding on this particular antler, the ridges had become most familiar to him. Any doubt he might have had vanished when he ran a finger across the flat of the blood-covered blade, exposing his name engraved in the metal.

Leroy valued the knife so much that when he wasn't wearing it on his belt, he hid the blade in his cabin—in a spot only one person knew about.

"Damn, Edie," he said, turning the bloody knife in his hand. "What have you gone and done?"

When the barn door opened, Leroy quickly slid the knife down his boot.

"Hey, Leroy," Billy said. "Red thought you could use some

help."

Leroy frowned. "He should know I don't need no help. This is my last load."

"He told us to remove some of the topsoil, so the blood won't leave a smell that could upset the horses," Jake explained. "If you want, we can take the rest of the straw out and get the pile burning before we get to work on removing the dirt."

Leroy considered only a moment before nodding. "I'll leave it to you boys then." He handed the pitchfork to Billy and strolled calmly down the aisle. Once he was outside, Leroy looked around and, seeing no one, rushed to his cabin. He opened the door, pausing to make sure he was alone before stepping inside. After closing and bolting the lock, he pulled the knife from his boot and carried it to a plastic wash tub. "You'll need a good cleanin' before I hide you away."

LATER THAT MORNING, Red entered the gathering room and found Noah standing at the gun case, staring at his John Wayne rifle.

"Would you like to take a closer look?" Red asked.

Noah nodded eagerly.

Red pulled a key from his pocket, unlocked the case, and took the gun out. He knew it wasn't loaded, but he checked it out of habit before handing it off to Noah.

Noah stared down at the rifle with awe. "I've never held a gun before."

Red took a .22-caliber rifle out of the case and performed the same procedure of checking it before offering it to Noah. "This is a better choice for learning."

Noah looked surprised. "I get to shoot it?"

"Every young person should know how to safely handle a gun." Red took his prized rifle from Noah and handed him the .22. "There have been a lot of people killed by guns they mistakenly presumed to be unloaded. Therefore, your first lesson is to never trust anyone's word that a gun is unloaded.

Make it a habit to always check for yourself." He demonstrated how to open the chamber and look for bullets, nodding when Noah did the same with the .22. "You'll be learning more safety rules before firing that thing. Once I'm convinced you won't shoot your foot off, you'll take to shootin' targets at the range across the meadow." He set the John Wayne Winchester inside and locked the case. "Well, let's get to it then."

As Noah followed Red to the door, the bearskin lying in front of the fireplace caught his eye. "Hey, Red, what kind of gun would you use to shoot a bear?"

"A loaded one," Red said straight-faced as he held the door for Noah.

"Shooting lessons?" Woody asked as he met them on the path.

"Yup." Red paused to look at him. "Good, I'm glad we ran into you. I'll have Jake round up the other campers while you and Noah set up the targets. Once I gather some ammunition, I'll meet you out on the meadow. Billy can help you. He's already out there throwing knives."

"Yeah, he says knife throwing relaxes him." Woody smirked. "By the looks of how good he's getting at it, I'd say he's been tense a lot lately." He motioned to Noah. "Come on, son. Let's get you out to the range."

Noah looked as though he could burst from excitement as he followed Woody across the meadow with the gun cradled in his arms.

Red collected the ammunition from his secret hiding place, grabbed another rifle, and walked out to join the others. He was crossing the path running along the landing strip when he was stopped by two middle-aged, female backpackers coming off the Moss Springs Trail.

"This isn't hunting season, so what on earth do you plan to shoot?" one of the women asked, looking annoyed.

Noah ran to Red. "Woody wants me to bring him the bullets."

"I hope you don't intend to kill some harmless animal." The other woman glared at Noah.

Noah looked at Red and back at the women. "We're only shooting targets."

"So you're just in training to become a killer," the first woman said.

"Go on over to the targets, son," Red said. Once Noah was out of earshot, he turned to the women. "Ladies, I'm Red Higgins. I own the ranch you're standing on. I appreciate your concerns, but I can assure you we take every precaution in teachin' our young men to respect a gun."

"Young men?" The first woman huffed. "They're nothing more than boys. How can you be so irresponsible?"

"Yes," the other chimed in. "Don't you see that by putting guns in their hands, you've equipped them to become violent killers?"

"Well, ma'am," Red said, pausing to strike a match and light his pipe. "One might say you're equipped to be a prostitute, but you're not one, are you?"

CHAPTER 12

"Now see here," Edith said smugly as she came bustling into the kitchen before noon. "You don't see me tuckin' my tail and runnin' off after havin' a little disagreement."

Sometimes I wish you would, Red thought. "No, I can always count on you, Edith."

She grabbed an apron off a peg and tied it around her plump waist. "No sir. And who's here to save the day when Lee don't show? Old Edith, that's who." She pulled a big pot from under the counter and set it on a burner. "I told you last night that you'd be makin' the choice between me and him. Looks to me like he made the decision for you. No loss, I'd say. Anyway, it's high time you sent that cantankerous munchkin back to the Emerald City where he belongs."

Red groaned internally. "Edith, I'm not gonna send either of you anywhere. You know you and Lee go through this at the start of every summer. Eventually, you work out sharing time and space in the kitchen."

She whirled, pointing a large metal spoon at him. "Last night was the last straw." She lowered the spoon and made a huffing sound as she turned toward the refrigerator. "Lee has a lot of nerve tryin' to tell me how to make pie. I've made plenty of pies in my time, wouldn't you say?"

"Yes, of course."

"And wouldn't you say they were good?"

"You make tasty pie, Edith."

"Damn right I do. And I don't need no pucker-faced high

and mighty, glorified chef tellin' me otherwise." She opened the refrigerator and bent over, exposing the full size of her backside as her floral dress pulled tight over her ample buttocks.

Red looked away.

"I tell you, if he goes and humiliates me in front of the youngsters again, I won't be able to hold my temper." She carried a container of hamburger to the stove and turned her back to him.

Was last night an example of her holdin' her temper? Red looked up at the remnants of one of the pies the boys hadn't gotten off the ceiling. *Then I'd hate to see her out of control.*

The door from the dining hall opened, and Woody led all five campers into the kitchen. "Here you go, Red. All present and accounted for." He placed his hands on the shoulders of the boy standing in front of him. "You might want to go easy on Carlos. He's still a bit green around the gills from this morning's ordeal."

"I can see that." Red studied his pale face and decided to take pity on the ailing boy. "Working in the washhouse should be mild enough for you. County Commissioner Reynolds and his wife have booked the Nez Perce cabin for their traditional stay over opening weekend. We might as well get the cabin ready. Mrs. Reynolds' special satin sheets are kept in a plastic container on a shelf in the washhouse. They'll need freshening up. While they're washing, clean the cabin spotless. Once the sheets have dried on the clothesline, get them on the bed. You do know how to make a proper bed?"

Carlos nodded.

Red turned to Woody. "Be sure to check that for me. The commissioner has enough to find fault with, I don't need complaints about bed making. Show Carlos where the supplies are kept. The three large bouquets of roses she flew in are sitting in the cold house, along with a throw made of beaver fur that she requested be laid out in front of the fireplace."

"Beaver fur? What's that about?" Nathan asked.

Red pinned his eyes on him. "We don't ask, and neither will you."

"When she gets here, you'll see why." Woody grinned. "Mrs. Reynolds is…well, let's say eccentric." He walked to the kitchen door and motioned to Carlos. "Come on. The quicker you get to it, the quicker you can enjoy your afternoon free time."

Red watched Carlos follow Woody out the door. When he turned to the others, he discovered Noah and Carlton, looking over Edith's shoulders, watching her brown hamburger for chili. "I see you have your volunteers for cooking duty."

"Oh good," Edith said, looking delighted. "After lunch, I'll teach you two how to make a real pie. But first, we'll have to get some cornbread bakin'."

Red opened the supply closet and brought out two mops and a bucket. "While they help Edith, you two can wash the pie off the ceiling."

Noah looked up. "Shoot, we didn't see that when we were cleaning up last night."

Nathan and Sean followed his gaze

"How did that get there?" Sean asked.

Red glanced at Edith and saw she was happily giving orders to Carlton. "That would be another thing you don't need to ask."

IT WAS MIDAFTERNOON when Nathan and Sean climbed the ladder to the hayloft. They walked to the large opening and sat down on the ledge under the hay hood, allowing their feet to dangle freely under the extension of the barn roof.

They could see most of the ranch buildings from where they sat. Below them was the corral of horses, and to the right, near the front of the barn, they could see Red sitting on Sugar. He was puffing on his pipe while he waited for Jake to finish saddling a flashy paint gelding named Rowdy.

Nathan kicked his heels back against the side of the barn in an even rhythm. "God, I'm so fucking bored. I can't even tell you how much I could go for a joint right now."

"Me too," said Sean. "What good is it to have our afternoons free when we have nothing to do?"

"Where do you suppose they're going?" Nathan asked, pointing to Red and Jake.

"I heard Red say they're going to ride through the campsites outside his property, looking for the person who killed the calf."

"What does he expect to find?" Nathan scoffed. "It's not like he's going to come across words written across someone's chest saying, 'I killed the calf, and all I got was this lousy T-shirt.'"

Sean laughed as he got to his feet and walked to the claw-like device hanging from a track running the length of the rafter and out through the opening under the hay hood. "No, but you have to admit Red has a look that could make an innocent person break a sweat. I swear he could stare down a priest and make him spill every single thing he'd ever heard in a confessional." He grabbed hold of the metal hook, and pulled it back to the end of the loft. Turning, he pushed it as he ran toward Nathan and the opening. Halfway across the loft, he picked up his feet and rode the hook.

Nathan jumped up out of the way as Sean sailed out the opening, coming to a jarring stop under the hay hood.

"Help!" Sean yelled, kicking his legs. "Pull me in."

Sitting on his horse below, Red scowled up at the boy dangling from the hay hood. "Ah hell." He began to get down from Sugar, hesitating when he saw Nathan clutch the side of the opening and reach out to haul Sean in by the legs. "It's a damn shame stupid don't hurt," Red grumbled as he settled back in the saddle.

"You say something, boss?" Jake asked as he slung a saddle over his horse's back.

"Yeah, shake a leg. I could have been gone and back by

now."

In the barn above them, Sean released the hook and dropped to the loft floor.

"You didn't exactly think that through, did you, dumbshit? That was a bonehead thing to do without a soft pile of hay to break your fall."

"Hey, I was just trying to find some kind of entertainment." Sean got to his feet and watched Nathan walk across the loft. "Where are you going?"

"You gave me an idea," Nathan said, walking to the ladder. "I'm going to score something a lot more fun than riding that stupid thing." He paused to look up at Sean, who stood over the ladder, staring down at him. "If anyone is likely to have pot, it's the dudes with the dreadlocks, and guess who Red and Jake are going out to search for? I'll weasel my way into going with them and while they're interrogating the hairy dudes, I'll be going through their gear."

"Do you have a death wish? That man has eyes behind his head," Sean said, climbing down the ladder behind Nathan.

"Ha, you haven't seen me in action. That foolish old man won't be any the wiser. I kind of know my way around a good con."

"You did hear me say they're going to ride. And we're not talking ATVs. Aren't you the one that keeps saying you'll never get on one of those smelly, four-legged creatures? So how do you expect to accomplish a ride, Mr. I Hate Horses?"

"With a double-handed grip on the saddle," Nathan said as his feet touched the ground.

Sean rushed to catch up to him at the barn door.

"Hey, Red, can I ride with you?" Nathan asked as he came out of the barn.

Red eyed him suspiciously. "Since when do you want to ride?"

"You said I needed to learn, so why not now?"

Red considered for a moment before looking at Jake. "I

don't have time to saddle another horse. He'll have to take Rowdy."

Jake shrugged. "You're the boss." Then he turned a glare on Nathan as he handed him the reins to the sorrel paint. Walking away, he paused to pat the gelding's rump. "Do me a favor, Rowdy. Toss the snot-nosed brat on his Hollywood ass."

Nathan ignored Jake's remarks as he gathered the reins and stuck his foot in the stirrup.

With his hands rested on his saddle horn, Red patiently watched Nathan fumble his way onto the horse.

"Now that you've finally got your butt where it belongs," Red began, "there are a few things you should remember when riding. The first is to keep your heels out of his flank. That would be this area here." He reached back and gently ran his hand over the area below his mare's hip. "The reins are your steering wheel." Red raised his hand slightly, and over to the left, laying the right rein tight against the right side of Sugar's neck. "See how she's pulling her head around, but not turning her body?"

Nathan nodded.

"That's because I haven't given her any gas." He squeezed his right leg against her side, and the mare immediately turned to the left. "It's pressure, not a kick." Red took his leg off of Sugar and centered his hand in front of the horn. She stopped. "Lean forward when goin' uphill and back when goin' down. That should be enough to get you by for now. Rowdy will stick to Sugar, so you don't need to worry about him takin' off somewhere."

Nathan held tightly to the saddle horn as Rowdy followed Sugar to the thick grove of trees running along the ranch side of the river.

"Where's your dog?" Nathan asked. "I thought she was always with you."

"She and her brothers caught wind of somethin' on the other end of the property. She'll catch up to me once she's lost interest in whatever they're chasin' after." Red gnawed his pipe, pondering. "Unless they got a cougar treed. None of them will leave then."

"Cougar?" Nathan looked around. "Should I be nervous?"

"Nah. If there's one near, the dogs will make a fuss."

"Aren't you worried about it killing your dogs?"

"In nature, mass wins. For instance, a single lion can easily take down a hyena, but when there are enough hyenas to outweigh the lion, they win. A cougar would be no match against four large dogs."

"Good. I'm glad to know those idiot dogs have a purpose."

Red turned to look back at Nathan. "You can say what you want about her brothers, but I'd be careful how you talk around Tan Dog. She tends to know when someone's thinkin' badly of her, and she doesn't take well to it. Those were just nips she gave you your first night here. Just think what she'd do if you really made her mad."

"I'm not a fan of animals, so your clairvoyant dog is just going to have to get over it."

Red shrugged. "She'll react to whatever you're puttin' out there. So you might want to consider adjusting your attitude toward her."

"I've never understood the whole man and his mutt thing and I see no purpose in having the flea-ridden things around."

"Come face to face with that cougar we were talking about, and tell me you don't see a purpose then."

Nathan gulped and scanned the trees. "Maybe you should call your dog."

Red smirked behind his pipe.

They were nearly to the end of the property when they came across a campground of several tents. As they rode into the camp, they saw three women and an adolescent girl sitting around a campfire.

"Mornin', ladies," Red said, tipping his hat. "I'm looking for three teenaged male hikers. They have long matted hair and were wearing long straggly shorts and carrying bedrolls. Have they come through here?"

"No, we haven't seen anyone of that description. But you might want to check with our husbands." The woman pointed. "They're down at the river with the kids."

"Thank you, miss. Please excuse our intrusion." Red touched the tip of his hat and turned Sugar toward the river.

"You think the hikers killed the calf?" Nathan asked as they rode through the trees.

"Could be, but I won't know 'til I talk with them."

"Then they probably booked it out of here."

Red glanced back at Nathan. "You sound disappointed."

Nathan shrugged. "Why would I be?"

That's a good question.

They rode out of the woods and stopped along the rocky riverbank. Down river, two men and several children were searching for colorful rocks. Not far upriver, was a man fishing with his young son. They rode to the two fishing.

"I did see three boys of that description last night." The man pointed across the river. "They were walking the trail over there. And by the looks of them, I was glad to see they were on that side."

"Dad said they were trouble," the man's six-year-old son lisped through two missing teeth.

The father rubbed his son's head. "I did say that, didn't I?" He looked at Red. "Is that why you're looking for them? Did they cause some kind of trouble at your ranch?"

"They broke into our supply shed."

Nathan frowned. "And they…"

"You folks have a fine day," Red said, cutting Nathan off.

Nathan looked bewildered, but kept his mouth shut.

"Are you a real cowboy?" the boy asked, stopping Red from turning Sugar.

"Got the hat and the horse, so I guess that makes me a cowboy."

The boy dropped his fishing pole on the bank and walked to Sugar. "Can I pet your horse?"

"Tyler, don't bother the man," the father scolded.

"No bother," Red said, tipping his hat back to better see the boy. "But you'll have to pay her." He took two sugar cubes from his pocket and leaned down to drop them into the boy's small hands. "Hold them flat on your hand."

The boy giggled when Sugar's lips grazed his palm. "That tickles."

"Now you can pet her face."

Sugar kept her head down to the boy's level, allowing him to run his tiny hand down her nose as she chewed her treats. Finished, Sugar raised her head and blew breath in his ear as she nuzzled the side of his face.

The boy squealed with delight.

Red grinned. "She likes you."

"Tyler, leave the nice man alone and come get your fishing pole," called his father.

Red saw how torn the boy was between petting Sugar and doing as his father asked. "You know there are some fish in that river bigger than you. You catch yourself one, you bring it on over to the ranch and I'll cook it up right for you."

The boy beamed. "Okay!"

As Red watched him run back for his pole, his thoughts drifted to the memory of another boy and that fateful night so many years ago. Just as if it were yesterday, Red remembered how Timmy had smiled when he had placed the fire helmet on his head. The memory made his gut wrench with the all-too-familiar pain of regret. Annoyed with himself, Red pulled his hat back in place and turned Sugar. *Get a grip, old man. This isn't the time to be thinking of the past and what you can't change.*

As they rode along the river, Red slipped the flask from his pocket, took a long drink, and tucked it away.

"Why didn't you tell them about the calf?" Nathan asked, breaking their silence.

"And cause the boy nightmares? No, sir, he didn't need to hear of such gore. He's already bombarded with horrible images on television. This is one place where he should feel safe and removed from all that. You saw his face. He was having the time of his life with his dad. What would you want him to remember of his trip to the mountains, the slayin' of the calf, or what a great time he had with his father? I'm sure you remember how important a connection with your father was when you were young."

"Yeah, well, that kid's lucky his dad takes him fishing." Nathan stared down at the saddle horn he was choking with both hands. "Dad was always too busy with work to do anything with me. Even when we went on vacations, the nanny would have to take me swimming or whatever. Mom and Dad were always off doing grown-up stuff without me."

"It's never too late to have a relationship with your father. Have you ever told him you wanted to spend time with him?"

"No. But it wouldn't change anything if I did. He's got his world, and I've got mine. I really don't care anymore."

I think you do. "I believe your recent dive into the pool of stupidity proves otherwise."

"What are you talking about?"

"You get in trouble, and your dad pays attention to you. It may not be the type of attention you really desire, but it is attention just the same."

"What kind of bullshit psychology is that?" Nathan grumbled.

As the mare continued to walk, Red fished a match from his shirt pocket and struck it across the decorative silver concho on his saddle horn. He lit the pipe, shook out the match, and turned in his saddle. "It doesn't take a psychiatrist to figure that one out. You're a little more transparent than you think. Have you ever considered that if you were to spend less of your dad's time bailin' you out of trouble, he might have more time to do enjoyable things with you?"

"Like that's going to happen. Dad's great at making promises, but he's lousy at keeping them. Besides, he thinks everything I do is wrong. Maybe I'm not the golden boy he was when he was a kid, but I don't think I'm all that bad."

Son, you don't know your father. In your case, the apple really doesn't fall far from the tree.

They came to the bridge spanning the Minam River. Some of the wider areas were already low enough to cross on foot, but that was not the case in this narrow portion of the river.

"Oh, please tell me we're not going up there," Nathan said, looking at the steep path.

"Unless you can sprout wings, there's no other way to get to the bridge."

Sugar's hooves dug into the path as she bounded up the slope. Nathan tightened his already white-knuckled grip on the horn as Rowdy leap up the hill behind her.

Red made it over the crest of the hill and turned toward the bridge, looking back at Nathan. "Unless you're lookin' to kiss the ground, you better lean forward." He pulled Sugar to a stop and watched as Nathan leaned so far forward his nose nearly touched Rowdy's neck.

"Get your heels out of his flank or he's gonna…" It was too late. As Rowdy cleared the hill, he pinned his ears and lowered his head. Giving a loud snort, he bucked his hind end up, sending Nathan flying over his head onto the hard surface of the bridge.

Nathan groaned and rolled onto his back, where he lay struggling for breath.

Red stepped down from his saddle. "Whoa," he said, patting Sugar's rump as he walked past her. "Are you hurt, boy?"

"No, just got the piss knocked out of me, thanks to your goddamn son of a bitch horse."

Red stood over Nathan. "I clearly recall telling you to keep your heels out of his flank. Don't blame the horse for something that was entirely your doin'. He had every right to object to you puttin' the hurt on him. Here, let me help you up." He leaned down, but instead of reaching for his hand, he pulled Nathan to his feet by his armpit, pinching it hard.

"Ouch! What the hell?" Nathan shouted as he jerked free, glaring and rubbing his sore underarm. "What kind of asinine move was that?"

"I figure you for one of those people who just has to put his hand on a hot stove even when someone tells you it'll burn. A horse's flank is as sensitive as your armpit, so maybe now you can have a little empathy for the pain you caused him."

"I think I've had enough of this cowboy shit for one day."

"You volunteered for this, and you'll see it through. Now get on your horse and stay out of his flank."

"Fine, but if he tries anything again, I'm going to beat his ass."

Red gathered Sugar's reins, stepped up into the saddle, and looked back at Nathan. "Son, as you just witnessed, if you teach mean to an animal, you'll find they learn their lesson well." He nudged Sugar forward across the bridge.

"Whatever," Nathan grumbled as he put a foot in the stirrup. Before he could pull himself up, Rowdy began to follow Sugar. "Hey! Stop you stupid fleabag."

Red looked back and saw Nathan bouncing on one leg beside Rowdy. He finally succeeded in pulling himself up, but instead of throwing his leg over, he lay across the saddle.

"Are you takin' up trick ridin'?"

"Real funny. I think this stupid horse has it in for me." Nathan grabbed the horn and squirmed until he finally got a leg over his horse and sat upright in the saddle.

"Yeah, the horse is the stupid one," Red said, chuckling to himself.

A MILE FROM THE ranch, Red and Nathan came upon a small cabin. "That's not good." Red pointed to the open door as he pulled Sugar to a halt. "The Keeler family owns this cabin, and they never come out before the Fourth of July weekend." He dismounted and dropped his reins to the ground. "You stay here with the horses."

"You're taking a gun?" Nathan asked, staring at the rifle Red pulled from the leather scabbard hanging on the side of his saddle.

"Yes, I'm taking a gun. Now stay here until I call you." Red walked down the path to the cabin, pausing to look at the broken door lock lying on the porch. He took a moment to peer through the door and walked into the cabin with his rifle raised. A few moments later, he came back out and motioned to Nathan. "It's clear. Leave the horses. They won't go anywhere."

Nathan jumped down and raced into the two-bedroom cabin, coming to a stop in the living room, where he looked around. "Wow, look at all the wrappers. Someone must be on a mega sugar high." He scanned the floor of crumpled up paper, foil, and plastic. "And here you thought I was bad for stealing a few bars of candy from the supply shed. It looks like they got away with box loads."

"Yup. They must have hauled off with cartons of candy and had come back for more when Lee caught them. I hope it gives them a king-sized bellyache." Red looked around the cabin for anything else they might have left behind. That's when he caught Nathan's expression in a mirror. "Why so glum, chum?" he asked as he continued inspecting the cabin. "So what was the plan? Weed? Pills?"

"What?" Nathan said, looking surprised.

"Like I told you, you're more transparent than you think. Come on, they're halfway to Timbuktu by now." Red followed Nathan out, closing the door behind him. "I'm as sorry as you we didn't find them."

"Because you think they killed the calf?"

"There was that, but I was also anxious to see how you planned to look for drugs with me standin' right here."

"I suppose I'm in trouble, even though I didn't do anything

wrong?"

Red slid his rifle into his scabbard and gathered his reins. "You were never out of trouble."

IT WAS NEARLY DINNERTIME when Red and Nathan rode past the dining room windows on their way to the barn.

Sean saw them and ran out to meet Nathan. "Well, any luck?" he whispered, walking beside Rowdy.

"No." Rowdy automatically stopped next to Sugar at the hitching rail. "We found their camp, but they were gone." Nathan groaned as he swung his leg over Rowdy's rump. "I'll tell you later. Right now all I can think about is getting my sore balls off this stupid horse." He slid down to the ground. "Holy shit, that's not the only thing that hurts!" He grabbed his butt with both hands.

Woody was waiting outside the barn for Red. "I thought young Hollywood was afraid of horses."

"By the way he choked the horn the entire time, I'd say he still is." Red dismounted, untied the girth strap, and pulled the saddle from Sugar's back. Woody grabbed the saddle pad and followed him into the tack room.

"At least he put his fear aside to help you," Woody said. "That has to mean something."

Red harrumphed as he plopped the saddle down on a rack and turned to take the pad from Woody. "He came to look for somethin', but it wasn't a calf killer."

"What was he looking for?"

"Trouble." Red picked up a brush on his way out. As he came out of the barn, he saw Nathan walking away with Sean. "Hey, where do you think you're goin'? What makes you think it's okay to walk off and leave your horse? You get back here and take care of Rowdy."

Nathan groaned. "God, does the fun ever end?"

"Since you don't have anything better to do, Sean, you can

go round up the kitchen scraps. Nathan should be done with Rowdy by the time you get back. Maybe this time you can feed hogs without incident.

"Great," Nathan grumbled. "Another fun-filled day at the ranch."

CHAPTER 13

The Slam of the lodge door made Tan Dog jump up from where she lay in front of the fire.

"There you are," Leroy said, walking into the room where Red sat smoking his pipe, waiting for dinner.

Something in the tone of Leroy's voice made Red turn in his chair to look at him.

"I think one of them snot-nosed kids is gettin' their hide chewed by a hog again." Leroy stood in front of Red's chair, ignoring Tan Dog as she circled him, sniffing his legs. "There be banshee screams comin' from Pig Island. Jake and Woody are headed over to the pond now."

Red jumped to his feet and headed for the door. "If those two got into another fight, hog bites are gonna be the last of their worries." He didn't wait for Leroy as he rushed off the porch and walked briskly down the path.

"Are they hurt?" he asked as he approached Jake and Woody pulling the boat to the bank.

Woody grabbed Nathan's arm and helped him out of the rowboat. "Don't appear to be. But something sure has scared the bejeebers out of them."

Red looked down to Nathan collapsed on the ground. "What's this all about, boy? Did a hog bite you?"

Nathan shook his head, moaning.

"We found bones," Sean said as he jumped from the boat. "Nathan didn't tie the boat up, and it drifted away from the usual spot. I was going after it when I tripped over bones."

Woody offered Nathan a hand up. "That was the calf. Best way to get rid of a carcass is to feed it to the hogs. I've seen them pick a dead horse clean of meat, then crunch right through bone to get to the marrow." He scratched his head. "Seems odd there'd be anything left of something as small as a calf."

Nathan looked annoyed. "Do you feed them humans? Because that's what these bones were."

"Human?" Red repeated, turning to look at the island.

"Maybe it was an Indian skeleton that worked its way to the surface," Jake offered.

Nathan shook his head. "I saw an eyeball and some hair on top of the skull."

Woody stood beside Red, staring at the island. "You don't suppose…"

Red kept his eyes on the island. "I sure would like to say no, but my gut is tellin' me otherwise. Guess there's only one way to find out." He looked at Nathan and Sean. "Which one of you is gonna show me where the bones are?"

"I'm not going back there," Sean said, shaking his head and backing away.

Red motioned to Nathan. "That leaves you, Hollywood. Come on, get in the boat."

"I can't imagine anything I'd rather do less," Nathan grumbled as Red pulled him to his feet. Red held the boat steady as Nathan reluctantly stepped aboard.

"You want me to go with you, boss?" Jake asked as Red got into the boat.

"No, that's not necessary. Just give us a push."

Jake stood with Woody, watching as the boat slowly slid across the water. "You think it's Lee, don't you?"

"I hope not, but he is missing, so it's definitely a possibility."

"So, what's all the hullabaloo about?" Leroy asked as he walked up. "I got waylaid by Edith. What did I miss?"

"The boys came across a human skeleton while they were feeding the hogs," Woody explained.

"We think it might be Lee," Jake added.

Leroy's thin, wrinkled face looked shocked. "Holy Moses." He turned his head to spit chewing tobacco on the ground. "Skeleton you say?"

"But Lee hasn't been missing more than a day," Sean said, coming to stand with the men. "Is it possible to turn a man to bones in such a short time?"

"I'm afraid it's very possible," said Woody. "It wouldn't take more than a few hours for ten hogs to chew the meat off a body. Then they would have come back after the bones when they got hungry again. And no amount of mud would have stopped them from finishing off what was left."

Leroy looked perplexed. "I didn't see no bones when I dropped the calf carcass off on the island. You be thinkin' Lee went to the island after the scuffle with Edith? But why would he do that? It don't make no sense."

Woody shrugged. "That's the million-dollar question we're all asking."

AS THEY GLIDED TO shore, Nathan jumped out of the boat and pulled the bow up on the bank. Red followed him out and tied the rope around a bush.

"Well, show me the bones."

Nathan glanced nervously at the hogs eating from the feed trough and hurried past. "It was this way." He led Red along the bank and stopped to search the ground around him. "It was somewhere here." As he took a couple steps back, he tripped over something and fell backward. Covered in mud, he quickly rolled over and came face-to-face with a skull. He sucked in a breath and pushed away from the skeleton, but as he did, he shook the bones, and the movement broke a lone eyeball free from its socket. Nathan screamed as he scrambled to his feet and ran for the boat.

Red crouched next to the skeleton and stared at the skull that no longer had a face to identify. The only flesh left was the eyeball and a patch of hair at the top of the skull. He pulled a handkerchief from his pocket and wiped the mud from the hair. It was black. *Black as Lee's hair.* He moved down the bones. The clothes were torn away and tromped into the mud. As with the fingers on the hands, the feet had missing toes, presumably snapped off by sharp teeth.

Beyond the bones of the feet, a brown object caught Red's eye. He pulled it from the mud.

His heart pounded in his ears as he stared down at the blood-drenched tongue of Lee's brown loafer.

CHAPTER 14

Finished with breakfast, Red sat down on a rocking chair in front of the lodge, took his hat off, and rubbed his pounding head. It had been a miserable night. The one time he'd managed to close his eyes and drift off, Timmy had appeared. *Like the little demon does every time I'm most in need of sleep.* He placed his hat on his head and watched Nathan and Sean walk back from feeding the hogs. *From the looks of them, I wasn't the only one not sleeping well last night. At least the campers did their chores without so much as a single whine for once.*

Breakfast had been a solemn and silent event for the campers and ranch staff alike. Through the closed kitchen door, they could hear Edith blowing her nose for the umpteenth time. Red knew she felt guilty for fighting with Lee, and he had done his best to console her after she heard of the discovery, but ultimately she'd found solace in a bottle.

Lee's death was having a profound effect on everyone, but none so much as Carlton, who sat at the end of campers' table, staring down at his untouched plate. The rest of the campers had eaten in silence.

Last night, after making the call to the sheriff, Red and his men had returned to Pig Island to remove Lee's remains. Together they'd lifted the skeleton from the mud, carefully placing it on the old door they had brought with them. Laying the door across the bow of the rowboat, Bud and Leroy rowed across the pond while Red and the others gathered what they could find of Lee's clothing. The one thing they had no luck finding was the solid gold medallion Lee always wore around his neck. Red knew Lee's relatives would want to have the family heirloom, and it had disturbed him not to find it.

Red scanned the island. *It could be anywhere beneath six inches of mud and hog crap.*

"I don't think there's a lick of hope of finding it in this mess," Woody had said as he came to stand with Red. "You know what might help is Lee's metal detector."

"I was just thinkin' the same thing," said Red.

"He was always looking for gold with that thing. Maybe it'll finally find it."

Red nodded. "Sounds like a job for one of the young wranglers."

Jake and Billy had been determined to go to the island with the other men. But for Billy, it had turned out to be a mistake. One look at the lone eyeball dangling from its socket and he had run off to the bushes to throw up. Until the remains were removed, he stayed as far from them as possible. Even then, he only moved slightly closer to where the men were searching.

"I think it's gonna be a while before Billy's gut settles," Woody had said. "I'll ask Jake to go over the area with the metal detector. Mucking around in hog shit shouldn't be a problem for his iron constitution."

Tan Dog ran onto the porch and shook her wet coat, waking Red from his thoughts of the evening before. "Here now," he said, turning his face when she shook again. "I realize you enjoy takin' a morning dip, but maybe the rest of us don't share in your fondness for being wet." He wiped his face with his hand and reached down to stroke Tan Dog's head.

Tan Dog wagged her tail and nuzzled Red's hand. He was going to give her another pet, but she jumped up and ran to the end of the porch, staring with pricked ears toward the far end of the canyon. It was a moment before he heard what she did.

Red searched for the source of the engine sound, finally spotting the glimmer of the silver plane heading their way. His brow furrowed at the odd way the wings dipped back and forth as it flew over his property. "Well now, wonder what that's all about?"

When the plane was halfway to the end of the meadow, Red saw a white object fly out of the passenger window and fall with feathers trailing after it. Tan Dog's three siblings sprinted past on their way out to the meadow. "Looks like your brothers are gonna have chicken for breakfast." She stayed by his side, watching with interest as the brother who grabbed the chicken was chased into the woods by the others.

The plane turned back and flew directly over the barn, where a second bird was launched from the window. This one landed on the barn roof, slid down, and tumbled off the edge, spooking the horses as it fell into the corral. Red's eyes followed the plane as it flew out of the canyon, turned, and came back for its final approach.

Red rocked in rhythm with the puffs of his pipe, watching as the plane's wheels touched down on the landing strip. "Well, girl, what say we go meet our visitors?"

Tan Dog followed him off the porch and stayed by his side as the plane taxied to a stop in the grass. The propeller stilled, and Tan Dog wagged her tail and looked up at Red. "Okay, I know you're dyin' to say hello. Go on with you then." She barked once and raced across the grass toward the plane.

The pilot side door opened—the only door in the front of the cockpit—and pilot, Joe Perkins stepped down, brushing feathers from his shoulders.

His passenger, Wallowa County Sheriff Rich Cason, followed him out, shaking feathers from his hat as he walked around the wing. He paused to flick a spot of bird manure off the brim before pulling his hat down over his short brown hair. In the center of his hat, a metal star glistened in the sunlight. His uniform shirt and slacks were a medium brown with a contrasting dark-brown stripe running down the side of each pant leg. The wide black belt at his waist was weighted heavily with his gun on one side and a radio on the other.

The sheriff left his pilot with the task of cleaning the plane. Eyes hidden behind aviator sunglasses, Sheriff Cason waved at Red, but it was the barking dog racing toward him who made the nearly six-foot-tall, fifty-seven-year-old man smile. "Hey, girl," he said, reaching into his pocket. "I bet I have something here you might want."

Tan Dog could hardly contain herself as she sat staring up at the puppy snack he waved in the air.

"So what are you going to do for me today?"

Tan Dog dropped to the ground, rolled over, and jumped to her feet with her tail wagging.

"Okay, that was pretty good." He tossed the dog bone. She caught it in the air and trotted off toward the porch.

"Hello, Red. Sorry to hear about Lee."

"We are too." Red shook the sheriff's hand. "It's a morbid bit of business, that's for sure. But before we get into all that, you mind telling me why you were bombin' my ranch with chickens?" He pulled a handkerchief from his pocket and handed it to Sheriff Cason, pointing to the streak of white droppings on his sleeve.

The sheriff frowned as he wiped his shirt. "Obviously, they started it. Talk about getting bombed." He rubbed at the stubborn stain. "What do they feed those birds, cement? Last time I ride in any plane making a chicken run for Edith."

"I wasn't aware she had called for a delivery."

"She told the chicken farmer that a weasel got away with a few of her laying hens." The sheriff lifted a brow at him. "I have a feeling the weasel is of the two-legged kind. You run low on chicken for dinner again?"

"It was a weasel. That's my story and I'm stickin' to it." Red grinned. "You do know that chickens can't fly."

"I really didn't give a damn. I was more concerned with keeping those confounded birds from blinding my pilot. If a landing were left to my doing, there wouldn't be a prayer of getting a plane safely on the ground. You can tell Edith that I chose to give them the boot in the name of self-preservation."

Red lit a match and held it to his pipe, puffing the smoldering tobacco to a glowing red. "You know, most people find it easier to transport chickens in a crate."

"And here we thought they were lap dogs." The sheriff rolled his eyes at Red. "They started out in a crate. The door must have gotten jostled open when we hit a patch of rough air. Edith is lucky only two of the bastards escaped. Otherwise you'd have four more extremely tenderized birds to pick out of your meadow."

"Don't need to worry about that. The dogs are on it. Just hope they don't get a chicken bone caught in their gullet."

"I think I'll be burning this shirt," the sheriff said, inspecting his stained sleeve. "Here's your handkerchief back."

"Keep it. You can burn it with the shirt."

The sheriff tucked the handkerchief in his pants pocket. "Do you have any idea what would make Lee go to the island after dark?" the sheriff asked as he strolled beside Red.

"No, but I suspect whiskey probably had somethin' to do with it."

"Were you aware of any heart or other medical problems?"

Red looked down at the ground as he walked. "No, though he wouldn't be one to broadcast such things, but I didn't find any medications in his cabin that indicated he was sick in any way." He took a key from his pocket and stepped down to the below-ground door well of the cold house.

"Somehow I think I'd feel better if I knew he was dead before the hogs got to him," said the sheriff as Red unlocked the door. "What's your guess?"

Red shoved the door open and turned to face the sheriff. "I see the probability of two scenarios. He could have passed out in a drunken stupor, and the pigs killed him. Or maybe alcohol poisoning finally caught up to him, and he was dead before the hogs got to him. Either way, since the hogs picked him clean of everything but bones and one eyeball, I doubt we'll ever know for sure."

Sheriff Cason followed him into the underground room. They stepped over the channel in the concrete floor where cold river water flowed, chilling the room as it drained into a pipe that emptied into the nearest pond. Thick stone walls rose from the twelve-foot-square floor up to the low-lying ceiling. Shelves of food staples sat along one wall, and skinless slabs of pork and beef hung from hooks along the other.

The men walked to the raised butcher's block at the back of the room. Lying across it was the door holding Lee's bones. The sheriff took hold of the sheet and carefully raised it. He immediately stepped back.

"Wow, that's a powerful smell."

"Swamp mud and hog shit," Red said. "It's sure better than the smell of decomp. Had my fair share of that, I tell you."

"True enough." The sheriff stepped closer and scanned the skeletal remains. "And here I didn't think anything could get worse than dragging dead hunters and hikers out of the mountains."

"And exactly when was it that you ever did that? I remember the many calls you made asking that I conduct a search for missing persons. I remember the times I scoured the mountains in the midst of winter storms, and I remember packing out the injured or the dead. But in all my recollection, you've never been there."

"Consider me there in spirit." The sheriff hid a grin as he picked up the plastic container sitting next to the skull. He opened it and looked inside. "At least the bodies you delivered had eyeballs where they belonged." He frowned, quickly closing the lid and setting it down. "Seriously, this is all that's left of him?"

"Stripping the meat from a human body wouldn't take ten hogs much longer than it would for you to eat a good-sized rack of pork ribs."

"That's one sick circle of life and one I'd just as soon step out of." The sheriff stared down at the skeleton. "My wife's been tryin' to talk me into going vegan. After this, she just might get her way. Please tell me you don't plan to serve those hogs to any of your guests."

"I hadn't thought that far ahead." Red bent down and picked up a plastic bag. "Here's what we found of his clothes and shoes. Hogs probably got some of it. They're not all that discriminating in what they eat."

"And you're sure it's Lee?"

Red sent puffs of smoke into the cold air as he considered. "Lee's missing, and his loafers and shredded clothing were found with the bones, so I'd say yes, I'm sure." He dropped the bag to the floor. "I'd like nothin' more than to share your doubt." He looked down at the remains and back to the sheriff. "But then we'd both be wrong."

"I'll have to collect hair from his brush for DNA comparison. The test will confirm positive identification, but for now, I'll take your word for it. I have a body bag in the plane. It seems like a bit of overkill for so little that's left, but I better go by the book just the same. I'll get the remains wrapped up, and then I'll need to speak with the boys that discovered the bones and anyone that might have been the last to see Lee alive."

They walked out, closing the door behind them, leaving it unlocked.

Red and the sheriff paused in front of the cold house. "I'll round up the two boys first and have 'em wait in my cabin. As far as who saw him last, there are four—Edith, two campers helpin' in the kitchen, and me. I'll gather them after I get the boys." While the sheriff headed to the plane to get the body bag, Red followed the path to the campers' cabin, thinking of the fight between Edith and Lee the night he disappeared. Red groaned. *I hope this is one time Edith knows to lock her loose jaw. If I thought it'd do any good, I'd put a muzzle on her.* He frowned. *I know none of my people had anything to do with Lee's death and the last thing I need is for Edith's ramblings to cause the sheriff to question that. I should talk to her before she meets with him. Otherwise, she's likely to not only hang herself, but make the rope with which to do it.*

"HEY BUD," Red said as he came walking up the path toward him. "Could you take Nathan and Sean into my cabin and wait for the sheriff to come interview them? I've got to have a chat with Edith before she confesses to things she hasn't done."

"Sure, come on, guys," Bud said, motioning to the two boys.

Red stepped off the path, allowing the boys to pass. As Sean walked on, Nathan hesitated. "What exactly is he going to ask us?"

"It's simple. He'll want you to walk him through how you came to find Lee's remains." Red noticed Nathan's look of concern. "You're not on the hot seat here, so why the worry?"

Nathan shrugged. "I've never been sober during an interrogation. I guess I'm not sure how to act."

"This isn't an interrogation. It's an interview."

"What's the difference?"

"What side of trouble you're on." Red walked beside him. "You'll be fine. Just give the sheriff the respect he deserves, and he'll do the same for you. But I should warn you, he isn't a fan of vulgar language. So you might want to broaden your vocabulary when you speak with him."

Nathan gave a nod and turned off the path, following Bud as Red walked on alone.

"The old man looks pretty beat up today," Nathan said when he caught up to Bud.

Bud paused at the cabin door, looking over his shoulder to Red. "His crust isn't as thick as you might think. He's taking Lee's loss as hard as the rest of us. Probably more so, considering he's spent a good amount of his adult life working to save people from harm. I'm sure the senseless way Lee died weighs heavily on him."

"When you say he worked to save people, are you talking about mountain rescue?" Sean asked, following Bud through the door.

Bud led the boys across the great room to the sofas in front of the large windows overlooking the Minam River. "He's done plenty of that through the years, but I was referring to his days as a fire captain in Portland."

"It's hard to picture him as anything other than a cowboy," said Nathan.

"I can't see him living in the city," Sean said.

"He tells some great stories about his days fighting fires." Bud chuckled. "You'll have to ask him about it."

"It looks like we have time. Why don't you tell us some?" Sean said.

"I suppose I could entertain you until the sheriff gets here. Say, did anyone ever tell you boys how Red came to own the ranch?"

"No," Nathan said.

Sean shook his head.

"Well then, that's a good place to start." Bud rubbed his chin. "From what I understand, Red really enjoyed firefighting, but his first love was always the mountains. Even before he became captain, most of his free time was spent hunting, fishing, and exploring on horseback. As the years went on, he began to obsess over getting his own spread, but he never had enough cash to make it happen.

Then a man came up missing while hunting alone in the Steens Mountain down in southeast Oregon. When the local officials gave up, the missing man's brother, a Portland dentist, wanted to arrange a private search. He was directed to Red, who found the man's body within half a day. Turns out the man had died of a heart attack.

Red had told the dentist about a ranch in eastern Oregon he wanted to buy, and in appreciation for finding his brother, the dentist gave Red the rest of the money he needed to purchase it. Unfortunately, running the ranch eventually ended his firefighting career, and not by choice.

Much to the disapproval of the newly elected Portland mayor, Red kept his position as a station captain, splitting his time between firefighting and the ranch. He followed the rules set for taking leave, but it still irked the mayor that he would do so for up to six months at a time. So when the mayor forced him to make a choice between his job and the ranch, he chose the ranch."

Bud crossed his ankles up on the coffee table and leaned back on the sofa with his hands resting behind his head. "He must have had a good crew working under him." He paused, staring up at the ceiling. "Let me see now. Oh yes, I know a good one for you.

Red's men were competent at fighting fire," Bud began. "It was between the fires that brought them trouble. Red would discover just how much when he returned to the station late one November. As he was walking from his car, his eyes caught a shadowy movement in the narrow alley beside the station. On closer investigation, he found a long ladder positioned with one end in a window on the second story of the station and the other secured to a window in the building next door. He stood there, watching as one of his crewmen crawled on all fours across the ladder to a beckoning prostitute. No sooner had he tumbled through the window than a second crewman started across to another waiting woman.

When Red entered to find the station all but deserted with only a few men scattered about the building, he was livid. So he called his men together and told them they were to take the catwalk to the whorehouse down immediately, and that he expected half of his on-duty squad to be standing at the ready at all times."

"Half of his squad? Why only half?" Sean asked.

"I questioned that myself," Bud said, chuckling again. "Red claims his men were so efficient at firefighting it only took half his on-duty men to fight any fire. And with Red in charge, I'm sure that was true."

"WELL, SHERIFF, you've talked to everyone now. Did you discover anything useful?" Red asked as he walked across his cabin's great room, taking a seat on the couch across from the sheriff.

"Not one blessed thing," Sheriff Cason said. "Nothing unusual popped up, other than the fight Lee had with Edith, which all your men reported to be fairly normal behavior for the two of them. Speaking of Edith, she's a hard one to keep up with. She went on about something to do with pies and lard, but I never did get clear as to what she was talking about."

Red smiled slightly. "Edith has always been blessed with the ability to use the most words to express the smallest thought."

"I can see that," the sheriff said. "Anyway, the consensus seems to be that Lee must have gotten drunk after the fight and for some unexplained reason took a boat ride over to Pig Island."

Red stared at the sheriff. "I knew somethin' was out of place, but I couldn't put my finger on it." He groaned. "It's the damn boat."

"What about it?"

"It was waitin' for the campers when they went to feed the hogs. If Lee rowed over to Pig Island, why would the boat be on this side? It doesn't make any sense."

"Maybe it got away from him and floated across the pond."

"And crawled up on the bank? I don't think so." Red took the pipe from his mouth and dumped the ashes into an ashtray on the coffee table. "Then again, I suppose if someone happened to see it drifting close to the bank, they might have pulled it to shore." He packed new tobacco in the pipe and held a flaming match to it. "But if it were one of my staff or the campers, they would have mentioned it."

The men sat in thought for a moment before the sheriff

broke the silence. "I could see how Lee's death could have been a strange accident, but who the devil would kill and mutilate a calf? No matter how you run this thing, it doesn't make any sense, especially since Lee happened to come up missing the same night the calf was killed. I'm having a hard time swallowing the coincidence of that."

Red nodded. "That night was the last either was seen alive. The calf was found the next morning, and Lee couldn't be found anywhere after he didn't show up for his breakfast shift. We didn't think much of his absence because when somethin' gets stuck in Lee's craw, it's not unusual for him to tie one on. So after the fight with Edith, we thought he'd just gone off on one of his benders."

"Maybe that's exactly what happened, but it doesn't explain why he'd end up on the island."

"Men do strange things when skunked on bug juice." Red took the pipe from his mouth and studied it. "And Lee was known not to stop drinkin' until he was facedown somewhere. I couldn't tell you how many times I've had to sober him with a toss in the pond." He placed the pipe back in his mouth and looked at the sheriff. "Maybe he decided to go for a boat ride, fell out, and made it to the island, only to be done in by the hogs."

The sheriff frowned. "But that's just it. In the condition you suspect, I very much doubt he'd have the balance to get in a boat, let alone maneuver the paddles." The sheriff gazed out the window, watching a heron land on the riverbank. "Do you think there's any chance Lee killed the calf to spite Edith? I know he had a temper. I remember more than one story about him chasing you with a meat cleaver."

Red shrugged. "When it came to cooking, Lee took offense to anyone giving him direction, me included. Now as far as killin' goes, I see a better chance he'd go after Edith, but never the calf. Buttercup was the first animal Lee ever grew an attachment for."

"Buttercup?"

"That's what he named the calf. He spent a lot of time doting on her."

"So what's your theory on who killed the calf?"

"I'd put money on the long-haired hikers that Lee caught stealing from the supply shed. Yesterday morning, I heard shouting coming from behind the lodge, and when I came around the corner to investigate, I saw a kid with dreadlocks fly out of the supply shed. I knew Lee wasn't the one throwing the kid. It had to be Carlton."

"Is he the one built like a boxcar?"

"That's the one. Anyway, two more bodies flew out the door, and then Lee and Noah, the youngest of the campers, chased them off with brooms." He grinned behind his pipe. "It was all I could do to contain myself. Those longhairs ran like their dreadlocks were on fire." His expression sobered. "Had I known they'd retaliate, I wouldn't have seen the humor in it. After findin' the calf, I searched the woods for them and found they had broken into a nearby cabin, but I missed them."

"How do you know they were the ones who broke in?"

"They left behind wrappers of candy and snacks they had stolen from our supply room."

"I sure would like to have a talk with them," the sheriff said.

"I'd like to do more than talk." Red scowled. "I'd drive the little bastards to the Oregon Zoo and throw them in with the chimpanzees, wearin' nothin' but banana underwear."

"I'll give you credit for creativity, but right now we're long on speculation and short on evidence, so unless we can somehow reverse those two, there's not a whole lot we can do." The sheriff's expression grew thoughtful as he stared at Red. "When you called, you said the calf had been dissected. You know, sooner or later we're going to nab the hikers. And if they still have the knife on them, I'll bet my life it has traces of blood matching the calf. Did you happen to keep the remains?"

"No. We fed them to the..."

"Hogs." The sheriff rolled his eyes. "I'm really starting to hate pork."

"Me too, and for the time bein', it's off the menu here."

The sheriff shook his head. "This whole situation smells a little hinky to me."

"That it does," Red agreed. "Maybe the medical examiner can shed some light on it."

"You're welcome to come with me," the sheriff offered. "Damn if all the color didn't just drain from your face. I take it you're not fond of flying?"

"I much prefer my feet on the ground or in the stirrup. But out of respect for my old friend, I'll ride the bird with you."

The sheriff followed Red to the far end of the room, where he waited while Red rummaged inside the built-in side bar. He stared at the bottle of whiskey Red pulled from the cupboard. "Liquid courage?"

"Damn straight."

As they walked around the corner of the lodge, Red called Jake off the porch. "Do me a favor and untack Sugar and put her in the round pen. I won't be needin' her any more today."

"Yes, sir," Jake said.

Sheriff Cason watched Jake untie Sugar and walk her toward the pen outside the barn. "I can tell you one thing. Riding in a plane is a hell of a lot safer than getting on that crazy mare. I half expected to hear you'd had her made into Alpo by now."

"Watch your tongue. That's a perfectly fine animal. She's just a bit testy at times.

The sheriff laughed. "Testy, my ass. I remember a hunting trip I took with you back when she was in training. What a battle. I wasn't sure which of you would be standing when the dust settled."

"We've come to an understandin' since then," Red said, standing at the door to the plane. "She don't set her teeth in me, and I don't knock 'em out."

CHAPTER 15

"This is one for the books," Dr. Douglas Stanford said as he flipped on the lights in his Enterprise, autopsy room. "Death by hogs—you don't hear that every day." He propped the door open and walked into the center of the room, where he waited for his guests to join him. "I've forgotten my manners. Could I get you boys some coffee and donuts?" he asked as Red and the sheriff carried the remains into the room and set them down on the exam table.

"Ah, no thanks." The sheriff stepped back. "I'm thinking this is the last place I'd want to eat anything."

"Oh sure." Dr. Stanford smiled. "I forget how difficult this can be for people who aren't used to it. Obviously, I don't get many visitors to an autopsy. Well, not ones who are still breathing."

"Where would you like the clothing and eyeball?" Red picked up the plastic kitchen bag they had carried in on top of the body.

The doctor pointed to behind him. "Just drop it on the counter there."

"I see your decorator was going for the white monochrome style." Red scanned the room as he walked back to the table. "It's so bright, add a pearly gate, and the dead could mistake it for heaven."

A grinning Dr. Stanford shrugged. "I've never had any complaints from my patients." He walked to the wall cabinets and pulled hospital gowns, paper face masks, and rubber gloves

148

out of a drawer. "I realize the remains have already been compromised, but once they hit my table, I have to keep protocol. You're welcome to stay, but you'll need to wear these." He passed gowns, gloves, and masks to his guests before pulling on his own. "Now let's have a look." He unzipped the bag and gazed down at the remains. "When you said hogs cleaned the flesh off the bones, you weren't exaggerating." He looked at Red. "Let's get the bag out of the way. I'll need to clean the bones before we can get on with it."

The doctor slid his hands under the torso as Red reached in for the legs. Together they lifted the remains while Sheriff Cason slid the bag off the table, zipping the muck inside before placing it on a chair in the corner.

Red and the sheriff stood by watching the doctor spray water over the bones.

"I've seen a lot of things in my thirty-five years as medical examiner, but this definitely takes the cake," said the white-haired doctor when he finished washing the skeleton.

Then he looked over his glasses at Red. "You say this is the Chinese feller you had cook for me and my boys during our hunting trip last fall?"

"The same."

"What makes you so sure?"

"His shoes." Red used his unlit pipe to point to the bag on the counter. "I don't know anyone else who would go to the mountains wearin' a white cooking jacket and soft leather loafers."

"But we did bring his hairbrush for DNA comparison, just to be positive," the sheriff added.

The doctor pulled a measuring tape from a drawer. "If my memory serves, he was about four inches shorter than me." He ran the tape from the top of the skull to the bottom of the foot bones. "I get five foot two. Well, that certainly fits." His eyes scanned the length of the skeleton. "The only time I've seen bones picked this clean is when my brother-in-law comes over for barbecue." He peered over his glasses at Red again. "And you think your man here…"

"Lee."

"You think Lee," the doctor corrected, "got liquored up and took a nighttime boat ride over to the pigs? Was there a logical reason for him doing that?"

"No," the sheriff answered before Red could. "But everything about this surpasses logic. We're hoping you'll find something that sheds some light on it."

"An eyeball and a tuft of scalp, that's not leaving me much external tissue to examine. But with any luck, the brain hasn't been contaminated." The doctor walked to a cabinet and came back wearing a rubber body apron and a face shield. He put a strap over the skull, holding it in place, and reached under the table for a power saw. "There's only one way to find out."

Red and the sheriff looked at each other and backed away from the table.

"Wise move." Dr. Stanford grinned as he flipped the shield's plastic barrier down over his face. He turned the switch, and the shrill from the spinning blade instantly filled the room. Bone dust drifted in the air as he cut a circle in the crown of the skull. He set the saw aside and picked up an instrument he used to pry the piece of bone from the top of the head. "This is something you two don't have a chance to see every day. Come on over and have a look."

Red moved to the head of the table and watched the doctor set the skull piece in a specimen tray.

"If it's all the same to you, I think I'll stay where I am," the sheriff said from where he stood at the far wall. "I'm not all that fond of the smell."

"Ah, that's nothing," said the doctor. "Bone dust smells like roses compared to most of the things that come across my table. I'll give you a call the next time I get a floater, and you can come by and get a whiff of that."

"No thanks. I'll take your word for it."

The doctor removed the brain from the skull and placed it on an organ tray. He weighed and measured it before slicing the brain in half with a surgical knife. "This is interesting," he said as he inspected the halves. "I wonder if this tumor had anything to do with his death."

"Tumor?" Red repeated. "That's news to me."

The doctor measured the tumor and recorded the results. "This should have given him miserable headaches." He looked at Red. "Did he complain of any?"

"No, but he wasn't the type to share such things."

"Did he ever lose his balance?"

"Only when he drank too much—which he did nightly."

"Are you thinking he could have committed suicide?" Sheriff Cason asked the doctor.

"Given his illness, it's a possibility."

Red stared at the tumor. "Seems strange that he would do so on Pig Island."

"Maybe he thought the hogs would save you the mess," the sheriff said. "If he shot himself, the bullet's probably sitting in one of their bellies.

"If he committed suicide, I doubt he did it by gun," said the doctor. He set the brain on the counter behind him and moved to the side of the table. "It's an interesting fact that women tend to shoot themselves in the chest, so as not to mess up their face. Men are much more likely to shoot themselves in the head, but there's no indication of that here. And a shot to the torso is much like shooting through a dense forest—you're bound to hit something. I'm not seeing any evidence of that in these bones." He paused, looking across the room at the sheriff. "Could you wheel that magnifier lamp over here for me? Right where Red's standing would be perfect."

Red stepped out of the way as the doctor positioned the magnifier over the skeleton. "I sent one of my young hands to the island with a metal detector to search for the medallion Lee always wore. If Lee shot himself, the gun wouldn't have been far from the remains. We didn't find the medallion or a gun."

"I only met Lee that one hunting trip," the doctor said as he leaned over the magnifier. "The two of you knew the man. If not a gun, what method do you think he'd use to kill himself?"

The sheriff considered for a moment. "I don't know. Maybe poison?"

"I would think poison would transfer to the hogs," said Dr. Stanford. "But I guess with a number of hogs sharing the meal, the effects of the toxin might be greatly reduced. I understand hogs can take snake venom without any troubles. Their heavy fat layer insulates them from poisonous bites, but maybe they have a tolerance for ingested poisons as well. I'm not a vet, but I can certainly research it."

"I doubt he'd take poison," Red gnawed on his pipe, thinking. "He'd probably keep it simple. Whiskey and pills would be my guess."

"That would make sense," Dr. Stanford said. "As advanced as the tumor looks to be, it's likely he'd have a prescription for pain meds. Do you know if he was under a doctor's care?"

Red shook his head. "He didn't share much about his private affairs. What I know of his life came from a conversation with a nephew who came to visit a few years back."

"We didn't find any kind of drugs when we searched his cabin," said Sheriff Cason.

"I guess we'll have to wait for the toxicology results to give us an answer to that question," the doctor said.

Sheriff Cason groaned. "So far, all we have is a growing list of questions and speculations."

"Hold on." The doctor adjusted the magnifier closer to a rib. "I just found something that could throw a monkey wrench at that list of yours."

"What's that?" Red came around and looked over the doctor's shoulder.

Dr. Stanford pointed to a rib and stepped back from the table. "Take a look at the marks on the third and fourth ribs.

Those aren't teeth marks."

Red peered through the magnifier and then motioned to the sheriff. "You'll need to take a look at this."

Sheriff Cason took his turn at the magnifier. "Is that a knife cut?"

"I'd say so," Dr. Stanford said. "I believe you finally have one answer—cause of death."

"Doc, do you think he could have done this to himself?" the sheriff asked as he adjusted the magnifier.

"Was he right-handed, Red?" asked the doctor.

"Yes."

"Then no. The angle is wrong. But I'll tell you one thing. The knife that made this cut was as sharp as any surgical tool I've ever seen." He pointed to a mark on the rib. "The point hit the fourth rib here, gouging a deep nick in it. As it continued in, the blade sliced through the top edge of the third rib, leaving a deep trench." He pulled a small measuring device from his lab coat pocket. "I'll take some measurements and compare them to the knives on the forensic weapons list."

"I know exactly what kind of knife leaves marks like those," said Red, watching the doctor make measurement notations on a pad. "It's a field-dressing knife with a trailing point."

The doctor looked up at him. "Do you know anyone with a knife like that?"

Red nodded. "Probably a hundred or more. Every hunter between here and Cascades has one." *There's one I'm particularly aware of. But no one needs to know that until after I've had the chance to talk with the owner.*

"That's certainly not going to help us," the doctor said, staring down at the remains. "The state police forensic lab has a lot better equipment than I do. I was going to have them run toxicology tests on tissue samples. Now that this wrinkle has presented itself, I think it's best to send them the whole shebang, clothes and all."

"That sounds like a plan," the sheriff said. "But before you do, could you use that fancy camera of yours and take a picture of the knife marks for us? I know tests results could take a couple weeks. If we come across a knife, it would be good to have something to compare it to."

"Not a problem. I take pictures of all evidence before I send it off anyway. I'll go to my office and make a copy of my measurements, and then take those pictures for you." The doctor walked out of the room, leaving the sheriff and Red alone with the remains.

"What's got you thinkin' so hard?" Sheriff Cason asked Red.

"You know that coincidence you were having a hard time swallowing earlier? Well, I don't believe in coincidences. There has to be a connection between the slaughter of the calf and killin' of Lee."

"You told me you thought the hikers killed the calf out of revenge for Lee running them off. Maybe he walked in when they were in the process, and they had to cover their tracks."

"That could be," said Red.

"If they killed Lee, then I imagine they're as far from the ranch as they can get by now. And since they were stealing food from you, they probably didn't come with provisions of their own. If they're still in the mountains, they won't be able to stay there for much longer. You give me a description, and I'll put out an Attempt to Locate."

"You might want to give the park rangers at Wallowa Lake a heads up. It's likely the hikers will go where they know there are plenty of people to steal from." Red paused for a moment. "I agree they're probably long gone by now, but just the same, I need to get back and put my own men on watch."

"I hear that," said the sheriff. "As soon as we get the pictures, I'll drive you to the airport."

"IS THAT WHO I think it is?" asked the sheriff as they drove off the paved road onto the graveled parking lot at the Enterprise airport.

Red groaned to himself when he saw the woman standing next to a cherry-red Mercedes convertible. "That would be Faye Reynolds in all her painted glory. Damn, with all that's happened I forgot she and her devil of a husband are stayin' at the ranch this weekend. And for some untold reason, she's coming in a day ahead of the commissioner."

"I take it you aren't a fan of our infamous county commissioner?" the sheriff asked as he parked near the small building that served as airport office and home of Perkins Air Service, the charter business operated by pilot Joe Perkins.

"Since the man has all the virtues I dislike and none of the vices I admire, can't say that I am." Red watched Faye, dressed in a sheer low-cut pink top and tight white capris, struggle to wheel one of three designer travel bags across the gravel. "I find it difficult to respect a man that preaches morality out of one side of his face, while the other lies and cheats ranchers out of their property. Banking, real estate, and politics—could one man be a worse mix?"

"Only if you add lawyer to the list," the sheriff replied. "I'll tell you one person Bruce Reynolds missed giving his morality sermon to: Choo Choo."

Red looked confused. "Choo Choo?"

"It's the nickname my deputy gave Faye, referring to her likeness to train tracks." He grinned at Red's questioning look. "She's been laid across the county."

"Does Bruce know of her infidelities?"

"If he does, he's doing a great job of pretending not to. Then again, Bruce Reynolds is a self-made man who worships his creator. From what I've seen, he's so wrapped up in self-adoration I rather doubt he'd take notice of anything his wife was doing."

Red watched as the pilot took the bag from Faye and loaded it into his six-passenger Cessna Skywagon sitting beside the office. "It could be that Bruce doesn't care what his wife does as long as she looks good on his arm."

"And boy it must take a lot of money to keep her looking the way she does. I don't think there's an inch of her that hasn't been tucked, sucked, lifted, or enlarged."

"Isn't he quite a bit older than her?" Red asked, watching Faye walk gingerly across the gravel on spiked heels.

"I think there's better than twenty years between them. I went to a big shindig he threw for her fortieth birthday a couple years ago. He even hogged the spotlight that night, turning the whole thing into an election campaign fundraiser. Poor Faye probably doesn't see the writing on the wall. It won't be but a handful of years before she's too long in the tooth to grace his arm. Then he'll trade her in for a younger model, just like he did his first two wives." Sheriff Cason frowned. "I guess I should watch my tongue. He gets wind of any bad-mouthing and he'll see to it my department budget gets cut. You might want to be careful too. I hear Faye can be very aggressive, and if her husband thinks she's taken an interest in you, he's likely to use his political clout to damage your business."

"No danger there. Faye obviously likes men with money and positions of power and status. I certainly don't fit that bill."

"Didn't you say two of your men are pretty well off?"

"Yup. I'm not sure about Woody, but Bud could buy Bruce about one hundred times over."

"Don't let Faye hear that."

"Don't worry. My men are scared to death of her. The last thing Bud needs is another woman in his pocket. And Woody fears his wife too much to touch another woman. It's the young ones I have to watch around her. They don't have the experience to know when a female is putting them in a compromising situation. Just last year I had to pull Billy's heinie out of the wringer when Faye had him backed into a corner. The experience had him sweatin' bullets. When he sees she's come to the ranch, I expect he'll make himself scarce."

Red stared at Faye's opened-toed heels. "Would you look at what she's wearin' on her feet? How the devil does she expect to walk around the ranch in those things?"

"Who's looking at feet? I'm watching to see what pops out first. As low as that top is, and as tight as the pants are, she bends over again, and one end or the other is bound to burst out."

"Capris," Red corrected.

"What?"

"The short pants are called capris."

"Since when did you become a fashion expert?"

Red shrugged. "Sometimes I run out of things to read while I'm soakin' in my tub, so I pick up whatever the guests have left lying around. Surprising what you can learn from reading a women's magazine." He pulled his gaze from Faye and looked at Sheriff Cason. "Did you know that it's fashionable for women to bleach their assholes? Who does that? I've never had a look at mine, but since I have no intention of parading it around like a show pony, whatever the color, I'm leavin' it be."

The sheriff laughed. "What other things have you learned?"

Red considered and with a straight face answered, "Purple will be the popular color worn at the Academy Awards this year."

"So glad to see you're getting in touch with your feminine side."

Red chuckled. "I best let you get to your duties."

"And miss this show?" The sheriff took his phone from his pocket. "Not on your life. She's gonna have to climb up into that plane, and when she does, her ample butt is likely to bust right out of those pants. And I'll be ready with my phone to record it for posterity."

"Well, as much as I've enjoyed the distraction, I'd say it's time to get back to reality." Red released his seat belt, and paused with his hand on the car door. "You let me know when the hikers are found. I'd like to be there when you talk with them." He stood outside the door, waiting for a response.

"You'll be my first call." The sheriff pushed a button on his phone and focused it on Faye as she struggled to climb into the seat behind the pilot's. "Shoot." He said, pushing another button and tossing the phone on the passenger seat. "That was just plain disappointing. There must be industrial-strength material in those pants."

"HERE'S RED NOW," Bud said as he watched the plane taxi to a stop beyond the flagpole.

"About time he got back here." Woody pushed his chair back from the table. "It's been driving me crazy not knowing if they found out what happened to Lee."

Joe stepped down from the plane and rushed around to assist his passenger with getting out of the back seat.

"That's not Red," Woody said of the high-heeled foot coming out of the plane.

Faye held tightly to the pilot's hand as she sought the step with her foot. Once she was soundly on the ground, Joe began pulling her luggage from the cargo area.

Red got out of the front and walked around the plane to his waiting guest.

Bud motioned to Nathan and Carlos as they came out from the lodge. "You two are just in time."

"Time for what?" Nathan asked, stopping on the porch beside Bud.

"To take Mrs. Reynolds's bags to the Nez Perce cabin," replied Bud.

"Good," Carlos said, looking relieved. "If you said anything about Pig Island, I'd be making a run for it."

"No need to sweat that," Woody said. "Red has Jake and Billy feeding the hogs from here on out."

"You won't hear me complaining about that," said Nathan. He stepped off the porch with Carlos following behind him.

Woody watched as Red lent Faye an arm and led her through the grass. "Is it my imagination, or is Mrs. Reynolds's topside bigger this year?"

"I'd say so," Bud replied. "And her pile of hair gets a little more platinum each summer."

"Whoa!" Nathan exclaimed as Tan Dog and her three brothers ran across the path, almost tripping him as they raced for Red and Faye.

"Keep them away from me," Faye screeched, releasing Red's arm, and ducking behind him.

"We best see if we can help keep the mutts from her white pants," Woody said. He and Bud were half way to Red and Faye when Bud whistled. The three male dogs ran to Bud and Woody and they grabbed them by their collars, holding them off the path.

Tan Dog ignored the whistle and sat at Red's side, panting up at him. He gave her head a pat and turned to Faye, offering his arm again. "Don't worry, she won't jump on you. Let me help you inside."

Faye grabbed his arm, smiling coyly and batting her long false lashes at him. "You're a true gentleman, Red. I'll have to think of some way to reward you." She winked, but once she caught sight of Nathan, her flirtations had a new target. "Well, well. What do we have here?" She stared at the young man walking the path toward her. She dropped Red's arm and stopped to look Nathan up and down. "Oh my, you're just as cute as that dreamy Billy Boy."

"He's seventeen, Faye," said Red.

"That only makes him more delicious." She scanned Nathan's body, lingering on his crotch before raising her eyes to his. "You be sure to save some of that whopper for me, Cupcake." She winked at him.

Nathan blushed and stepped back, running into Carlos.

Faye laughed at the look on his face. "I'll look for you later, Sugar." As she walked past him, she clipped him under the chin with one of her long fingernails and sashayed up the path alone.

Bud and Woody nodded as she passed them.

"That was the scariest thing I've ever seen," Carlos said,

looking spooked.

"I knew you had cougar up here, but I didn't know you had that kind," Nathan said as Bud and Woody joined them.

"My generation referred to a woman like that as 'rode hard and put away wet." Woody turned to watch the sway of Faye's skin-tight capris. "Criminy! Her pants are so tight you can see Lincoln smiling on the penny in her pocket."

"Did you see the size of her ass?" Nathan exclaimed.

Red biffed him on the back of his head. "Quiet, boy. Unless it's got four legs and haulin' coal from a mine, I don't want to hear you make mention of any ass." He turned his glare on Woody. "And you're no better."

"Sorry, Red. I was so taken aback, I forgot my manners."

Red looked at the faces around him. "It would do all of you good to remember—you can't stick a foot in a closed mouth." His angry gaze landed on Nathan. "She's a paying guest, so please try to control your afflictions while you take her bags in."

Confused, Nathan asked, "What afflictions?"

"Constipation of thought and diarrhea of mouth."

CHAPTER 16

"I'm having a hard time wrapping my head around the fact that Lee was murdered," Woody said as he and Bud followed Red into his private cabin in the midafternoon. "And you think the long-haired hikers killed him and the calf?"

"It's the only scenario that makes any sense," said Red. Tan Dog trotted ahead of him as he led the men through the great room to the twin spotted cowhide sofas by the back windows. He sat opposite his men, puffing on his pipe as Tan Dog circled twice before settling at his feet. "We better hope they're the ones that did it. Otherwise we may be lookin' at one of our own."

"How's that?" Bud asked.

"The stab marks in the bone were made by a unique cutting tool. It sticks in my craw to say it, but Leroy's homemade huntin' knife would leave the exact same marks. I'll compare his knife to the measurements I brought back with me. If it's a match, I'll have to call for a plane to take the blade to the medical examiner." *I sure as hell hope it doesn't come to that.*

"There must be more than a dozen hunting knives in one place or the other here. What makes Leroy's so special?" asked Bud.

"I've seen enough of its use to know the unique marks it leaves,"

"You don't actually think Leroy killed Lee?" Woody asked.

"I might believe him killing Lee, but not the calf." Bud stretched his legs out on the coffee table. "It's got to be the

161

hikers."

"I hope you're right, but I'll have to rule out his knife, just the same. And that is not a conversation I'm looking forward to having. No matter how I dance around it, just the asking is the same as accusing him of murder. He's bound to be insulted, and I don't blame him."

"If I killed someone with a knife as easy to trace as his, it'd be at the bottom of the deepest pond by now," said Bud.

"That knife is his pride and joy." Woody shook his head. "I doubt he could bring himself to give it up, no matter what."

Red stood. "Well, we can sit around and discuss this all day, but it's not gonna get us any closer to the truth." He walked to his bar, opened a cabinet, and took out a full bottle of whiskey.

"Is that your form of truth serum or Novocain?" asked Woody.

"Both," Red said as he held the door open for Tan Dog. "With any luck, it'll work for apologies as well." He closed the door behind him and walked to the shoeing shed, where he knew Leroy was sharpening the teeth on the old hay sickle mower.

"Leroy, could you take a break? I have something I need to discuss with you."

Leroy froze. "Right this very minute?"

Red heard the nerves in Leroy's voice. "Yes, Leroy, right now."

Leroy set the sickle tooth on the table, and turned to face him.

"Let's talk in your cabin." Red waited for Leroy to walk past him. *He's not lookin' me in the eye—that can't be good.*

"What's this about?" Leroy asked as Red followed him through the door of the one-room cabin.

"You got glasses?" Red held the bottle of whiskey up.

Leroy searched through a tray of dishes sitting on a brown dresser. "Edith ain't had much time to tidy up since takin' over the cookin' job full time. I'll take these back to the kitchen as soon as were done here." He finally reached for two short jelly jars sitting on the windowsill above the dresser. "Would these do?" he asked, flipping a dead fly from one of the jars.

"Just right." Red opened the bottle.

Leroy wiped the dust from the jars and carried them to a small table at the end of the bed. He stood by, watching Red pour whiskey into each jar.

"Have a seat, Leroy." Red pointed to one of the two mismatched wooden chairs sitting on either side of the table.

"It must be serious for you to be pourin' your top-shelf whiskey. Should I be worried?" Leroy asked as he slid onto the chair across from the one Red took.

"I hope not. But I have to ask to see your huntin' knife. The one with the elk-antler handle."

Leroy reached for his jar of whiskey and drank all of it. "I was really hopin' the doc wouldn't find nothin' that would circle back to my knife."

Red emptied his glass and poured two more. "I wish he hadn't." He drained his second glass and slammed the jar on the table, making Leroy jump. "What the hell, Leroy," he shouted. "What would make you take the life of another man?"

Leroy looked shocked. "I didn't kill no one."

"Then how the hell did your knife leave marks on Lee's bones?"

Leroy stared down at his whiskey. "She didn't mean to do it," he said softly. "Lee just pushed her too far that last time." His pleading eyes rose to meet Red's. "Please, Red, she's too old to go to prison." He gulped down his drink.

"Are you tellin' me Edith did this?"

"Edith did what?" Edith asked as she walked through the door, wearing a bright red dress with big purple flowers. She eyed the bottle. "Well now, isn't it nice to find you two sittin' on your backsides, pullin' at a bottle in the middle of the day," she scolded with her hands on her hips. "If you ain't got nothin' better to do, I'll give you both a peeler and you can gab all you want while you skin taters for dinner."

"He knows, Edie." Leroy reached for the bottle and poured another drink.

"He knows what?"

Leroy drank his third jar full, and set the empty glass down. "They found stab wounds on the bones. He knows you killed the calf and murdered Lee with my knife."

Edith stared at him. "Have you finally gone completely loco?" she shouted. "I didn't kill no one, you crazy old coot." Sure, I threatened to kill Lee almost every day I worked with him, but you'd have to be dumber than a hairball to think I'd actually do it." Her eyes drew to daggers as she raged on. "If it weren't a waste of good whiskey, I'd take that there bottle and ring your bell with it." Then she whirled and pointed a finger at Red. "And I suppose you were right there to jump on his crazy train."

"Now, Edith," Red began.

"Don't you, now, Edith me, Buster Brown. You should know better than to believe an old fool."

The sudden sad change in her expression made Red reach for the bottle. *Oh no, here come the waterworks. Hell, I'll take her yellin' over tears any day.* He quickly poured a drink, handed it to Edith, and watched her toss it down her throat.

She set the jar on the table and raised her apron to dab at her tears. Her voice softened with sadness when she said, "I might understand how you'd be dumb enough to think I'd kill Lee, but you should have enough sense to know I could never hurt that precious little calf—the poor thing." She sniffed. "How could anyone who's known me as long as you have, even think I'd do such a thing?"

"You're right," Red said. "I know you didn't have anything to do with the killings."

"I'm sorry, Edie," pleaded Leroy. "When I found my bloody knife in the calf's stall, I thought it had to be you that done it. Ever since my old knife got stolen right out of this here cabin,

I've kept my new one hid away. And you're the only one that knows where my hidin' place is."

Red stood and walked to the four-drawer dresser sitting against the wall. He pulled the second drawer open and ran his hand over the bottom surface of the drawer above it. "I see you finally found a new hiding place," he said when he discovered the leather sheath was empty.

"What? No, I put it right back in there," Leroy said, looking confused. "And how the devil did you know where I keep my knife?"

"You've told every livin' soul on this ranch," said Edith, crossing her arms over her chest. "You know how the drink loosens your tongue."

Leroy got up and inspected the drawer for himself. "It's not here."

"You sure you weren't pickled on juice?" Edith asked. "Your memory ain't too good when you've hit the bottle too hard."

"I clearly remember puttin' the knife back in the cover after I cleaned it. And no, I wasn't skunked when I did it. I put it right back where it lives because with you bein' the only one knowin' of its whereabouts, I thought it'd be safe there. Once I heard that Red suspected them long-haired kids of doin' it, I thought the whole thing would blow over with time. I was gonna talk to you 'bout the calf killin', Edie, but when Lee come up dead, I didn't know what to think."

"Lord, have mercy, how on earth did I marry such a ninny-headed man?" Edith shook her head at Leroy. "You were actually thinkin' that I killed the calf just 'cause Lee and I had a squabble? And then I stabbed Lee and left the knife for the whole world to find? Good Lord, I would certainly hope to be a little smarter 'bout it."

"That's what doesn't make sense," Red said, drawing the Meyers' attention to where he leaned against the chest of drawers. "Even the longhairs couldn't be dumb enough to come back for the knife. What would be the point in that? And after the mess they made of the supply room, I don't see them conducting a soft-handed search of anything. When they were through, this place would have looked like a tornado blew through. Besides," he pointed to the loaded rifle hanging over the door and the kitchen knives sitting on top of the dresser. "You've got plenty of weapons for easy takin', and with the close distance to the lodge I doubt they'd dillydally." He rubbed his forehead. "Ah hell, here I was set on proving the hikers' guilt, but I only succeeded in testifying to their innocence. It had to be someone who knew right where you kept the knife, and that means we may be lookin' at one of our own."

The Meyers followed Red's movements as he walked across the cabin to the small woodstove.

"You're not thinkin' to look at me for this?" Leroy said, looking alarmed.

"No, Edith was right about the calf. Neither of you would have killed her." Red opened the wood compartment door and emptied his pipe ash into the belly of the stove. "But I rather doubt the authorities are going to share in my confidence." He latched the door closed. "They're sure to put blinders on once they hear it was likely your knife that sliced Lee and the calf. From then on, they'll be looking for anything that points to you, and it won't be hard for them to find enough to arrest you. You provide them with the trifecta of means, motive, and opportunity. You own the missing murder weapon, you were angry about Lee fighting with Edith, and you always said Edith could sleep through a herd stampeding through your cabin. You could have easily slipped out of bed while she was asleep."

Leroy paled and gulped. "How about keepin' my knife to yerself for the time bein'? Maybe long enough for me to get out of Dodge?"

Red watched the lines on Leroy's face deepen with worry. "I won't lie to the sheriff, but nothin' says I have to offer anything he doesn't ask. You're not goin' anywhere, Leroy."

Leroy brightened slightly. "You tell the sheriff that if he

searches them delinquents' cabin, he's sure to find my knife."

"I won't be tellin' the sheriff anything just yet, but we will be searching their cabin along with all the others." Red packed his pipe with fresh tobacco. "The only way to keep the sheriff from fixating on you is to figure out who took your knife, and we can only do that by finding the blasted thing. If it takes pullin' the logs off every building on this ranch, so be it. Before we look for an outsider, I want to know it wasn't one of my people." He paused to strike a match on the stove and lit his pipe. "Everyone should be together when we conduct the search. You gather the men, and I'll get the young hands."

"They ain't here," Leroy said.

Red shook the match out and tossed it into the stove. "Where the hell are they?"

"Bud got a call that the lumber you ordered for fixing the walls in the staff cabin are ready to be delivered to Moss Springs. Jake and Billy set out with a pack string soon after you left this mornin'. They won't be gettin' back 'til early evening. I say we start with the campers' cabin. Why bother with the others when we know that's where we're gonna find my knife?" He reached for the whiskey, but before his hand closed on the bottle, Edith grabbed it off the table.

"No, sir, you'll be gettin' no more of this." She shook the bottle at Leroy. "First you accuse me of murder, and now you point the finger at them poor boys. I'll have you know, Carlton and Noah have been nothin' but sweet help to me in the kitchen. And the other three went and done their chores without a single gripe this mornin'. They were all plum sick over Lee's death. There's no killer in any of 'em. They're just boys bein' boys, that's all. Last I saw they were headed back to their cabin with a pack of cards. They deserve a little fun after bein' exposed to such a horrible thing as Lee's death." She stalked past Red, opened the door, and glared back at Leroy. "You'll be makin' your bed in the barn tonight, and maybe every night from here on out." She walked out the door, slamming it closed behind her.

Leroy stared at the door for a moment before turning to Red. "Maybe gettin' arrested for murder don't seem so bad after all. Prison could be a heap safer than livin' with Edith when she's got her angry on. She's gonna be chewin' on this for a long time."

"Hell hath no fury like a woman scorned," Red said as he walked to the door.

CHAPTER 17

Red was deep in thought as he walked with Bud and Woody. He hated the thought of searching the next cabin. The invasion was such a violation of the campers' privacy, but it had to be done. He had thought it best to begin the search with the staff cabin, so as not to make the campers feel singled out. But since he felt it only right each person be present when their things were searched, they had to wait to begin until Jake and Billy had returned from hauling lumber. Although they didn't find the knife, that first search hadn't gone well.

His confidence that the knife wouldn't be found in the possession of one of his staff began to waver when Billy adamantly protested the search of his belongings. They soon discovered he was hiding something, but it wasn't a murder weapon.

"I sure feel bad about upsetting Billy that way," Woody said, breaking into Red's thoughts as they followed the path to the campers' cabin.

"I don't know why he'd care about anyone knowing he takes prescription drugs," said Bud. "Hell, my doctor's got me taking four different things."

"Not to mention the tiny blue pill for special occasions." Woody grinned. "Yeah, I saw it."

"Like you don't take Viagra." Bud glared at him.

"I probably have more occasions to use it than you do."

"Sadly, that's all too true," Bud replied. "I forgot it was in that bag from when wife number three and I took our

European vacation last year. Went away with high hopes, came home with a full bottle, and divorce papers."

"What could Billy be takin' that would make him so embarrassed," Woody asked Bud. "What did the label say?"

"I'm not the nosy Nellie that you are. It wasn't a weapon, so there was no reason to look any further."

"That would be a good thing to remember when searchin' the campers' gear," said Red. "It's humiliating enough that we're goin' through their skivvies. We don't need to add any unnecessary embarrassment to it. We're all aware of exactly what Leroy's knife looks like. We ignore everything we see, except the knife. That is, unless we come across somethin' that could cause harm."

"I still don't see the point of the killer taking the knife back," said Woody. "The antler handle would be too rough to hold a print, and after Leroy's meticulous cleaning, I wouldn't expect there would be a trace of any evidence left on it. It seems it would be to the killer's benefit to leave the knife in Leroy's cabin. It would certainly point the finger of guilt at him."

"That's the knot we have to unravel," Red said. "It all comes back to someone knowing where Leroy keeps the knife. Unfortunately, his drunken bragging could have caused that number to be in the triple digits."

"Yes, but none have more cause for suspicion than Edith," said Bud. "No matter how you spin it, it's not Leroy, but Edith the finger of guilt ends up pointing to."

"I'm well aware of that. Even more of a reason to find that damn knife," Red said, turning off the path.

They reached the cabin just as a panicked-looking Noah came rushing out the door. He saw the men and quickly turned, throwing up off the side of the porch.

"Damn, boy, you got a stomach bug?" Bud asked.

"Hey, Noah," Sean called from inside the cabin. "You're holding up the game. Get back in here and take your shot." He tripped coming out the door, and fell at Red's feet. He slowly raised his head and struggled to focus his bloodshot eyes on the angry face looking down at him. "Uh-oh, busted."

Red reached down and grabbed the back of Sean's jeans, lifting him up close to his face. "By the smell of this one, I'd say they've been bit by the whiskey bug." He dropped Sean to the porch, stepped over him, and walked into the cabin. There he found the rest of the boys sitting in a circle on the floor in front of the fireplace. All had a shot of whiskey in front of them, and two additional glasses waiting for Sean and Noah. In the center of the circle, he spied a bottle of his best whiskey. Beside that bottle lay an empty one, and beer cans were scattered throughout the room. "What the hell do you think you're doin'?" Red growled.

"Are they all in the same condition as these two?" Bud asked as he and Woody herded the Sean and Noah back into the cabin.

"Where did you get the whiskey?" Red stared angrily around the circle of red-faced boys. "Answer me, damn it!"

"We know where they got it," Jake said as he and Billy walked into the cabin. "We went to search Lee's cabin again, like you told us, and found the place had been tossed."

"We dent have nothun to do wid dat," Carlton slurred.

"Yeah, that was all Nathan," Sean said, shrugging at Nathan's glare. "Sorry, man."

"You broke into a dead man's cabin and went through his things?" Red was appalled. "It's just one jackass move after another with you."

"Chill, dude. It's not like it's a big deal." Nathan looked up at him through half-lidded eyes.

"What did I tell you about calling me dude?"

"Whatever, dude."

"Hey, dude, stop calling him, dude." Carlos shoved Nathan's shoulder. "You'll get us in more trouble."

Nathan tipped over, laughing.

Red chewed on his pipe, staring down at Nathan, crumpled

on the floor. "Glad you're in such a jovial mood—dude. We'll see if we can't give you a fun night you'll never forget." He turned to Woody. "Is there still a bottle of castor oil in the shoeing shed?"

"Yup."

"Make sure each gets a big spoonful. Then we'll have ourselves a relay race to the top of the ridge and back."

"Shoot, your punishments are usually a little more creative." Bud looked disappointed.

"Did I forget to mention that each person will be carrying Noah on their back during their leg of the relay? And there won't be any stopping or slowin' down, not even if Noah blows chunks all over them. Any violation of this rule will result in an automatic start-over for that person. Is that creative enough for you, Bud?"

"Much better." Bud grinned.

"In all fairness, I think Carlton should have to carry someone heavier than Noah," Billy said.

Red looked at Billy's smiling face. "That's a prime idea. Glad you volunteered."

"What? Me? Hey, that's not funny."

"Kinda is," Bud said, laughing. "I'm gonna get my camera."

"Once you're done with the race, we'll have ourselves a rodeo in the round pen," Red said. "Jake, be a good lad and fetch Satan for me."

"Sure, boss." Jake walked out of the cabin, grinning.

"Satan?" Sean repeated. "I don't think I like the sound of that."

"Don't worry, he's just a little donkey," Nathan said.

"A little donkey with a giant mean streak." Woody chuckled. "This should be a good show."

"But before we get on with the fun." Red looked around at the campers. "I'll need everyone to grab your gear and set it out on your bed."

"What for?" Carlos asked.

"Yeah," Sean said. "If it's whiskey you're looking for, that was the last of what Nathan found."

"That's not what we're lookin' for." Red's stern expression grew with his annoyance.

"Don't you need a warrant to look through our stuff?" Noah asked.

"On this ranch, I'm the law. Now do as you're told."

The boys staggered into the next room and gathered their things from under their beds.

Going down the row of bunks, Red and Woody searched one side of the cabin, while Bud and Billy took the other.

Red was going through Noah's belongings when he spotted a lump inside the lining of the metal-sided suitcase. He ran his hand over the bump and froze when he felt a strange shape. "Noah?" he said, turning to look into the boy's pale face.

Noah reached out and gripped Red's arm. "Please, don't." Beads of sweat formed across his brow as he looked up at Red with pleading eyes. "I didn't mean to."

Woody pulled Noah off Red and held him back.

Drawn by Noah's outburst, everyone except Nathan gathered around his bed. They watched as Red pulled the Velcro loose from where it fastened the lining to the case, releasing a stream of items that fell from their hiding place onto the bed.

"Well, this is an unexpected turn of events," said Bud.

"Hey! That's my phone," Sean exclaimed, grabbing it off bed.

"That's my watch," Carton said, picking up the antique pocket watch. Looking confused and hurt, he turned to Noah. "You knew I was going crazy trying to find this, and you had it the whole time? I thought we were friends. How could you take my grandfather's watch? It's the only thing of his I have left."

"I'm sorry, Carlton. I don't know why I take things," Noah said, fighting the tears that threatened to spill from his eyes.

Carlton sat down on the bed and stared silently down at his

watch.

The others were too busy looking over Noah's stash to notice Nathan extract an item from his bag behind them, shoving it into his jeans pocket.

Red reached into Noah's pile of stolen property and picked up a gold lighter taken from the gathering room mantel. Then he brushed Edith's handkerchief aside, exposing an item the men all recognized.

"Damn!" Billy exclaimed. "Is that Leroy's?"

Noah shook his head. "No, it's Nathan's."

"What did the little thief take of mine?" Nathan said, coming to look over their shoulders.

"Your knife." Carlos pointed to the weapon.

"What?" Nathan struggled to focus on the knife Red held in his hand. "I don't have a knife. Noah is too shitfaced to know his ass from his mouth."

"It is too," Noah argued. "I got it from the side pocket of your duffel bag."

Nathan glared at him. "Don't you try to point the finger at me, you little shit." He looked at the faces staring back at him. "I tell you, that isn't mine. The little fucker is lying." He crossed his arms and turned angry eyes on Red. "You won't listen to anything I say anyway, so believe what you want. So what if the knife is mine?"

Red tapped the flat of the knife across his palm, staring at Nathan. "Actually, Billy was right about it belongin' to Leroy. It was stolen from his cabin and used to kill Lee. So in claiming the knife as yours, are you also admitting to killing Lee?"

"Are you crazy? No, I didn't kill Lee!" Nathan pointed at Noah. "He's the one with the damn knife. If anyone is a killer, it's him."

"No, he didn't do it," Carlton said, surprising them all.

"You know that for sure?" asked Red.

Keeping his eyes lowered on the watch in his hand, Carlton shrugged. "Yeah, he and I were up all night together."

"Doing what?" asked Bud.

Carlton's cheeks colored. "Throwing up mostly. After Lee and Edith's fight over how to make pies, Noah and I stayed behind to clean the kitchen. After they left, we got the last of the pies out of the oven and realized we were hungry. So we sort of ate all of them."

"I ate one. Carlton ate two," Noah said. "They made us sick, and we sat up all night in front of the fire, taking turns in the bathroom."

"Other than the restroom, was Noah ever out of your sight?" Red asked Carlton.

Carlton shook his head. "Nope."

"Thanks, Carlton," Noah said, looking relieved.

Carlton shrugged again. "It's not like I'm doing you a favor. It's the truth, that's all."

"When did you take the knife from Nathan's gear?" Red asked Noah.

"When everyone else was out doing chores this morning, I told Edith I needed to take a break from helping with breakfast. She'll tell you, just ask her."

"That's why you disappeared for so long?" Carlton asked. "I thought you were sick again."

"When you two returned to the cabin after eating the pies, did either of you happen to notice Nathan?" Bud asked.

"No," Noah replied. "We didn't go into the bunkroom. We were still feeling sick by the time we got back, so we stayed out in the living room."

"Nathan could have slipped out the back door without them knowing he was gone," Billy said.

"Wow, fuck you," Nathan snarled.

Billy glared. "Hey, you're the one that claimed the knife is his."

"Obviously I wasn't serious, you idiot. And what I said was: what if it is mine—not that it is mine." He dragged a hand through his hair. "Dammit, I was just upset because you jerks won't believe the truth. I didn't kill anyone or anything, and I've never seen that knife before."

"How are we supposed to know when you're telling the truth when we've never heard you do it before?" Billy asked.

"Suck it, Billy," Nathan said.

"Enough!" Red shouted. "None of this is helping."

While the boys glared at each other, Tan Dog trotted through the open cabin door and into the bunkroom room. There she went from bed to bed, sniffing the piles of possessions. As she passed Nathan, she stopped and ran her nose from his feet up to his pockets.

"Get your nose off me," Nathan grumbled, pushing her head away. When she came toward him again, he kicked at her. "Get away from me."

She jumped back, growling at him with the hair on her back bristling"

Empty your pockets," Red ordered.

"Why?"

"Tan Dog doesn't usually show interest in people's pockets, so I'd be curious as to what she's found in yours. Now turn 'em inside out, or I'll be doing it for you."

Nathan hesitated. Flinching when Red stepped toward him, he threw up a hand and jumped back. "Okay, okay, I'll do it." He put his hands in the front pockets of his jeans and pulled them inside out.

Tan Dog sniffed one of Nathan's hands and backed away, barking.

"Put your hands out, palms up," Red said. When Nathan didn't immediately comply, Red closed the distance on him, grabbed his hand, and pried the small bag of white powder from his fingers. *Is there no limit to this kid's stupidity?*

"I didn't know your stupid dog was a narc," Nathan said, jerking his hands free.

"Yeah, she's the stupid one." Billy laughed.

Red inspected the bag, while fighting to hold on to what

little patience he had left. "I suppose these drugs aren't yours either."

"I'll cop to the cocaine," Nathan said. "But no way is that knife mine, and no fuckin' way did I kill anyone."

"You had blow all this time and didn't think to share it?" Sean asked. "That's cold, dude."

Bud slapped the back of Sean's head so hard it made him stagger forward. "Have you got shit for brains, boy?"

"Any other time I'd be happy to watch you slap him senseless," Red said, looking at Bud. "But as it stands, we really can't spare the three seconds that would take." He searched the inebriated faces of his young campers. "Bud, you and Billy take the rest of these knuckleheads to the lodge and keep them there. Nathan's gonna stay to help Woody and I make sense of all this."

Billy's face fell in disappointment. "Damn, I was looking forward to the relay race and rodeo."

"It'll have to wait," Red said.

"You heard the boss." Bud motioned to the campers. "Let's go."

Carlton was the last to follow Billy and Bud to the door, but instead of going through, he suddenly turned and rushed Nathan. "You murderer!"

Red stepped in front of Nathan, blocking him from Carlton, but the massive boy kept coming. Red braced both hands against his chest, holding Carlton back at arm's length. *Good God, it's like trying to hold a raging bull.* He felt the strong pounding of Carlton's heart and the heaving of his breath as he pushed against him. *I've got to get this boy's temper down to a simmer.*

Woody rushed to help Red hold Carlton back.

"Look at me, son," Red shouted, drawing Carlton's eyes from Nathan. "I know how you felt about Lee, but you can't go off half-cocked and beat Nathan to a pulp when we don't even know if he's guilty." Seeing the pained look in Carlton's eyes, Red softened his voice. "I understand your rage. I've had plenty of it myself. But unleashing it on the wrong person doesn't get us anywhere." He thought he might actually be getting through to Carlton when he felt him ease. He was wrong.

Carlton turned his eyes from Red, saw Nathan, and let out a loud growl as he pushed the men back a step.

"Listen to me," Red shouted, bracing his feet. "Lee would want the truth." A moment passed before Carlton finally calmed, and another before he stepped back.

"Lee was my friend." Carlton glowered at Nathan cowering behind the men.

"I know he was." Red placed his hands on Carlton's shoulders. "But until we get all the facts, we can't have you killin' Nathan. Now, go on with you."

Red and Woody watched as Carlton strode out of the cabin. Once he was out of sight, Red turned his gaze to Nathan. "I hope you realize you dodged two bullets there—his need to tear you apart, and my inclination to let him do it. I warn you, boy. I have an ear for detecting lies, so unless you want Carlton turned loose on you, you might want to keep any untruths from rollin' off that silver tongue of yours. Got that, kid?"

Nathan gulped. "Yeah, yeah, I got it. Just keep him away from me."

"You want me to call the sheriff?" Woody asked Red.

"No, please," Nathan pleaded. "I didn't do it. You have to believe me. I'm telling you the truth. I'm being framed."

Red stared at Nathan's panic-stricken face. "We'll wait a bit on that call, Woody. For now, you can get Nathan started on puttin' Lee's cabin to rights. I'll join you later."

"What are you going to do?" Woody asked.

"I'm gonna flush these drugs and lock this damn knife away where no one will find it." Red's piercing eyes landed on Nathan. "Once that's done, I'll give our young outlaw one chance to convince me he had nothing to do with Lee's death."

CHAPTER 18

Red carried a large duffel bag and cardboard box into Lee's cabin, dropping them at Nathan's feet. "Clothin' in the duffel, and personal items go in the box. And make sure you fold the clothes nice and neat." He walked to the far wall where Woody sat in a rocking chair, watching Nathan sweep.

"He hasn't gotten much done in the time I've been gone." Red stood with his back against the wall, scowling at the broken glass Nathan dumped into a garbage can.

"Nope, in his condition, he's about as useless as tits on a boar," grumbled Woody. "He spent the better part of his time huggin' the porcelain throne and the rest mopping the floor when he didn't make it to the bathroom."

"I see why you chose to sit as far as you can from him."

"Damn straight. And until he reaches the point of dry heaves, I'll be keepin' my distance."

Nathan set the dustpan on the stack of kindling in the firewood box, propped the broom against the fireplace, and bent to pick up the first item of many strewn across the floor. "Son of a bitch!" he exclaimed, groaning as he stood up. Holding his head in one hand and a white chef's jacket in his other, he fought to steady the sway of his body. "God, I think I'm gonna hurl again."

"Boy, that's just karma giving your stupidity a good bitch slap." Woody grinned. "I'd say you earned that and a whole lot more."

They watched as Nathan ran for the bathroom.

"Here we go again." Woody groaned. "I'm not so sure this one isn't a lost cause."

Red shook his head, staring at the bathroom door. "He may be as dumb as a trumpet in a brass monkey's butt, but I'm not ready to throw in the towel just yet."

"I figured since you didn't bring a rope to string him up, you don't believe him to be a murderer," Woody said.

"He's guilty of a lot of things, but murder isn't one of them."

"What makes you so sure he's innocent?"

"My gut mostly, but I also remember the look on his face when he fell over Lee's remains. Nathan may be astute at lying and scheming, but he doesn't have the acting skills to fake the terror I saw." Red's gaze scanned the destruction of the cabin, landing on the broken windowpane. "The person who stole the knife from the Meyers' cabin had a lot more finesse with breaking and entering—a talent young Hollywood clearly does not possess."

"That's true enough," Woody agreed, looking around. "Besides that, even when the boy's sober, he moves at the speed of snail, so he'd probably be caught long before he found the knife. Unless Leroy told him where he kept it hidden."

"No, Leroy says he didn't tell the boys. I actually don't think he's said more than two words to any of them since they got here."

"Yeah, his favorite phrases are 'get out' and 'shut up." Woody took off his hat and scratched his head of gray hair. "I'll be thankful if it's not Gil's kid, but that only circles it back to Leroy. He never has hidden his feelings about Lee, or his annoyance with the campers. The sheriff is going to see it as two birds, one stone. To an outsider it would appear Leroy killed Lee and pinned it on one of the campers. But even as cantankerous as he is, I still don't believe him to be a murderer."

"No, me neither. However, I have to admit there was a

moment when I did."

"I heard all about that when I ran into Edith right after your conversation with her and Leroy. She was mad as a wet hen over Leroy thinking she had killed Lee. I think if she murders anyone, it'll be her husband."

"He's smart enough to lay low until she cools." Red stared at his feet. "If we don't figure out who really did this, Edith will be the least of Leroy's problems. With the evidence stacked against him, the sheriff will have no choice but to take Leroy in."

"For a while there, things weren't looking too good for our resident kleptomaniac," Woody said. "Noah's damn lucky Carlton came to his rescue after he violated their friendship the way he did. His sticky fingers could have cost him a lot more if Carlton hadn't come forward. Were you aware of Noah's problem before he came?"

"No, that was a bit of information his father failed to pass on to me." Red paused to light his pipe. "Then again, it could be a brand-new habit he started here at the ranch. I probably won't have the chance to look into it though. Since we have no way of knowin' whether there's a killer still lurking around, the campers will have to be removed from the ranch.

"Yeah, I can see how that would be best." Woody glanced at the bathroom door. "You actually believe it was dumb luck that Noah chose to lift an item that the killer happened to have planted on Nathan?"

"We had better hope the murderer chose a random bag. If Nathan was the killer's intentional target, he could be in real danger."

"If what you're saying is true, the killer is going to a lot of trouble to pin the murder and calf's slaughter on someone here at the ranch. First, he used Leroy's knife and left it to be found in the barn. And I presume when that didn't work, the plan was for the knife to point to Nathan when it was discovered during the police investigation." Woody looked perplexed. "The question is why Nathan?"

Red nodded. "If we knew the why, we'd know who, but since we are clueless on both counts, all the more reason to get the campers a safe distance from here. It's too late to deal with it today. I'll call Joe to fly them out first thing in the morning. I think his plane might be able to haul all five out at one time, as long as we leave their gear for another trip."

"I'm not so sure. Carlton weighs enough for two people, and that might put the plane over weight."

"What Noah lacks in weight should balance him out. Once the boys are safely out of here, we can concentrate on catching the killer."

Nathan came back into the room looking pale and drawn.

Red watched him for a moment before turning to Woody. "I fear this is gonna take some time. No sense in both of us coolin' our heels. You might want to let Jake know that we've cancelled the punishment of the campers for now. After he turns Satan out, have him bring buckets from the barn. I don't want anyone puking in the lodge. As soon as Nathan is finished here, we'll join the rest of you, and make a plan for getting the evening chores done in groups. Until the mad man is caught, no one is to do anything alone."

"Will do," Woody said, rising from his chair.

"Stay in the clear on your way to the barn. I realize that if the murderer is still here, he most likely won't go on the hunt until after nightfall. But I'd keep to the open just the same."

Woody nodded. He opened the door, and Tan Dog trotted in with muddy feet. "I was wondering where you were."

Red frowned at the paw prints trailing behind her. "She's been disappearing a lot lately."

"Maybe she's declared war on a pesky critter. You know how irritated she gets when a squirrel takes to teasing her."

"I just hope she isn't following the scent of a killer."

Woody looked down at the smiling dog. "She'd be safer going after a mountain lion."

"Hey, my head is spinning," Nathan whined from across the

cabin. "Can I sit down for a while?"

"No, keep workin'," Red snapped as he followed Woody out onto the porch. "If the killer chose to plant the knife on Nathan, there would have to be a reason. The first thing the sheriff will ask is if there's been any trouble between Leroy and the boy. Have you seen any?"

"No. Leroy treats him with the same piss and vinegar he gives to the others."

Red puffed smoke into the air, thinking. "We're missing something, and I'll be damned if I can put a finger on what it is."

"Let me know if there's anything I can do," Woody said as he stepped off the porch.

Red walked back to the rocking chair and dragged it to the center of the room. Tan Dog settled beside him, resting her chin on Red's knee as she closely watched Nathan.

Nathan picked up a small, framed portrait of a Chinese man. "Who's this?" He began to take a step toward Red, but the low growl coming from Tan Dog made him freeze. "Is she going to bite me?"

Red stroked Tan Dog's head. "You gave her good reason when you kicked at her earlier."

From where he stood, Nathan turned the picture around and held it up for Red to see.

"That was Lee's great-grandfather. He was the lone survivor of the Chinese massacre that took place in Hells Canyon in May 1887. The newspapers reported that none survived the attack, but according to Lee, they had it wrong."

"Indians?" Nathan asked.

"No, the murderin' gang of deviants that did this were all white folk from Wallowa County. A gang of three known horse thieves, another local man, and two foolish schoolboys on a lark, ambushed and brutally murdered thirty-four Chinese workers minin' gold at Deep Creek. The crime was discovered when a number of the bodies floated down the Snake River to

Lewiston in the Idaho Territory, some forty-eight miles to the north of where the miners were killed."

"Wow. This guy survived?"

"According to Lee, his injured great-grandfather clung to a log until plucked from the river by a fur trapper. Over the many weeks the trapper nursed the miner to health, a friendship developed between the two. As it turns out, it would be a profitable relationship. After learning of the survivor's knowledge about minin', the two set out in 1888 to stake a claim in South Dakota, where they later hit gold. Other than his business partner, Lee's great-grandfather never spoke to anyone but family about his experience on the Snake River. Back then, Chinese people weren't treated any better than insects in this country."

"Were the killers ever caught?"

"They were, but the three horse thieves broke from jail— probably with the help from some of their equally unscrupulous friends. After they got away, the lone adult massacre participant was released after pinnin' the whole thing on the gang of horse thieves. And the three young ones were found innocent by a jury, mostly because the boys came from local families. In the end, no one was ever punished for the crime. That was likely the reason Lee's great-grandfather didn't want his survival known—the killers might have looked to silence the only witness to their crime."

"What happened to the gold?"

"It was rumored that the leaders took some of it with them and buried the rest. Today, most believe this to be a fable."

"Do you?"

"I suppose it's as likely as not. Lee believed the gold was buried here somewhere on the ranch and spent twenty-six years looking for it."

"Why here? Wouldn't they bury it closer to home?"

"This would be a likely place for them to run. It was where they hid the horses they rustled from Idaho. After the dust settled, they'd run them up through Washington state into Canada. I imagine that's where they stayed after fleeing prosecution."

"I thought Indians used to live here?"

"They did, up until all the land in this area was taken away from the Nez Perce in a fraudulent 1863 treaty. After that, the isolation became a perfect hideout for horse thieves and bandits."

"So that's what Lee was looking for with the metal detector?"

"Yup. He must have run that thing over every inch of this canyon—twice. But he never found a speck of gold dust. It's too bad. He planned to set up a college scholarship program for decedents of the murdered miners. Pretty damn noble, if you ask me."

Nathan placed the picture in the box. "You would have let him keep it? If the gold were found on your land, why wouldn't it belong to you?"

"That's what you take from this story?" Red stared at him. "I guess I'm not as greedy as you and your 'me' generation. I wasn't gonna break a sweat looking for it myself, and I figure if he spent the time and effort to find it, he deserved to keep every ounce of it. I admire someone with the ambition to dedicate himself to a mission, and Lee certainly did. Have you ever been dedicated to anything?"

Nathan looked confused. "What do you mean?"

"Besides your passion for getting into trouble—Have you ever taken on a challenge and stuck with it?"

"I'm a celebrity." Nathan shrugged as he folded a shirt and shoved it into the duffel. "I really don't need to work at anything."

"So what you're saying is: as a failure, you are a big success." Red frowned. "I realize your father is a well-known movie producer and former actor, and your friend is a movie star. Their celebrity status was obviously a result of their work. For you, fame came by association with those who earned it and later by acting like an idiot while cameras recorded your stupidity. How long do you think people will take interest in you now that your show has been cancelled?"

"Have you seen the tabloids lately? I'm on every cover."

You smug little shit. "Not something to be proud of when the picture is a mug shot. And if we don't get this murder straightened out, you might be wearing jail rags on the next cover."

"I told you I had nothing to do with Lee's murder. God! What does it take to convince you?" Nathan flopped across Lee's worn leather chair with his head resting on one arm and his legs dangling over the other. His arm fell across his face, covering his eyes from the overhead light. "Look, I'm a lot of things, but I'm not a killer."

"It's not me you'll be needing to convince. You might want to check your attitude and try having at least a little respect and empathy for others. Until you change that, you won't be anything more than an empty shell of a person. But I also know you aren't a killer."

Nathan drew his arm away from his face, exposing his surprise. "You do?"

"Sure."

"You believe me?" Nathan grabbed his head from the pain of sitting up too fast.

Serves you right, boy. Red fought a grin, holding fast to his gruff expression. "I'm not in a habit of repeating myself, and I never told you to stop working." He looked down at Tan Dog. "How would you like to sink your teeth into his lazy ass for me?"

"I'm up, I'm up." Nathan rolled from the chair, throwing his arms out when dizziness caused him to teeter. "Whoa! When did we get on a boat?"

Tan Dog jumped to her feet, growling.

"Hey, call off the hound!" Nathan backed up and fell over a pile of Lee's things.

"Come on, girl," Red called. Tan Dog ran back to him. "Boy, I sure hope you didn't break anything."

"No, I think I'm okay," Nathan said as he pushed from the floor.

"I was talking about Lee's things."

"Oh."

Red sat puffing on his pipe, silently watching Nathan fold clothing. Once all the clothes were packed away, Nathan began picking up the pictures he had dumped from a drawer when he was searching the cabin. Each of the photos appeared to be family events.

"Are any of the children in these pictures Lee's?"

"No, his wife died of cancer early in their marriage. He never married again."

"Wow, he's actually smiling in this picture with all the kids."

"Those are his nieces and nephews. He sent most of his pay to help with their college expenses." Red rocked in the chair with Tan Dog panting at his side.

Nathan sent Red a sideways glance. "So he did have a good side."

"He was as charitable as any man I've ever known. But he didn't want anyone knowing it." Red ran a hand down Tan Dog's back. "If it weren't for him asking me to make his paychecks out to several relatives, I wouldn't have known. He'd keep a little cash for gambling, but the rest was sent on to family members."

"I didn't believe Carlton and Noah when they said Lee had a sense of humor. I never saw him smile, except for the time I caught him playing with the calf without him knowing it." Nathan took one last look at each picture as he set them in the box. He took a picture from the wall and placed it in the box with the others. "Why do you think someone would want to kill Lee?"

"That's a question we're all asking ourselves."

"It couldn't be for money." Nathan pointed to the duffel.

"Shoot, everything he owns fits in a bag and box. I can't picture him in a love triangle, and I doubt he was a member of a Chinese gang. So why slice the shit out of him and feed him to the hogs?"

"The only theory we can come up with is that he walked in on the person killin' the calf."

"That's the other thing. Who the fuck kills a calf? I mean, what's the point? I didn't like the little shit machine, but I wouldn't have butchered her because of it." Nathan hesitated. "Wait—the knife. If Noah got it from my bag, then it was the killer who put it there."

"I'm glad to see the fog is finally startin' to lift from your brain."

"What if he chose me on purpose?" His panic began to build. "What if he decides to come after me?"

"That's why you'll be stayin' in my cabin tonight." Red took the pipe from his mouth and frowned at the burned-out tobacco.

Nathan inspected the ivory handle on a mirror before setting it into the box. "The men say you never let anyone but family and friends stay in your personal cabin."

"You're neither, but since the safest place for you is with me, I'll have to make an exception."

Nathan grinned. "If I didn't know better, I'd say you care what happens to me."

"Don't get cocky." Red stared down at his pipe. "I just don't want to be put in the spot of explaining to your father why I had to send you back in a body bag."

Nathan glanced at the box of family pictures. "What are they going to do now that Lee won't be sending them any money?"

Red smirked. "Careful, now you're starting to sound like you care."

"Surprises the hell out of me too." Nathan smiled as he picked up items from the pine dresser.

"Maybe you find yourself relating to Lee. Both of you put

up a wall of protection, presenting yourselves as someone you really weren't meant to be. In your case, insecurities drew you to crave public attention, and it was far easier to attract that attention through outrageous behavior than from doing something noble."

Nathan cringed. "Ouch. You don't like to soft-sell it, do you?"

"No reason to dance around it."

Nathan grew silent as he continued to pack Lee's possessions. "This really sucks," he finally said.

"You made the mess."

"No, I mean the killer. I'd do anything to help you catch the bastard."

"You can help by staying safe and doing what I tell you."

"Where's the noble in that? After how I misjudged Lee, I wouldn't feel right about not helping to bring justice down on his killer. Besides, I'd like nothing more than to serve up a little payback for the dirty son of a bitch trying to frame me."

"I owe it to your dad to send you home alive and in one piece. You let me worry about catching Lee's killer."

CHAPTER 19

"This is just great," Billy said, picking up an empty bottle from the floor of the campers' cabin. "They had the fun, and we get to clean it up." He shoved the bottle into a black plastic garbage bag.

"You're sure in a grumpy mood. What's up with you anyway?" Jake dropped an empty bottle into Billy's bag.

"I got a call from my dad. He wants me to cut the summer short and come home to start my job. I'm not looking forward to leaving here to work where I know I'll hate it."

"Have you told your father you have doubts about the job?"

"I've tried, but he just goes into some long speech about ancestors, family traditions, and obligations—blah, blah, blah."

"I'm seriously having a hard time feeling sorry for you, especially when you're wearing five-hundred-dollar boots, and those aren't even your good ones."

"I'm sure you've heard that money can't buy happiness," Billy said, frowning at the empty beer cans he tossed in the bag.

"Try going without yours for a while and see how you feel. You give the word, and I'll gladly trade places with you." Jake picked up a couple beer cans and turned to find Billy sitting in one of the wooden rocking chairs. "Don't worry about helping, princess, I'll get it. You just rest your royal bum." Glaring, he walked across the room, jerked the bag out of Billy's hand, and turned his back on him. "I'd like this not to take all day."

Jake gathered more beer cans from the corner of the living area and turned around to find that Billy had moved to the floor. "What are you doing?" He watched as Billy downed a shot of whiskey.

"Bud told us to clean up the whiskey in the campers' cabin." Billy reached for a second glass. "But he didn't say how we had to do it." He threw the shot down his throat, made a face, and then picked up another. "Might as well not have it go to waste. Here, have one."

Jake shook his head. "And have Red kick my ass for drinking on the job. Not on your life."

Billy rolled his eyes. "You've become such a goody-two-shoes, you know that?"

"I'm not a goody-two-shoes. I just respect Red too much to piss him off."

Billy shrugged. "Okay, more for me." He emptied the glass and slammed it upside down on the floor. "Booyah!"

There were two more glasses of whiskey, but since they were out of his reach, Billy grabbed the bottle.

"Don't do it," Jake said.

Billy only paused for a moment before he pulled the cap off and took a long drink.

"Shit, Billy, you're as juvenile as the campers."

"You gonna tattle on me, Mr. Goody-Two-Shoes?"

"No. Of course not, but you better perform a disappearing act until you sober up. Your cheeks always turn red when you drink. One look at you and they'll know what you've been up to."

"What's the big deal? I can handle my liquor. Besides, Red drinks twenty-four seven. Isn't that the black calling the kettle pot? Wait..." Billy rolled on the floor, laughing. "I screwed that up."

"Yeah, you can handle your liquor all right." Jake grabbed the bottle out of Billy's hands and set it on the mantel. When he turned, Billy was crawling on all fours toward the two remaining glasses. Jake was too late to stop him from drinking one, but he kept him from the second glass by kicking it over, spilling it on the floor. "You're such a jackass, Billy." He reached down, grabbed him by the arm, and pulled him to his feet.

Billy swayed as he poked a finger in Jake's chest. "And you, sir, have a stick up your ass."

"Can you walk?" Jake asked, as Billy staggered forward.

"Hell, I can fly like an eagle." Billy broke from Jake's hold and flapped his arms, screeching more like a peacock than a bird of prey.

"Jesus, Billy, could you tone it down? You're loud enough to call the dogs."

"Let them come. I'll claw their eyes out with my mighty talons." He ran around the room pretending to be a bird.

"Let me get this picked up, and then we better get you somewhere the men won't see you. With all that's been happening, Red's likely to snap you like a twig." Jake gathered the glasses from the floor, set them on the mantel, and turned around in time to see Billy go out the door. "Shit!" He grabbed the bottle and the garbage bag and ran outside. Billy wasn't on the path to the right or to the left. When Jake heard a woman's laugh, he followed the sound to the porch of the closest cabin. He moaned when he saw his drunken friend talking with Faye Reynolds. "Damn you, Billy."

Billy was leaning against the cabin wall, staring down at Faye's ample bosom, barely concealed by the lace-adorned collar of her shimmering white chiffon robe. Through alcohol-glazed eyes, he moved down to the sash tied at her waist. He watched as she slid her leg out from behind the fabric, exposing ivory flesh from thigh down to the high, thin-heeled sandals strapped to her feet with a crisscross of tiny strips of leather.

Faye stroked Billy under the chin with one of her long painted nails, bringing his eyes up to hers.

"Ah hell, that's not good," Jake groaned as Faye took Billy by the hand and pulled him through the door, closing it behind them.

"Hey, Jake," Bud called as he walked up the path with

Woody. "Did you get the campers' mess cleaned up?"

"Yeah, this is the last of it." He held up the bottle. "I'll put the whiskey in Red's cabin."

"Where's Billy?" Bud asked. "Dinner should be ready soon."

Jake hesitated. "I think he might have taken the glasses to the kitchen."

"Lord have mercy on his soul." Woody shook his head. "Edith is on the peck on account of not having any help with the cooking. He's liable to get commandeered."

"She's in a piss-foul mood all right," Bud said. "I didn't get much of a peek at what was cooking in the pot before she chased me out with one of the giant metal spoons. I could only see that it was reddish brown."

"That could be any of her three signature dishes: spaghetti, chili, or beef stew," said Woody. "Doesn't really matter which—they all taste the same anyway."

"We're gonna get cleaned up for dinner," Bud said. "Could you check on the campers? We left them cutting weeds along the airstrip."

A loud thumping sound diverted the men's attention to Faye's cabin.

"What the hell is she doing in there, moving furniture?" Bud asked.

"She probably just dropped one of her suitcases," Jake said. "I'll check on the campers after I drop this bottle off in Red's cabin." He walked past the men. "See you at dinner." Jake strolled slowly down the path, looked back at the men, and dashed around to the back door of Faye's cabin.

He stepped under the cover of the back door, held his hand against the bedroom windowsill, and peered in. The bed was empty, so he tried the door handle, but it was locked. "Damn you, Billy. Red's going to kill you." Then he looked beyond the bedroom, down the short hallway to the living area. There stood Billy, wearing nothing but socks and a shirt that was torn open, exposing his chest. "You idiot," Jake groaned when Billy buried his hands in the tangle of Faye's blonde hair, holding her head as he kissed her hard.

Faye's lips parted, taking his tongue deep into her mouth as she ran her hands through his hair. Billy pulled away and tore the knotted sash from her robe. Then he slid his hands along either side of her hips and tightened on her buttocks. Her breast heaved heavily and her mouth dropped open. When he lifted her up against the wall, she wrapped her legs around him.

Billy took her hands and pinned them against the wall above her head. Lowering his head, he trailed his tongue down her neck to her breasts, pausing to tease and suck her nipples.

She threw her head back and rode the rhythm of his hard thrusts.

Jake turned from the window, pulled the cap from the whiskey bottle, and held it up in a toast. "Here's to you, Billy Kirkpatrick. Red's gonna kill you, but you sure picked a great way to go."

CHAPTER 20

Later that night, Red moved Nathan into his private cabin.

"This place is sick," Nathan said as he walked into the great room.

"Don't get too comfortable. It's only for one night." Red opened the door to the bedroom directly across from his. "You'll stay in this room. The bathroom is the next door over."

"Man, I could get used to this." Nathan walked into the bedroom and set his bags on top of the southwestern-patterned bedspread.

"Don't mistake my hospitality as a reward, boy. You attract trouble like fleas to a dog. And the only reason you'll be stayin' here tonight is so I can keep an eye on you."

"This time it wasn't my fault." Nathan looked sheepish when Red raised a brow at him. "Well, the cocaine was mine, and I lifted the whiskey and beer from Lee's cabin, but I had nothing to do with the knife."

"I'm aware of that. But we can't ignore the fact that the killer might have deliberately chosen to point the finger of guilt your way. If that's the case, you aren't safe."

"You don't really think he's still here at the ranch? I mean, if it were me, I'd be long gone by now."

"I had hoped not, but finding the knife after Leroy had hidden it again makes it possible. At the time the knife was planted on you, only two people knew it had been used to slaughter the calf: Leroy, and the killer. And Leroy didn't know it was the weapon used to kill Lee until I got back from the medical examiner."

"Maybe he was just acting like he didn't know. Killers are good at that, you know. And now that I think about it, Leroy never has liked me. I can totally see him planting the knife on me."

"Nah, Leroy can't bluff worth a damn," Red said, leaning his shoulder against the doorjamb. Don't go and jump to conclusions, boy. Leroy doesn't show a fondness for anyone, and I'm pretty sure he'd cut his own leg off before he'd let his prized knife out of his possession. He's not our man, and at this point we aren't any closer to finding him."

"So this killer, whoever he is, may still have it out for me."

"It could be. But he won't be gettin' to you here."

Nathan looked concerned. "I sure would feel better if you had an alarm system."

"We've got the best." Red looked over his shoulder to his dog lying in front of the fire. "If anyone tries to break in, Tan Dog will raise holy hell. And I'll be armed. Stay here." He walked into his bedroom and came out with a gun, checking to make sure it was loaded before setting it down on a table next to the sofa. "You don't need to worry. Tanny and I have your back."

"Aren't you worried about the safety of the other campers? What if the killer goes after them?" His eyes grew large. "What if one of them *is* the killer?"

"No. There's no evidence any of them have an inclination for murder. Bud and Woody are watching over the campers tonight. And, yes, I am concerned for them, and that's why all of you are leaving in the mornin'. Then hopefully we can get this mess sorted out."

Nathan's face lit up. "We're going home?"

"After a stop in Enterprise, where the sheriff and state police will be waiting to take fingerprints, collect DNA, and get statements from each of you. Then you and the other three California boys will fly out on the plane your father has chartered, and Noah will take a bus to Pendleton, where he can catch a flight home to Portland."

"I can't believe it. I'm finally going back to civilization!" Nathan opened one of his bags and searched out his cell phone. "I've got to get a charge on this bad boy." He tossed clothes aside, digging for his charging cord. "I finally got sick of playing the same games on it and gave up keeping it charged. God, I can't believe I'll actually be able to call, send texts, and email again. If my stomach and head didn't ache, I'd be doing a happy dance right now."

"I'll get you some aspirin and Sprite. The last thing I need is you throwin' up in the plane tomorrow."

Nathan plugged his phone into the outlet behind the bedside table and followed Red across the great room to the wall bar.

"Here you go," Red said, handing him a can from the miniature fridge. He reached into the overhead cupboard, took out a box of first-aid supplies, and tossed a bottle of aspirin to him. Setting the first-aid box on the counter, he opened another cupboard and removed the items hiding his whiskey. The box felt much too light. He pulled it out and stared down at the lone bottle in the case that had held six. *Damn you, Lee.* Annoyed, he grabbed the bottle by the neck, tossed the empty box on the floor, and took a glass tumbler from a bar tray. As he turned around, he found Nathan holding two aspirin tablets in his hand and staring at the whiskey bottle.

"My stomach may not agree, but I'd rather have a glass of that." Nathan tossed the tablets in his mouth and washed them down with Sprite.

"I'm sure you would, but there won't be any hair of the dog for you." Red walked past him and sat down on the sofa, where he poured half a glass of whiskey and set the bottle on the side table.

Nathan took a seat on the opposite end of the sofa. "You're a hypocrite, you know?"

Red gave him a sideways glance. "How's that?" He gulped

down a generous amount of the whiskey.

"You bust my chops for a little cocaine, yet you spend the better part of the day sucking whiskey from a flask and draining a bottle at night. You do know that's the definition of an alcoholic."

"If you're determined to put a label on me, I'd prefer experienced drinker." Red lifted his glass in salute and tossed the rest of the drink down his throat. "And my drinking habits aren't breakin' any laws. Hell, you don't see me running a bicyclist off the road while crashing a car into someone's backyard, do you? My actions don't hurt others. You, on the other hand, crap all over them. So now that you're through with your Carrie Nation speech, I'll ask that you go to your room."

"Okay, okay, don't get bent out of shape." Nathan drained his soda and set it on the side table. Then he rose from the sofa and paused to look at Red. "I was just making an observation."

"Do us both a favor and keep your observations to yourself." Red watched Nathan walk to his bedroom, waiting for him to close the door before he reached for the bottle and poured another drink. "Well, girl, maybe now we can finally have some peace." Tan Dog opened her eyes, and thumped her tail on the fireplace rug.

RED WAS JUST BEGINNING to sleep on the sofa when Tan Dog jumped to her feet, growling. "What is it, girl?"

The hair bristled on her back and her ears pricked as she stared across the cabin. She stood motionless for a moment before letting out a bark and sprinting to Nathan's room.

Red grabbed the rifle and ran to where his dog leapt against the door, barking.

Hearing a scream come from inside, Red threw the door opened and raised his gun. A scan of the room found Nathan alone on his bed huddled against the wall, scared and staring at the window.

"What's going on in here?"

"Someone was trying to break in." Nathan pointed to the partially opened window. "It was one of the hikers—the one with the dreadlocks and blue bandana. Your dog scared him off."

"He had better run fast and far." Red turned around, whistling for Tan Dog as he walked to the front door. "Go on, girl. Chase that bastard over the ridge."

Tan Dog raced out the door, barking.

Red flipped on the light as he entered Nathan's room. After slamming the window shut he turned to the terrorized boy. "No worries, son. Tan Dog will see to it he doesn't come back. Not tonight anyway." His words did nothing to alleviate the tense look on Nathan's face. "Come on." Red motioned to him as he walked to the door. "Grab a blanket. I'll take the sofa, and you can make a bed out of the two chairs."

Nathan grabbed the bedspread off the bed and scurried out to the fireplace, where he opted for the rocker over the other chairs. Wrapped in the bed cover, he had one leg draped over the wooden armrest, and the other on the floor, rocking as he watched the glowing embers shoot flames around the stack of wood Red fed to the fire. His eyes tracked Red to the sofa, and to the whiskey he poured into the tumbler. "I don't suppose you'd want to share with a guy who just had the shit scared out of him?"

"You know the answer to that." Red lifted the drink to his lips, almost sighing as the warm burn of liquor flowed down his throat. He swallowed another drink and rested his head back on the sofa with his eyes closed, listening to the soothing sounds of the crackling of the fire.

"He was going to kill me." Nathan's soft voice broke through the silence.

Red kept his lids shut. "I very much doubt that's true. The kid is nothing more than a thief, looking to break into the cabin."

"With a knife in his mouth?"

Red opened his eyes and looked at Nathan. "You got that good of a look at him in the dark?"

"Not so much his face. It was covered up to his eyes with the bandana. But I did see the knife in his mouth behind the gross dreadlocks hanging down." Nathan pulled his phone from his pocket and turned it to flashlight mode. "I shined my phone on him."

"Is there anything those things can't do?"

"Yeah, stop a guy from stabbing you."

Red heard a scratch. "She's back." He got up and opened the door and Tan Dog trotted to the fireplace with her head held high, wagging her tail the entire way. "You certainly look pleased with yourself."

"What is that?" Nathan stared at the odd object Tan Dog dropped to the floor.

"She must have gotten away with part of his clothing." Red locked the door and walked to the fireplace, pausing to give Tan Dog's head a rub before picking up what she had brought back with her. As he stepped closer to the fire, it became all too clear what he held in his hand. *Damn.* "We can cross the hikers off our list of suspects."

"Why do you say that?"

"Because most people don't survive a scalping." Red slowly turned with the scalped dreadlocks.

"Shit," Nathan exclaimed as he sprang from his chair. "But I just saw those dreadlocks on a living head."

"You saw someone who wanted you, or anyone who might see him, to think it was the hiker."

"He put someone else's scalp on his head?" Nathan paled. "Who does that?"

Red gazed down at the dreadlocks. "A killer."

THEY SAT IN SILENCE, staring into the fire. After a time, Red looked over at Nathan and saw he was sound asleep with his head back and mouth open. A few drinks later, Red also slipped into slumber. The two dozed for a couple of hours before Nathan was startled awake by the sound of frantic shouts.

"No, Timmy! Stop!"

Tan Dog jumped to her feet, whining and licking Red's hand.

Nathan raced over and shook him. "Wake up! You're having a bad dream."

Red's eyes flew open, and he dropped his glass to the floor as he stood up. Disoriented, he scanned the room. Realizing where he was, he sat back down and rubbed his face while Tan Dog whimpered up at him. He stroked her head.

"Who's Timmy?" Nathan asked.

"A constant reminder of my biggest mistake."

CHAPTER 21

"They might have looked like a scene out of a zombie movie, but the campers finally got their morning chores done, boss." Jake grinned as he came up on the lodge porch. "But I'm not sure how many have the stomach for breakfast this morning." He sat in the chair next to Red.

Tan Dog leapt up from Red's feet and gave chase after her brothers as they ran past the lodge barking.

"If they look anything like Noah and Carlton did when they dragged their asses into the kitchen, we may have plenty of food for once." Red took a sip of coffee from his steaming mug and leaned back in his chair, resting his boots on the railing.

Jake tipped his chair back against the wall and placed his arms behind his head.

"Probably best they don't eat anyway," Red said, puffing on his pipe. "Joe won't be any too happy if they toss their cookies in his plane. Just to be safe, we better gather barf bags to send with them on their flight out."

Jake looked confused. "Are the campers going somewhere?"

"With all that's taken place of late—I've decided it best to send them home." Red turned to look at the plane flying into the canyon. "That's probably Joe coming to get 'em now. I promised him breakfast before he flies out. That should give you and Billy enough time to have the campers pack their gear. Where is Billy? I haven't seen him this mornin'."

"Oh, he's around somewhere." It wasn't a complete lie.

The plane flew over and circled, going out the end of the

canyon where it would turn and come back to land.

"What's with the worried look, Jake?" Red asked. "Don't tell me you're gonna miss the boys."

"Hell no, they're a giant pain in the ass. It's just with them gone, after this murder thing blows over, I'm not sure how Billy and I are going to keep up with the added chores and help take care of the guests. In another week, all the cabins will be booked, and we'll have a full schedule of pack trips and trail rides to guide. We're going to be stretched thin."

"Everyone's gonna have to pitch in to help pick up the slack."

"Leroy's going to love that, especially since he has the hay to cut. And without the extra manpower of the campers, getting it put up in the barn isn't going to be fun for any of us."

"It can't be helped," Red said, watching the plane touch down on the landing strip. "I won't have the boys in danger."

"But what if one of them killed Lee? You'll be setting him free."

"None of them did it."

"What makes you so sure?"

"Years of experience handling teenagers," Red said, standing to greet the plane taxiing to a stop in the grass beyond the hitching rail. "Eyes don't lie."

"Joe is coming in early this morning," Bud said as he walked out onto to the porch. "Who's his passenger?"

Red stared at the short, chubby man getting out of the plane. "That would be the dishonorable Commissioner Reynolds."

"That reminds me, I didn't see Faye at dinner last night. Come to think of it, Billy wasn't there either."

"Jake said Billy was under the weather," Red said. "And Faye was mad at me for trying to convince her to allow Edith to stay with her last night. Even after I spun a tale about a cougar prowling the ranch, she refused. Then I tried to convince her to take a room in my cabin, but she turned that down as well. Damn if she isn't as pig-headed as her husband. Now I've got to come up with a story that will make the commissioner pack his wife up and leave the ranch."

Bud watched as the commissioner barked orders to Joe. "The man can't say hello without adding some barbs to it. But at least he always gives us something to look forward to."

Jake looked confused. "What's that?"

"His departure," Bud replied.

"Got that right!" Jake laughed. "I don't think I've ever been around a bigger jerk. He treats everyone like it should be their pleasure to lick his boots."

"Comes from being a big frog in a tiny pond," Red said, turning to Jake. "Be a good lad and fetch his bags and take them into the lodge."

"Shouldn't I take them to his cabin?"

"No, Faye is a late sleeper. If anyone's gonna wake her, it should be her husband."

Red walked out to meet his guests at the flagpole. "Hello, Commissioner."

"Hello, Red, always a pleasure," replied the man with hair dyed raven black. He forced a smile and shook Red's hand.

Red didn't show his annoyance at the commissioner's overly forceful squeeze. *Oh how I loathe this pompous ass.* He shook off his thoughts and turned to Joe. "Good mornin', Joe. I hope you brought an appetite. We have quite the spread."

"Don't have to ask me twice." Joe headed for the lodge.

Red turned to the commissioner and saw that he was staring at the barn. "Would you like to join us, Commissioner?"

The commissioner glanced at Red and back to the barn. "When are you going to take me up on that loan I've offered you? Just look at that old barn. You could throw a cat between the boards." He waved a hand at the lodge. "And you could have a lodge twice this size. It's time you took this business seriously and put some money into it." He looked at Red through thick dark-rimmed glasses. "You can't tell me you couldn't use the money."

"Like I've told you so many times since you first made the offer, I feel we're doin' just fine as we are."

"Hogwash! This place needs a serious face-lift."

"Like cheese and wine, my ranch grows better with age." Red puffed on his pipe, gazing at the barn. "She was here long before us, and I'm sure she'll be here long after our names are worn off our gravestones."

"You're a foolish dreamer, Red Higgins. But one of these days you'll wake up and come to your senses. You better hope I'm in a generous mood when you do."

As they walked toward the lodge, the commissioner stopped to look back to the plane, watching Jake unload his bags. "I hear you've got one of those spoiled Hollywood boys staying at your ranch." He harrumphed and shook his head. "I don't know why you take on the foolish endeavor of caring for that sort. It's nothing more than a waste of energy. I've seen his television show. The boy is a lost cause, if you ask me."

Like anyone ever has to ask for your opinion. Red turned toward his guest. "I'm happy with the boy's adjustment." His brow furrowed. "How did you hear he was here?"

The commissioner's smirk did little to hide the darkness in his eyes. "You should know by now that I am privy to anything and everything happening in my county." He stepped closer to Red, lowering his voice as he leaned in. "I know about your cook." The puckered expression on his round face resembled that of a playground bully. "You see, nothing gets past me and it never will." He poked a finger in Red's chest. "It would serve you well to remember that."

Red wasn't sure what the commissioner meant by his last statement, but he definitely heard the threat in it. *You sorry bugger. Poke me again and I'm likely to break your stubby fingers.*

As though reading his mind, the commission pulled his hand away and turned his attention back to the young man unloading his bags. "Is that the Hollywood brat?"

"No, that's Jake." Red watched his wrangler pull a bag from

the plane. "You don't recognize him? He's been a ranch hand going on five years now."

"I don't make a habit of associating with the hired help." Commissioner Reynolds watched Jake set one of his bags on the ground. "Your boy better not rip my bags. I paid a small fortune for them."

"He'll be careful," Red assured as they walked to the porch, where Joe waited for them. Red held the door for his guests. "Congratulations on your reelection, Commissioner."

"Ah, yes." The commissioner grinned. "I almost feel sorry for my poor opponent. I really mopped the floor with him. Just goes to show, cream really does float to the top." He walked through the door and into the dining hall.

Red looked at Joe, saying under his breath, "So does scum."

JAKE POUNDED HIS FIST on the back door of Faye's cabin. There was no answer. He tried the handle, but it was locked.

"Fuck!" He raced around to the front door. Finding it unlocked, he ran in and tripped over the chair rockers as he struggled to maneuver through the room darkened by drawn shades.

"Ouch! God dammit!" He hopped on his sore foot, knocking over the upright lamp, shattering the bulb as it hit the floor. "Shit! There goes my only light." He nearly fell for a second time when he tripped over Billy's pile of clothes. Jake picked them up and staggered down the dimly lit hall, calling for Billy. Once he came to the bathroom, he reached in and flipped the switch, casting a faint light on the bed in the next room.

He found Billy asleep in Faye's bed, lying on his stomach with the upper half of his naked torso exposed and his left arm dangling off the side of the bed. Jake shook him hard. "Wake up, Billy! Come on. Faye's husband is here. You've got to get out, now!"

Billy groaned at the sound of Jake's voice, but he didn't open his eyes.

Jake grabbed the glass on the side table and rushed to the bathroom to fill it with water. He ran back and tossed it over Billy's head.

"What the hell?" Billy sputtered, sitting upright. He wiped the water from his face and rubbed his eyes, trying to focus on his assailant. "What the fuck, Jake?"

"Faye's husband is here. You've got to get out!"

"What? Oh shit! Where are my clothes?"

Jake shoved them into Billy's arms. "Get those on. And hurry up about it!"

Billy pulled his jeans on, tucked his underwear in his pocket, and tugged his arms through his shirt, ignoring the buttons.

"Come on, come on," Jake shouted from the back door. "Out this way."

"Quit yelling, you'll wake Faye." Billy looked down at his bare feet. "Have you seen my boots?"

"Dammit, Billy." Jake raced to where he saw them lying in the hall, ran back and shoved the boots into Billy's chest. "Would you hurry up? I don't want to have to explain why we're in Faye's cabin.

"Me neither." Billy bounced on one leg, pulling a boot on and dropping the other in the process. As he turned to pick it up, he caught sight of the empty bed. "Where is Faye?"

Jake scanned the bed. "How would I know? Maybe she went to breakfast. Come on."

Billy started for the door, stopping a few feet away. "Hey, where are my socks?"

"Goddamn it, Billy." As Jake felt around for the socks on one side of the bed, Billy rushed around to the other and got on his knees, searching the floor on that side. Then his hand touched something wet. "What the hell?" He reached for the switch on the nightstand lamp and turned it on. Startled, he fell back against the wall.

"I've got them," Jake shouted.

"Um, Jake? What the hell happened here?"

"Don't even try to tell me you were too drunk to remember what you did last night," Jake grumbled as he stood up with Billy's socks. "I found your..." He froze, staring at the blood on the wall above the bed. Then he looked down at Billy, sitting in a pool of red, gazing down at his blood-covered hands. Jake stepped across the blood and took Billy by the arm, helping his dazed friend to his feet.

"I sure don't remember any of this." Billy's ashen face turned to Jake. "Where did all this blood come from?"

Jake pulled the covers back on Faye's side of the bed. "Fuck, Billy. What the hell did you do?"

Billy gasped at the sight of the crimson sheets. "I didn't do anything, I swear. I mean, yes we had sex, and she likes it rough, but I didn't do anything to her that would cause this. God, that's a lot of blood."

"Way too much." Jake stared at the soaked sheets. "You know we have to tell Red."

"Bu-but," Billy stuttered. "I didn't do anything." He buried his face in his hands. "This can't be happening."

"Great, now you've got blood all over your face." Jake noticed the stain on Billy's jeans. "Holy crap, you're covered in it!"

Billy raced for the bathroom. He turned the water on, but one look in the mirror had him throwing up in the sink. He threw water on his face.

"Where are you going?" Jake called as Billy rushed for the front door.

"I've got to find her."

"COULD I HAVE A MOMENT, boss?" Jake asked.

"Can it wait?" Red said as he poured coffee for the guests sitting across from him. Receiving no reply, he looked up and saw Jake's stricken expression.

Red rose from the table and followed him into the gathering room.

"We think Faye might have been murdered," Jake whispered. "Her bed is covered in blood."

"What! Wait. What were you doing in her cabin?"

Jake flushed but didn't answer.

"I asked you a question, boy."

Jake glanced toward the dining hall. "I went to get Billy before Faye's husband found him in her bed.

The pipe nearly dropped from Red's mouth. "Are you tellin' me Faye and Billy…"

Jake nodded.

"Son of a bitch!" Red spoke louder than he meant to. He grabbed Jake by the arm, pulling him out the door and around to the back of the lodge. "Okay, so what's this about her bein' dead?"

"When I got there, Billy was passed out alone in bed, and the other side of the mattress was covered in blood."

"Where's Billy now?"

"He ran off to look for Faye." Jake looked past Red to the riverbank.

"You do know that women bleed once a month?"

"Not this much. You'll have to see for yourself."

Red's head pounded to the rhythm of his racing heart as he followed Jake into Faye's cabin. "It's dark in here, get the light, Jake."

"I knocked it over and it broke."

"Of course you did." Red walked to the curtains and pulled them open. "Stop," he shouted when he saw the blood on the floor.

Jake froze. "What is it?"

"You're tracking through evidence." Red's gut twisted in a knot as he gazed at the trail of blood leading from the bedroom to the front door.

"Crap, I didn't see that before," Jake said, stepping back

against the wall. "Sorry, boss, but Billy and I have already walked through it and me more than once."

"Do what you can to keep from compromising it any further."

They dodged the blood the best they could as they made their way to the foot of the bed.

Red stared down at the scarlet bedding. "Damn, that is a lot of blood. It looks like an animal has been bled for slaughter." *Or, in this case, a woman.* His eyes went to the blood splatters on the wall and down to the floor. "Flip that other lamp on for me."

Jake walked to the nightstand on what had been Billy's side of the bed and switched the light on. "What do you see, boss?"

"It's hard to make out with all the footprints, but I believe the double lines trailing down the hall must have been made by the heels of her feet as she was dragged backward to the door. Come on, we better see what Billy has to say about all this."

"Um, boss."

Red turned and saw Jake staring at something sticking out from under Billy's pillow. "What is it?"

Jake picked up the pillow and tossed it on the end of the bed. "Is that Leroy's knife?"

"Don't touch it!" He was too late. Jake already had the knife in his hand. "Damn, boy." Red groaned. "If there were a chance of prints, we won't be getting any off it now."

"Sorry, boss. I wasn't thinking."

"That seems to be a common theme around here lately." Red studied the knife Jake held. "It can't be Leroy's. I locked it away in my cabin."

"But it has an antler handle," Jake said.

"So does mine. Leroy used it as a pattern to make his. The biggest difference in our two knives is that the point of his blade is more swept than mine. I keep mine locked up in the lodge display case, but I suppose someone could have stolen it. If it is mine, it'll have an RH carved into the handle butt."

Jake turned the knife, showing Red the initials on the end. They were his.

Holy smokes! Red rubbed his head as he considered the situation. *Edith, Nathan Noah, Billy, and now even me. At this rate, the whole ranch could become suspect. This is getting worse by the minute.*

Jake looked down at the knife in his hand. "You know, boss, it's going to be hard for you to convince the sheriff you had nothing to do with this, this being your knife and all. I think I should clean it real good and slip it back into the display case. No one has to know."

"I appreciate your loyalty. But unless you want to share a jail cell, I wouldn't suggest tampering with evidence."

"But they're going to think you did this."

"Until we find a body, we don't even know what 'this' is," Red replied.

"You're right." Jake's face suddenly brightened. "Hey, maybe the campers pulled a stupid prank. For all we know, it could be chicken blood."

Red scowled at the blood-stained walls and floor. "I'm afraid that's wishful thinkin'. They would have had to get past Bud and Woody, and you know that wouldn't happen. Besides that, I don't think the campers are crass enough to pull something this soon after Lee's death. And Faye would have to play along, and I really can't see her doing that."

"Shoot, I hadn't thought of all that." Jake held the knife out. "What should I do with this?"

Red pulled a handkerchief from his pocket. "I'll lock it up with Leroy's."

Jake dropped the knife in Red's hand. "Sorry, I know I was thinking stupid. This whole mess has got me a little rattled."

"Believe me, you're not alone." Red placed a hand on Jake's shoulder. "I do appreciate your concern for my welfare. But, son, the other side of right is always wrong."

Jake nodded. "I get it. Don't like it. But I get it."

They were careful to seek dry spots as they started down the hallway.

"Boss, boss!" Billy shouted as he rushed into the cabin. "The trail of blood leads down to the river. She must have been tossed in there."

Red held his hand up, stopping him from coming any farther. "I can't allow the key suspect to tramp through evidence."

Billy looked horrified. "Hey, you don't really think I could kill anyone?"

"I'm not sure what to think." Red glared at Billy as he stepped out of the hallway. "But I have a good idea what Sheriff Cason is going think." Standing beside him, Red reached out and slapped Billy.

"Ouch!" Billy rubbed the back of his head. "What was that for?"

"For bein' dumber than a bag of rocks," Red growled, slapping him a second time. "And that's for breaking the number one rule." He pointed a finger in Billy's face. "How many times have I told you to never touch another man's hat, horse, or woman?"

"I'm sorry. I wasn't in my right mind."

"That's an understatement." Red glared at him. "Sorry isn't going to give us any answers as to what happened to Faye. Come on. Show me this trail of blood." He handed his keys to Jake. "Lock it up for me, and join us at the river."

Red followed Billy down the riverbank.

"Maybe she's still alive," Billy said, breaking their silence.

"I wouldn't get my hopes up. The blood spatters on the wall suggest her throat might have been slashed."

Billy looked defeated. "I'm going to be blamed for this, aren't I?"

"It's certainly not lookin' good. You were in her bed at the time. How do you think that looks?" Red raised his eyes from the trail of blood to look at Billy. "And you just happened to sleep through the whole thing? I doubt the sheriff is going to buy that." He followed the blood down to the rocky bank of the river and stood with his toes inches from the edge of the water, puffing quick clouds of smoke into the air as he gazed downstream. When Red finally turned to Billy, his expression had grown dark. "What in tarnation made you think sleepin' with the commissioner's wife was a good idea?"

"Whiskey," Billy said, looking like a whipped pup. "I remember drinking the whiskey left in the campers' cabin, but everything after is a haze." He rubbed his face with trembling hands. "I don't know what happened. Instead of dreaming a nightmare, I've awakened to one."

Been there, Red thought as he watched Billy closely. *If this kid is acting, he's doing a bang-up job of it. But to wash the color from his face would be quite the trick. Then again, it could be the whiskey kickin' back on him.*

"Find anything?" Jake called from the path above them.

"The blood trail goes to the river," Red said as he and Billy climbed up the gentle rise. "I'm afraid the body could be anywhere downstream by now."

The young wranglers fell silent as they waited for Red's orders.

"Jake, round up the campers and get them on the plane. I can't afford to risk their safety knowin' we still have a killer among us. Let Joe know we're ready for him to fly them to Enterprise and keep a close watch on them until they're all loaded on that plane." He paused to look downriver. "The body could be hung up on a log or stuck in shallow water. We'll need to search the river on both sides. Ask Bud and Leroy to saddle five horses for me."

"What if the commissioner decides to check on his wife?"

"Good point." Red thought for a moment. "Have Woody take him fishin'. He can make up some cock-'n'-bull story about the prize-sized salmon he spotted somewhere upstream. Have him tell the commissioner that the fish are bigger than the one he caught last year. That should stir his competitive nature."

"I thought it was illegal to fish Chinook out of the Minam."

"That doesn't stop the commissioner. Laws pertain to everyone but him."

Jake nodded and ran off toward the lodge.

"What do you want me to do?" Billy asked, looking pensive.

"I think you've done quite enough damage for one mornin'," Red grumbled. "Come on, you're with me. I'm not letting you out of my sight." He began to walk up the path, stopping when his young wrangler didn't follow.

Billy's bloodshot eyes grew large. "Please tell me you don't think I did this."

"If I thought you did, you wouldn't be standin' here right now. You'd be covered in honey and tied to a tree outside a bear's den." He turned and walked away, glancing at Billy when he ran to his side. "That's not to say others won't see it differently."

"What happened to innocent until proven guilty?"

"There's a thing called probable cause, and you served that up on a silver platter. Once the sheriff hears Faye disappeared while you were in her bed, he's gonna be all over that like fleas on a hound."

"You'll stand up for me, won't you?"

"Boy, you may not have invented stupid, but you certainly perfected it. But I doubt even you are dumb enough to stay in the bed of the woman you murdered. So, yes, I'll do what I can. What irks me the most is that you gave the son of a bitch killer the opportunity to frame you in the first place. Had I known you could be this dense, I would have never let you come back as a ranch hand."

"I'm sorry, boss." Billy stared down at his feet.

"Don't think for a minute that you're out of hot water with me. You can't even imagine the level of my disappointment. Lucky for you, I have bigger problems than a young befuddled wrangler lettin' his cock do his thinking for him. I have a crazy murderer to stop before the bastard has the chance to kill again."

"You have no idea who he could be?"

"No I don't. But he sure is hell-bent on pointing the finger at my people. I have no idea what the motive could be behind the insanity, but it appears well planned and carefully orchestrated to me."

They came to a split in the path, one way going to the lodge and the other to Red's cabin. Red motioned Billy to follow him. "I need to call the sheriff, but first, I have somethin' I want to check on."

As Red opened his cabin door, Tan Dog suddenly appeared behind him. She slipped through the door, trotting to the rug in front of the smoldering fire.

"I was wondering when I'd see you again," said Red as he walked into the great room. She responded with a thump of her tail.

Billy followed close behind him and sat on sofa Red pointed to. "Don't take your ass off that couch. I'll only be a minute."

Red slipped into his bedroom and closed the door. Then he opened his closet and removed the false panel in the back, exposing the safe. He pushed a series of numbers into the combination lock keypad and opened the door. Leroy's knife was sitting right where he had left it. Relieved, Red blew out a breath. *At least my safe hasn't been broken into. I'm not sure how I would have explained how Leroy's knife got taken for a third time. That would certainly be a hard pill for the sheriff to swallow.* He scanned the safe, taking quick inventory of the contents. Six bundles of cash, the deed to the ranch, his fire captain's badge, and the single-action army revolver Burt Lancaster had given him. It was all there. He closed the safe, waiting for the lock to set before placing the hidden panel back in place.

Red walked out to where Billy sat with his head resting on the back of the sofa, mouth opened, and snoring. Crossing his arms, Red scowled as he watched his young wrangler sleep. *So you think you're gonna sleep it off, while I see to fixing the mess you've made? Not likely.* He picked up the black rotary telephone from a lampstand and slammed it down on the coffee table.

Billy jumped up on unsteady legs. "Damn." He grabbed his head. "That wasn't funny."

"Maybe not from where you're standing, but it's pretty amusing from my side."

"Yeah. Real hysterical." Billy collapsed back onto the sofa as Red took a seat opposite him. "Remind me to laugh later."

The tinge of satisfaction passed as Red picked up the receiver and spun the sheriff's number with the antique dial. "Hello, Claire. It's Red Higgins. Is the sheriff available?"

"Oh, hi, Red," the dispatcher's warm voice said. "No, he's up to his eyeballs in alligators right now. He and the deputies are up at Wallowa Lake with the state police and neighboring county deputies. They're in the middle of a Mexican standoff between two biker gangs. Apparently both groups decided to hold a campout on the same weekend. The sheriff had to evacuate the resort before all hell broke loose." She paused. "I could patch you through, if it's important."

"It is, yes, please."

A few moments later, Sheriff Cason came on the line. "Hey, Red, what's up?"

"We have more trouble here at the ranch."

"How's that?"

"It's Faye Reynolds. We think she's been murdered."

"What? I realize my brain's a little fuzzy after pushing more than forty-eight hours without sleep, but did you say you *think*? You don't *know*?"

"We haven't found a body yet. But her bedroom looks like a slaughterhouse and a trail of blood leads through the cabin down to the Minam."

The sheriff groaned. "You're going have to shut the place down, Red."

"Already on it. The campers are gettin' on a plane as we speak. They'll be at your office within the hour."

"Great. And here I'm stuck here at the OK Corral with a bunch of feuding hotheads. I'll have to send one of my deputies back to watch them. That's not going to set well. None of my boys want to miss out on something as big as a biker war. But it can't be helped."

"Now that we know Lee's murder wasn't an isolated incident, I'm gonna have my staff warn the families camping in the woods. What's to say the killer doesn't take to them next? Or the Minam Lodge guests? I could use some backup. I know you've got your hands full. But could you ask Union County to send a couple deputies?"

"I doubt it. They're working with a skeleton crew, since most are up here helping us."

"Damn."

"Red, I know you called for my help, but I need to ask for yours. Consider yourself deputized, and your first order is to get the folks in the woods out of there. Tell them they have to vacate on orders of the sheriff. And contact Harold at the Minam Lodge and let him know he's going to have to close to guests for the time being. Then it's best if you get all your people, including yourself, out as well."

"No one runs me off my land," Red growled. "Besides, I couldn't leave my animals unattended."

"I thought as much, but I had to try." The line went silent for a moment. "Does Commissioner Reynolds know about his wife?"

"Not yet. I wanted to talk with you and look for the body first. I have little doubt that she's dead, but I'd like to have proof before I talk with the commissioner. My men are saddling the horses for a search along the river. If we don't find her, I'll tell him what we suspect."

Red heard shots fired in the background, followed by shouting.

"Red, I've got to go, things are heating up here. Good luck."

The line went dead.

"We need to start the search," Red said, looking at Billy as he set the receiver down on the base. "We'll gear up at the lodge." He held the door for Billy and looked at his dog resting in front of the fire. "You too, girl."

Tan Dog jumped up, ran to him, and sat at his feet, panting.

"Let's put that nose of yours to work. And later, I could use a good set of sharp teeth standin' between me and the commissioner when I tell him about his wife."

Tan Dog wagged her tail and raced up the path past Billy.

CHAPTER 22

"What in blazes?" Red said when he saw the campers sitting on the lodge porch. Exasperated, he walked out to the flagpole and waved Jake from the plane. "Why aren't they in the air?"

"The plane has a flat tire," Jake replied. "Joe says he'll have to get a new one. Bud already called Russell Elmer to ask if he'd pick one up in La Grande and fly it in, but it turns out he's out of town. So he called Russell's friend, Burt."

"Burr," Red corrected.

"Yeah, that's it. Anyway, Burr says he'll do it."

"Did Woody get the commissioner out on the river?"

Jake nodded. "They headed out with fishing poles about twenty minutes ago. Woody said he'd keep him out there until lunch."

"Good. Then why don't you go lend Leroy a hand with saddling the horses? Take Billy with you. He might as well be useful while under house arrest." Red pointed a finger at Jake. "You two stay together, hear? Just because its daylight, doesn't mean it's safe to be alone. And don't leave Billy, even for a moment."

"Sure, boss." Jake grinned. "I'll stick to him like the stink on his feet."

Red walked out to the plane, where Joe stood inspecting his engine. "You run over somethin' when you landed?"

"I think I would have noticed hitting something that leaves a gash the size of an ax blade." He closed the cowl and knelt down by the tire. "One of your boys really must not want to

219

leave the ranch."

Red stared down at the large gash. *Or someone doesn't want them to leave.* "That's not good. I'm sorry, Joe. I'll pay for the damages."

"I checked to make sure the engine wasn't tampered with. But it's good to go."

"I just got off the phone with Burr," Bud said as he walked to the plane. "He called back to let us know that when he checked, La Grande didn't have any tires of this size in stock. He called around, and Boise is the closest he could get one. He's on his way there now, but it'll be hours before he gets here."

Red's frown deepened. "Damn."

"Well, that shoots my day," Joe said. "I better radio the wife."

"I'll see if I can't speed things up with the horses," Bud said.

Red walked to the lodge, leaving Joe alone to talk to his wife. As he stepped up onto the porch, he motioned to the campers sitting there. "Well, come on. I think you can be doin' something more productive than sittin' here watching the grass grow. Carlton and Noah, you help Edith in the kitchen. Carlos, you and Sean grab a broom and mop and give the lodge a good going over. Nathan, you're with me. Everyone stay with your chore mate. I don't want anyone wandering off alone. In fact, unless you're with me or one of the men, no one is to leave the lodge."

"Why?" Sean asked. "Has something else happened?"

Red hesitated. "Faye Reynolds is missing. We're riding out to search for her now."

"Missing?" Carlos said.

Nathan curved his fingers into imaginary claws and made a growling noise. "Look out, the cougar's on the prowl." He laughed. "Since she struck out here, she'd probably stalk the men at the Minam Lodge." Red smacked the back of his head. "Ouch!" "Do you ever get tired of slapping me?"

"Do you ever get tired of sayin' stupid things?" Red pulled his glare from Nathan and looked at the others. "What are you waiting for? Get to work." He held the door, waiting for the last of the boys to rush through. Then he turned back to Nathan. "I'll be right back. Don't move from this spot, hear me?"

Nathan nodded.

Red disappeared into the lodge, leaving Nathan rubbing his head and grumbling under his breath, "If I have to spend much more time with that man, I'm going to need a goddamn football helmet."

Red walked through the gathering room straight to the display case. There he saw the bare spot where his knife had been, but nothing else appeared to be missing. He ran his fingers over the marks on the keyhole where it had been jimmied open. Pulling a ring of keys from his pocket, he searched for the one fitting this lock. He shoved the key into the hole and turned it until he heard the click. *Nothin' like lockin' the barn door after the horses ran off. But for the time, it should keep my guns safe from the curious fingers of the young campers.* He walked out the door. "With me," he ordered as he stepped off the porch.

Nathan followed him to the row of horses tied outside the corral.

"What's he doing here?" Jake asked when he saw Nathan.

"He's comin' with us." Red pointed to the solid sorrel mare with a unique spot on her face that looked like the curved back of a dolphin jumping out of the water. "He'll ride Stella."

Nathan watched as Leroy looped the strap through the rigging D ring on Stella's saddle.

"Then we're a horse short," Leroy said as he finished tying Stella's cinch and pulled the stirrup down into place. He freed the mare's reins, backed her from the hitching rail, and handed the reins to Nathan. "I'll throw a saddle on Carrie."

"That works," said Red. "I'd be more comfortable if you were to stand watch while we're all gone from the ranch, Leroy. Take a rifle and ride up on the ridge. If you see anyone you don't recognize lurking around, fire off a shot."

Leroy nodded and walked into the barn to gather tack.

"What happens if the commissioner decides to come back and go to his cabin in search of Faye?" Bud asked.

Red pulled Sugar's reins loose from the hitching rail and stepped up into the saddle. "Woody has the plan for that." He backed Sugar out of line as the others collected their horses. "He'll tell him that I've decided to accept his offer of a loan, and the greedy devil will rush to my cabin like his tail feathers were on fire. Then Woody will leave him with a notebook and calculator, and tell him that I'll meet him there after he's had a chance to run all the numbers. That should keep him busy long enough for us to search the canyon."

"That could work," Bud said, mounting his horse.

"Hey, Bud, before you and Billy search the other side of the river, ride to the families camping in the woods and let them know that the sheriff has ordered an evacuation of the area. They'll want to know why. Take the adults aside to tell them. We don't need to alarm the children."

"We can do that."

Waiting for Leroy to finish saddling Carrie, Red, Bud, Jake, and Billy watched as Nathan struggled to get up into his saddle.

Billy sat on a tall chestnut quarter horse named Max, rolling his eyes at Nathan's awkward attempt at mounting his horse. "Nothing worse than a greenhorn."

"Got that right," Jake smirked from the back of Rowdy.

"You two should know," Bud said, getting up on Dipsy, a mostly white mare with patches of brown spots. "It took both of you the better part of three years to learn the head from the tail."

"I wasn't that bad," Billy said, frowning at Bud.

"No, you were worse," grumbled Red as he watched Nathan finally settle into the saddle. Then he turned angry eyes on Billy. "After the numbskull act you pulled last night, it might be wise for you not to criticize anyone for anything."

Billy's pale cheeks finally found some color. "Sorry, boss. It won't happen again."

"Boy, your reins are all catawampus," Red called to Nathan as he rode Sugar to Stella's side. He took the reins from Nathan's hands and pulled them up evenly on both sides of the mare's neck. "There you go. That should work better for you."

Red looked back at his men. "Bud, you and Billy might as well start off for the woods. Once you begin your search for the body, be sure to pay attention to snags in the water. It's likely to be hung up on something. Fire off a shot if you spot her. Nathan and I will search the shallow bend in the river near the Minam Lodge. Jake, you stand watch with Leroy."

"I think I'd be of better use riding with you, boss." Jake tossed his head in the direction of a nervous looking Nathan, gripping the horn with both hands. "Nathan's useless on a horse. You might as well send him with Leroy."

"No, I want him with me where he won't be able to invite trouble. And, until we catch the killer, you younger hands will be ridin' with one of the men. You're with Leroy, Billy's with Bud." He turned to Bud. "Do me a favor, every time Billy says somethin' stupid, give his head a good rattle for me."

"Hey," Billy exclaimed, rubbing the back of his head. "What was that for?"

Bud shrugged. "Just practicing." He gathered his reins and turned his mare toward the Minam bridge near the lodge.

"I'm begging you, please don't lope. My head can't take it with this hangover," whined Billy as he fell in behind Bud.

Bud caught Red's eye as he rode past. "Did I just hear him say he wanted to lope?"

"That's what I heard."

"Crap," Billy said as his horse jumped into a lope behind Bud's.

"Stop," Nathan shouted, raising his rein hand up to his face when Stella started to follow the other horses.

"You'll find 'whoa' works better," Red said.

"Make her stop," Nathan pleaded when Stella began backing in a circle.

"She's only doin' what you're telling her to do. If you want her to stop, quit pulling back on the reins."

Nathan put his hand down, and Stella came to a halt.

"I told you he's worthless on a horse," Jake said. "He didn't learn anything from the last ride."

"Is your head itchin' for a slap too?" Red glared at Jake. "We just haven't had the time to teach him properly." Red rode up beside Nathan. "Put your rein hand in front of the horn and keep it there. This horse is as well trained as Rowdy, the gelding you rode last time, but her go pedal is a bit touchier. Best not to pull on her mouth. And unless you want to play spin the top, keep your heels out of her sides. Just let her follow like you did on Rowdy. Let's go."

Tan Dog wagged her tail as she led the way on the path across the meadow, over the landing strip, and through the gate into the trees. Just on the other side of the gate, she paused to make sure they were following before running on ahead.

Red and Nathan turned their horses onto the trail that ran parallel to the fence separating Red's property from Forest Service land. As they approached the end of his land, a building in ruins came into view.

"What's that over there?" Nathan asked, not taking his hand from the horn he was choking.

Red glanced back and saw Nathan looking at the half-fallen building nearly devoured by overgrown brush. "That's my old sawmill we used to make the lumber for building the cabins on the ranch. Still had it up and runnin' when we built the Nez Perce cabin five years ago. Unfortunately, a couple years back a heavy snowstorm collapsed half the roof on top of the saw equipment. If there's a need for lumber now, we have to bring it in by horse." He turned in his saddle and saw how intently Nathan was staring at the broken-down building. "We don't go anywhere near the old sawmill now. It's too dangerous. It wouldn't take more than a bird landin' on the roof to make the rest of it fall."

"No worries there. I've had my fill of derelict buildings."

"Derelict?" Red repeated, frowning. "Most of my buildings are aged, and some are rustic, but to call any of them derelict implies disrepair and abandonment, and that's flat-out untrue. Just because something is old doesn't make it obsolete."

"No, but new is always better than old. I mean, think about it. Businesses hire young people over old because they want the fresh ideas that only the young can bring to the table."

"Horseshit. The only reason they hire the inexperienced is because the bean counters don't want to pay for experience. We're headed to the Minam Lodge. It's owned by an old duffer like me, and he's as attached to his place as I am mine, so if you can't hold your tongue, you'll be staying outside while I talk with him. I don't need you runnin' your mouth off about how little you think of his property."

"I'll keep my opinions to myself, even if they happen to be true."

"That's big of you." Then a grin came to his face as he nudged Sugar into a fast trot. *Let's see how well he flaps his smart mouth when his teeth are rattling.*

Nathan clutched the saddle horn harder as Stella zigzagged through brush and trees behind Sugar.

"If you're trying to make sure I never have kids, I think you've succeeded," Nathan called.

Red slowed Sugar to a jog trot and looked back at Nathan leaning forward as he bounced wildly in the saddle. "Concentrate on riding with the rhythm of the horse instead of against it. If you sit back and think of your butt as a heavy weight, you'll have a much easier time of it."

"I'm not sure anything can help."

"Riding is no different than any other challenge in life. Whether you think you can or think you can't—you're right. It's all in how you program your brain." Sugar held to a slow jog trot as Red rested a hand on her rump, leaning back to watch Nathan. "Sometimes it helps to give your mind somethin' else to concentrate on. The jog is a two-count rhythm. Try counting, one, two, one, two, one, two…" He saw Nathan relax slightly as he concentrated on counting. "There, now isn't that better?"

"It's less of a ballbuster, I'll give you that."

They rode quietly up the trail, passing the cross fence indicating the end of Red's property and the beginning of the Minam Lodge land. As their horses jogged along, Red's thoughts drifted to the horrific killing of his friend Lee and the bloody scene in the cabin of the missing woman. He'd like nothing more than to find Faye alive, but the knot in his gut said that wouldn't be the case.

This all started with the slaughter of the calf. How does that fit? Is this some kind of sick game? If I could discover the motivation behind killing the calf, maybe it would shine light on the killer. Was Lee an intended victim, or was he collateral damage after walking in on the calf killer? And now Faye… He was shaken from his thoughts by the loud shouts behind him.

"Hey, stop!" Nathan cried as Stella spun around and around. He shouted again, but she just spun faster.

"For the love of Pete, now what?" Red pulled Sugar to a halt and turned her. He groaned at the sight of Stella spinning in place. "She won't stop until you drop your hand down and get your damn heel out of her side."

Nathan clung to the saddle horn as he fought to stay on the horse. "Make her stop. I'm getting dizzy."

Red shouted, "Whoa."

Stella's abrupt halt sent Nathan tumbling to the ground. He was lucky to land in the soft dirt beyond the rocky trail.

Red could see that he was okay. "She's what they call a reiner," he explained as Nathan sat up and rubbed his elbow.

"What the hell is that, some kind of mental disorder?" Nathan grumbled as he got to his feet.

"She's trained for a western riding competition where the

horse performs patterns of circles, spins, and sliding stops. You had the reins pulled over her neck and your heel in her side, signaling for a spin."

"Yeah, well she was doing a great job of it. I felt like I was on the fuckin' teacups at Disneyland."

"You use that word again, and I'll strap you to her back and let her spin 'til she hits water."

"Okay, okay, I forgot."

"Get back on, and this time, keep your heels out of her sides." Red waited for Nathan to mount before he turned and rode silently up the trail.

"Do you always carry a gun with you?" Nathan asked, breaking the long silence.

Red glanced down at the rifle sheathed safely in the scabbard hanging from his saddle. "I'm not at all sure about yours, but my mother didn't birth no dummies. Only a fool wanders the wilderness without a gun. Old Betsy here has saved my hide more than once."

"You named your gun?" Nathan laughed.

"Yup. I call my pistol Pete."

"Pistol Pete, now that's original." Nathan rolled his eyes.

Red shrugged. "Fits, don't it?" He hit his pipe on the pommel of his saddle, knocking the tobacco onto the trail. Draping the reins across Sugar's neck, he reached in his pocket for the packet of fresh tobacco and packed his pipe.

"Have you ever had to kill someone?"

Red struck a match across his saddle horn and lit his pipe, puffing several times before answering. "I have never killed a man, but I have read many obituaries with great pleasure."

Nathan groaned. "Anyone ever tell you that you have the strangest way of saying things?"

When Tan Dog suddenly charged off into the brush, barking madly, Red threw a hand up, signaling for Nathan to stop. "Hold up, Tan Dog's found something." He jumped down from his horse and pulled the reins from around Sugar's neck, leaving them hanging down to the ground from her bit. "Whoa, girl." He patted her shoulder and left her standing on the path as he walked into the heavy brush.

"She's probably just after a squirrel. Isn't chasing rodents a constant activity for her?" Nathan asked.

"She uses different barks for different things. This is her bark of alarm." Twigs snapped beneath Red's dusty boots as he shoved past the thicket to where Tan stood whining down at a body. "Ah, shoot, it's Percy."

"Who's Percy?"

"The Minam Lodge owner's golden Lab." Red fell silent as he knelt down to inspect the gashes spread across the dog's body. *This wasn't done by a cougar.* His eyes traveled up to the exposed throat that had been cut nearly all the way through. *The cuts look to be done by Leroy's knife, but with less precision than the calf. The killing appears much more thoughtless and rushed than the calf. Harold's other dog, Lola, must have been after him.* He scanned Percy's body from one end to the other. *He took his goddamn tail as a trophy?*

"Was it shot?"

Red struggled back through the brush. "No, he was stabbed, and if I'm not mistaken, with the same knife that was used on Lee and the calf." He gathered his reins and jumped up into the saddle. "Come on, now I've got even worse news to give Harold."

A short time later, they came to a wooden gate with an overhead sign: Minam Lodge. On top of the sign sat a worn cowboy hat. They rode past the corrals, turning at the gray barn, and up a hill past a row of log cabins as they made their way to the hitching rail on the side of the main building. There they dismounted and tied their horses.

The lodge sat on a hillside with dense forest behind it. Directly below was a large meadow with a portion separated into a circular pasture by a crisscross of rough-cut wood pole fencing. A landing strip ran between the pasture and the sparkling waters of the Minam River on the far side of the canyon wall. Rising up across the river was a steep mountainside covered in rock and a sprinkling of trees.

"Hey, Red," Harold greeted his guests as they walked into the lodge.

"Hello, Harold."

"What brings you to my neck of the woods?" Harold got up from his leather chair in front of the fireplace. He set his newspaper on a side table and walked into the next room, motioning Red to follow him. From behind the bar, he pulled two coffee mugs off a shelf and placed them on the countertop.

"Bad news," Red said, taking a seat on a barstool. "And then some worse news."

Harold's smile faded. "Hell with coffee, I had better pour something stronger." He replaced the mugs with short glasses and grabbed a bottle of whiskey from the shelf, turning the label toward Red. "This is your choice of poison, isn't it?"

"That's the one."

"Soda, son?" Harold asked as he pulled a can from the refrigerator.

Nathan nodded and reached for the cola. "Thanks."

Harold began to pour the whiskey, pausing to look at Red. "Does this bad news call for two fingers or four?"

"Best make it to the brim."

"Damn." Harold filled the glasses.

Red picked up his glass and gulped down half before setting it on the counter. "Found Percy dead along the trail on our way over here. He'd been stabbed numerous times."

"Stabbed? So it wasn't a cougar."

"I know Bud told you about Lee's murder and the mutilation of the calf."

"Yeah, I'm real sorry to hear about Lee."

"Lee was a big loss, but chances are he wasn't the last to die at the hands of the son of a bitch. It appears the killer started with your dog, then the calf, and then moved on to humans.

We fear his latest victim may be a female guest who went missing from my ranch. Do you know Commissioner Reynolds's wife, Faye?"

"Yes, she and her husband came over to have dinner with a couple of my guests while they were staying with you last year. Is she your missing guest?"

"Yes. You haven't seen her?"

"No, but maybe she ran off with a new beau. She does have quite the reputation, you know."

Red drained his glass. "The butchering of an elephant wouldn't leave behind the amount of blood we found in her cabin, so we're sure someone had to have been slaughtered there. If not her, I have no idea who it could have been. We followed a bloody trail from the cabin down to the river. I thought since the river has dropped down close to summer levels the last few days, if her body got carried downstream, it couldn't have gone past the shallow sandbar at the bend. My men are searching the river now—should be down along your place soon. Since I haven't heard a shot, I don't think they've found anything. If she's not in the river, I'll be blessed as to where she is. Haven't seen blood anywhere but going down to the bank, and there are no signs of her in any other building."

"That doesn't make any sense. Why drag her to the river if he didn't intend to throw her in?"

"The moon was bright last night. Maybe he dragged her down to where she couldn't be seen while he went after something to help move her, say a wheelbarrow, or a tarp. Leroy checked Pig Island to make sure we didn't have a repeat of Lee, but he didn't find any bones. We might have to search the ponds next."

Harold picked up his glass and drank it to the bottom. "Holy smokes, I've got to arm my men and have them stand guard over my guests."

"That brings me to another bit of news you're not gonna like. Sheriff Cason has ordered us to evacuate our guests immediately, and close up shop until he clears us to open again."

"Damn, you're just full of good news today." Harold poured a smaller amount in Red's glass, but took none for himself.

"Aren't you going to have another?"

"No, I'm trying to cut back. Getting older, you know. It might be wise for you to do the same."

Red glanced at Nathan. "More than one person's told me that lately. But I figure even if I eat healthy, stop drinking, and don't smoke, I'll die anyway. So what's the point?" He picked up his glass and drank it all. "I'd tell you to have a good day, but that ship's already sailed."

Harold picked up the bottle of whiskey. "Screw health! Percy deserves a toast." He filled his glass to half and the same for Red. "To Percy!" The men clinked glasses and tossed the liquor down their throats. "Thanks, Harold, we best be on our way."

Red held the door for Nathan, pausing to look back at Harold. "I tied a marker on the shrubs where Percy is. If I had the time, I'd help you give the old boy a proper burial."

Red led Nathan out to the hitching rail. They untied their horses, and Red bounded up into his saddle effortlessly. He saw Nathan staring at him. "What are you waitin' for?"

"I thought if I followed your moves, I might have a better go of it." Nathan reached for the horn with his left hand, the cantle with his right, and stuck his left foot in the stirrup.

"I'm quite sure you didn't see me put my hand on the back of the saddle." Red watched as Nathan came to the realization that his leg couldn't swing over with his arm in the way.

Nathan stepped down to the ground and studied his options.

"This is gonna take a while," Red said, patting Sugar's neck. By the time he fished tobacco from his pocket and had his pipe packed and lit, Nathan still wasn't on his horse. "You're not the most coordinated, are you, boy?" He frowned at the sight of Nathan lying over the saddle. "Okay, I can't watch any more of this." Red rode over beside Stella, reached down, and lifted

Nathan by the back of his pants, shoving his leg over Stella's rump. "Son, you're gonna have to practice getting on and off a horse. It really isn't all that difficult." His eyes traveled down to Nathan's untied laces. "Master that and maybe we can take on teaching you to tie your shoes."

Red gathered the reins Nathan had dropped, handed them to him, and rode away from the lodge.

As Nathan followed Red down the trail, he asked, "You really think Faye's dead?"

"Yup, but that's not to be fodder for gossip."

"I won't tell anyone."

"I know you won't, because you're stickin' with me."

WE DIDN'T SEE ANY sign of her, boss," Billy said as he brushed his horse down.

Red groaned. "Then she's not in the river." He dismounted and tied Sugar to the hitching rail. "You couldn't have missed seeing her as clear and shallow as the river is running."

"Yeah, we thought the same thing," Bud agreed as he carried his saddle to the tack room.

Leroy and Jake rode around the barn.

"Not a single blade of grass moved while you were gone," Leroy said.

"Like he would know," grumbled Jake as he stepped down from his horse. "He kept hogging the binoculars. Not that he could see anything through them anyway. As bad as his eyes are, binoculars do about as much good as a windshield wiper on a goat's ass."

"I see your ass clear enough to put my boot in it," Leroy snarled, spitting tobacco on the ground as he loosened the cinch."

The lunch bell rang as Nathan came out from delivering his saddle and pad to the tack room. "Good, I'm starved."

Red watched as Nathan ran a few strokes over Stella's back and then tossed the brush in the grooming bucket. "Boy, that was about the most half-assed excuse for a brushing I've ever seen. If you don't pick up that brush and put some elbow grease behind it, I'll have you brushin' every damn horse on the ranch."

"But I'm hungry."

"Well, son, you always have choices. Maybe you should ask yourself if it's more advantageous to stand here and debate with me, or to take proper care of your horse and be free to get some grub."

Nathan pinned his glaring eyes at Red.

"Best not direct your angry mule ears my way."

Nathan turned his back to him.

"Take one step toward that lodge and you'll find yourself spitting pond water."

Nathan whirled around, ready to lash out. Then he froze at the sight of the coil of rope in Red's hands. "Go ahead. I'll give you a running start."

"Fine, I'll brush the stupid horse." Nathan stomped to the grooming bucket.

"Never time to do it right, but always time to do it over," Bud said, chuckling as he led Dipsy past Red.

CHAPTER 23

"You stay in your room until I tell you otherwise," Red said, walking Nathan to his cabin after lunch. "I have to talk to the commissioner in private."

"That's not a conversation I want anything to do with anyway." Nathan followed Tan Dog inside and immediately went to his room and closed the door.

Red walked into his room to snatch a bottle from another hidden case of whiskey, gathered three glasses from the bar and carried them to the coffee table. Taking a seat on the sofa, he poured himself a shot, slammed it back, and poured another.

Tan Dog circled twice before finally lying down beside his sofa, only to jump to her feet again when she heard the knock at the door. She barked.

Woody poked his head in. "I have Commissioner Reynolds with me."

"Please come in." Red motioned to them. "I'm pourin'." He picked up the bottle. "Commissioner?"

"I don't usually partake in alcohol when talking business, but since this is a special occasion, by all means." The commissioner nodded as he walked in wearing a blue dress shirt, tan slacks gathered up over his bulging stomach, and a pair of brand-new ostrich cowboy boots. He flicked his cigar.

Red watched the ash fall to his floor.

"I waited for you here until lunch," the commissioner said, taking a seat on the sofa opposite Red. "Sure did take your time with whatever you were off doing. I was about to go rouse Faye when Woody told me you were back."

Red poured him a glass, and without asking, poured one for Woody. "Unexpected challenges have a way of popping up at the most inopportune times around here. I apologize for keeping you waiting. I assure you it couldn't be helped."

"Well then, that's fine," the commissioner said, blowing smoke into the air. He took a sip of whiskey and glanced at the bottle. "If nothing else is up to par here, at least you pour a good brand."

Red fought off a frown. *Too bad it's being wasted on the likes of you.*

Woody stepped past Red and settled on the window end of the sofa. Looking rather uncomfortable, he took his hat off, set it over his knees, and swallowed half his drink down.

"Get away from me, mutt," the commissioner said, kicking at the dog sniffing his legs.

Tan Dog jumped away from his foot, growling. Red snapped his fingers, and she sat on the floor next to him, growling softly as she stared at the commissioner. Red stroked her head, but she kept her eyes trained on the portly man. *I know exactly how you feel, girl.*

"I was pleasantly surprised when Woody told me you finally came to your senses about taking out a loan." The commissioner looked smug.

The man's like a broken record. "No, Commissioner, I'm afraid the news I have has nothing to do with a loan." Red took a moment to collect his thoughts. *How do I tell a man I believe his wife was murdered? I suppose there's only one way—the direct approach.* "It's Faye. She's missing and presumed dead."

The commissioner stared darkly but made no response. Finally, he drained his glass and slammed it down on the coffee table. "What the fuck are you talking about?"

"I'm very sorry, Commissioner, but the indications are that she might have been killed in her bed last night. We haven't found her body yet, but it's very unlikely that anyone could survive losing the amount of blood we found in her cabin. After discovering the blood trail led to the river, my men and I conducted a thorough search, only to come up empty-handed." He watched the commissioner closely. *Was that a flash of a smile I just saw?*

Eyeing Red through thick glasses, the commissioner slid his glass across the table. "Make it a double."

The unexpected calm in his voice made Red's skin prickle. *Strange reaction for a man who's just been informed his wife might be dead. But then, everything about this man is strange.*

Red filled the highball glass halfway to the top, slid it back to the commissioner, and watched him toss back the entire drink. When the commissioner looked at Red again, his expression had turned cold.

"I guess you won't be needin' that loan after all."

Red offered no response.

The commissioner stood. "Because when I get through with you, you won't have a ranch to worry about." He shook a finger at Red. "I'm gonna bleed you dry."

Tan Dog jumped to her feet, barking and growling loudly. The hair along the ridge of her back bristled as she stood in front of Red, stopping the commissioner from coming any closer.

"I left her in your care, and you were negligent in keeping her safe. You'll be hearing from my lawyer."

The angry outburst was loud enough for Nathan to hear it over the music playing in his earbuds. He jumped off his bed, opened his door a crack, and watched the commissioner storm out of the cabin, slamming the door behind him.

Woody blew out a breath. "Well, that went well."

"Did you really expect it to go any differently?" Red drained the rest of his glass.

"I expected to see an inkling of grief from a man who just lost the woman he loved."

Red poured whiskey in his glass and handed the bottle to

Woody. "There are only two things that man loves: himself and bringing ruin to others. And I'd be hard-pressed to tell which he values more."

Woody refilled his glass. "I can tell you one thing. That little weasel is set to make a mountain of trouble for you."

"Yeah, well he's been waitin' a long time for the opportunity to pull this ranch out from under me. He associates land with power and has trampled a lot of people in the pursuit of it. I doubt he'd give a second thought to using his wife's death to get one more.

"The man reeks of evil," Woody said, taking a drink from his glass.

"It's a vocational hazard often shared by unscrupulous bankers and politicians. In his case, you get a twofer." Red stared out the window at the deer licking the salt block across the river. "No need to strain your ears, Nathan. Come on out here."

A moment passed before the men heard the squeak of the bedroom door opening.

"Your eavesdropping skills could use some work, boy." Red scowled at Nathan as he emerged from his hiding place. "Soda's in the fridge if you want one."

"That guy is a prick with ears," Nathan said as he carried a can of soda to the vacant sofa across from the men.

"That would be a fairly adequate description." Woody chuckled.

"What are you going to do?" Nathan set his soda on the coffee table and looked across it to Red. "Shouldn't we put together a defensive plan? I mean, he made it clear he plans to ruin you."

"The kid's right," Woody said. "And I wouldn't be surprised to find he was behind all the killings."

"There's a problem with your theory," Red said, holding his pipe in his hand. "The commissioner flew in after Faye was killed, and according to Joe, the newspaper took his picture during a social affair the night Lee was killed. That gives him plenty of witnesses and a steadfast alibi." He paused, studying his pipe. "That doesn't mean he didn't have a hand in it."

Woody tossed his hat aside and lifted his feet up on the coffee table. "If he brought in a killer for hire, I suspect the bastard's nearby."

Nathan gulped down his soda and smashed the can in his hand. "I say we find him and squash him like a bug."

Red raised a brow at him. "I don't recall inviting you to join my posse." He studied Nathan's angry face. "You saw what lengths the murderer will go to get to his victims. If it hadn't been for Tan Dog, you could have been his next."

"And the fact that he wore a dead boy's scalp tells you how crazy this bastard is," Woody said. "What a scary bit of business that was."

"You're telling me." Nathan stared down at his feet. "Shouldn't someone go look for the hikers?"

"That's probably exactly what the killer wants us to do—split us up." Red petted Tan Dog's head. "I'm certain the murderer wouldn't leave any of the hikers alive to identify him. And I'm not willing to chance losing any more of my people. No, the dead will have to wait. Catching the killer is the only way to put a stop to this nightmare."

"I'm in," Nathan said. "Where do we start?"

Red shook his head. "I can't allow you to be involved in something so dangerous."

"I'm involved up to my eyebrows." Nathan frowned as his toss of the can missed the nearby trash container. "No one frames me and gets away with it. And I sure as hell don't plan to let him get another shot at coming after me." He looked at Red. "You shouldn't let that dirtbag commissioner get away with sticking it to you. We have a lot of his type in LA—vultures making fortunes from picking the bones of others. And I've seen enough detective shows to know the husband is usually to blame for the wife's death. Lee and the calf were probably killed to take suspicion from the real motive behind the murders—to get the ranch away from you."

Woody nodded. "Faye's death would provide the perfect opportunity to claim liability against you. He's probably making a call to his lawyer right now."

"No doubt," Red said. "You two have certainly got it all figured out. Now we have to prove it. As far as a defensive plan goes, first order of business is to get you boys to safety. As soon as the replacement tire gets here, we'll do exactly that." He turned to Woody. "Joe will make a second trip to take the staff members. Once I know you're all safely out of here, I'm gonna tear up this canyon, hunting for the killer."

"You can change that to *we*," Woody said.

"Unless I've got a rat in my pocket I wasn't aware of, there is no 'we.'"

"You don't actually think you can keep me from staying?"

Red's hot glare melted to a cool resolve. "I won't bother to waste my breath. Your mule ears are longer than old Ned's."

Woody smirked. "I'm sure my wife would agree with your comparison." His gaze was drawn to where Tan Dog lay, growling softly with her eyes trained on the front door. "I believe she smells a rat. I do too—a two-legged, and most pompous sort of rat."

Red ran his hand down the ridge of hair still bristling on Tan Dog's back. "The commissioner sure did get her dander up." He gave her head a rub. "I can't say I don't agree with your opinion of him. He's not to be trusted."

"No he's not," Woody grumbled. "What I can't understand is why he'd want to frame Nathan for killing Lee."

Nathan looked at Woody. "And why he'd want to kill me?"

"I've been thinking about that," Red said. "I believe your celebrity status probably had something to do with both of those actions. If what we suspect of the commissioner's involvement is true, his ultimate goal is to see to the closure of the ranch. He knows I can't afford to lose even one season and an unsolved murder would be just the thing to make that happen. It could be that when Lee's death failed to make a media splash, the killer looked for ways to draw attention to his murder. Placing the blame on a reality show celebrity would be a great way to achieve that. Of course that didn't work, so he had to step up his game. Killing a famed television star would have to draw huge media coverage, and result in closing the ranch for the entire season.

"And forcing you to sell out," Woody added, nodding. "I think that's a plausible scenario."

"If he has a hired killer, he'll probably try to make contact with him," Nathan said.

"And that's why we're going to keep a close watch on him," said Red.

The front door opened and Bud and Carlos walked into the cabin.

"Are the families camping in the forest about ready to leave?" Red asked Bud as he approached.

"Yes, they're already packed up and waiting at the lodge. The pilot that flew them in isn't available to come get them today, so I told them we'd pack them out to Moss Springs. Billy is saddling horses, and Sean and Leroy are loading their gear on Ned and Nell."

"Good. I'll feel better when I know there aren't any children in the area. At least that's one less thing to worry about. And it's probably a good idea to have Billy away from the ranch until we get the commissioner out of here. He hears that Billy and Faye were together and there'll be hell to pay. Any word about the tire?"

"That's the other thing. That Burr feller has been trying to call all morning. Says he got nothing but a busy signal. We must have a short in the wire again. Anyway, it turns out his trip to Boise was a bust. He flew all that way just to discover they didn't have the correct size of tire after all. They made noise about a computer error, which in my experience always seems to lead back to a human error. Anyway, they're shipping one overnight to the La Grande airport. It probably won't get in until midday tomorrow. Burr said he'd bring it to us, but since tomorrow's going be a warm one, he'll be forced to wait for cooler temperatures later in the day."

"Great," Red grumbled. "Give Joe the bad news and let him know he'll be sleeping in the lodge. I want to keep everyone under one roof tonight. You can take the campers out to collect mattresses from the cabins. Since they'll be making their beds on the floor, might as well make it comfortable."

Bud nodded. "The second reason for our interruption comes at the behest of Edith. She tells me she can't spare the two boys she has slaving away in the kitchen, and she was wondering if Nathan and Carlos could take on the chore of peeling potatoes."

"Don't see why not, as long as they stay together and you watch them." Red looked at Nathan. "You'll find spud bags in the cold house. Twenty-five big ones should do."

"I think I could be of better use here working on a plan," Nathan said.

"You have your plan—kitchen duty and bedding." Red saw Nathan's face flush in mulish discord. "Take warning, young man. I'm not in the mood for any arguments."

"Are you going to just sit there while grass grows under your feet?" Bud said, motioning to Nathan.

"Swell." Nathan moaned as he stood.

"Come on." Bud walked the boys to the door. "Let's get this done while the gettin's good. You'll start with the peeling, and then gather the bedding after." Bud followed the boys out of the cabin, closing the door behind him.

"At least Nathan shouldn't be able to find trouble while he's peeling spuds," Woody said.

"I wouldn't put anything past that boy. He doesn't find trouble—trouble finds him."

CHAPTER 24

Nathan and Carlos followed Bud down the path, stopping in front of the cold house. He unlocked the door, and propped it open with a canister of butter before waving them through. "Don't bother looking for a light. The sun shining through this door is about as bright as it's going to get in here. You boys gather the spuds. I'm going to wait outside where it's not so cold." Bud grabbed a basket from the shelf, handed it to Nathan, and walked out.

"Do you see any potatoes?" Nathan asked, looking around the room.

"No." Carlos slammed a fist into a side of beef hanging from the rafters. "Ouch! Shit, that hurts."

"Hey, Rocky, you want to help me find the stupid potatoes so we can get out of here? It's cold."

Carlos rubbed his hand. "I guess I can rule out becoming a boxer."

"Boxers aren't dumb enough to hit a slab of meat barehanded."

"I sure wouldn't do it twice." Carlos looked at the stack of boxes sitting in the corner. "Wait, I see some burlap bags back here behind this pile of crap." He slipped past the hanging beef, picked up a box of carrots, and set it on the butcher block along the back wall. Then he shoved a box of lettuce aside. "Gross. The beef dripped blood all over the side of this bag."

"Just toss me the potatoes already," Nathan said.

Carlos opened the top of the bag and filled his arms with

potatoes. "Catch." He threw two potatoes at Nathan as he came around the slab of beef.

The first landed directly in the center of Nathan's chest, dropping into the basket he held. He dodged the second as it whizzed past, hitting the wall behind him. "Damn you, Carlos!" Nathan took the potato from the basket and threw it back at him.

And the battle was on.

Carlos blocked the potato and then threw one after another, only letting up when he had to gather more ammunition from the bag.

Each time Carlos went back for more potatoes, Nathan rushed to collect the ones on the floor around him.

"Take that," Carlos shouted, laughing as he threw two potatoes in quick succession.

Nathan caught one, but the second was a direct hit, splattering something wet across his chest. He looked down at the red stains. "Hey, you got cow blood on my T-shirt."

"Ah crap, it's all over my shirt too." Carlos dropped his potatoes to the floor and looked down at his blood-covered hands. "Yuck, I thought that was potato slime." He reached in the bag and pulled out two more and immediately dropped them. "They're all covered in it." He slid the bag to the side and pulled another forward. "This one should be clean." He wiped his hands on his jeans, opened the next bag, and inspected a couple of the potatoes sitting on top. "These are good." This time he tossed them slowly, making it easy for Nathan to catch them with the basket.

"Hold up. Let me take a count," Nathan said when his basket was nearly full.

Carlos juggled a potato back and forth in his hands, waiting for Nathan's count.

"We need six more."

Carlos threw Nathan the one in his hand and reached in the bag for another, hesitating. "What the…? I think there's something besides potatoes in this bag." He tried to look at the strange object his hand was touching. "Damn, it's so dark back here I can't see a fucking thing." He pulled the bag wider, pushed potatoes aside, and reached in, blindly exploring with his hand. "I can't figure out what this is, but I know it isn't a potato.

"Just lift it out, stupid."

Carlos entwined his fingers in the long strands and jerked the object from the bag, sending droplets of liquid flying. "Gross!" He wiped his face with his sleeve and watched as the object hanging from his hand turned, revealing a face.

His breath caught. He screamed and shook his hand free from the hair, dropping Faye's decapitated head onto the bag. Panicked, he stumbled backward, slamming against the hanging beef as he tried to flee from the corner.

"What the hell, Carlos?" Nathan shouted when he stumbled into him.

Carlos pointed, but no words came out.

The side of beef swung back into the potato bag, knocking the head from its perch. It rolled to the center of the room, coming to a stop with open eyes looking up at the boys.

They screamed and ran into each other as they raced for the door. Nathan dropped the basket and shoved Carlos out of his way as he frantically sped out of the cold house.

"What in the Sam Hill?" Bud exclaimed as the boys tore past him. "Come back here!" He watched as Carlos tore around the corner, running for the lodge, while Nathan sprinted in the opposite direction to Red's cabin.

"What nonsense is this?" Bud grumbled as the boys disappeared from his view. "Horseshit, that's what it is. It's most likely nothing more than a rodent." He walked down the slope to the cold house entrance and stopped inside the door. Once his eyes began to adjust to the dark, he slowly made his way to the center of the room. "What the hell was that?" He reached down and picked up the object his foot bumped. As

Faye's face came into focus, Bud's breath caught in his chest. "Hell no!" He dropped the head, and took a step back.

"What's the problem?" Red asked as he rushed into the cold house with Woody behind him. "Nathan ran into the cabin, looking like he'd seen a ghost. What's got the boy so upset?"

Bud didn't answer.

"We couldn't make head nor tails out of what Nathan was rambling on about," Woody added, stopping beside Bud. "Holy mother of God!"

Red stood on Bud's other side, staring in muted disbelief at the lifeless blue eyes looking up from the decapitated head. Moments passed.

"Where do you suppose the rest of her is?" Woody asked, breaking the silence.

Red walked to the potato bags and peered into the closest one. Then he grabbed both bags, slid them closer to the light in the center of the room, and opened the second. "Arms and legs are in this one, and the torso is in that one. That answers the question as to why he dragged her down to the river. It kept the butchering nice and tidy."

"I did not see this comin'," Bud said, shaking his head.

"No one could have seen this coming," said Woody. "This is one crazy bastard we're dealing with."

"And there stands the problem." Red's eyes narrowed with anger. "We're *not* dealing with him. Time we turned the tables and made the hunter the hunted."

"And put the blasted animal down," Bud growled.

"I'll go load every goddamn weapon on the place." Woody headed for the door.

"Good, and tell Jake he's to stand watch over the campers. I'm sure Edith can find somethin' to keep the boys busy in the kitchen. And light a fire under Leroy and Billy. I want those families out of here, now! I won't have a child's life at risk."

"I'll talk with Edith and Joe about staying in the lodge, but I doubt the commissioner will concede to anything but his own castle. Since his choice cabin is no longer in shape for staying, he's been making noise about taking yours. That being the case, I'd expect him to kick up a fuss about being locked up with people he believes to be below his status. It's never easy to reason with someone who has a Napoleon complex."

"Without an army behind him, Napoleon was nothing more than a short man on a tall horse," grumbled Red. "I'll deal with the commissioner's delusions of grandeur after I make a call to the sheriff. If I'm forced to chain the bastard in the lodge, so be it."

"SHERIFF?" RED SAID, using the phone in his cabin. "By the sounds of it, you must be in the middle of a war zone."

"You're gonna have to speak up," Sheriff Cason shouted into the phone. "We've taken a few of the gang's lead rabble-rousers into custody and the rest are spittin' mad about it. Say, where are the boys you were supposed to send me? Claire says they haven't made it to the office."

"There's been a delay. Someone slashed one of the airplane's tires, so Joe is grounded until we get another flown in tomorrow."

"Did you say slashed? Damn, I can't hear myself think. Let me get inside the marina store, away from the ruckus."

Red heard the open and close of a door. The background shouts softened to a muffle.

"There, that's better. I tell you, for a bunch of guys with limited vocabulary, they sure can find creative and loud uses for the few words they do know." The noise outside increased as a group of state police troopers broke up another scuffle between two opposing bikers. "Anyway, you were saying?"

"We have a pilot bringing us a replacement tire tomorrow."

"It sounds like someone doesn't want the campers leaving. Do you think it's one of them?"

"I can only hope. I'd hate to think the killer is trying to keep them at the ranch. But the only ones that show any disappointment in leaving are the two working in the kitchen. The other three would gladly walk out barefooted with suitcases strapped to their backs, if that's what it took to leave."

"Just to ease your mind, take a look at your kitchen knives. Slicing a tire might leave rubber residue on the blade. That is, as long as they didn't have the foresight to clean it. Of course, if it were a teenager, he probably wouldn't think to cover his tracks."

"I'll take a look," Red said. "Now for the real reason I called. We found Faye."

"From the sound of your voice, I take it not alive?"

"No, we found her in the cold house—in pieces. Her dismembered body was hidden in potato bags."

"Tell your pilot to make a swing over to pick me up on his way in with the tire tomorrow."

"Will do. And, Sheriff, there's somethin' else you should know. The men and I looked over the body parts the best we could without touching or removing them from the bags. And we came across somethin' disturbing."

"More disturbing than a woman hacked into pieces?"

"It appears the mentally deranged bastard kept a piece of her, I suppose as some kind of sick trophy. He skinned a spot low on her back where she had a palm-tree tattoo."

"I believe you're describing a tramp stamp. Now how would you know about a tattoo in that location? If you tell me you had an up-close-and-personal look at it, we're gonna have ourselves a whole nother conversation."

"Of course not!" Red huffed. "You know I have enough sense not to dip a toe in that pool of temptation. Unfortunately, I can't say the same for Billy. That young fool got himself pickled on my best whiskey and dove in head first. His brains might still be a pile of mush, but he's adamant about seeing the tattoo. Once he heard what part of Faye's body had been whittled on, he knew exactly what had been cut from her."

"Well, isn't that just dandy." Sheriff Cason groaned. "You

know that since Billy was the last to see her alive, he now tops the list of persons of interest."

"Yeah, I'm aware of that. I figured you should know Billy was with her before she died, especially since forensics is bound to find his DNA on her and in the cabin where she was killed."

"Does the commissioner know this piece of the puzzle?"

"No, I left Billy out. I also left out the details on how she was killed. He just knows her body was found in the cold house."

"Where is Billy now?"

"He and Leroy are gettin' set to pack the camp families out to Moss Springs."

"Good, I'll have Union County deputies pick him up there."

"He didn't do this, Sheriff. Billy just doesn't have the stomach for killing."

"Maybe you don't know him as well as you think. Could be you've got a Dr. Jekyll and Mr. Hyde."

"I've known the boy for years and I can't see how he could fool me like that."

"Even if I believe you, we still have to play this by the book. We can't risk anyone even thinking we swept anything under the rug. If the commissioner were to find out, he'd see to both of our crucifixions."

"Then I guess there are a couple more things I should share with you."

"Why is it that I have a feeling I'm not going to like this?"

"You're going to hate it. I know I do. But you might as well know the knife that killed Lee belongs to Leroy, and the knife that killed Faye belongs to me. Both were locked away at the time they were stolen, and both were left for us to find. I've got them in my safe now. Unfortunately, they've been compromised. I doubt you'll find any prints of the killer's, but you'll find plenty from my people."

"Well, isn't that just swell," the sheriff snapped. "That certainly doesn't set well for you or Leroy. I'll have Union

County pick up Leroy along with Billy. I'll deal with you and your knife when I get there." He paused. "Exactly how many people contaminated the crime scenes?"

Red considered for a moment. "Jake, Billy, and I were all in Faye's cabin. And two campers, Nathan and Carlos, along with Bud, Woody, and I were in the cold house where the body was found."

The sheriff blew out a long breath. "In other words, it's a forensic nightmare."

RED WALKED THROUGH THE back door of the kitchen and straight to the sink. He picked up one of two dirty knives, tossed one aside, and ran his fingers down the sticky blade of the other. "Who used this knife last, Edith?"

Edith slid the loaf pan in the oven, closed the door, and wiped her hands on her apron as she turned to look at the knife he held up. "Well now, I believe..." She hesitated, glancing at Carlton, who was stirring a pot of stew next to her. She grabbed a rag and busied herself with wiping down the stove. "I'm not sure. Why do you ask?"

"Never mind, I think I have my answer," Red said, watching Carlton's cheeks redden as he stared into the pot.

Noah stopped kneading bread on the wooden butcher block and lifted a dough-covered hand. "It was me."

Red raised a brow at him. Then he turned to Edith and saw that she was doing her best to act like she didn't know he was eyeing her. "I appreciate the loyalty that has grown among the kitchen crew, but I'd appreciate it even more if you weren't lyin' to me. Noah, I'm glad to see that you have a better understanding of the value of friendship, but you can't do something right by doing something wrong. And Edith, I fully understand your desire to protect the boys, but please don't insult my intelligence."

Edith grabbed an empty pan from a shelf, carried it to the butcher block, and took over kneading for Noah. "We best get this in the oven, or we'll be short on bread for dinner."

Noah stepped aside, but was too preoccupied with watching Red to respond to her.

Red walked to Carlton. "Son, you want to explain how the film of tire rubber came to be on this knife?"

Carlton set the metal spoon on the stove and turned with his eyes lowered to the floor. "I'm sorry, I shouldn't have done it." He spoke so softly Red could barely hear him. His eyes darted to Noah and back to his feet. "Don't be mad at Noah. He didn't have anything to do with it. He even tried to stop me from cutting the plane's tire." His eyes slowly rose to Red's. "I just couldn't stand the thought of going home yet. I like it here. I have a friend, and I really like learning to cook. I was…upset."

Red watched Carlton's embarrassed expression turn to sadness.

"Sometimes I lose control. But this time I took it out on a pilot, and he didn't even deserve it. I feel bad about that. I know it was wrong of me, and I'll do anything to pay the pilot for the damage. Please don't blame Noah for something I did. It wasn't his fault. Whatever punishment you decide should only go to me."

Who needs punishment when this boy is doing such a fine job of beating himself up? Red looked at Noah and back to Carlton. "Well, aren't you two a peach of a pair? Noah steals from you, and you stand up for him. Then you do something stupid and Noah tries to take the blame for it." He shook his head. "I don't know whether to be proud or mad as hell at the both of you." Red shrugged. "At least that's one answer to a growing number of questions we have popping up around here."

Edith plopped the dough in the pan, placed her hands on her hips, and tapped her foot, glaring at Red. "See here, he explained himself jest fine. Now, if you're expectin' to have dinner anytime tonight, best if you don't let the door hit your backside on the way out."

"Subtlety has never been one of your strong suits, Edith."

Red turned to walk to the door. "We'll talk about this again another time, boys." As he reached for the doorknob, the double barreled shotgun resting near it gave him pause. "Edith, what is this gun doing here?"

"You said Jake and I was to protect the boys. The way I figure it, any stranger who comes sniffin' round here is gonna leave with a rump of buckshot. Yes, sir, shoot first, ask questions later. That's what I intend to do."

"I said Jake is to guard the boys. You're supposed to keep them busy." Red picked up the gun and inspected it.

"I can do both at the same time."

Red stepped back to let Woody lead Nathan and Carlos in through the kitchen door.

"Hey, Red, the boys and I got the animals fed early." Woody saw the shotgun. "Say, isn't that the gun Leroy complains about having a defect? You're not planning to use that one?"

Edith slammed the oven door closed and turned to face the men. "Now see here, no one's using my gun but me. It belonged to my father, and if it was good enough for him, it sure as shoot is good enough for me. We may be old and rusty, but the both of us can still get the job done. Besides, as long as I'm aimin' in the general direction, I'll surely hit somethin'."

"That's what I'm afraid of," Woody whispered to Red.

"Edith..." Red began.

"Now you just put that back where you found it and go about your business." Edith pointed to the door. "You've taken enough of our time. Get!"

Red began to follow Woody out, pausing at the door to make sure there wasn't a round in the chamber before setting the gun down against the wall.

"It's impossible to win an argument with that woman," said Woody as he walked with Red.

"You've been around women long enough to know that they always get the last word. Anything a man says after that is just the beginning of a new argument."

CHAPTER 25

"Need more soap," Nathan said to himself. Grabbing the bar, he lathered his body for the third time. He rinsed, turned off the shower, pulled a towel from the rack, and stepped out onto the mat to dry off. Then he dressed in clean clothing, ran a comb through his dark hair, and tossed it into the duffel on the floor next to the pile of bloody clothing. Gathering the soiled garments in his arms, he walked out of the bathroom and straight to the rock fireplace in Red's cabin.

"Hey, what are you doing?" Carlos asked from the sofa in front of the fireplace.

"That's the last I ever want to see of those." Nathan threw the cloths on the burning fire and turned to walk to his room.

"Red told us to take showers and get right back to the lodge." Carlos stood. "You're taking too long. You can dally all you want, but I don't plan on getting into trouble. I'm going on without you."

"I'll be right behind you. I just need to get my phone. If we're going to be stuck in the lodge, I want something to entertainment myself."

While Carlos walked to the lodge, Nathan went to his room and unplugged his phone from the charger. He was almost to his door when the front door opened. He hesitated, listening to the odd sound the boots made as they walked across the plank floor. It wasn't the same noise made by the well-worn boots the ranch hands wore. There was no jingling of spurs, only the click, click, click of brand-new heels hitting wood.

Nathan hid behind the door and peeked through the open crack at the wide-bodied figure walking through the cabin. "What's he doing here?" he whispered, watching as the commissioner took a seat on one of the sofas at the windows.

"I keep telling Red this place needs some serious updating," the commissioner griped as he reached for the phone. "The least he could do is trade out these old phones for some that were made in the twenty-first century." He placed his finger in a hole and spun the first of a series of numbers on the dial. "Rotary phones and Red have one thing in common: they're both obsolete." He chuckled at himself, sat back, and put his feet up on the coffee table.

"Hi, baby, it's daddy," the commissioner said, his voice sugary.

"Fucking disgusting," Nathan said from behind his door.

"I have some great news for you, darlin'." The commissioner paused. "No, I won't be filing for divorce." He laughed. "Hold on, baby, I haven't changed my mind. It's just that I don't need a divorce now that she got herself killed." He laughed loudly. "Can you believe that? The bitch is dead. Yes, you heard me right—she's dead. But we'll need to wait an appropriate length of time to marry." He went silent again.

"Now, don't be like that, sunshine. You know you're my girl, but I've got to play the grieving widower for at least a little while." He chuckled again. "I should be able to ride on the back of pity clean through the next election. You want to be the commissioner's wife, don't you, baby? Good. When I get home, I'm going to buy you a diamond so large you're going to need both hands to lift it. But you won't be able to wear it out in public for a while—you want what? Faye's convertible? No, baby, that won't look good. But I'm about to come into some sizable money, and when I do, I'll get you the prettiest little baby-blue Porsche...I thought that would make you happy. Now you go buy something real sexy for me to tear off you. See you soon, baby." He hung up and sat back with his hands behind his head, smirking up at the ceiling.

"Piece of shit," Nathan said under his breath as he watched the commissioner pick up the receiver and dial another number.

"Frank? It's me. I got a job for you. It's time to dust off the federal land-swap deal that went south on us a couple years back. Those bastard feds said they wouldn't consider land that wasn't adjacent to national forest. Well, the perfect property just fell into my hands, and they'll be hard-pressed to turn it down since it's surrounded by the Eagle Cap Wilderness. That's right—Red Higgins's place. No, we won't need any more inspectors coming up here, and we can forget hooking him with a loan. Turns out he's a much larger fish than we thought, and he's about to jump right into my boat—thanks to my lovely wife providing the bait. What? No, you can toss the divorce papers. I have something much bigger for you to handle. You're finally going to earn the outrageous retainer I pay you by filing a lawsuit against Red Higgins for the wrongful death of my wife. Yeah, they just found her body. No, they don't know who did it. If it was one of your guys, throw the bastard a party for me.

Anyway, I want Higgins and everyone associated with this place, including his damn dog, to be named in the lawsuit. How much? No, I want to squeeze him harder than that. I was thinking more like in the tens of millions. Yes, I know he doesn't have that kind of money. That's exactly the point, you idiot. The ranch is the only card he holds. Higgins will have no choice but to fold, and we'll finally get our land swap." He hesitated, listening. "It can't take that long. We're going to have to figure out a way to speed things up." He strummed his fingers on the wood armrest.

"Hmm…what if evidence were found linking Red to Faye's murder." He laughed. "I don't care if he didn't do it. You worry about getting the ball rolling on the paperwork, and I'll handle things here. Okay, good. Oh, and Frank, I heard the sheriff is planning to fly in tomorrow, so be sure to have the papers ready to send with him. I want to be here when he serves Red.

There's nothing I enjoy more than seeing a man's expression when the realization of impending doom hits. I'll let you go. You have lots of work to get done before morning." He hung up the phone, stood, and whistled a tune as he walked across the cabin. It looked as though he was going to leave, but halfway across the great room he made a left turn, opened Red's bedroom door, and walked inside.

Nathan pushed his door wider, craning to see through the doorway opposite his. When the commissioner walked out of view, Nathan crept out, snuck across, and tucked behind Red's open door. Snuggling against the wall, he peered through the crack, watching as the commissioner rummaged through Red's closet. Taking his phone from his pocket, Nathan touched the video symbol and held it up against the narrow opening.

"Ah, perfect," the commissioner said, lifting a dirty shirt from the laundry basket and carrying it into the adjoining bathroom.

A few moments later, Nathan heard the approach of clicking heels and dove for cover. Peeking around the end of the sofa, he watched the grinning man walk out of Red's bedroom with a shirt tucked under his arm.

"Thank God for technology," Nathan muttered as he slid his finger over the stop record on his phone and shoved it into his pocket. Then he ran to his bedroom, grabbed his sunglasses off the bed, and rushed to the front door. He peered out and when he saw that the path leading to the lodge was empty, he opened the door wide enough to stick his head out and spotted the commissioner lumbering toward the guest cabins.

The commissioner stepped onto the porch of the first building—Faye's cabin. When he found the door locked, he walked around to the back.

Nathan closed the door behind him, ran down the path, and slipped onto the front porch of the Nez Perce cabin. He crouched down, and peered through the corner of the window. From his location, he had a clear view of the commissioner entering the bedroom through the back door. He watched as the portly man paused to close the blade on the pocketknife he had used to force the lock, sliding it into his pant pocket as he walked into the bedroom.

Nathan used his phone to record the commissioner laying Red's shirt across the blood on the floor near the bathroom door. Next, he saw him pull a folded tissue from his pocket as he walked to the head of the bed and out of view.

Nathan quickly moved to the other side of the window, where he could just barely see the pudgy hands sprinkling something on the bed. "Oh, aren't you the clever bastard. So that's what you were doing in Red's bathroom—collecting hair from his brush." He pushed the zoom button on his phone, enlarging the picture on the bed, cutting the commissioner out of view as he tried to catch the falling hair on video. As he made the picture smaller again, something caught his eye.

"What's that?" Nathan zoomed in on an object lying under the bed. He stared at the item, but couldn't make it out. "Shoot, I got off target." He turned the video back to normal, but the commissioner was no longer in sight. Nathan lowered his phone, and put his face against the window, blocking the light with his hand. "Where is that nasty bastard?"

"If you're thinking of becoming a Peeping Tom, you chose the wrong profession," Commissioner Reynolds said as he grabbed Nathan from behind and shoved him up against the door of the cabin.

"Let me go!" Nathan shouted, struggling to break free of his grasp.

The commissioner pressed against him, flattening Nathan against the door. "I'll take that." He grabbed the phone from Nathan's hand and threw him onto the cement floor of the porch. Phone in hand, he turned and strode across the path and down the few yards to the bank of the river.

Nathan struggled to his feet, rubbing his bruised arm as he rushed after him. "No!" he shouted as the commissioner threw his phone into the river.

Commissioner Reynolds turned and grinned at him. "That'll teach you to play with the big boys." The slope was gentle, but it was enough to make the commissioner huff as he made his way up the bank.

Nathan stood on the path, flushed with anger. "I don't need my phone to tell them what I saw. Tampering with evidence is a criminal offense, and I'd be more than happy to testify against you."

The commissioner's laugh was menacing. "Stupid boy. Who do you think is more believable, the pillar of the community, or a snot-nosed delinquent?" He rubbed his chin. "Let's see now. How should I tell it? I know—Sheriff, I was out walking off my grief when low and behold, I saw this young man break into Faye's cabin. To my horror, I watched him lay a man's shirt in my darling departed wife's blood, and then he sprinkled something over her bed." He clutched his chest dramatically. "As if the pain of losing my sweet Faye weren't bad enough, this disrespectful heathen has to go and taint the very place she breathed her last breath. It's shameful, that's what it is." He stepped close to Nathan and poked a finger in his chest. "You should never enter a battle of wits unarmed, boy."

Nathan stared at the commissioner for a moment before shoving his hand away. "I'm not afraid of you."

Eye to eye, the commissioner smirked when Nathan's angry expression turned to surprise. "That's my sweet thirty-eight tickling your ribs. It's not a big gun, but it's enough to blow a good-sized hole in you."

Nathan stepped back with his hands up. "Don't shoot."

"Now there's a good boy." The commissioner gave Nathan's cheek two soft pats and a third one hard enough to make him flinch. "You might be hot stuff where you come from, but here, you're nothing more than a pathetic pissant that no one would think twice about me squashing. Any good politician knows how to spin stories in his favor, and I'm not just good at it, I'm great." He raised the gun, pointing it to Nathan's head. "You open your mouth about what you just saw, and I'll shoot you between the eyes." He shrugged, adding, "In self-defense, of course."

"You crazy bastard!"

The commissioner looked smug. "Big talk for a punk-ass with a gun aimed at his head. You really don't get the self-preservation thing, do you, kid?" He considered for a moment. "Maybe I'll just shoot you and feed you to the hogs like that miserable Chinese cook."

"So, you know about Lee?"

"Boy, I make it my business to know everything."

"Maybe you know about Lee because you're the one who murdered him."

"Too bad you'll never know."

Beyond the commissioner, Nathan caught sight of Jake as he peered around the corner of the Nez Perce cabin. Jake signaled for him to stop staring, and Nathan quickly turned his eyes back on the commissioner.

The commissioner shook his head. "You don't actually think me stupid enough to fall for the 'look behind you' gag? Nice try, but I'm quite aware that everyone else is at the lodge. And since I have a clear view of the path leading from there, I'd be the first to know if anyone were to be heading this way."

Jake crept from the corner, sneaking up the path behind the commissioner. As he narrowed the distance, he signaled Nathan to break to his right. Then he bent low and rushed Commissioner Reynolds, ramming into him as Nathan lunged for the brush along the path.

A shot fired from the commissioner's gun as he fell on his face.

Startled, Nathan crawled through the brush and crouched behind the cover of a tree.

Jake jumped on the commissioner, wrestled the gun from his hand, and tossed it aside. Pulling his belt from his waist, he tied the commissioner's hands together behind his back. "Nathan, you can stop hiding now. I've got him." Jake stood, leaving the commissioner lying face down on the ground. "You're safe."

Nathan got to his feet and came to stand next to Jake.

"You mind telling me what this idiot was doing in a locked crime scene?" Jake asked, giving the commissioner's rump a kick with his foot.

"Here now, that's enough of that," Red said as he rapidly walked down the path with Bud and Woody. "What in tarnation is goin' on here?"

"I came late to the party, so I'm not all that sure," Jake said. "I was coming from the barn when I saw Commissioner Jackass here come out the back door of the Nez Perce cabin. By the time I got over here, he had a gun pointed in Nathan's face."

Red turned to Nathan. "And what were you doin' here? As I recall, your orders were to come directly to the lodge after your shower."

"I meant to, but then the commissioner came into your cabin and made a couple interesting phone calls."

"Eavesdropping again?" Red looked annoyed.

"This time, I think you'll be happy I did. I heard him talking to his girlfriend about how glad he is that his wife was murdered. Then he called a lawyer and told him to draw up papers suing you for the wrongful death of Faye. And there was something about using your ranch in a federal land-swap deal. I was going to tell you all this, but then he told the lawyer he was going to frame you for the murder. So I took a video of him planting evidence in the cabin. You'll find your shirt lying in a pool of blood, and he sprinkled your hair on the bed."

Red turned his piercing eyes on the commissioner. "Get him on his feet."

Bud and Woody grabbed the commissioner by the crook of his tied arms and pulled him up.

"I've underestimated the depth of low you will sink to." Red stared darkly at the commissioner.

"You can't believe anything a delinquent says," the commissioner said. "He was the one planting evidence on you. I was just trying to stop him."

"That's not true, and if I can find my phone, I'll prove it." Nathan rushed down the bank to the river.

"Where are you going?" Jake asked.

"He threw my phone in the river."

"Don't bother searching. It's ruined by now," Red said.

"No, it's not," Nathan said, pausing to look back at Red. "It's waterproof." He pulled his shirt over his head, kicked his shoes off, and removed his socks and jeans.

As Nathan tiptoed into the water, Red turned to investigate the sounds coming from the path behind him. He scowled at Sean, Carlos, and Noah as they ran up. Behind them, Carlton lumbered at his usual slow pace, and beyond him, Edith gave chase with her shotgun cradled in her arms.

"Dammit, Edith, I told you they weren't to leave the lodge."

"I tried to stop them," Edith said. She stopped beside Sean, placed a hand on his shoulder, and bent to catch her breath. "Goodness gracious, I think my heart is near ready to sprout legs and run off on its own."

Edith looked up at the foul expression on Red's face. "Don't you blame me none for this. I told them boys a smart person never runs toward a gunshot—he runs away. But they couldn't contain their curiosity no better than a cat." She stood up straight, placed a hand on her hip, and glared at the boys standing around her. "And you know what killed that damn cat—curiosity, that's what. Oh my," she said when she saw the commissioner standing with his hands tied behind his back. "Well now, this is certainly a turn of events. Looks like I was smart to come armed." She aimed the gun at the commissioner. "I knew you weren't no good. Just try and make a wrong move, bucko, and I'll see to it you'll be pickin' buckshot out of your ass 'til Christmas."

Red fought a smile when he saw Bud and Woody take a step

away from the commissioner. "Wise move." He nodded to his men as he turned to walk down to the riverbank.

Nathan was wearing nothing but boxer shorts and sunglasses as he waded through the thigh-high water.

"Where was he standin' when he threw it?" Red asked as he came to a stop along the water's edge.

"Right about where you are," Nathan replied.

"Did you see where it landed?"

"Yeah, somewhere out in the center."

Red looked at the campers on the path. "Any of you boys have a cell phone on you?"

All four pulled phones from their pockets and held them up.

"Are any of them the same brand as Nathan's?"

"Mine is," Noah said.

"Well, bring it on down here and let's have a look."

Noah raced down the bank and handed his phone to Red.

"Watch and see how far the current takes it as it sinks," Red said, throwing the phone close to Nathan.

Noah sucked in a breath. "My phone!"

Red looked down at the stricken expression on Noah's face. "Don't worry. We'll be able to find it with Lee's metal detector if we have to."

"It's not that."

"You said it was like Nathan's. So what's the problem?"

"Same brand, but different model. His is waterproof."

"And yours isn't?"

"Nope."

Red looked out over the river. "That is a problem. But at least you learned a lesson from it."

Noah looked confused.

"Now maybe you can sympathize with the feelings of your fellow campers. Not much fun in havin' your things taken from you, is there?"

"No, there sure isn't." Noah looked sheepishly down at his feet. "I know it was a bonehead thing to do. And I promise I won't be stealing ever again, not from anyone." He rolled a pebble with his foot. "I started stealing to get back at people who picked on me, but these guys weren't that bad. Well, maybe Nathan, if I hadn't had Carlton to protect me, but the others not so much. And then I had to go and kick Carlton in the nuts after he was good to me. I'm such an idiot." He turned and looked at his large friend. "I'd do anything to make it up to him."

"Just make sure you aren't tradin' one bad habit for another."

"Yeah, sorry I lied about the tire. I thought it was my turn to stand up for Carlton for a change."

"Ah, it's all water under the bridge now. I'll tell you what. I read you can draw the moisture out of a cell phone by placing it in rice. We'll give that a try after we find it. Maybe we can save your phone after all."

"I got it!" Nathan shouted, waving Noah's phone in the air. "The current made it drift about ten feet from where it went in."

"Okay, you stand where you think it dropped." Red looked at Noah. "You up for helpin' him out?"

"Sure!" Noah bounced on one foot as he pulled his shoe and sock off the other. He repeated the process with the other foot, yanked his shirt off, tossed it on the pebble-covered bank, and followed with his jeans.

Nathan pointed to where Noah needed to search.

"The rest of you want in on this hunt?" Red called up to the other campers. He watched Sean and Carlos shed their clothes as they ran down to the river and jumped in wearing only boxers. Carlton, on the other hand, sauntered slowly, pausing on the bank to kick his shoes and socks off. He stuffed the socks in his shoes and set the pair neatly together. Then he rolled his pant legs up under the knee and walked into the water.

"There's a different tempo beating on that boy's drum,"

Woody said, stopping beside Red.

"I asked for his help. I didn't say what speed." Red watched the boys walk tenderly across the rock-covered riverbed.

Woody tossed his head in the direction of Commissioner Reynolds. "What do you want us to do with his eminence?"

"He can cool his heels until we're done here. Then we'll take him to the lodge and strap him in a chair until the sheriff gets here in the mornin'."

Woody followed Red's gaze to the boys searching the river. "You believe the kid?"

"No reason not to." Red glanced back to the path where the commissioner now sat on a stump with Edith standing guard behind him. "What Nathan relayed of his phone conversations rings all too likely."

"I believe him too. I took a look through the cabin window and your shirt is right where Nathan claimed the commissioner put it. Of course, the commissioner will tell the sheriff the boy put it there."

Anger deepened the lines across Red's forehead. "Reynold's is an accomplished liar, and a hypocritical, self-absorbed bastard. But there's one area the underhanded crook hasn't perfected."

"What's that?"

"Breaking and entering." Red glanced back at the captured man again. "You see any gloves on those stubby little fingers?"

"Nope, sure don't."

"He had to touch the knob in order to get in."

"Yeah, but he'll just cover that with another cockamamie story. I wouldn't be surprised if he claimed he went by earlier and tried the door. And when no prints are found to be Nathan's, he'll say he saw him wipe them off. It's hard to keep ahead of a pathological liar."

"That's why we need to find Nathan's phone. If there really is a video, it'll be damn impossible for him to dig his way out of that one."

Woody began to turn, hesitating at the sight of Edith holding her gun on the commissioner. "You want me to take that gun from Edith? I know her aim isn't all that good."

Red reached in his pocket and pulled out two shotgun shells. "No need. I unloaded it while her back was turned in the kitchen." He shoved them back in his pocket. "No reason for the commissioner to know that."

"I got it!" Sean shouted, waving Nathan's phone in the air.

"Well done. Bring it on up here, boy," Red called.

Sean rushed up the bank and handed the dripping phone to Red. "What's so important about the phone?"

Red wiped it on his sleeve. "Hopefully, it holds the rope for the commissioner to hang from."

CHAPTER 26

"Keep walkin'," Edith said, poking the commissioner's back with the muzzle of her gun. "You're a horrible excuse of a human bein', that's for sure." She poked him again. "No one picks on one of my boys and gets away with it, no, sir."

"You think she'd actually shoot him?" Sean whispered to Carlos as they walked behind Edith and her prisoner.

"I'm pretty sure she would," Carlos replied.

Nathan stepped off the path, leaving the other campers to go on without him. As Jake walked by, he fell in beside him. "What you did back there. Thanks, dude. I would have been toast if you hadn't come along."

Jake gave Nathan a sideways glance. "Save it. It's not like we're going to become buddies just because I did what Red would expect of me."

"You really like him, don't you?"

"Not so much like as respect. With the way you two have become hinged at the hip, it appears your attitude has changed toward him as well."

"He's beginning to grow on me." Nathan held his index finger and thumb a centimeter apart. "But only about that much." He gave Jake a grin but got none in return. "Don't get me wrong, I still think he's from another planet. But I have discovered that there might be more to the crusty old coot than he likes people to think. What's your deal with him?"

Jake shrugged. "He was there for me when no one else was."

"The whole ignorant cowboy thing doesn't get on your

nerves?"

"Ignorant?" Jake repeated, finally turning to look at Nathan. "Man, you sure know how to underestimate people. I would have thought the commissioner would have taught you a lesson about that." He laughed. "You really are a slow learner, aren't you?"

Leaving Nathan to walk alone, Jake stopped to wait for the men following them at a leisurely pace. "You think the phone will work after being in the water?"

"Well, since you're probably much more tech savvy than I am, why don't you give it a try?" Red handed Jake the phone.

Jake ran his finger across the phone, turning it on. "It's working. I would have lost a bet on that one. All we need is Nathan's password."

"Nathan, what's your password?" Red called up the path.

Nathan stopped and looked back at them. "Seven-eight-eight-three."

"Get the cotton out of your mouth, boy, we can't hear you," Red scolded.

"Just spell out the word *stud*," Nathan shouted.

Jake rolled his eyes and touched the numbers corresponding to the letters. "It figures that would be his password."

As the screen filled with colorful symbols, he found the one for videos and touched it with his finger. Jake scrolled through the clips, tapping the last one taken, and started it. "It's here, but it's hard to see in this light." He moved the phone in different positions and squinted at the screen. When the video stopped, he touched the arrow and played it again. "I don't think you'll be able to make this out until you get inside." He turned the phone off and handed it to Red.

Walking ahead of the men, Jake turned onto the path leading to the back door of the kitchen.

"Where are you goin'?" Red asked as he and the men stayed on the path taking them around to the front of the lodge.

"I'm starved and the way things are going we'll be lucky if

we get fed by 10:00 tonight. The smell of fresh-baked bread is calling to my stomach. I'm gonna sneak me a piece before Edith gets back to the kitchen."

"You better not let her catch you, or the commissioner won't be the only one bound to a chair."

"WELL, YOU'VE BEEN VERY busy, haven't you, Commissioner?" Red said, watching Nathan's video from one of the stuffed chairs in the gathering room. He brought the phone closer to his face, squinting at the screen. "What's this that you zoomed in on?" he asked Nathan, who was leaning against the cold fireplace.

Nathan stepped over Tan Dog lying stretched out on the floor.

Red turned the phone around and held it up for Nathan to see.

"That's just the ceiling on the cabin porch. It's when he jumped me."

Red turned the phone around and saw that the video was frozen. "No. Not that. How do you run this thing back?" He handed the phone to Nathan and watched him touch the screen. "I need the spot where you widened the shot on the bedroom."

Nathan replayed the video, pausing where it zoomed in. "You mean under the bed? I'm not sure what that was." He turned to look at the angry-faced commissioner, who sat in a corner with his hands and feet tied to a wooden chair. "Whatever it is, he's probably the one that dropped it." He ran the video back and watched it again. "I think it might be a keychain, but I'm not sure."

"Go ahead and shut it off," Red said. "I wouldn't want to lose the video to the battery goin' dead."

"There's plenty of charge left. And it'll be there until it's deleted anyway." Nathan shut off the phone and handed it back to Red.

"If the object under the bed doesn't belong to the commissioner, it might have been left behind by the killer," Woody said from the other stuffed chair.

"What if they're one and the same?" asked Nathan, tossing his head in the commissioner's direction. "Porky the Politician has the motive. And from what he was saying on the phone, he's been messing with you for a long time. My theory is when his tactics failed to close the ranch, he turned to the one thing he knew would—murder. But even after Lee was killed, the ranch didn't close, so he offed the wife he was about to divorce. With a second murder, the sheriff couldn't do anything but close the ranch down. Framing you for Faye's murder was his insurance policy in case the whole thing started to go south."

"I wasn't anywhere near the ranch when Lee or Faye were killed, you stupid little punk!" the red-faced commissioner shouted.

"You wouldn't have to be here to hire it done." Nathan shrugged. "Cowards like you don't get their hands dirty. They hire someone else to do it."

"Keep talkin', city boy. I'm sure your daddy will love paying for a slander lawsuit. As for the rest of you, I hope you don't have plans for the next few years. False imprisonment carries a three-year sentence in the federal pen."

Bud calmly got up from the couch along the back wall and pulled the handkerchief free from around his neck as he walked to the corner. "I don't know about the rest of you, but I've heard enough of his jackass dribble." He gagged the commissioner, tying the handkerchief tightly at the back of his head, and leaned down into his face. "The salty taste of the gag comes from honest sweat. I'm sure you wouldn't recognize that for yourself." Bud gave the commissioner's cheek a pat before walking across the room to a collection of guns on a table. He scanned the weapons and began setting the appropriate ammunition next to each.

"I can agree with Nathan about the commissioner's

motives." Red stood. "And I also agree that if he had anything to do with this, he probably had help. But the thing I don't understand is why he'd feed Lee's body to the hogs? If the intent was to use a murder to get the ranch closed down, wouldn't it make sense to leave the body where it would easily be found?"

"Maybe the murderer messed up when he killed Lee and had to get rid of the body because there was evidence that could lead back to him," Nathan speculated.

"Evidence is exactly what we need," said Red. "And hopefully that's what we'll find in the cabin." He turned and called to the campers watching from the dining hall doorway, "Is Jake in there?"

"Yeah, I'm here." Jake shoved the last of a piece of bread in his mouth as he walked through the campers.

Looking hostile, Edith scolded, "Someone's been helping himself to a snack. I ought to get me a strap and tan your hide for gettin' into my bread." Fuming, she turned around and headed for the kitchen. "Land sakes alive! A woman can't turn her back for a bloody minute around here. I best protect the rest before another one of you two-legged varmints gets into it. Lord knows it's damn impossible to make food fast enough to keep up with you boys."

Red waited until he heard the kitchen door swing shut. Then he looked at Jake. "You help the men finish loading guns. The rest of you get to helping Edith with dinner. And no nibblin'."

"Where are you going?" Jake asked as Red walked to the front door.

"Nathan and I need to take a look under Faye's bed."

The sound of creaking hinges made Tan Dog jump up and race to beat Nathan through the door Red held.

"She doesn't like to miss anything, does she?" Nathan said, walking off the porch with Red.

"I wouldn't say much gets past her," Red replied. As they neared the Nez Perce cabin, Tan Dog was already coming back off the porch with her nose to the ground.

"She's caught a scent." Red stepped out of her way as she ran back toward the lodge, sniffing madly. "Glad she's preoccupied. Tan Dog has a tendency to get her feelin's hurt when she's shut out from anywhere I happen to be. And the last thing I need is a dog tracking through the killer's footprints. Jake and Billy already did a bang-up job of that." He unlocked the door, pushed it open, and threw a hand across Nathan, stopping him from entering. "You watch yourself as well. Step nowhere but right where I step."

"Why don't we go in through the back where it's clear of blood?"

"We don't need to add more prints to those already there."

Nathan followed him through the door, only taking a few steps before bumping into Red when he stopped abruptly. "What's wrong?"

Red chewed on his pipe as he stared down. He pointed to the boot prints running along the trail of dried blood. "Those weren't here earlier. Someone's been in here since I locked it up."

"Duh, it was the commissioner."

"All right, genius, take a good look at the tracks and tell me what you see."

"They're cowboy boots."

Red groaned. "Now it's my turn to say duh. Take a closer look. The commissioner wore brand spankin' new boots with a rounded toe and traction clips on the heels. The tracks here show a boot with sharp pointed toes and no heel clips. And then there's the direction. Which way would you say the tracks are heading?"

"From the bedroom to the front door," Nathan said.

"Did the commissioner come out through the front door?"

"No, I was at the front, he had to have gone out the…oh." Nathan looked confused. "I don't get it. If these are the killer's prints, why would he come back?"

"I don't know, but I've got a nagging feelin' in my gut, and that's never a good thing. Come on. We'll go across to the other side of the cabin and shoot through the bathroom."

He led Nathan across the living area, stepping on the beaver skin that lay between the fireplace and wooden rocking chairs. This side of the cabin was an exact mirror of the other with a bed area and a door to the shared bath. They made a right turn into the bathroom and crossed to the doorway on the opposite side.

"How good's your jump?" Red asked.

"Why?"

"I need you to jump over the blood and land on the clean floor in the bedroom."

"That's only a couple of yards. I should be able to make it."

"Then give it a whirl."

Nathan jumped through the doorway, coming down near the end of the bed. His toes landed in the clear, but the rest of his feet were another matter. He circled his arms madly as he fought to keep from setting his heels down in the blood.

"Boy, watch where you place those clown feet of yours."

"I'm trying," Nathan said, finally falling forward.

"That was one lousy landing." Red groaned. "There won't be any gymnastics in your future."

"At least I made it. Now let's see you do it, old man." Nathan got to his feet.

You're damn lucky to be out of my reach, or I'd give that smart mouth a swat. "I don't see the need for both of us to crawl under the bed. You got that sandwich bag I gave you earlier?"

"Yeah." Nathan pulled the bag from his pocket and dropped to his knees. He disappeared from view for a moment before raising his head up to look at Red.

"What's the problem? You should fit easily under there."

"It's not here," Nathan said, tucking his head down to look under the bed again. "Whatever it was, I guess we know it didn't belong to the commissioner."

"Well, ain't that just a kick in the head," Red grumbled. "Someone sure didn't want us seeing it. Most likely because it would tell us exactly who the killer is."

"But...then it would have to be something you'd seen the person with."

"Bingo. And that means it belongs to someone I know quite well. The most disturbing question is whether this person knew we saw the object on the video, or whether he simply discovered he'd lost it and went back to get it? I hope it's the latter, because it makes my skin crawl to think the killer could have close enough to hear our conversation." Red took his hat off and rubbed his pounding forehead. "Damn, if that don't beat all." He placed his hat back on his head and stared across the room at the blood-stained wall. "Did you catch the name of that fella the commissioner was talkin' with on the phone?" he asked as his eyes traveled down to the sticky footprints that ran from the bed to the front door.

"I only heard him call him Frank. I didn't hear a last name."

"Frank," Red repeated. "I know five or six people by that name, but none of them are lawyers."

"It couldn't be him anyway. I'm sure the commissioner was calling the lawyer at his office. Besides, cell phones don't work up here, so he couldn't have been lurking anywhere nearby."

"True. Unless..."

"Unless?"

"Never mind, just thinkin' out loud." Red stared down at one of the prints. "Can your phone take decent indoor pictures?"

"Sure. Do you want me to take pictures of the crime scene?"

"That's not a bad idea, but what I really want is a clear picture of that boot print over there." He pointed to where the blood covered a large area of the floor on Faye's side of the bed. "There's something about that print that I'd like to see up close."

"I'm not sure how close I can get without stepping in the

blood." Nathan hung on to the short corner post on the bed and tried to lean out over the floor.

"Why is it that when there are two ways of doing somethin', you always choose the hardest?"

"Huh?"

"The corner of the bed next to you doesn't have any blood on it, right?"

"Yeah, so?"

"Do me a favor and slap yourself on the back of the head. With any luck, it'll rattle your sleeping brain cells awake."

Nathan looked down at the bed. Then his face lit up in realization. "Oh, I get it." He crawled across the corner diagonally and stretched his arms out over the side. He snapped a picture, checked it, and took another. "Got it." He rolled off the bed and proceeded to take pictures of the wall, bed, and trail of blood. "It looks like he came in through the back door, grabbed whatever was under the bed, and ran out the front door."

"It makes sense, since there's less of a chance of him being seen going out the front. Well, I guess there isn't anything we can do here, so you might as well go out the back door. Just be sure and use the sandwich bag as a glove. Try to touch the knob as little as possible, so you don't smear any prints that might be there. And don't touch the outside knob. We should have three sets of outside prints, including Jake's. I don't need you adding yours to the others. We can only hope the killer left his mark on the front door when he went out. Luckily, we left it open. I'll catch you outside."

Nathan picked up the sandwich bag from the floor where he had dropped it earlier and shoved his hand inside. Heeding Red's instructions, he used his bagged hand to open and close the door. Then he ran around to the front of the cabin, where Red was waiting in the shade of the trees.

"Let's have a look at that boot print," Red said.

Nathan took out his phone, pulled up the picture, and

zoomed in on the print made by a boot with a sharply pointed toe.

Red looked over Nathan's shoulder, his eyes narrowing. "Can you enlarge the spot where it looks like a chunk of the heel is missin'?"

Nathan touched the screen and spread his fingers apart, enlarging the pie-shaped area of the print.

Red studied the mark and then nodded.

"Does that mean anything to you?" Nathan asked as he turned off his phone.

"If I find the boot that made those marks, it will. I know the shape is wrong for it to have been made by the commissioner's shiny new boots." Red turned and walked down the path.

Nathan slipped the phone into his pocket and jogged to catch up with Red. "It can't be any of the campers, we all wear sneakers. Do you think it belongs to one of the men?"

"No. To my knowledge, none of the staff have boots with that pointy of a toe. I have to conclude the prints were made by an outsider."

"But you said it had to be someone who knew where Leroy keeps his knife."

"Yeah, and that could be anyone visiting the ranch over the last ten years. Leroy finally admitted he's taken quite a few people to his cabin to show off his blade. The man has a tendency to lose his senses when he's had a few." Red puffed on his pipe, contemplating.

"It's too bad we couldn't make out what the killer left under the bed." Nathan quickened his pace to keep up with Red's long strides. "If it was important enough for him to come back after, it was probably something he knew you'd recognize."

"Yup."

"Now what?"

"Now you go to the lodge and stay with the other campers. The men and I will take it from here."

"But I'm getting kind of good at this investigation stuff. I know I could be of help."

"I've appreciated your help up to this point, but the game has changed. Had I known how wrong I was in thinkin' Lee was murdered by a teenage hiker set on revenge, I would have never involved you in any of this. There is no doubt in my mind that this isn't the work of a random person on a killing spree. Every act of bloodshed has been way too carefully orchestrated. The murdering bastard doesn't simply kill, he means to shock and terrorize. And I don't intend to let him get to any more of my people—including you. Best you can do for me is to stay safe in the lodge with the other campers, while the men and I put a stop to this madness."

"But…"

"This isn't up for debate," Red said as Nathan followed him through the back door into the kitchen.

Tan Dog barked and raced across the kitchen to give Red's hand a quick lick before running back to Sean.

"She was scratchin' at the back door, so I let her in," Edith said from where she stood at the stove, spooning stew into a serving bowl. "She was sniffin' around like a hound after a fox when she first came in, but the smell of cookin' got the best of her and she took to beggin' from the boys. They're havin' a lark seein' how far she'll jump to catch bites of stale bread and cheese. I think they darn near fed her a whole loaf by now."

"Watch this," Sean said, throwing a chunk of cheese up toward the ceiling.

Tan Dog ran and caught the cheese before it hit the ground.

"She hasn't missed one," Noah said, beaming as he tossed her a piece of bread.

"I take it you didn't tell these boys what happens when a dog eats cheese?"

Edith chuckled at Red's frown. "I thought it a lesson best learned for themselves."

"Great, I'll make sure Tan Dog stays in the lodge with all of you tonight."

"That's okay with us," Sean said.

"It won't be." Red walked through the swinging door into the dining hall. A few steps into the room he stopped and turned to discover Nathan following him. "You help the others get dinner on the table." He held a hand up, stopping Nathan before he could protest. "No arguments. Go on. Do what you're told for once."

Nathan turned and slammed his fist into the door, swinging it open.

"Hey, watch it," Carlos shouted as the door nearly knocked the platter out of his hands. He turned and backed through the swinging door, glaring. But his hostility was wasted on Nathan, who was gazing through the open door, watching Red turn into the gathering room.

"Would it be too much to ask for you to pull your head out of your ass?" Carlos snapped when Nathan almost ran into him again as he came back from delivering food to the dining hall.

"What the hell, Nathan?" exclaimed Sean when the door swung back and almost hit the bowl of stew he was carrying.

Ignoring both of them, Nathan walked to the far end of the dining hall and hid behind the corner of the doorway, listening to the men in the gathering room.

As Red walked across the room, he nodded to Joe and Bud talking on the couch and continued on to where Woody was hanging up the telephone on the end table.

Jake got up, giving his seat in the stuffed chair to Red.

"There you are," Woody said. "I was just about to go look for you. That was the sheriff on the phone. He said the Union County sheriff's deputies picked Leroy up at Moss Springs, but Billy wasn't anywhere to be found."

"What?" Red said. "Oh holy hell!"

"Leroy told them that somewhere along the end of the ride he looked back and Billy was gone. The people they were guiding out didn't notice when he dropped off from his position at the end of the string. If he doubled back, I would think he'd be here by now."

Red groaned. "What does it take to get that boy to do what he's told? He's as bad as Nathan, and here he's supposed to be a mentor to the younger boys. When I get my hands on him…"

"Dinner's served," Edith called, startling Nathan. He turned and saw her wink at him. "That's one of my favorite spots for eavesdroppin'," she whispered. "I find if you have a cleanin' rag in your hand, no one gives you no mind. You might wanna give that a try next time." She gave his arm a pat.

Nathan watched her walk back into the kitchen. "God, she's so weird."

"But she's a lot better snoop than you are," Red said, making him jump for a second time. "You keep this up and I'm gonna nail a bell to your ass."

Nathan flushed.

"Go get some grub before it gets cold. And when you're done, grab a bucket and rag. You'll be scrubbin' the dining room floor on your knees."

"On my knees?"

"Good, you heard me. Jake will stand watch to make sure you get it done right."

Nathan muttered obscenities as he walked to where the campers were taking seats around a table nearest the kitchen door.

Red motioned Joe to follow his men to a table on the opposite end of the dining hall. He sat between Joe and Jake and began filling his plate along with the others.

Woody raised a brow at Red as he passed the bowl of stew across the table. "You do know we have a mop?"

"Sure, but I'm hopin' sore knees might help to slow him down a bit." Red glanced over his shoulder to Nathan, who sat silently staring down at his plate, ignoring the conversations of the other boys. "The kid is hell-bent on sleuthing after the killer. Thinks himself a Sherlock Holmes, and that in itself is troubling. The fact that he doesn't have a lick of reasoning is just plain dangerous."

"Earth to Nathan, come in, Nathan," Sean said when Nathan didn't respond to his request to pass the milk.

"Sean wants the milk, Nathan," Noah said. Receiving no response, Noah looked at Carlton.

Carlton shrugged.

"I know how to get his attention." Carlos threw a spoon, hitting Nathan in the head. "Wake up, idiot."

Nathan rubbed his head and glared at Carlos. "You could ask."

"We did," Sean and Carlos sang in unison.

Nathan picked up the pitcher of milk and slammed it down in the middle of the table, splashing milk across the surface. "There's your stupid milk."

Surprised, Sean and Carlos jumped up from their chairs before the spilt milk flowed into their laps.

"What's with him anyway?" Carlos asked, watching Nathan storm into the kitchen.

"I'm not sure," Sean said, watching the stream of milk flow onto the floor. "If I didn't know better, I'd say it's his time of the month.

CHAPTER 27

"What did Harold have to say?" Woody asked as Red hung up the telephone in the gathering room after dinner.

"Something very interesting." Red scanned the faces of Bud, Woody and Joe. "Harold said one of his guests refused to leave his place. The man's been quite a loner. Other than his Los Angeles address, Harold doesn't know much about him. He always requests sack lunches, then disappears until after dark and takes his dinner in his room. Harold said that when he first got to his lodge, he had lots of questions about my ranch and how to get around on trails."

"How long has he been there?" Bud asked, getting up from his chair to stoke the fire.

"Six days, which gave him plenty of time to study the activity of our people, and wait for opportunities to cause the havoc he's thrown our way."

"That makes sense." Bud set the poker in the fireplace stand, and turned a scowl on the gagged commissioner sitting tied in the corner chair. "He could very well be the commissioner's henchman."

"And the killer," Woody added as Bud returned to his chair next to him. "So when do you want to ride over and have a chat with this mysterious man?"

"If he's true to form, he won't be back to the lodge until after dark. In the meantime, Harold has agreed to open his room for us."

"What do you want to do about getting our prisoner fed?"

Bud asked, looking at commissioner.

"I think he could stand to go a few hours without eating," Woody huffed. "Tell him to think of it as one of those pricey weight-loss spas. We'll add the service to his bill."

Red nodded. "Woody's right. He won't waste away overnight. And I'm not feelin' all that hospitable toward him." He turned to Joe. "Would you mind keeping an eye on him while we're gone?"

"Not as long as his restraints are tight,"

"I can make sure of that," Woody said. "Duct tape and zip ties should do the job. I'll see to making sure that devil is tied up tighter than a tick."

Red watched Woody go through the lodge front door. "I think our astronauts were damn lucky Woody didn't work on shuttle maintenance. If he had, they'd likely be shot into outer space with nothin' more than duct tape and zip ties holdin' their rocket together."

"YOU MISSED A SPOT," Carlos said, laughing.

"Maybe you'd like to come closer and show me where." Nathan glared across the dining room at him.

"Sorry, pal, I'm about to win this hand." Carlos laid his cards on the game table, grinning at his fellow poker players. "Read 'em and weep, boys."

"Ah crap." Sean threw his cards down. "What are you, some kind of card shark?"

"I think we should check his sleeves," Noah said, turning to Carlton. "Better yet, why don't you turn him upside down and give him a good shake."

"I'm not cheating. I'm just really good." Carlos collected the cards from around the table and shuffled them. "I was doing real well in Reno until a friend of my father's caught me playing blackjack and snitched me off to my dad."

"Bet that didn't go well," said Sean.

"Let's just say my ass was grass, and my dad was the lawn

mower." He groaned. "Really wish he hadn't put my fake ID through the shredder. Man, I miss being Francisco Mendez." He laughed. "What a great name."

"Hey, guys, come here," Nathan said, staring at the floor.

"Right, like we're gonna fall for that," Carlos said, fanning the cards across the table. "You're not going to con us in to helping you clean the floor."

"Cool," Noah said as Carlos made the cards stream back and forth in a wave.

"No, really, come here and look at this," Nathan insisted. "Red and I saw these same tracks in Faye's cabin."

"What are you talking about?" Sean asked as he jumped up from the table.

"I'm telling you, I think the killer has been in this room, and recently."

The boys rushed to see the print Nathan was pointing at.

"These are the same prints Red showed me in Faye's cabin. The killer had to have tracked through the milk we spilled."

"We?" Sean repeated. "As Red would say, you got a rat in your pocket?"

Nathan looked annoyed. "Okay, the milk I spilled. Would you just take a look at this?"

"So it's a boot print," said Carlos. "How can you possibly tell it from all the others worn on this ranch?"

"Because the notch in the heel leaves a mark." Nathan pointed to the wedge-shaped imprint tracked across the floor toward the dining hall fireplace.

"Well, it's none of us," Carlos said, looking around at everyone's feet. "We're all wearing sneakers."

"Then it has to be one of the staff," said Sean.

"What about the pilot?" Noah whispered, nervously glancing at the entryway to the gathering room.

Nathan shook his head. "He's wearing work boots, not cowboy boots. The soles would leave a waffle pattern and the toes are rounded. Cowboy boots look like these prints, smooth on the bottom and more pointed in the toe. But none of the men have toes this sharp."

"The commissioner is wearing cowboy boots," Carlos said, bending to look at the tracks.

Nathan shook his head. "No, the prints are wrong, and he's been tied to the chair since before the milk spilled."

Jake walked through the swinging door, frowning. "What are you pissants doing now? Watching the floor dry?"

"Geez, what crawled up your ass?" Sean asked.

"The fact that I have to waste my time babysitting a bunch of teenage rejects when I should be out with the men." Jake looked around the circle of boys crouching on the floor. "What the hell are you doing anyway?"

"We found the killer's prints," Noah said.

"What?" Jake walked to the boys.

While the others stood around the old prints, a bewildered Nathan was staring down at the new ones made by Jake's boots as he crossed the wet floor. "It was you! You killed Lee and Faye!"

"What are you talking about?" Jake asked, looking equally perplexed. "Are you out of your..." But before he could say more, someone growled behind him.

"Lee was my friend!" Carlton shouted as he slammed into Jake, knocking him back against the wall.

Jake rubbed his sore ribs with one hand and held off Carlton with the other. "Wait! You've got this all wrong. I didn't kill anyone."

"Your boots tell a different story," said Nathan.

"My boots?"

"Yeah, your boots, asshole." Nathan sneered. "Red and I found your prints in Faye's cabin when you went back to get whatever it was that you left under the bed."

"Look, I haven't been in Faye's cabin since going after Billy this morning, and I didn't leave anything there. I did walk through here earlier, but these boots aren't mine. They're Billy's and I've only been wearing them for a few minutes." Jake pulled the leg of his jeans up, exposing the hand-tooled and ornately painted tops of the boots. "These are the Black Jack ostrich boots he only wears for special occasions. I can't even begin to afford fancy shit kickers like these. I only borrowed them because the whole side of one of my boots just busted out, and I had to have something to wear on my feet. They were just sitting at the end of his bed, and I didn't think he'd mind me wearing them, so long as I weren't doing anything that would tear them up."

"What about the cut in the heel?" Carlos asked. "If Billy is so careful with them, how did he get that?"

Jake looked exasperated. "I don't know. How about you clowns ask Billy the next time you see him? Red said he's on his way back. He'll probably come looking for grub the minute he gets in, so you can ask him then."

"Unless he's trying to keep from being seen." Nathan turned his gaze to Jake. "He might have thought there was a chance Red would recognize marks made by his everyday boots. If that's the case, wearing the dress boots where he knew he'd be tracking through blood would have been a wise move to make."

Jake rolled his eyes. "I tell you, he's not that smart. You can't seriously be thinking Billy is a killer. Besides, if he was, and he thought someone was on to him, don't you think he'd want to get out of here? Why would he come back to the ranch?"

"Maybe he remembered something else that could point to his guilt, or maybe he isn't done killing." All eyes set on Nathan. "Hey, this murdering bastard is as nuts as they come, I wouldn't put anything past him."

"But when was Billy alone long enough to get into Faye's cabin?" Sean asked. "Wasn't someone watching his every move this afternoon?"

Carlos frowned at the heel marks. "You know how unaware Leroy is. Billy could have easily snuck off from saddling horses and old guy would never know it."

"Or he could have doubled back soon after hitting the trail with Leroy," Noah said. "No one knows when he dropped off from behind the pack string."

Sean glared down at the tracks. "I always thought there was something off about Billy."

"Oh, come on," Jake exclaimed. "You don't actually see Billy as a killer. He doesn't have the guts to cut someone up. He'd be tossing his cookies before he made it through the first slice. Believe me, I know Billy's a goof-off and a king-sized idiot, but he's no murderer. Heck, I've even had to kill spiders for him."

"Then who wore the boots?" Carlton asked.

"It could have been anyone. Like I said, he keeps them at the end of his bed. You ever think that maybe someone's trying to frame him?" He turned to Nathan. "The knife was in with your stuff before Noah took it. Does that make you a killer?"

"Yeah, I get it," said Nathan.

"Well, we know it wasn't Carlton," Sean said. "His feet would never fit in those boots."

"Red believes it isn't anyone we know," Jake said, calming. "He, Bud, and Woody are on their way to the check out a suspicious guest staying at the Minam Lodge. They believe he might be the commissioner's minion."

"Shouldn't they wait for the sheriff?" Noah asked. "If he's the killer, it could be dangerous to go after him."

"They took guns. Besides, Harold said his guest doesn't return until dark." A strange expression suddenly came over Jake. "But that means he could be lurking around the ranch and Billy wouldn't know it. You guys stay here. I've got to find Billy and warn him."

Jake hit the swinging kitchen door with such force it startled Edith. She jumped and held a hand to her chest, watching as he raced across the kitchen, grabbing her shotgun on his way out the door.

Nathan stared hypnotically at the kitchen door as it swung back and forth. "What if the killer *is* Billy?"

"What are you talking about?" Sean asked.

Nathan shook himself from his trance. "Nothing. I'm just talking to myself."

Sean laughed. "Dude, you're getting goofier by the minute."

"What the devil was that all about?" Edith asked as she came through the swinging door, wiping her hands on her apron. "Red told me and Jake to watch over you boys. Now what's got Jake all fired up, and where's he runnin' off to with my gun?"

"He's going to warn Billy that the killer might be close by," Noah replied.

"Oh, Lordy," Edith exclaimed, holding a hand to her bosom again. "I'm sure glad I checked the gun earlier. I loaded that thing to the hilt when I discovered it was empty." Her expression hardened. "I suspect Red had somethin' to do with that. Just like him to leave a poor old woman defenseless to protect her chicks. And now Jake's done run off with the gun. Now, don't you boys worry your noggins over it, Edith has more than one card up her sleeve."

The campers looked at each other and followed her to the gun cabinet in the gathering room. They stood behind her, watching as she pulled kitchen scissors from her apron pocket.

"Aren't scissors a little large for picking a lock?" Nathan asked.

"Who said anything about pickin' a lock?" Edith took her apron off and wrapped it around her hand. "Stand back, boys."

They moved several feet back and watched as Edith covered her eyes with her arm and hit the cabinet window with the handle of the scissors, shattering the glass.

"And here I bet you thought the only thing old Edith's good for is cookin'." Her wide grin showed her missing teeth.

"Actually, I don't think she's all that good at cooking," Sean whispered to Carlton.

Edith freed her hand from her apron, set the scissors on top of the cabinet, and reached for the prized rifle John Wayne had given Red. She cradled the gun in her arms, admiring the pristine wood stock. "If my gun were a broken-down plow mule, this here would be a sleek Thoroughbred." She put it back and took out the old rifle. "But this here will have to do. Red would scalp me if I were to use the Winchester. He's never even fired it."

Edith walked to the corner where the commissioner sat. She stood directly in front of him, glowering. "You might want to shove back in your chair, 'cause your southernmost part is sittin' right where my knee is 'bout to land."

The commissioner's eyes grew round as Edith lifted her leg. He tried to scoot back, but his large body was already taking up every inch of the seat. Panicked by the knee coming at him, he let out a muffled scream and quickly spread his legs apart.

Edith set her knee on the edge of the chair. When she swayed, Joe jumped from his couch and grabbed her arm, steadying her.

"Oh, thank you, Joe. You're always the gentleman." She frowned at the commissioner. "You could take some manner lessons from him." As she rose up, her stomach smashed into the commission's face. "Quiet," she scolded when he grumbled behind his gag. "Could one of you boys bring me them scissors?"

Sean grabbed them off the cabinet and handed them to her.

She reached up and pried open the door hidden in what appeared to be a short log and took a box of ammo from the hollowed center. "That should do it." She slammed the door back in place and stepped down from the chair with Joe's help.

"Did any of you know that was there?" Carlos watched the others shake their heads. "I wonder what other hiding places they've got around here."

"There," Edith said as Joe returned to his seat on the couch. "We should be right as rain now that we're armed to the teeth." She walked to the front door and locked it. "But we'll be keepin' the doors locked just the same. And none of you boys are to set foot out of this here lodge. Do you understand me?"

All but Nathan nodded. He was too busy staring at the lone rifle in the case.

"Come on, boys, no sense frettin'," Edith called as she walked to the dining hall. "Might as well go back to your card game, and I'll make you one of my famous chocolate cream pies."

"You better make it two," Carlos mused. "One for Carlton, and one for the rest of us."

"I'd like to help, if that's okay," Carlton said, following Edith.

"Why sure, I never turn down company."

Nathan stayed behind as the others walked to the game table. He picked up the scissors from the side table where Edith had left them and walked to the commissioner. "Watch your balls," he ordered as he stepped up on the edge of the chair. He opened the hidden compartment, took out a box of rifle ammo, and closed the door. Jumping back from the chair, he went to the cabinet and took out the Winchester rifle. As he turned, he caught Joe staring at him. Nathan shrugged. "Can't hurt to have backup."

As Nathan approached the doorway to the dining hall, he suddenly turned and darted down the short hallway leading to the restrooms.

The Commissioner looked at Joe, mumbling something behind his gag.

Joe shook his head. "Don't ask me, I have no idea what that was all about."

CHAPTER 28

"I realize we still have a few hours before sunset, but I sure hope this guy doesn't decide tonight's the night to come back early," Harold said, stopping at the door to room 202 on the second floor of Minam Lodge.

"No worries there," said Red. "Tan Dog's outside keepin' an eye out for us. She'll sound the alarm if anyone comes near." He eyed the shiny new room number. "Ten rooms up here, and you got them numbered in the two hundreds. What's the thinking in that?"

Harold smirked as he looked for the key. "The wife bought herself a hotel management book. Chapter three says guests don't like rooms numbered in single digits." He continued to fumble through his ring of keys. "After what you said you suspect this man of doing, I'd feel more comfortable with a pack of dogs, and maybe a rocket launcher for good measure. Here it is."

"Thanks, Harold," Red said as his neighbor unlocked the guest room door.

"I'm sure this is breaking a good handful of laws," said Harold. "So do me a favor and save me a cot. I'd prefer to share a jail cell with someone I know."

"If your elusive guest turns out to be our killer, all should be forgiven," Red said.

"And if he isn't?"

"You can have the top bunk." Red placed his hand on Harold's arm, stopping him from opening the door. "I smell smoke." He looked behind him at Bud and Woody. "Don't you boys smell smoke?"

"What?" Bud said, confused. "I don't smell anything."

"I smell it," said Woody, elbowing Bud.

"Oh, yeah, I smell it now. We better get in there."

Harold pushed the door open and followed the others inside.

Red stood at the foot of the bed, staring down at the laptop computer and another rectangular object lying on top of it. "Now would be a good time for you not to be here, Harold. Why don't you take your time findin' a fire extinguisher?"

"Plausible deniability?" Harold asked.

Red nodded. "It might earn me a private cell."

Harold walked to the door. "Just let me know when the fire's out."

Once the door was closed, Red's attention returned to the items on the bed. "What do you fella's make of the odd-looking radio?"

"It's a satellite phone," Bud said, picking it up. "People use them in areas where there aren't any cell towers."

"You might want to think about getting one for the ranch," Bud said as he placed the phone back where he found it. He walked to a dresser and began exploring the black case sitting on top.

"Yeah, at a cost of fifteen dollars a minute," Woody said.

Red made a snorting sound. "I'll pass." Then he pointed to the laptop computer. "Well, Woody, you know your way around a computer. Do you think you can pull anything up on that thing?"

"Not without a password, but..." Woody paused as he reached down and unplugged the flash drive from the side of the laptop. "With this, we don't need one."

"I found three more flash drives in the pocket of his computer bag." Bud handed them to Woody. "Each has a date on it, the earliest being the day before Lee was killed."

"Well isn't that interesting?" said Woody.

"It'd be even more interesting to find out what's on those things," Red said.

Woody headed for the door. "I bet Harold has a computer that could help with that."

Bud fell in behind him. "Poor Harold. Just when he's free from any involvement, we have to go and pull him back in."

"It can't be helped. With any luck, these files will tell us what this guy's been up to." Woody paused in the hallway. "We'll want to get the flash drives back where we found them as quickly as possible. No sense giving the man a reason to come looking for us. I don't know about you, but I'd just as soon not have a murderer strolling into Harold's office while we're taking a gander at what he's been doing."

"I'm with you there," Bud said, waiting in the hall with Woody. They watched as Red went through a pile of laundry on the floor. "You got any idea what he's doing?"

"Like most of the time, no."

Red walked out, carrying a dirty sock in his hand.

"You runnin' low on socks?" Bud asked.

"Yeah, I like to collect them one at a time." Red shoved the sock in his pocket. "Tanny's gonna need his scent if she's to track the man for me."

"There's always a reason for your madness," Bud said, walking to the staircase.

"YOU'VE GOT TO SEE THIS," Woody said as Bud came back from returning the flash drives to room 202.

"Whatcha got?" Bud peered down at the aged desktop computer.

Woody scrolled through page after page of photos. "There's nothing but pictures on any of the flash drives."

Bud looked over Woody's shoulder. "They seem to all be taken at the ranch."

"And from a distance," Woody added, enlarging one of the

pictures.

"Who is that?" Bud pointed to a blurred figure.

"It's one of the campers. I think maybe Nathan." Woody clicked on another picture. "There he is again." He clicked another. "If fact, I think Nathan is in all of these pictures."

"Hey, Red," Bud shouted through the office door. "Come take a look at this."

Red set his glass of whiskey on the bar, stepped down from the stool, and followed Harold to the closet-sized room beside the bar. "What is it?" he asked, standing in the doorway.

"It looks like Nathan has a stalker." Woody pointed at the computer screen.

"I think this guy might be a paparazzo," Bud said as he came out the door, making room for Red to enter.

Red stared silently at the photos scrolling down the screen.

"Each flash drive is full of pictures like these," Woody said. "They're all taken at the ranch, and Nathan seems to be the prime focus. If he isn't a paparazzo, I'd like to know why the fascination with Nathan."

Red walked out, passing Bud and Harold. "I say we go ask him." Returning to the bar, he threw back the rest of the whiskey, and headed for the door. "Hold down the fort, Harold. I'll call when we have him."

Harold walked behind his bar and pulled a rifle and box of ammunition from a low shelf. "If he's the son of a bitch that killed my dog, do me a favor and knock a couple of his teeth out for me." He reached for his glass and downed the whiskey.

"If he's the one that killed my people, there won't be a tooth left in his head." Red walked through the door.

"Wait," Harold called, stopping Woody and Bud at the door. He ran to his office and came back with a paper. "This is the man in room 202. It might be handy to take a copy of his ID with you. That way you might be saved the embarrassment of mistakin' an innocent person for him."

"Thanks, Harold," Woody said, taking the printout. He

folded the paper, shoved it in his pocket, and followed Bud out.

Red whistled, and Tan Dog jumped up from where she had been lying in the shade and ran to him with her tail wagging. Her happy expression turned serious as she sniffed the sock he held down to her.

"Go find him, girl." She let out one bark and raced off with her nose to the ground. Red tucked the sock in his back pocket and walked to his horse.

Tan Dog zigzagged back and forth across the ground, searching for the scent. She passed over a spot, doubled back, and froze. Pausing to look at Red, she barked again and ran down the path with her nose to the ground.

Red pulled Sugar's reins free from the hitching rail, jumped into the saddle, and spun her on her haunches.

Woody and Bud scrambled to mount their horses and follow Red as he galloped down the path toward the woods skirting the edge of Red's property.

As he entered the thicket of trees, Red turned Sugar sharply where Tan Dog had veered off the path and raced through the forest. He kept Sugar to a gallop, reining her around trees, dodging shrubbery, and jumping her over logs. Leaping over a small creek, he pulled the mare to a halt near where Tan Dog stood barking up at a tree. The ridge hair along her back rose as she growled at the feet hanging from a branch.

"You don't care for the likes of him, do you, girl? Well, you've always been a good judge of character." Red pulled his rifle from the leather scabbard hanging from his saddle. He racked a round in the chamber and rode forward with the gun pointed above the dangling legs.

Red stopped and gazed up the frightened man sitting on a thin limb. He looked to be in his mid-thirties and not at all comfortable being off the ground. *That's not exactly the look I expected to see on a cold-blooded killer. Too tan to be a local this early in the season.*

The man's sun-bleached hair stuck out under a black ball

cap, and he wore a tan fishing vest over a short sleeve shirt.

Red smirked. "I see you stopped by a Columbia Sportswear outlet before coming into the mountains. You're lookin' pretty sharp for fishing, but where is your pole?"

"I'm...I'm not here for fishing," the man stuttered. "I'm here to take pictures."

Red looked down at the photo bag sitting at the base of the tree. "So why the fishing getup?"

"I wanted to look like I fit in." He shifted on the branch.

Tan Dog sprang from the ground, jumping up at his feet.

Startled, the man jerked his feet up and almost fell backward off the limb. "Call off your damn dog!" he shouted, clutching the tree.

Seeing the man had both arms wrapped around the trunk, Red lowered his gun and laid it across his lap. Taking the pipe from his mouth, he used it to tip his hat up off his forehead, improving his view of the nervous man.

Tan Dog braced her front feet against the trunk, barking and snarling up at the treed man.

"You might want to keep your insults to yourself. Tan Dog's liable to take offense." Red rested his hands on his saddle horn and turned to look at the pack of barking dogs running through the trees behind him. "Those would be her brothers comin' to her defense. They must have heard her from the ranch."

The man groaned, "Not them again."

"I take it you've met Gray, Black, and Brown Dog?"

"Every time I line up a good shot, those mutts go and ruin it for me. I've spent more time up a tree than taking pictures." His distraction gave Tan Dog the opportunity to make a successful jump, grazing the tip of the man's hiking boot with her teeth.

"Stop that, you stupid bitch!" He pulled a pinecone from a branch and threw it at her.

Tan Dog dodged it, bared her teeth, and growled up at him.

"Tsk, tsk." Red shook his head. "Taunting Tan Dog isn't the

smartest move you could make at the moment. She doesn't have to understand the words to recognize the intent of your tone. I let you down now and she's liable to take a bite out of your ass. Can't say I'd blame her, and can't say I'd stop her. Although I can't really see the offense in calling her a bitch—all female dogs are—but calling her stupid is downright insulting. You might want to take a good look at where you're sittin', and then tell me who looks to be the stupid one here."

The man looked down at the male dogs barking up at him and then to their much angrier-looking sister. "I don't think the others will bite me, if you hold the tan dog back."

"Tan Dog's brothers aren't the sharpest tools in the shed, but if she tells them to attack, you'll definitely have more than one chunk missin' from your rump."

"Then call off all the dogs, so I can get down," the stranger pleaded.

"I've found Tan Dog's opinion to be worthy of note, and she seems to think you're up to no good. That bein' the case, you'll be staying put while you explain a few things."

Tan Dog jumped at the man's foot again.

"I'm telling you, if she bites me, I'll sue."

Red chuckled. "You'll have to get in line for that one. Lately that seems to be a common theme among you lowlanders." He looked down at the burnt-out tobacco in his pipe. "I might remind you that you're trespassin' on my land, and I have a right to protect myself and my property. And Tan Dog here is just defending me from what appears to be an intruder with malicious intentions."

"Listen, old-timer, there's nothing malicious about taking nature pictures," the man snapped, keeping his eyes on the pack of dogs barking at the base of the tree.

"The name is Red Higgins. If you can't remember that, sir will do." Red held his gaze on the man as Woody and Bud pulled their horses to a halt on either side of him.

"We lost you," Woody said.

"Then we saw the dogs headed this way and figured Tan Dog must have called them." Bud pulled the rifle from his scabbard and aimed it at the man in the tree.

"I don't think he has a weapon." Red slid his rifle back into his scabbard. "But if he lets go of his grip around that tree, I give you permission to shoot him."

"With pleasure." Bud nodded.

"Come on, you can see the only thing I carry is a camera. Get the dogs out of here, so I can get down. I'm not good with heights, and this limb keeps making creaking noises. I think it's going to break."

Red didn't reply as he tapped his pipe against his saddle, emptying the cold ash. Draping the reins over the neck of his sweating horse, he ignored the stranger as he pulled a packet of tobacco from his shirt pocket and filled his pipe. He slid the tobacco back in his pocket, pulled a match from another, and struck it across his saddle horn. Cupping his hand around the flame, he raised it to his pipe, puffing until the tobacco glowed red.

"The way I see it..." Red paused to spit on his fingers and wet the end of the match. "...you'd be safer sittin' up there for now." He took the pipe from his mouth and whistled loudly, immediately silencing the barking dogs. "Down," he ordered. All four dogs settled around the tree trunk and stared up at the man. "There. Now maybe we can hear ourselves think. Let's start with your name and where you're from."

"I'm Terrance Tucker, on vacation from LA."

Woody pulled Harold's copy of the man's driver's license from his pocket and studied it. "That fits with what Harold gave me."

"There's one thing I know isn't true. You're not here on vacation." Red glowered up at Terrance. "See this rope?" He touched the coil hanging from his saddle horn. "One more lie from you, and I'll be throwin' this rope around your heels and dragging you through the prickly brush." His eyes set on Tan

Dog momentarily before rising back to the photographer. "And I sure hope you're not too attached to your face, 'cause it won't be Jack Frost nippin' at your nose."

"Okay, I'll admit that I'm not here on vacation, but I don't see how taking a few pictures could be any of your concern."

"You're takin' pictures of a minor in my charge, so that makes it my concern."

"How did you know…holy crap, you went through my things, didn't you? That's a violation of my privacy."

"Well, if that ain't the pot callin' the kettle black," Bud said, grinning.

Woody laughed. "Are you actually going to pull that card when you're the one sneaking through the woods with a telephoto lens?"

"Why are you stalking Nathan?"

"I make a living taking photos of celebrities. And since Nathan Harper and Trey Campbell are inseparable, I fully expected to get shots of Trey as well. But my source was wrong about him being here." His expression suddenly brightened. "I could spare a few bills, if you tell me where they've got Trey locked away."

Red let out a snort. "If I did know, I wouldn't tell you."

The photographer's hopeful look faded. "There's a bigger payoff for the two of them, but at this point, I'd settle for one good shot of Nathan." He looked down at the dogs circling the tree. "It should make you happy to know that thanks to your dogs, I haven't gotten one decent picture the whole time I've been in this goddamn place. The only pictures I got this morning were of one of your hillbilly ranch hands."

"Turn on your camera and give it to me," Red ordered, riding Sugar under the branch.

"Do you know how much cameras like this cost?" Terrance asked.

Red turned and looked at his men. "Did I begin that statement with 'if it pleases your highness'?"

"Nope," said Bud.

"I didn't think so." Red turned back to Terrance. "Now give me the damn thing, or I'll throw you and your camera in the river."

Terrance released one arm from the tree, pulled the strap over his head, and pushed a button on the camera before lowering it into Red's waiting hands. "Push the right arrow to change shots."

The lines on Red's forehead deepened as he scrolled through the photos. Then he ran through the pictures again, studying each carefully before moving to the next. "When did you take these pictures?"

"About two hours ago."

"What is it?" Bud asked.

Red went back through the photos. "The first pictures show Billy leaving Stella tied in some brush and running through the woods. This one shows him going into the staff cabin. And here's one of him hiding behind a tree near Faye's cabin. You can't see Nathan, but Jake appears to be sneaking around the cabin, so Billy must have been watching the commissioner hold Nathan at gunpoint, meaning he's been back for a while."

"What?" Terrance exclaimed. "I missed someone attacking Nathan Harper? Shit, that could have been worth a year's salary."

"Shut up," Bud shouted, raising his gun.

"Here's one of Billy entering Faye's cabin. And the last are of him going back into the staff cabin." Red continued.

"Ah, please tell me we're not about to find out Billy's the one behind all the killings," Woody said.

"Whoa," Terrance said. "Who's been killed?"

"Didn't I tell you to shut up?" Bud glared up at him.

"It doesn't look good." Red looked troubled. "It would explain a lot. He had the means to do all of it. And it looks like he was the one who went back for the item under Faye's bed. Damn it all to hell, Billy!" Angry, he tugged the memory card from the camera and shoved it in his pocket.

"Hey!" Terrance shouted. "I need that."

"It's evidence." Red looked up at him with indifference. "Looks like you won't be makin' any money on this trip. The sheriff has ordered the evacuation of the area. You head back to the Minam Lodge, and Harold will make arrangements to get you out of here." As he turned Sugar, he tossed the camera up.

Terrance released the tree, freeing both hands to catch it. "Oh crap," he said as the limb creaked beneath him.

As Sugar broke into a lope, Red whistled for his dogs. Tan Dog raced after him with her brothers following, barking noisily until they veered off to chase after a squirrel.

"Wait. Help me down!" Terrance shouted as Bud and Woody turned their horses to follow Red. The limb cracked and gave way, slamming him on the ground. Terrance moaned as he rolled over on his back.

Bud grinned at Woody. "He did say he wanted down."

CHAPTER 29

Behind the locked door of the bathroom, Nathan emptied the ammunition into his pocket and threw the box in the garbage can. Then he jumped up on the closed toilet lid, reached up to the window, and slid it open. When his attempts to push the screen from the window casing failed, he slammed the butt of the rifle in the center, tearing the screen loose from its frame. Using the toilet tank as a stepping stool, he dropped the rifle out the window and began to follow it.

Halfway out the window he became stuck. "Shit." He squirmed and kicked his dangling legs, struggling to inch his body through the tight frame. "Dammit," he growled as he tried to free his back pocket from where it had gotten hung up on the metal window frame. "Screw it." He reached down and grabbed the lower edge of one of the siding planks and pulled hard. The force finally tore the pocket, releasing him to tumble out the window headfirst. He broke the fall with his hands and flipped on his back, landing on the sharp point of a broken tree limb.

"Ouch!" Nathan sprang to his feet, raised his shirt, and looked around at the bleeding gash in his side. "Son of a bitch!" He kicked the branch, sending it flying into the outside kitchen wall. "Shoot!" He grabbed the rifle and sprinted for cover behind the supply shed. After a few moments, he peeked around the corner at the kitchen door. Seeing no one, he dragged a hand through his hair, groaning, "That was real stupid, Nathan. Get it together, man."

He loaded the rifle's tubular magazine as Red had taught him during shooting lessons. When he looked up, he glimpsed Jake darting from the back of Lee's cabin into the grove of trees behind the staff cabin.

Nathan held the rifle in both hands across his chest and ran down the path past the row of guest cabins.

"I THOUGHT I MIGHT FIND you here," Jake said as he walked through the back door of the staff cabin.

Startled, Billy dropped the small metal box he was staring into, spilling the contents across the floor.

Recognizing Lee's medallion, Jake raised the shotgun, pointing it at Billy as he walked closer. "What a disappointment you are, Billy Boy. I have to tell you, I did not see this coming."

"That makes two of us," Billy said, glaring at Jake. "I see you're wearing my good boots."

"I didn't think you'd mind, seeing that mine are out of commission." Jake shrugged. "Since you won't need them where you're going, I figure they're mine now." He sobered. "I can't believe you came back when you could have escaped all this. And just when I thought you couldn't be a bigger idiot, you had to go and prove me…" He hesitated, looking out the window at Nathan sneaking through the trees. "Great, that's all I need." He heard the click of a switchblade springing open.

It happened so fast Jake didn't have time to jump out of the way of the knife. He dropped the shotgun to the floor, screaming in pain as he pulled the blade from his right shoulder.

Billy rushed him, knocking him to the ground. They rolled on the floor, wrestling for the switchblade. Billy slammed his elbow into Jake's bleeding shoulder, grabbed the knife, and scrambled to his feet.

Adrenaline rushing through him, Jake seized Billy's legs, tripping him. Then he crawled on top of Billy, wrapped his left arm around his neck, and squeezed hard.

Nathan ran through the back door of the cabin just as Billy

went limp. "What's going on?"

Jake released Billy and rolled onto his back, panting. "Isn't it obvious, Sherlock? I was trying to keep from ending up Billy's next victim."

"So, it was Billy. Hey, you're bleeding, Jake."

"That's what happens when you get stabbed, you idiot." Jake moaned. "Help me up."

Nathan grabbed Jake's good arm and pulled him to a standing position. "Then I was right."

"About what?" Jake groaned as he bent to pick up the knife. He wiped the blood on his pant leg, closed the blade, and slid it into his pocket.

"I knew Billy had to be the killer, and I was right about the evidence his boots left behind at the crime scene. I was right about all of it." Nathan laid his rifle on a cot and walked to the items scattered near the metal box.

"I'll throw you a damn parade." Jake slipped his shirt off his shoulder and inspected his wound.

As Nathan scanned the items, a large gold coin attached to a chain caught his eye. "Hey, this must be the medallion that belonged to Lee." As he raised the chain off the floor, the medallion caught on an item encased in plastic wrap. He tore the plastic loose and took a close look at the item within. "Gross, that's the calf's ear." He dropped it, along with the medallion.

"They're kill trophies," Jake said as he walked past Nathan. "I'm going to get a towel and see if I can stop the bleeding."

"You sure are calm for someone who almost got killed."

A little more cautious, Nathan bent over, looking at the next item without touching it. It was also covered in plastic. "I can't figure out what this is." Curiosity getting the best of him, he picked it up and pulled the wrap tight, bringing the green and black palm tree into focus through the plastic. He sucked in a breath, dropping it as he jumped back between two cots. "Jesus! That's a person's tattoo." He turned angry eyes on Billy, walked to him, and kicked him in the side. "You sick bastard."

"It'd be more effective if you waited until he's conscious," Jake said as he came from the bathroom, pressing a towel to his wound. "The tattoo is Faye's."

Nathan walked to a cot and sat down next to a pair of boots.

Jake picked up Edith's shotgun from the floor and carried it to a cot behind Nathan, moaning as he sat down.

"Aren't these your boots? You might be able to fix them with duct tape. Woody seems to think it's a cure-all." Nathan picked up one of the boots and inspected them. "I don't see a tear in either of these." He felt moisture on the outside leather and ran his hand down the inside of one of the boots "And they're soaked inside and out." He laughed. "Dude, what did you do, fall in the river?" His smiled faded when he looked over his shoulder and saw Jake's dark stare. Nathan gulped and turned back to the boots. "You aren't wearing Billy's boots because yours tore. You're wearing them because you ruined yours while murdering Faye..." He froze at the sound of a switchblade clicking open and slowly turned to look at Jake. "Holy shit!" He jumped off the bed just as Jake lunged across it, swinging the knife.

Nathan dove under the next cot and crawled like a lizard to the other side. He popped up, grabbed the John Wayne rifle off the bed, and pointed it at Jake. "I would have never thought that Red's golden boy would turn out to be a murderer."

"There you go underestimating people again." Jake groaned as he struggled to push off the bed he had fallen on. His face was set in a sneer as he straightened. "You've become quite the little detective." Turning the knife handle in his hand, he slowly walked out from the beds with his eyes pinned to Nathan's. "I'm sorry you won't be getting that pat on the head you were so hoping Red would give you. You and Billy have made things a bit more difficult, but it's nothing I can't fix. See, I'm smarter than anyone here. They'll believe me when I tell them that Billy killed you, and I had to kill Billy. It'll all work out—for me anyway."

"I'm the one holding the gun, you moron."

Jake ignored him as he continued to walk forward. He paused beside Billy and kicked him hard. "If this bastard hadn't come back to snoop in my business, no one would have ever been the wiser."

"Stop!" Nathan shouted as Jake turned toward him. "Come on, man. Don't make me shoot you."

Jake looked at the rifle and smiled oddly. "I have a hunch that won't be happening." He stepped toward him.

Nathan pulled the trigger, but the rifle didn't fire.

"I figured you'd forget to rack a round into the chamber." Jake raised the knife and ran at him.

With no time to load the rifle, Nathan turned the gun horizontally and used it to block the knife Jake slashed down at him. He pushed with all his strength, raising Jake's arm up, and kicked his exposed abdomen.

Jake staggered back, holding his stomach as he struggled to catch his breath. "Well, look at you going all Jackie Chan on me."

Nathan fumbled with the large loop lever, trying to cock the rifle, and almost dropped it when Jake rushed him again. In a flash, he jumped to the side, dodging the blade. But Jake was just as quick to turn back, forcing Nathan to scurry backward between two beds. Then, Nathan grabbed the rifle by the barrel and swung the gun like a bat, knocking the knife from Jake's hand. It spun across the floor, coming to rest under a bed on the other side of the cabin.

Jake looked down at the gash the raised metal *J.W.* initials on the rifle stock had scraped into his hand.

Nathan finally succeeded in racking a round, but when he aimed the rifle, Jake was already in the process of going for Edith's shotgun two beds over. Nathan fired, missing Jake as he grabbed the gun and dove between the cots. Shaken, Nathan fired again, hitting the bed behind his target.

"You do realize that even left-handed, I'm a better shot than you." Jake kept his head down as he rested the gun barrel on the edge of the bed, placed the butt up against his good shoulder, and took aim.

Nathan darted for the exit, and dove out just before a shot riddled the door behind him. Gun in one hand, he got up and sprinted for the woods.

"Shit," Jake shouted. "Stupid, fucked-up gun." He stood up and looked out the window, catching sight of Nathan as he disappeared into the forest. "That little prick hasn't seen the last of me."

Billy groaned.

"There you are, old buddy. I was thinking I might have killed you." Jake walked to the center of the room and stood over him. "We can't have that yet. The game's not over." He tapped Billy's face with his foot. "But you'll help me end it, won't you, old pal?"

Beginning to stir, Billy groaned and opened his eyes just as the butt of a gun slammed into his head.

RED HAD A GENERAL IDEA as to where to find his horse. He had recognized the area in the paparazzo's picture as being somewhere along the base of the ridge near the trailhead to Moss Springs. He might as well collect her, since he'd be going right past.

"Stella!" Red called as Bud and Woody followed him on horseback.

She nickered in response, and Sugar took him right to where Stella was tied to a tree hidden behind a wall of thick brush.

Red was winding his way through the heavy overgrowth when he heard the first shot. He pulled Sugar to a stop and scanned the woods as he tried to determine the direction of the sound echoing across the canyon walls. Bam! Another shot rang out.

Billy! If he hadn't seen the pictures for himself, he wouldn't have believed that his bungling young wrangler could actually be a killer. *But there's no good explanation as to why Billy would come back to the ranch and absolutely none for why he would hide his horse. The series of incriminating photos of him sneaking around the ranch are more than a little suspicious. And I very much doubt that these gunshots and his reappearance could be a coincidence.*

Red was reaching to untie Stella's reins from the tree when Sugar spooked from another booming gunshot. "Easy girl," he said, stroking the dancing mare's sweaty neck. "There now, no need to get your tail in a knot. No one's shootin' at you." The squeeze of his heels nudged her forward. Taking Stella's reins from the tree, he turned Sugar and led the younger mare out of the brush.

Stella nickered at the two horses loping through the woods toward them.

"Got any idea where the shots are comin' from," Bud asked as he and Woody pulled their horses to a stop.

"No, but Tan Dog does." Red watched her stare motionless through the woods. "The first two shots came from a rifle I don't recognize, but the third came from Edith's shotgun. It didn't sound like they were coming from as far away as the lodge. I can't imagine that Edith would leave the boys, but I do know one of the shots came from her gun."

"Maybe Jake's got Edith's shotgun," Woody offered.

"It could be, but even though he's a better shot than Billy, he couldn't hit the broad side of a barn with that broken-down heap of metal. It pulls hard to the right of the target. You men better go help protect the gang at the lodge. Take the trail along the ridge and cut across the meadow to the back of the barn. The shoeing shed and cabins will give you cover. Be mindful that if Edith is armed and rattled, she might have a jittery trigger finger."

"Where are you going?" Bud asked, watching as Red tied Stella's reins up on her saddle horn.

"Tan Dog's taken off through the trees. I'm gonna follow

her in case she has Billy in her sights. You boys take care, and keep the campers safe. Don't leave them, no matter what." Red spurred Sugar into a lope, dodging trees as they worked their way through the dense forest with Stella following freely behind.

"That man will never fail to amaze me," Woody said as he turned his horse to follow Bud to the trail along the ridge. "I'll never understand how he can tell the sound of one gun from another."

"It's uncanny, isn't it?" Bud replied.

"He may be a gun whisperer, but I think he feels he failed as a kid mentor," Woody said.

"I don't think anyone could have seen that comin'. It's Billy, for God's sake." Bud shook his head. "He's always been a knucklehead, but a killer? I still can't say I see it."

"He flew under all of our radars," said Woody. "As much as we both liked the damn kid, we can't let him pull the wool over our eyes any longer. And we're gonna need to watch each other's backs."

"You got a deal. And I'll gladly watch yours while you knock on Edith's door."

"Gee, how kind of ya."

RED KEPT HIS EYES trained on Tan Dog as he galloped through the trees after her. It was dangerous to run a horse through a thick forest laden with obstacles the likes of downed logs and low tree limbs, but he had to maintain the pace to keep up with his sprinting dog.

He jumped Sugar over a log and turned sharply at the same tree where Tan Dog had changed direction. "Whoa," he shouted, pulling Sugar to a sliding halt when he saw his dog suddenly stop. Stella halted beside them. The horses stood, breathing heavily as they joined Tan Dog in staring at the trunk of a large tree.

Tan Dog stood with her tail straight out, and the hair

bristled along her back. Hearing her growl, Red pulled his rifle from the scabbard and aimed it at the tree. "Whoever you are, come on out here where I can see you."

"Red?" Nathan peered around the tree. "It's me. Please don't shoot. I've had enough lead shot at me for one day."

Red lowered his gun, and Nathan slowly came out from behind the tree.

Tan Dog stood her distance.

"What in blazes are you doin' out here? I thought this once you'd actually do what you were told."

"This time, you'll be happy I disobeyed because I know who the killer is. It's—"

"We know," Red interrupted. "It pains me to think someone I've mentored for so long is the one doing these horrible things." Then he noticed the gun Nathan held. "What the devil are you doin' with my John Wayne rifle?"

"Jake wouldn't listen to me when I told him that I thought Billy was the killer. So when he decided to go out looking for Billy, I took the only gun I could find and followed him in case he needed backup. I didn't realize until too late that it was Billy who needed protection."

Red rubbed his brow as he stared at Nathan. "Why would you do that?"

"What do you mean why would I do that? Because Jake was set to kill him, that's why. It was lucky for Billy that I walked in when I did, and even luckier for me that Billy stuck a knife in Jake's shoulder before he took him down with a stranglehold. If Billy hadn't stabbed Jake's shooting shoulder, I'd be full of buckshot right now. And you should know, even left-handed Jake's wicked mean with a knife."

"Did you get knocked in the noggin? Because it sounds like you're saying Jake is the killer."

"He is. I thought you knew that."

"No, we thought it was Billy." Red gnawed his pipe, staring at Nathan. "It can't be Jake."

Nathan pointed in the direction of the staff cabin. "There's a box of kill trophies that say otherwise. I saw Lee's medallion, the calf's ear, a blue bandana, and a hunk of Faye's tattooed flesh. There's more, but after seeing the piece of Faye, I was too grossed out to look at the others. Billy must have figured something out, because he was going through Jake's things when he walked in on him. And then I had a look at Jake's boots. They were soaked from him wearing them into the river when he cut Faye to pieces. Once he realized what I knew, it was all over. His face changed. He changed. It was like looking into the eyes of a crazed animal." Nathan paced nervously.

"You were in the staff cabin when all this took place?"

"Yes." Nathan looked through the trees behind him. "We have to get out of here."

"Did Jake follow you into the woods?"

"I don't know, but I'd just as soon not stay here to find out." Nathan looked around. "I'm telling you, he's flat out crazy."

Red heard the crack in Nathan's voice.

"I just took off running and didn't stop until I heard horses running toward me."

"We better hope he followed you."

"What? Why would you want that?" Nathan stared in shock. "You do know that he has a gun."

"If he didn't chase after you, Billy could end up becoming his latest victim. Here, give me that gun and climb aboard Stella. We've got to get to the cabin and see about Billy." Red laid his gun across his lap.

Nathan walked to him. "But if Jake's coming this way, we'll run right into him."

"Not since we'll be takin' the long way round to the river side of the cabin."

Nathan handed the gun to Red, collected the reins from Stella's saddle, and bounded up into the seat.

"That's the first time I've seen you set your butt in a saddle like a real rider." Red slid the John Wayne Winchester into his scabbard. "See that you keep it there and lay low. We're gonna be ridin' fast." With rifle in one hand and reins in the other, he spurred Sugar into a gallop.

Nathan gripped the saddle horn as Stella bolted behind Sugar.

They ran through the trees onto the trail taking them on Minam Lodge property. Then they rode past the barn, across the landing strip in the middle of the meadow, and finally to the river. The horses' hooves sent water splashing into the air as they galloped into the shallow water and turned upstream. Once they came to Red's property, they rode up onto the bank, stopping their horses at the front of the staff cabin. Red motioned for Nathan to stay put while he rode to a side window and peered inside. Seeing that the cabin was vacant, he rode around to the back, where he studied the area. All was quiet. Then he noticed Tan Dog sniffing along a trail of bent grass. He turned and waved Nathan to him.

"The grass is mashed from here to the old sawmill." Red pointed to the broken down building. "He must have dragged Billy with him."

"Do you think he killed him?"

"I don't see any blood, and if he'd killed him, there wouldn't be any point to moving him since he no longer has anything to hide."

"Don't you think he'd make a run for it at this point?"

Red stared across the meadow to the collapsed sawmill roof. "I'm afraid he's chosen fight over flight."

"But why bother taking Billy?"

"Bait."

"For who?"

"The one person he knows will come looking for him— me."

"But he respects you. He told me so."

"I wouldn't give much credence to anything said by a person

diseased in the head." Red looked down at Tan Dog. "My dog respects me. But if she were to come down with rabies, she'd tear me from limb to limb all the same. And unfortunately, there's never a happy ending to the story."

"What are you going to do?"

"The only thing distinguishing humans from animals is reason. Hopefully Jake hasn't completely lost all of his humanity. Otherwise, I might be forced to do the same thing I'd have to do to Tanny if she were to go mad." Red tore his eyes from the mill and turned them on Nathan. "You ride to the lodge and tell the men what's happened. And..." He pointed his finger at Nathan. "You listen to me good this time. Tell my men that I want them to keep watch from the lodge. If they get Jake in their sights, tell them to take the animal down. And you are not to set foot out of the lodge. Do you hear me?"

"I hear you. But I don't think it's a good idea for you to take him on alone. You didn't see the crazed look in his eyes. He's one bat-crap crazy son of a bitch. I really think you should have some backup. Shouldn't I send the men?"

"No. I need them protecting all of you."

"Then I think I should help you."

"By doin' exactly what I just told you to do, you are. That's not up for debate, son. Now get." Red slapped Stella on the rump, making her leap into a lope.

Nathan floundered in the saddle as the mare loped across the small grassy meadow behind the guest cabins.

Red watched until Nathan disappeared behind the Meyers' cabin. Then he pulled the flask from his pocket and took a long drink as he studied the mill.

The structure once had a roof covering three open sides with a solid wall at the back. The roof was still attached to the standing back wall, but the front had collapsed on top of the iron saw equipment in the center of the building, leaving a skeleton of support posts.

He took another drink, capped the flask, and tucked it away.

"Well, girl, I expect it's time I knocked on a door." He squeezed his heels, moving Sugar into a walk. As he drew closer, the large iron saw flywheel came into view under the fallen roof. He pulled to a stop, staring at the figure hanging from the wheel. The red shirt and straw cowboy hat told him it was Billy. "Let's make that the back door." Red turned and rode deep into the woods, making a wide circle and coming up behind the cover of the solid wall in the back.

Rifle in hand, he dismounted, wrapped the reins around a bush, and walked to the edge of the trees where Tan Dog stood in the open. "Where is he, girl?" he whispered from behind a tree.

Tan Dog growled as she stared at a corner of the wall.

Red saw the shotgun muzzle pop out from a knothole and dashed to the cover of a larger tree. The shot sent splinters of bark exploding from the tree he had just left.

Startled, Tan Dog jumped back into the brush behind Red.

"Jake," he called with his back to the tree. "Son, you know this is finished. Throw the gun down and come out. I want to help you." The menacing laugh he heard sent a shiver down his spine. Red knew his rifle was loaded, but he opened the slide and checked the round in the chamber just the same.

"Help? That's a laugh. Good try, old man, but you know you can't bullshit a bullshitter. I'll be the one to say when this game is finished."

Red snapped the slide closed. "And how do you see it playin' out?"

"As much as it disappoints me." Jake sneered. "I only have one last play before calling the game. Damn, and here I had expected to kill me a sheriff during the bonus round. I guess you can't have everything."

"Is Billy alive?"

"He won't be if you move from where you are."

"He's served his purpose as bait. I'm here. You don't need him any longer."

"Actually, that's not entirely true. See, he really isn't the bait. You are."

What the hell is this crazy boy talking about? Then Red turned to look at the horse galloping toward them. *Nathan.*

"He's a predictable little asshole," Jake said.

"Nathan, stop!" Red shouted as he broke cover to wave him off.

Jake fired.

Nathan slid Stella to a stop, rolled her back, and galloped into the cover of the trees. He stopped the mare and jumped off, quickly tying the reins around her neck before slapping her on the rump. As she trotted off in one direction, Nathan ran through the woods in the other. It wasn't a long distance, but he was still breathing heavily by the time he made it to the trees behind Sugar. He slowed to a walk as he crept down to her.

With the mare blocking him from Jake's view, Nathan watched as Red looked down at the blood flowing profusely from the buckshot wounds in his side. Then Red collapsed to his knees, wavered for a moment, and fell to the ground on his face.

Nathan slid the John Wayne Winchester from Red's scabbard, pulled Sugar's reins free from the brush, and tapped her side with the butt of the gun. As the mare trotted away from the line of fire, he ducked behind a tree.

"Well, I finally hit something with this piece of shit gun," Jake said as he came out of the mill, walking calmly with the shotgun resting on his good shoulder. He stood over Red. "I was actually aiming for your chest. But I'll take it any way I can get it. Hey, are you dead old man?" He tapped him with his foot. Getting no response, he kicked him over on his back and pointed the gun at his face.

Red's eyes were closed, his breathing labored.

"Never take your eyes off your target. You taught me that. Too bad you didn't take a rule from your own playbook." Jake chuckled as he tossed the shotgun aside and bent to pick up

Red's gun. As he began to rise, he was caught off guard when a snarling Tan Dog leaped from the brush, biting the arm on his injured side. Jake screamed in pain and kicked her off. She fell on her side, jumped up, and lunged at him again. This time he was ready with the gun, slamming the butt as hard as he could into her shoulder.

She yipped as she was knocked to the ground, rolling twice before coming to a rest a few yards away.

He walked to the motionless dog, set the rifle down, and pulled the switchblade from his pocket. "I'm going to cut your heart out and eat it, you stupid mutt." Jake crouched down with the knife raised. Then he heard the cocking of a rifle and froze.

"Drop the knife," Nathan said.

Jake hesitated and then slowly turned.

Nathan's senses prickled at the sight of his insidious smile.

"Well, well, if it isn't Red's little hero, here to save the day. I've got news for you. I just killed the old bastard, so it's just you and me now. But don't worry. You'll still die a hero, because if you had hid behind Edith's skirt, like I'm sure Red told you to, I would have had to kill her and everyone at the lodge. Now it's just you and me." He took a step forward, stopping when Nathan aimed the gun at him.

"Are you forgetting who's holding the gun?"

Jake glanced down at the rifle he had dropped. It was just out of his reach.

"Don't even think about it," Nathan growled. "This time I'm locked and loaded. Even I couldn't miss from this distance."

The sound of a low moan drew Nathan's attention to the body lying behind the trees. He only took his eyes off his captive for a split second, but it was all Jake needed to grab Red's rifle and fire a hasty shot.

Nathan jumped in the brush and fired a wild shot back.

Jake fired as he ran for cover.

Nathan got off another shot, hitting the corner of the mill as

Jake dove behind it. He kept the gun aimed at the corner, waiting for Jake to reappear. Time ticked by as he held his position, straining to hear Jake's movement over his pounding heart. As he swept his sweating forehead across his sleeve, his eyes caught a flash of blue coming out from the front of the mill. He stood up and watched Jake run across the grass, disappearing into the trees.

Red moaned again.

"Red!" Nathan shouted, running to his side. He shook him. "Red?"

"Would you stop that?" Red's eyes opened to a slit, and he groaned as he tried to reach for his flask. "Get my drink." He rolled slightly, and Nathan pulled the flask from his back pocket. "Help me sit up." Nathan grabbed Red's arm and pulled him up with his back resting against a tree.

Red tipped the flask, drank it dry, and tossed it aside. "I'm really gonna need a whole lot more of that." He opened his eyes wider, trying to focus on Nathan. "Are you completely incapable of doing as you're told? I swear, either you have shit for brains, or there's somethin' not hooked up right in your head. Did you at least talk to the men before you ran off on a suicide mission?" He moaned.

"Yes, I warned them about Jake and told them they're supposed to protect those at the lodge."

"You just left out the part where you were supposed to stay there with them."

"I couldn't leave you to take on Jake alone. I'm real sorry. I didn't think I'd get you shot."

"It was my fault." Red coughed, spat out blood, and wiped a sleeve across his mouth. "Where is he?"

"He ran into the woods. You don't look good. We have to get you back to the lodge."

"No, you have to go." Red's voice went weak. "He's after you."

"It's okay. He's gone. I'm not going to leave you."

Red slumped to the side and fell over on the ground. As Red drifted into darkness, he heard Nathan calling his name.

CHAPTER 30

Nathan tore the sleeves from his shirt and pressed them against Red's bleeding side. He was holding both hands against the wounds when a sound behind him made him jump. He blew out his breath when he saw Tan Dog limping toward him.

She licked his arm and settled on the ground next to him.

"Hi, Tan Dog, glad to see you too." Nathan lifted Red's arm and draped it over the torn sleeve, trapping the material over the wounds.

Tan Dog sniffed Red's wounded side, and looked up at Nathan.

"Don't worry, I'll get help." He gave her shoulder a pat.
She flinched.

"You're hurt." Nathan looked her over and discovered a deep gash in her shoulder. "That's going to need stitches." He stroked her head. "Sorry, girl, but we'll have to take care of you later. Right now, I've got to get Billy out of the mill." He studied Red for a moment. "You watch over your owner while I'm gone." As he started to walk away, he looked back and took pause at the sight of Tan Dog crawling over Red, settling her weight across his wounded side. "Damn, I take back any bad thing I've ever said about that dog."

Nathan stepped through the opening between the broken-down boards and stopped to allow his eyes to adjust to the dark. As he took in the shambles around him, the rusted engine and the tall iron flywheel resting dormant in the center of the ruins came into view. "Billy!" he shouted at the sight of him hanging from the giant wheel. Billy's back rested against the thick black grease that covered the equipment. His wrists were bound in ancient gray rope. One arm was tied to a spoke high over his head, the other to a lower spoke on the opposite side. His head drooped motionless against his chest with his face hidden behind a straw cowboy hat. His red and white checkered shirt was torn and stained with blood.

"Billy!" Nathan ran to him and set the gun down along the track of the movable platform that held the log as it slid along the saw. He searched Billy's neck for a pulse and found the beats to be strong. "Let's get you down from there." He leaned against Billy, keeping him upright as he reached up to untie his wrist. But when he tugged on the rope, Billy's arm dropped freely without the need of untying. Nathan braced for Billy's body to crumble, but it didn't. Instead, Billy stood on his own accord and slowly raised his head. The hat lifted off his face, and he looked Nathan directly in the eyes.

Nathan tensed. "Jake," he gasped.

Jake flashed a wicked smile. "This is where I say *gotcha*."

Nathan turned to run, but Jake grabbed his arms.

"What's the hurry?" Jake whirled him around, smashing him back against the wheel and held a knife to his throat. "This is going to be great fun. Well, for me anyway."

Nathan struggled until the knife cut into his skin. He froze.

Jake used his teeth to tear the loop from his wrist and placed it on one of Nathan's. Then he threw the end of the rope over a high spoke, pulled it tight, and ran the rope down to a bar, securing it with a clover hitch knot, which he easily tied one-handed. He repeated the process on Nathan's other wrist. Although he didn't raise his injured arm very high, he no longer showed much pain when using it.

Jake finished tying Nathan, and stepped back to pat him on the cheek. "Poor stupid little asswipe. You should have hid in the lodge when you had the chance." He placed the tip of the blade against Nathan's cheek and drew it down, trailing blood as it sliced into his skin.

Nathan cringed.

"You really didn't think I'd take off without completing our business?" He laughed, but there was no humor in his expression. "We wouldn't want to disappoint Red. You know how he's always preaching never to leave a job unfinished, and you and me are far from done." He patted his face again, this time harder. "I could have just shot you, but that just seemed way too impersonal. This way we can take our time and do it right." He scoffed in Nathan's face. "No matter how clever you think you are, I'm smarter."

"You're a sneaky bastard, I'll give you that." Nathan stared at the bloodstain on Jake's shirt. "Nice touch changing clothes with Billy. Is that his blood or yours?"

Jake turned the knife in his hand. "It's mine. I'm bleeding, but you know the funny thing? It's like I don't even feel it. It must be the adrenaline. I don't know if I've ever felt more alive. You should have seen the look on your face." His laugh was pure evil. "While you were crying over that old dead bastard, I was slipping back in to set up my ambush."

"Where's Billy?"

"Ah, he's around." He snickered. "Woody sure is right about one thing. Duct tape comes in handy when you need to tie someone up. I probably should have killed him, but Billy and I have been buds for so long. I just couldn't take the time to do him right."

"You're one sick bastard, you know that?"

"Yeah, I've heard that a time or two."

CHAPTER 31

Red woke to a thick mist. As his eyes began to focus through the low-rolling fog, he realized he was no longer outside the mill. *I don't know this place,* he thought as he surveyed his surroundings.

It would have been dark under the thick canopy of trees if not for the strange glow of the mist illuminating the forest floor. *That's odd. I've never known fog to sparkle this way. Wait, wasn't I shot?.* He ran a hand down his side and felt the holes in his shirt and the wet of the blood, but what he didn't feel was pain. He stood on his feet and turned a circle, scanning the area.

"Hello, Mr. Higgins." A tiny voice came from somewhere behind him.

Red turned quickly, staring through squinting eyes at the small figure walking out from the fog. "Timmy?"

"Yeah, it's me," the boy said as he stopped a distance from Red.

"You've never talked in my dreams before."

Timmy shrugged and kicked a rock with his foot. "That's because it isn't a dream. The other times weren't neither."

Red stared. "If I'm talking to a ghost, I must be dead."

Timmy picked up a stick, threw it, and watched it bounce off a tree trunk. "You're not dead for reals yet. This is a special place where I can talk to people before they go on to somewhere else."

"These people, they're dead?"

"Yes." His eyes brightened. "I've seen a lot of men with

319

guns."

"Hunters?"

Timmy nodded. "And a man that went splat into the mountain."

"That must have been the pilot that was killed years ago." Red's expression showed his puzzlement. "If I'm not dead, how is it that I came to be here?"

"You're almost dead." Timmy shook his head with a sad face. "I didn't want you to go someplace else. I wished you here, so I could talk to you."

Red looked around again. "Do you come here often?"

Timmy nodded. "I come here to play sometimes. But I can go anywhere." He placed his fingers on his temples, closed his eyes, and scrunched his face. "I just have to think real hard of Mama, and poof!" He opened his eyes and threw his arms out. "I'm with Mama." His expression turned sad. "Mama can't see me, even when I hug her hard. Bubba don't neither."

"Bubba? Is that what you call your brother?"

"Yeah, I play with him, but he don't know it. He's big now." Timmy picked up a broken branch that was as tall as he was. "He plays a game with a shiny silver stick." He swung the thin branch, hitting a pinecone. "The ball's sposed to go in a hole."

"That's golf."

"Yeah, golf. Sometimes I like to make the ball go in the hole. But sometimes I get mad that he don't see me and I kick it into the water." He giggled. "That makes Bubba say real bad words. If Mama heard him, he'd get a time-out this big." He stretched his arms out wide.

"That big, huh?" Red grinned. "I sure like it better when you talk to me."

"I talk to you a lot of times. You're just a bad hearer." He ran around Red with his arms stretched out, making zooming sounds. "I like the airplanes that come to see you. I watch them all the time."

"What other things do you see when you watch my place?"

Timmy stopped in front of him, dropped his arms, and looked up with a serious expression. "Bad things."

"Like what?"

"Bad things that man does."

"Jake?"

Timmy stared down at his feet, nodding. "He shouldn't have done that to the baby cow. I liked her. She let me pet her, and it tickled when she licked my fingers. He killed the other man's doggy too." He kicked the dirt with his toe. "Jake is a bad, bad man."

"Have you seen other people like you?"

"Yeah. The man with the flat white hat." Timmy smiled. "He talks funny." He picked up a rock and threw it.

"That would be Lee. What did you talk about?"

"He's mad at bad Jake too. Says he don't care he killed him, 'cause he was gonna die anyway on account of that rock in his head."

"It's called a tumor."

"He don't care about the tumor, but he's real mad 'cause Jake killed his baby cow." Timmy threw another rock. "And the lady with the yellow hair was here. She was nice. But she don't remember names too good, 'cause she kept calling me pumpkin." He smiled again. "She's madder at the fat man than she is bad Jake. She didn't like that he was going to dee...dee...it was a grown-up word I can't remember."

"Divorce?"

"Yeah, that's it. She said she's gonna haunt the fat man and his tramp too." He frowned. "I don't know why she's mad at his dog. I like the movie with Lady and the Tramp. I like Tan Dog too. She's my friend."

"That's not what she meant by..." Red hesitated. "Never mind."

Timmy turned with a puzzled look. "What is haunt?"

"It's when a ghost does bad things to scare people who are still alive."

Timmy's face fell. "You used that word about me. I heard you. That was mean. I'm not bad."

"I know you aren't. I didn't know you were real. I thought you were a dream."

"What's a demon?"

Red cringed internally. "I did say that, but you aren't a demon either. I thought my head was punishing me for not saving you from the fire."

"That wasn't your fault." Timmy shrugged. "I got scared and wanted my mama."

Red got down on a knee, and looked Timmy in the eye. "It was my job to keep you safe. I failed. I'm sorry, little man." Red stood up as Timmy ran off to a nearby stump.

"I know." Timmy stepped up on the stump. "You tried to stop me, but I didn't listen." He jumped off. "I'm sorry for that. It made Mama sad, and I didn't get the toy."

"Toy?"

"The fire truck you promised if I went down the ladder."

"You have no idea how much I wanted to give you that truck."

"I try to do better now." Timmy climbed up on a bigger stump. "I tell you when bad things are happening, but you don't hear me." He jumped off and rolled on the ground. "You just get mad, and it scares me when you yell."

"I won't ever do that to you again. I promise."

"Hey, where's that thing that blows smoke."

"My pipe? It must have fallen out when I came here."

Timmy got to his feet and stepped back up on the stump, where he paused to look at Red. "Want to know a secret?"

"Sure."

"I know what was under the yellow-haired lady's bed. It was a rabbit's foot with a chain on it. Bad Jake has it in his pocket."

That's why Jake went back for it. He knew I would recognize his lucky keychain.

Timmy made a face. "It has yucky blood all over it. Bad

322

Jake's daddy was a bad, bad man too. He made Jake kill a bunny when he was a little boy. Then he cut a foot off and put a chain on it and made Jake wear it to remember the first time he killed something. Jake's daddy was mean. He made Jake mean. Jake likes to kill people, just like the bunny. He killed a girl too."

"What girl?"

Timmy didn't answer. He was looking over his shoulder to the dark woods beyond the mist. "You have to go back and save the boy."

"Nathan?"

Timmy faced Red. "I didn't like Nathan at first, but now he's good. You have to go back and save him." He walked to Red, grabbed his sleeve, and tugged on it. "Go now, Mr. Higgins. You go now!" He tugged harder.

Red suddenly found himself lying on the ground with something tugging at the cuff of his sleeve. He felt the brush of fur on his wrist and opened his eyes. Tan Dog released his sleeve and licked his face.

"Son of a bitch." He groaned in pain when he struggled to sit up. "Sorry for the language, Timmy. I'll give myself a time-out when this is over." He looked around and discovered he was back outside the mill. And his tiny friend was nowhere to be seen.

Red tried to stand but found he had no strength. "Blast," he said, plopping back against the tree. Then he heard a horse snort somewhere behind him. He put two fingers in his mouth and whistled.

Feeling naked without his pipe, he looked around and saw it lying out of reach. "Hey, girl, fetch my pipe for me. Tan Dog limped over, carried his pipe back and dropped it in his lap.

Using his good arm, he gave her head a rub. "Atta girl. Can't think straight without that." Red wiped the pipe on his pant leg and shoved it in his mouth. Then he saw the cut on her shoulder. "Damn, girl. Jake do that to you? Now he's really pissed me off." He tried to stand again but was too weak to get up. *Where is that damn horse?* No sooner had he thought it than he felt a nudge on the back of his shoulder. Sugar brought her nose up to nuzzle his ear. "Get around here where I can get ahold of you."

Sugar turned and started eating grass.

"Get over here, you flea-bitten nag."

She swished her tail, ignoring him.

Red slid a hand in his pocket and pulled out two sugar cubes. Before he had a chance to call her, she was right there. "I thought that would get your attention."

As she gobbled them up, Red grabbed ahold of her mane high on her neck and held on tight. She raised her head up, dragging him to his feet. "Whoa." He clung to her as he struggled to stand.

Sugar stood still, crunching the cubes as Red reached for the saddle. He grabbed the horn, pausing to catch his breath before asking her to walk. She stepped forward a few feet, stopping when he said, "Whoa."

Red stared down at the shotgun lying on the ground. *This is gonna hurt like the devil.* He held on to the stirrup, sucked in a breath, and crouched down to pick up the weapon. "Aagh!" he cried as pain shot through him. He stood panting for a moment, tucked the gun under his arm, and dug the shotgun rounds he had taken from Edith's gun from his pocket. Red leaned against Sugar, freeing his hands to load the gun. *Two rounds. Hopefully that's one more than I need.*

He clucked to her and tapped her side with the stirrup. Sugar walked to the corner of the mill, where he released her, grabbed the corner post, and hobbled through the broken-down boards with Tan Dog limping in after him.

His vision blurred as he fought to keep from blacking out. *Come on, Red, now's not the time to be takin' a nap.* He staggered through the last of the obstacles and came to a stop behind a barrel. Then he heard Jake tell Nathan he was going to cut his skin off nice and slow. Red followed the voice to the center of what was left of the structure. He shook his head, trying to force his eyes to focus. He could make out Nathan bound to the flywheel. Standing in front of Nathan was a figure in a red shirt. *That isn't Jake, he was wearing blue.* Confused, Red called Billy's name. He watched as the person turned around. *Damn you, fool, that is Jake. So much for taking him by surprise.* He leaned against a post and raised the shotgun, but his vision blurred even worse.

Jake hid behind the metal framework constraining Nathan. "Well, would you look at who we have here? You just refuse to die, don't you, old man?" He looked up at Nathan. "Don't worry, I'll get back to you after I finish with the boss."

Tan Dog growled and bared her teeth.

"And you brought Cujo with you. Great, I can take care of both of you at the same time." Jake slapped the flat of the switchblade in his palm repeatedly. "But who do I begin with? Maybe I should start with your loyal companion. She's been a real pain in my ass—tracking my every move—constantly interrupting my work."

"So you were the one she tracked from Faye's cabin to the kitchen earlier today?" Red asked.

Jake chuckled. "She was right on my trail until the idiot campers distracted her with food. Other than that time, the bitch has been hard to shake. The only time I could get anything accomplished was while she was locked up in your cabin at night. And even then she made me miss a great opportunity. I was really looking forward to seeing the look on your face when you discovered your little buddy here sliced up nice and neat the next morning. Not only did your damn dog ruin my plans, she ended up getting one of my favorite trophies away from me. No worries, I'll just replace it with her hide."

"You crazy bastard. You had no reason to kill the hikers," Nathan said, struggling to free his hands.

"I only got the leader, but I can guarantee the other two won't be breaking into the supply shed again. I did that one for you, boss."

"You know damn well that he wouldn't want you to kill anyone," Nathan said. "You could have just scared all of them off."

Jake's expression turned smug. "Now what fun would there be in that? Unfortunately, there's not a lot of challenge in killing a dumb doper, so I had to get creative with that one." The false smile spreading across his face was a contradiction to his cold eyes. "As much as I enjoyed the hiker, cutting through Faye's throat with Billy passed out right next to her had to be my favorite so far. I'll never forget the look in her eyes as the knife sliced across her neck. But with the two of you and your stupid hound, I know the best is yet to come."

"How do you suppose to do all this killin' after I fill you with buckshot?" Red coughed and spit up blood.

"You're not doing too well, are ya, boss?" Jake grinned at the sight of Red slumped against the post. "I'm guessing you can't see all that well. Be careful, I wouldn't want you to hit Nathan. That could make a mess of my canvas." He looked up at Nathan. "Could you just fall down dead already? I'm itching to get to work on Hollywood."

Red didn't need to see Jake's eyes to know how cold they had grown—he could hear it in his voice. *Why haven't I seen this before? How could he have hid his evilness so well?*

"This is my grand finale." Jake turned an eerie smile on Nathan. "It's going to be epic. And to think the boss man was the one who gave me the idea."

"I'm pretty certain we've never had a discussion about your perverse hobby." Red coughed again.

"It wasn't really a discussion. It was something you said in the heat of the moment about skinning Nathan alive. I couldn't get it out of my head. It was so perfect. I was planning to make a belt out of Faye's tattoo, but now I'm thinking I might want to make matching moccasins out of Nathan's back. Good thing he's not too hairy."

Nathan paled and tugged harder at the ropes.

"Did you set out to kill, Lee?" Red asked.

"No, that was a bit of luck, or in Lee's case, bad luck. I had my sights on a girl at the Minam Lodge for my first human kill here. But Harold's stupid dogs ruined that. You have no idea how satisfying it was to kill that mutt. I only wish I could have stayed to skin him, but when the other dog took after me, I figured I'd better get out of there."

Red blinked repeatedly and gave his head another shake. *Come on, Red. You've got to keep him talkin' 'til your eyes clear.* It wasn't hard to do. Jake obviously enjoyed boasting about his kills—proof he has no intention of leaving them alive. "So you're the one who's been killin' Harold's animals?"

While Red kept Jake talking, Nathan was working to loosen his ropes.

"Yeah, I've been picking off a few every year. You, of all people, should understand. You enjoy killing and butchering animals, just as much as I do."

Red struggled to follow the sound of Jake's voice. "There's a big difference between hunter and sociopath."

"Careful," Jake hissed. "Insults will only get you killed painfully slow." He saw Nathan looking down through the metal at him. "Once I take care of you, old man, I'll give rich boy here my full attention."

"What did I ever do to you?" Nathan asked.

"Are you kidding?" Jake scoffed. "I want to hurl every time a spoiled asswipe whines about how horrible his life is. You with your daddy cancelling your television show, and Billy with his constant complaints about being forced to work for his father's company. *Boo fucking hoo!* You two are worse than the privileged tools I went to school with." His ominous laugh made the hair stand up on Nathan's neck. "I almost killed Billy our first year at the ranch together, but then I thought it would be more fun to watch him suffer over something that would really matter to him."

"Watch him suffer over what?" Nathan asked.

"Well, let's just say Lee wasn't my first human kill."

Red groaned, but it wasn't from pain. "You killed Billy's sister."

"Ding, ding, ding, we have a winner." Jake laughed. "Pretty little thing with skin as soft as a rose petal. But she fought like a wildcat. I hadn't expected that of such a little package. She must have really wanted to live. It's true what they say—you always remember your first." He snorted. "Didn't see a killer in my eyes, did you, gramps?"

Nathan stopped working the ropes and stared down at Jake. "You're a fucking psychopath!"

"What I am is smart. If it weren't for finding my boots, no one would have ever suspected me of any of this. Even went so far as to save your sorry ass from the commissioner." He turned his glare from Nathan, across the mill at Red. "You pretend to be my friend, but you're just like all the rest, another person trying to control me. So who's in control now, old man?" He shouted. "These stupid rich punks you coddle year after year aren't worth the time. And then you two had to get all cozy. No way was a Hollywood prick going to take my place as your right hand wrangler. That's why I decided to make this my last year at the ranch—and *yours* too. When Noah screwed up my chance to frame Nathan for Lee's murder, I figured I could spread suspicion of Faye's slaying on Billy. Two killings would have closed the ranch for the season—breaking you. Then I could have watched you die slowly from the loss of your beloved land, but now I'm forced to take it another direction." He sneered. "I just wish you'd die so I can get on with it."

Red struggled to stay on his feet. "I guess we don't always get what we wish for."

Hearing the weakness in Red's voice, Jake stuck his head out from behind the metal, grinning when he saw that Red was barely able to stand. "Don't think for a minute that I didn't know what you were doing. Keeping me talking isn't going to buy enough time for the men to come to your rescue. Actually, I've been the one staling. I know my craft well enough to know when someone is about bled out. My favorite thing is that last moment when the life is draining out of a subject and you can see they know they're about to die. I just bet you're almost there. For every second that passes, you get weaker and closer to death. The problem is I've lost patience in waiting." Seeing Red's eyes close, Jake crept from his hiding place, crossing in front of Nathan as he headed for the gun resting along the saw.

Nathan saw what he was about to do and lifted his legs, wrapping them around Jake's chest, stopping him. "He's going for the rifle!"

Red opened his eyes and took aim, but he couldn't pull the trigger. He knew with certainty that the spray of buckshot would hit Nathan as well as Jake.

With his upper arms trapped by Nathan's legs, Jake twisted, trying to break free. He finally turned the knife in his hand and jabbed upward, stabbing Nathan in the calf.

Nathan screamed and dropped his legs.

Jake yanked the knife from Nathan's leg, making him scream again. Then he turned and leaned close to his face. "We'll have to finish this later." He slid the knife behind his belt and dashed for the rifle.

Red fired, but he didn't hit Jake. The splattering buckshot pinged as it hit the iron framework along the track. The spray knocked the rifle off the ledge, coming to a rest under the saw equipment.

Jake dove behind a barrel. "Nice try, old man. Glad to see even the great marksman has trouble with that gun."

"What makes you think I missed?" Red teetered as he wiped the sweat from his forehead.

Nathan pulled at his ropes, stopping when he saw Jake creep from behind the barrel, slowly sneaking around downed boards and rubble as he closed in on Red. "Watch out, Red! He's coming your way."

Red raised his gun, but his feet could no longer hold him and he slid down the post to the floor.

"Red!" Nathan shouted. He grabbed a spoke in each hand, muffling a scream as he lifted his legs up and stood on the iron wheel frame. Without the weight of his body pulling on the ropes, Nathan was able to twist his hands until one of the loops loosened. He jerked his hand free, skinning his knuckles in the process. Ignoring the pain, he tore the rope from his other hand and climbed down to stand on one leg. Holding on to the machinery, he quickly hopped around behind the wheel and crawled under the saw to retrieve the Winchester rifle.

Tan Dog straddled Red, snarling and baring her teeth as Jake edged closer. "Down, girl," Red said, pushing her off him. She lay next to him, growly loudly as Jake advanced. Still, Red failed to find his legs. He braced the gun in his lap. *One shot left. Maybe I'll be lucky enough to shoot the legs out from under him.* He closed his eyes, and when he opened them, Jake was rushing forward.

Nathan took a shot, missing Jake and hitting the two-by-four bracing the rotten roof over him.

Jake covered his head as debris and scraps of wood rained down on him.

Red fought to keep his eyes open, straining to focus through the cloud of dust. He heard Jake cough as he staggered out of the haze. "Hell and damnation," Red said, seeing the deranged look in Jake's eyes. "How did I not see how demented you are?"

Tan Dog jumped to her feet and leaped at Jake, knocking him back against a post so hard it tore all but one corner of the bottom loose. The broken down roof shuttered, groaning and creaking above Jake's head.

Seeing his chance, Nathan ran to the center of the room, picked up an empty barrel, and threw it, knocking the brace free. The roof gave way, dumping pounds of material on Jake and Tan Dog.

Nathan watched for movement under the debris. Seeing

none, he hobbled across the mill to Red. "Are you okay?"

"Just peachy," Red mumbled before passing out.

"I'll get help." Nathan limped through the same downed boards he had come through earlier. Outside, he found Stella and Sugar grazing not far from the mill. When he reached for Sugar's reins, she let out a snort and trotted away from him. He turned to Stella who stood watching him with great interest. "Please don't run," Nathan said as he limped toward the mare. "That's a good girl." He brushed a hand along her neck and collected the reins.

He held the rifle in his right hand, grabbed the horn with his left, and stood up in the stirrup. That was as far as he got before hands gripped his waist and pulled. Nathan dropped the rifle to the ground as he struggled to hang on to the saddle, but his attacker pulled harder. Clutching the horn in one hand, he grabbed the reins with the other and pulled them over Stella's neck. She spun, turning into his assailant and knocking him off his feet. "Whoa," Nathan shouted, stopping her. He quickly pulled himself up into the saddle and gathered the reins.

"We have unfinished business," Jake shouted as he scrambled for the gun on the ground. He picked it up but didn't have a chance to fire before Nathan kicked him in the face as he galloped by on Stella.

Jake fell, taking the gun with him. He struggled to his feet and aimed the rifle at Nathan's back.

A shot rang out.

Nathan looked over his shoulder as Jake fell. He pulled to a halt and spun Stella around. Red was lying face down in the opening of the mill with the shotgun in his hand. Nathan turned Stella and raced for the lodge.

CHAPTER 32

"Blessed day for a memorial," Edith said, dabbing a tissue to her eyes. "I know it's been more than a week, but I still can't get used to the idea of not ever seein' that cantankerous old fool again."

"Least he died on the ranch, liken he'd want," said Leroy. "When we gonna get this shindig on the road anyway?"

She turned angry eyes on him. "Would it kill you to show a little respect for someone you've known forever? Lord knows, sometimes it takes all the patience I have just to keep from wringing your scrawny neck."

Bud rode up on Dipsy. "We're going to start as soon as this last plane lands."

"Great, one more plane to mash the hay," Leroy grumbled.

"Button it, Leroy," Edith said, glaring. "It's lovely all these fine folks came to give their respects." Her expression softened as she gazed across the meadow. "It looks like a patchwork quilt down there with all them colorful planes." She dabbed her eyes again. "You know, I've never been up here on the ridge before. I now understand Red's fondness of it."

"That's why we thought it would be the perfect place to spread the ashes," said Bud, watching a plane touch down. "That's Russell Elmer. I didn't think he'd miss the memorial."

The plane parked near the others, and the passenger got out.

"Who does Russell have with him?" Bud pulled the pocket binoculars from his saddlebag and focused them on the plane. "Holy smokes!"

"Well, don't keep us in the dark. Who is it?" Edith asked.

"Um."

"Here, give me those things." She grabbed the binoculars out of Bud's hand. "Land sakes! That man don't listen to no one."

"I'm sure he just couldn't miss sending his old friend off," Bud said.

"Well, I'll be givin' that Russell Elmer a piece of my mind," Edith huffed. "You just wait and see if I don't."

Ten minutes later, Russell rode up the trail on Rowdy, with Red following behind him on Sugar.

"You might want to stay on your horse," Bud said as Russell stopped Rowdy next to Dipsy. "It'll make it harder for Edith to reach you."

"I take it she's mad that I helped Red break out of the hospital?"

"Steaming."

Russell cringed at the dark look Edith shot him. "She should know by now when Red gets a notion, there's no stopping him."

"Morning, Edith," Red said, tipping his hat as he rode past her.

Hands on her hips, her eyes shot daggers at him. "Don't waste your pleasantries on me, buster. Soon as Lee's ashes are spread, you're gettin' yourself right back to that hospital."

"You got a better chance of bloomin' daisies out your ass," Red said, grinning. He rode Sugar around the crowd of mourners gathered on the ridge, stopping between Nathan on Stella and Gil on Max.

"You do know Edith is planning to skin you alive?" Gil asked.

"Ugh," moaned Nathan. "I'd just as soon never hear that again. I came too close to experiencing it for myself."

Gil cringed. "Sorry, it slipped my mind."

"How's the leg?" Red asked.

"Fifteen stitches," Nathan said, proudly. "But the doctor says it should heal fine. How are your bullet holes?"

"I no longer leak when I take a drink of water, so I must be on the mend. The doc taped me up real good." Red scanned the waiting crowd. "Good turnout. Sorry we held things up. I had to bust Tan Dog out of the vet's."

"How is she doing?" asked Gil.

"Doc says she'll be good as new in time, but right now she's havin' a hard time getting around. She's resting in my cabin."

"I'm so glad she's going to make it," said Nathan. "She's a special dog."

"That she is," Red agreed. "She'd have to be to change your opinion of her."

"I understand the sheriff found the body of the hiker downriver," Gil said. "The other two were lucky to have gotten away."

"Yeah, I guess they were scared out of their wits when the deputy picked them up in Wallowa. Probably the first time those two ever ran *to* the police." Red looked around at the people waiting. "Well, I guess we better get this started." He turned Sugar to face the crowd of pilots, packers and locals. "Thanks for comin' out to remember our friend," he began. "Lee could be as cranky as a constipated bear, but lord knows that man could cook. Did I ever tell you about the time he went after Edith with a frying pan?"

DURING THE SALMON BARBECUE following the memorial, Nathan paused among the picnic tables to talk to Billy. "Your head is looking good. I bet you don't even end up with a scar."

Billy shook his head. "Nah, it takes more than the butt of a gun to get through this thick skull."

"I've been sayin' that for years," Red said from a nearby lounge chair.

Billy laughed. "Yeah, look who's talking. My thick head

doesn't even compare to your stubborn will to live. What *does* it take to kill you?"

"I'd just as soon not find out." Red's expression turned sullen as he looked at Nathan. "I took no pleasure in killing Jake, but I am thankful I could stop him from taking your life."

"Not as much as I am."

"Jake fooled us all," Billy said. "It's like he was two different people—the friend I knew one minute and a bloodthirsty killer the next. I'm still having a hard time believing it."

"Jake's grandfather didn't believe it either," Red said. "Not until the police found your sister buried in his very own backyard."

"It may have started there, but thanks to you it ended here." Billy's expression of sadness turned to joy when he saw the bowl of strawberry shortcake Edith set in front of him.

"That'll keep him occupied for a while." Red pointed to a chair. "Why don't you take a load off, son?"

Nathan sat down. "I owe you an apology. I was wrong about so many things, but I think my head's on straight now."

"Your dad told me he could see the change in you."

"Yeah, well that's what happens when someone tries to remove your skin while you're still using it. I have to face the music back home, but I know I won't be making any of the same mistakes. I'm done with all that bullshit."

"You don't think you'll go back to your old ways once you get back to California?"

"No, I've had my fill of doing boneheaded things. I'm also going to try to keep Trey out of the trouble we usually get into. I think there are better things we could spend our time doing, like maybe starting a foundation for troubled kids. I was thinking that since the ranch did so much for me, maybe it could help a lot more messed up kids. I was thinking we could expand on your boy's camp." Nathan smiled at Red. "I don't suppose you know anyone who could help us with that?"

"I just might." Red said.

Nathan's expression turned serious. "Do you think people will ever look at me differently?"

"Well, you can't change the past." Red paused to blow smoke from his pipe. "But you can let go of it and embrace the future. You may not realize it yet, but you are the master of your destiny."

"I hope you're right. I'd hate to find out I'm fated to be nothing more than a screw up."

"Fate is what happens to us. Destiny is what we do in spite of fate. People can change."

"According to Dad, you haven't."

"Perfection has no need of change." Red smirked.

Nathan returned his grin. "Right. Anyway, I plan to be more careful from now on."

"Not too cautious, I hope. I've always believed that takin' a risk is the difference between living and just plain existing. You just have to make sure the risks you take are for the positive." Red caught sight of Gil heading their way. "I'm sure if you're anything like your father, you'll choose living over existing."

"How's it going over here?" Gil asked.

"I'm glad you came over," Nathan said. "I wanted to ask both of you a question."

"Shoot." Gil took a seat.

"I was wondering if I could stay at the ranch for the rest of the summer."

Gil looked at Red. "As long as you aren't planning any more shootouts at the OK Corral, I'm good with that."

Red grinned behind his pipe. "He can stay, but I can't make any promises about shootouts."

LATER THAT AFTERNOON, Woody found Red in his cabin with Tan Dog. "Russell's pulled his plane up to the lodge. Is he taking you back to the hospital?"

"No, but that's what we're tellin' Edith."

"So where are you really going?"

"He's flyin' me to Portland. I owe a little man a fire engine."
Red grabbed the hand Woody offered and slowly rose off the
sofa. Together they walked out to the plane, where Woody
helped him into the passenger seat.

"Where's he going?" Bud asked as Woody came to stand on
the porch with him.

"Portland."

"Portland? Why?"

Woody shielded his eyes, watching the plane taxi down the
airstrip. It lifted out of the canyon and rose over the trees,
becoming a silver blip in the clouds before it disappeared.

Woody turned to Bud. "That's a story we'll have to wait
for."

A WORD FROM THE AUTHOR

Loyal fans of Red's Horse Ranch will notice that I took creative license with descriptions of the true life setting of the fictional story, *Red Reins*. I mention the wash house, which actually burned down years ago, added a staff cabin, and put stalls in the barn. In some cases, other buildings have a change in location, were altered, added, or deleted to better fit the story.

The 1887 Chinese massacre at Deep Creek was a truly low point in Eastern Oregon history. However, there is no need to bring your gold mining gear to Red's ranch. To my knowledge, the missing gold was not buried there.

Although I grew up a short mountain range from the ranch, I never had the opportunity to meet the real, Red Higgins. Red passed away in 1970 at the age of sixty. For my fictional story, he is alive and well, living in modern times.

After his death, the ranch was managed by his daughter and son-in-law, leased to outside operators, sold and finally traded to the federal government. In 1994, it became part of the Eagle Cap Wilderness in the Wallowa Mountains.

The public is no longer allowed to stay in the ranch buildings, but the air strip is still functioning and volunteers are on site throughout the summers. Many of these volunteers have fond memories and entertaining stories to tell about the notorious, Red Higgins they knew.

The easiest way to get to Red's Horse Ranch is by small plane. Joe Spence charters flights out of Enterprise. You can also hike or ride horses in from Moss Springs Trail Head above Cove, Oregon, or take the longer route from the Wallowa side.

It's well worth the trip to experience the beauty and history of the location. For more information and to view pictures and videos, visit my website at sgcourtright.com.

S.G. Courtright

Made in the USA
San Bernardino, CA
03 February 2016